Hearts *in* Darkness

Collection

LAURA KAYE

Embrace the darkness! to Laura Kaye

Hearts in Darkness Collection

FIRST EDITION August 2021 by Laura Kaye

Hearts in Darkness

SECOND EDITION May 2013 by Laura Kaye

FIRST EDITION April 2011

Lovers at Dawn

FIRST EDITION August 2021 by Laura Kaye

Love in the Light

FIRST EDITION January 2016 by Laura Kaye

Forever in the Light

FIRST EDITION August 2021 by Laura Kaye

HEARTS IN DARKNESS COLLECTION © Laura Kaye.

ALL RIGHTS RESERVED.

ISBN 978-1-952428-09-8

Front Cover Art by Tricia "Pickyme" Schmitt

Back Cover and Interior by The Killion Group

❀ Created with Vellum

To all the readers who have loved Caden and Makenna,
thank you for ten wonderful years!

HEARTS IN DARKNESS COLLECTION

Hearts in Darkness
Lovers at Dawn
Love in the Light
Forever in the Light

Love looks not with the eyes, but with the mind;
and therefore is winged Cupid painted blind.

~William Shakespeare

When the cloud in the sky starts to pour
And your life is just a storm you're braving
Don't tell yourself you can't lean on someone else
Cause we all need saving
Sometimes

~Jon McLaughlin
We All Need Saving

Hearts *in* Darkness

CHAPTER ONE

"*W*ait! Can you please hold that?"

Makenna James huffed her frustration at her crappy day as she jogged toward the waiting elevator. Her cell phone rang in her suit jacket pocket. She shifted her bags over her right shoulder to pull it out. The bleating ring tone was as annoying as an alarm clock in the morning, but it was probably just that the damn thing hadn't stopped ringing all afternoon.

She glanced up just long enough to glimpse a big tattooed hand holding the elevator door open as she finally freed the small black phone. She spun it around in her hand to answer it and fumbled, sending it crashing and skidding along the dull marble floor.

"Shit!" she muttered, already fantasizing about the bottle of wine she was going to demolish once she got home. At least the phone skittered toward the still-waiting elevator. God bless the patience of the Good Samaritan holding it.

Makenna bent down to retrieve the phone, then stumbled into the elevator. Her long hair swung into her face, but she didn't have a free hand to push it back.

"Thanks," she mumbled to the Good Samaritan as her laptop strap fell off her shoulder bringing her purse with it to the floor. The elevator beeped its impatience even as the man removed his hand and the doors eased shut.

"No problem" came a deep voice from behind her. "What floor?"

"Oh, um, lobby, please."

Distracted by her purse and the day in general, Makenna hiked her laptop strap higher on her shoulder, then reached down to grab her purse. She slung it over her arm once more and looked down at her phone to see whose call she'd missed. The LED screen was black.

"What the...?" She flipped the phone around and found a gaping rectangular hole where the battery should be. "That's just perfect."

There was no way Makenna could be without her phone. Not with her boss calling every five minutes to check on the progress of her work. That it was Friday night and the beginning of the weekend made little difference to him toward the end of a project. She'd be glad when this contract was up.

With a sigh, she reached a tired hand over to the panel and jabbed at the button to return to the sixth floor. From the corner of her eye, she glimpsed just how tall her Good Samaritan was.

Then the elevator jolted to a stop and everything went pitch black.

---

*C*aden Grayson tried not to chuckle at the frazzled redhead careening towards the elevator. Why did women carry so many bags anyway? If it didn't fit in the pockets of his worn-soft jeans, he didn't carry it.

As the woman reached down to scoop up her phone—another thing Caden refused to carry unless he was on call—he found himself mesmerized by the way her hair tumbled over her shoulder in a long waterfall of soft, wavy red.

When the woman finally made it into the elevator, she murmured distractedly that she was going to the lobby too. He stepped back against the rear wall and bowed his head as he always did. He didn't really care if people stared at his piercings and ink, but that didn't mean he went out of his way to see their looks of disapproval or, worse, fear.

Caden shook his head in amusement as the woman continued to juggle her belongings and spat out a string of expletives under her breath. His day had been a complete pisser, so he was almost ready to join in with her—though his particular coping mechanism usually had him looking for the humor in a situation. And he found Red damn funny. He was grateful for the distraction.

Red reached in front of him to press a button. Caden almost laughed when she punched it at least five times. But the laughter died in his throat when he caught the scent of her shampoo. One of the things he loved about women: their hair *always* smelled like flowers. And that scent, combined with the redness and the softness and the waviness...Caden shoved his hands in his jeans pockets to keep from running his fingers through the thick mass of her hair. But, Christ, how he wanted to, just once.

And then Red disappeared, along with everything else, as the elevator jerked to a stop and the lights went out.

Caden gasped and stumbled back into the corner of the elevator. Clenching his eyes, he lowered his head into his hands and counted backwards from ten, trying to remember his breathing techniques, trying to keep from flipping the fuck out.

The confined space of the elevator was one thing—years of therapy had gotten him past that. Mostly. But confined spaces with no lights? No way. The pounding of his heart and tightness in his chest told him that was a complete fucking deal breaker.

He was on five when he realized Red was making a noise. He managed to push through his fear enough to hear she was laughing. Hysterically.

Caden opened his eyes, though they were useless. But he could tell from Red's laughter she was still near the bank of call buttons. And, amazingly, the more he focused on her, the faster his panic receded— or, at least, it didn't worsen.

God, he wished he could see her. He could almost imagine her shoulders shaking and her eyes tearing and her clutching her stomach from the force of her now breath-stealing laughter. When she snorted, Caden quirked a grin, as her less-than-graceful noises set her off to laughing once more.

But he didn't mind, because he found himself standing upright again, breathing more normally. He'd beaten back the panic. Thanks to her.

---

*M*akenna would've shouted if she could've, but she was laughing so hard she could barely breathe. *Perfect! This is just freaking perfect!*

Nobody would believe the big steaming pile of crap her day had been. It started when she broke the heel on her favorite pair of strappy sandals walking up the stairs out of the metro. She'd had to turn around and make the twenty-minute trip back to her apartment to change shoes, simultaneously making herself late for work and earning herself blisters on both pinky toes from choosing the only other shoes—a pair of new heels—that matched her suit. It had all gone downhill after that. And now this. It was like...some stupid sitcom. With canned laughter and all. She snorted at the thought. The ridiculousness of the sound and the situation and her whole blasted day had her laughing again until her right side cramped and her cheeks burned from how wide she was smiling.

Finally, she dropped her bags somewhere on the floor next to her and reached out a hand until she encountered a cold metal wall. Bracing herself as she tried to calm down, she used her free hand to wipe away tears and fan the heat crawling up her face as she remembered Good Sam was in there with her.

Oh God. He probably thinks I'm a complete lunatic.

"Sorry, sorry," she finally choked out as the laughs turned into occasional chuckles. Now she was laughing at herself.

Good Sam didn't reply.

"Hello? You still with me?"

"Yeah, I'm here. You okay?" His voice resonated in the confined space, surrounded her.

"Um, yeah. I have no idea." She brushed her hair back off her face and shook her head.

The low sound of his chuckle made her feel a little less ridiculous. "That bad, huh?"

"The worst," Makenna said and sighed. "How long do you think we'll be in here?"

"Who knows. Hopefully not long." His voice had an edge to it Makenna didn't understand.

"Yeah. Don't these things usually have emergency lights?" She ran her fingers over the bank of call buttons and randomly pushed some looking for the alarm button, but none of them seemed to do anything. And she knew from working in this building for the past two years that the receiver was missing from the emergency phone cord. The hazards of working in a 1960s-era office building, apparently.

"The newer ones do."

Makenna finally gave up on the buttons. She turned towards the door and rapped her knuckles against the metal three times. "Hey! Anybody there? Can anyone hear me? We're stuck in the elevator." She pressed her ear against the cool surface of the doors, but after several minutes it was clear no one had heard. Makenna bet the elevator stopped somewhere between the third and fourth floors, which housed satellite offices of the Social Security Administration. The agency closed at five and was a ghost town by quarter after. It would certainly explain the lack of response.

Sighing, she held her hand up, but couldn't see it, even when her palm got close enough to touch her nose. "Damn, this is the very definition of pitch black. I can't even see my hand in front of my face."

Good Sam groaned. Makenna dropped her hand. "What?"

"Nothing." His voice was clipped, tight.

Oookay.

He huffed out a breath and moved around. Makenna yelped in surprise when something hard crashed into her ankle.

"Damn, I'm sorry. Are you okay?"

Makenna reached down and rubbed where his shoe, apparently, had kicked her. "Yeah. Did you sit down?"

"Yeah. Might as well get comfortable. I really didn't mean to kick you though. I didn't realize..."

"What? You couldn't see me standing here?" She laughed, trying to make light of their situation and break the ice a little, but his lack of reply rang loudly in the small space.

Makenna sighed and used her hand to guide her way back over to "her side" of the elevator. She tripped when her left foot got caught in the strap of one of her bags. Her heel slipped off. She kicked the other one off in defeat. It tumbled...somewhere into the darkness.

"I guess I might as well get comfortable, too, then," she said, as much to fill the dark silence as to make small talk with him. She found the back corner of the elevator and sat down, then carefully stretched her legs out in front of her and crossed her ankles. She smoothed her skirt over her thighs and then rolled her eyes at her actions. It wasn't like he could get a peek right now anyway.

The darkness was so disorienting. Not a hint of ambient light filtered in anywhere. Her impulse was to use the LED on her cell phone to shed some bluish light on their predicament, but its battery was currently somewhere in the elevator lobby of her floor. And, because this day was what it was, she'd drained the battery to her laptop earlier, so it wasn't any use either.

She wished she knew what Good Sam looked like. His aftershave was clean scented. She bit back a laugh as the thought of running her nose up his throat dashed through her head.

Makenna couldn't tell how much time was passing. She twiddled her thumbs, counting to a hundred twiddles as she also shook her ankles back and forth.

Why isn't he saying anything? Maybe he's shy. Or maybe you shocked and awed him with your graceful entrance, elegant nervous breakdown, and sexy snorting. Yeah, that must be it.

*C*aden wished Red would laugh again, or at least talk. Her reminders about just how goddamned dark it was in this suffocating box of an elevator had quickly reawakened his anxiety. When the tightness settled back into his chest, he'd sat down so he didn't embarrass himself by passing out or some shit and kicked her when he'd stretched out his legs. She hadn't uttered more than two sentences since.

Good going, man.

He heard her over there fidgeting and sighing and shifting. He started concentrating on the sound of her legs shaking against the short-knapped carpet of the elevator floor, and the distraction helped him slow his breathing. The deep breath he finally pulled into his lungs relieved and surprised him.

Caden was kind of a loner. He had a few close friends—people who'd known him most of his life and knew what happened when he was fourteen—but otherwise he didn't spend much time talking to people he didn't know. Part of that he did himself. The ink and the piercings and the skull trim all gave off an antisocial vibe, even if that was more image than reality. So it was odd for him to siphon calmness off another person the way he was doing with Red. He didn't even know what she looked like, for God's sake, or what her name was.

There was one way to fix that. "Hey, Red?" His voice sounded loud in the small space after the long moments of quiet. "What's your name?" he asked in a quieter voice.

She cleared her throat. "Everyone calls me M.J. You?"

"Caden. Is M.J. your name, or just what everyone calls you?"

She chuckled. "Well, *Caden*"—her emphasis on his name brought an unexpected smile to his face—"my name is Makenna, but M.J. seems to have stuck."

"What's the J for?"

"My last name is James."

"Makenna James," he whispered. He liked the name. It fit all that thick, luscious red hair. "You should go by Makenna. It suits you."

Caden grimaced as he waited for her reaction to his unsolicited opinion. His mouth had worked faster than his brain.

"Hmm," she replied noncommittally. He thought he'd offended her until she continued, "Well, one advantage of M.J. is it doesn't make me stand out in my firm."

"What do you mean?"

"I'm the only woman."

"What do you do?"

"Are we playing Twenty Questions now?"

He grinned. He liked a woman who gave as good as she got. For an instant, the darkness felt almost freeing—she wouldn't be able to judge his appearance. And he was enjoying her openness. "Why not?"

She laughed softly. "Well, in that case, I've answered a lot more than you. What's your last name?"

"Grayson. Caden Grayson."

"And what do *you* do, Mr. Grayson?"

He swallowed thickly at the sound of her saying his name that way. It...did things to him. "Um"—he cleared his throat—"I'm a paramedic." Caden had known what he wanted to be since he was a teenager. It wasn't easy seeing other people, other families, in situations like the one that'd changed his life, but he'd felt called to do it.

"Wow. That's great. Very impressive."

"Yeah. It pays the bills," Caden said, embarrassed at the compliment. He wasn't used to receiving them. As he thought, he brushed a hand back and forth against the short-trimmed hairs on the top of his head. His fingers trailed over his most prominent scar. "How about you?" When she chuckled, he wondered what amused her.

"I'm an accountant, and, before you die of boredom over there, I do forensic accounting, so it's not as bad as it sounds."

He found himself laughing, though he wasn't sure why. Something about her just made him feel good. "Well, that's very...interesting."

"Shut up." She chuckled again.

He grinned broadly. "Good comeback."

She huffed and her voice sounded amused. "If I could see you, I'd smack you."

The sudden reference to the darkness chased the smile from his face. He gulped down a deep breath through his constricting throat.

"Hey, where'd you go?"

"Nowhere." He couldn't help the shortness in his tone, though his frustration was more at himself than her. He didn't like losing his shit, certainly not in front of other people.

"I'm sorry. Um...I wouldn't really hit you, you know."

Just like that, she refocused him. "Oh, well, I feel better now," he said, amusement threading back into his voice. And it was true. He rolled his head on his shoulders and released some of the tension in his neck. She was quiet for a while, making him wonder if she really thought he'd been upset about her comment. He didn't like the idea she might be feeling badly. "Um, I'm a little claustrophobic is all. So, if you could, maybe, stop mentioning it's dark in here, even though...shit."

"What?"

"Well, obviously it's dark, but I can avoid thinking about how tight and...close it is in here when you're talking—just, talk about something else." He rubbed his hand roughly over his skull trim knowing he sounded like a complete idiot, which was why he didn't often get to know anyone beyond his small circle.

But her reply sounded completely earnest. "Oh, okay. Well, then, what should I talk about?"

CHAPTER TWO

"Hell, I don't know. How about that game of Twenty Questions?"

Makenna smiled at his gruffness but couldn't blame him. She'd be freaking out if she were claustrophobic and thought he had to be strong to sit there so calmly. She wondered if that was why he'd been so quiet earlier and decided to help him through their hopefully temporary confinement.

"Okay. You go first."

"Okay." He was quiet for a moment, then said, "What's a forensic accountant?"

"An accountant who analyzes accounting and business practices as part of an investigation, like for litigation."

"Oh, well, that actually does sound interesting. Like detective work."

She appreciated his effort, but was so used to people developing narcolepsy at the mere mention of being an accountant that she wasn't sure if he was being serious. "Are you making fun of me?"

"Not at all," he replied. The speed of his words confirmed his sincerity.

"Okay, then. My turn?"

"Fire away."

Makenna smiled. "Did I see a tattoo on your hand?"

He didn't answer right away. "Yeah. It's the head of a dragon."

Makenna didn't have any tattoos—she'd been afraid it would hurt to get one—but she'd also always been a little fascinated by them. "Is it just the head?"

"Hey, it's my turn now."

"That wasn't a new question," she argued, "that was simply a clarification of my previous question."

"I thought you were an accountant, not a lawyer." He chuckled. "Fine. The whole dragon's on my arm and its head's on the back of my hand. Now, is it my turn, counselor?"

Makenna couldn't help but smile at his sarcasm. Growing up with three brothers had taught her the fine art of banter. "You may proceed."

He laughed and she liked the ring of it. "How very magnanimous of you."

"Ooh, pulling out the SAT words now, are we?"

"What? A guy with a tattoo can't use a four-syllable word?"

Makenna sucked in a breath, then sighed. "I wish I could see your face so I could tell if you're being serious or not." Then, just in case her indirect reference to the darkness bothered him, she hurried to add, "That's *so* not what I was saying. Just yanking your chain. It's your turn, already."

His low chuckle made her smile in relief. "Yeah, yeah. Okay. What made a girl like you become an accountant?"

A girl like me?

"A girl like me?" Makenna frowned and awaited his explanation. She couldn't begin to fathom what he meant.

"Just..." Caden sighed and murmured something she couldn't understand. "You're pretty."

Makenna went from flattered to perturbed and back again. In the end, she couldn't decide which emotion to settle on. Growing up in a houseful of boys turned her into a tomboy from as early as she could remember. Although her college roommates introduced her to girly things like dresses and skirts and lingerie and makeup, she still thought of herself as just one of the guys. Nothing remarkable. Certainly not the kind of girl her brothers drooled over.

"Um, shit, that didn't come out right either. I mean, you *are* pretty, but of course pretty girls can be smart. I mean—shit, I'm just gonna stop talking now."

Makenna finally settled on amused and burst out laughing. "Yes, now would be a good time to put down that shovel." Getting more serious, she said, "Well, and this will no doubt up my geek factor to you, but I was always very good at math, and numbers just came easy to me. I didn't really want to go into the theoretical side of it and teach. And then my oldest brother became a cop. He told me about forensic accounting."

Caden didn't respond, and Makenna was almost certain she'd put him to sleep. Then he said, quietly, "I really like the sound of your voice."

Makenna's flush ran down into the neck of her silk blouse. Saying she was pretty hadn't gotten to her, but his saying he liked her voice set butterflies loose in her stomach.

"Me, too. I mean, I like it, too. Your voice, that is." Makenna bit her lip to cut off the spectacular stream of nonsense coming out of her mouth, then pretended to thunk herself in the forehead. In that moment, she was glad for the darkness.

---

*C*aden felt lucky Makenna was as easygoing as she was, because if he put his foot in his mouth one more time, he was sure she'd make good on her threat to smack him. First, he jumped to conclusions, assuming she'd judged him when she learned of his tattoo. He'd just been so disappointed she might disapprove of him even without seeing him. Then, his verbal filter failed, and he'd called her pretty. He'd been thinking of her red hair again and, without a doubt, it was pretty, beautiful even, but it slipped out without him thinking about the caveman way he'd phrased the question. And then he'd actually admitted he liked her voice. It was true, but he didn't need to be saying that shit out loud.

But then she'd said it too. And the dynamic shifted back in his favor. She'd stumbled over her own compliment. He thought maybe, just maybe, she enjoyed him saying he liked her voice.

He searched his mind to think of another question, one that ran less risk of him encountering bodily harm at her hand. He finally came up with "How many brothers do you have?" He probably should've thought of something else, but the words were out of his mouth.

Her voice sounded like she was smiling. "Three. Patrick's the oldest. He's the one who became a cop. Ian's next. And Collin's a year younger than me. Do you have any siblings?"

"His name was Sean. He was two years younger than me." Caden waited, suspecting Makenna would pick up on his use of the past tense.

Finally, her response came. "I'm sorry. I can't imagine losing one of my brothers. That must've been very hard. Can I ask how long ago he...you lost him?"

Something about the darkness made it safe to share some of this story. She couldn't see his grimace or the ticking of his clenched jaw. She couldn't wonder about the way he flexed his right shoulder so he could feel the skin over his shoulder blade move where Sean's name was inked. And she couldn't see the crescent-shaped scar on the right side of his head he always fingered when he got tangled in memories of his brother.

"I'm sorry. You don't have to talk about it."

"Don't apologize. I don't talk about him often, but maybe I should. He died when I was fourteen. He was twelve. That was fourteen years ago." As he said the words, Caden could hardly believe he'd been alive longer without Sean than he'd been with him. He'd been the best friend Caden ever had.

Makenna burned to reach out to him. She shoved her hands flat under her thighs to keep from seeking out a hand to hold or a shoulder to squeeze. She didn't know this man from Adam, but she hurt for him. Two years ago when Patrick had been shot in the line of duty, she'd experienced a kind of terror she never wanted to feel again. And she could only imagine the way that feeling would've been amplified if her brother hadn't pulled through. She could hear it in Caden's voice.

But she couldn't resist some small gesture, so she said, "Thanks for sharing that, Caden. That's so damn young. I'm really sorry."

"Thanks" came his whispered reply. "So"—he cleared his throat—"how old are you?"

Makenna figured he'd appreciate her lightening things up, so she said in her most haughty voice, "Why, Mr. Grayson, what kind of question is that to ask a lady?"

"You're fascinated with numbers, so I'd think you'd be happy to tell me about this one."

She smiled as the good humor returned to his voice. "Fine." She exaggerated a sigh. "I'm twenty-five."

"A mere babe."

"Shut up, old man."

He barked out a laugh that made her grin.

A comfortable silence enveloped them. But now, without the conversation to distract her, Makenna was hot. It might've been the end of September, but the daytime temperature still felt like the middle of the summer. The lack of air conditioning was starting to make a difference inside the old elevator and her silk blouse clung uncomfortably.

Makenna shifted up onto her knees and shrugged out of her suit jacket. She folded it as neatly as she could and tossed it gently in the general direction of her bags.

"What are you doing?" Caden asked.

"Taking off my jacket. I'm getting a little warm. I wonder how long it's been." She untucked her blouse and shook the hem to fan air onto her abdomen.

"I don't know. Maybe an hour, hour and a half?"

"Yeah," Makenna agreed, figuring it was somewhere around 8 p.m. Someone would surely figure out they were in here sooner or later, right? Sighing, she settled back into her corner, but turned on her hip a little. Even though it was carpeted, the floor was hard. Her behind was falling asleep. "So, whose turn is it?" she asked.

Caden chuckled. "No idea. You can go though."

"What big plans did you have for tonight?"

"No big plans, really. I was just going to meet some buddies to play pool. I work a lot of night shifts, so I don't get to hang out with them as much as I'd like."

Makenna thought that sounded nice. Except for her college friends, only one of whom was in the D.C. area with her, she didn't have many girl friends to hang out with. For some reason, she'd always had an easier time making guy friends. She blamed being surrounded by her brothers and all their friends growing up.

"How 'bout you?"

"Oh, I had a very important date with my couch and a bottle of wine."

"I'm sure they'll reschedule."

"Yeah." Makenna chuckled, then sighed. "They're pretty much always available. Okay…moving on from that depressing topic…"

"Are you seeing anyone?" Caden asked, *not* getting off the depressing topic at all.

"Obviously not. You?"

"No."

Makenna took more pleasure in his answer than she thought she should. Maybe she was just happy she wasn't the only single person left out there. All her friends seemed to either be getting married or engaged. It was like a line of dominos falling, only she didn't seem to be in line.

"Okay," Caden said with a clapping sound that rang loud in the small space, "favorite color."

"Seriously?"

"Down to basics, Red."

She smiled widely at the nickname so many others had called her but she'd never really liked until now.

"Blue. Yours?"

"Black."

She smirked. "How very boy of you."

He chuckled. And launched into at least another twenty questions of the kind of minutiae you learned about a person after a couple months of dating: favorite band, favorite movie, favorite food, favorite place, favorite-everything-else-he-could-think-of, most embarrassing moment, and best day ever, though he skipped asking about worst day ever. Makenna was glad—she didn't think she could resist touching him if he talked about his brother again.

Makenna enjoyed the conversation. Some time in the middle of discussing favorites, she stretched out on the floor and propped herself up on her elbow. Despite being trapped in a pitch black elevator for a couple hours with a stranger, she felt surprisingly relaxed. The smallest niggling thought snuck into the back of her mind—she was kind of not looking forward to when the power came back on and they'd go their separate ways.

And, even more than that, they had a surprising amount in common. They both loved Italian and Thai food. She could even overlook his love of sushi since he was such a huge fan of Kings of Leon, her absolute favorite band. They both enjoyed going to baseball games, mostly to sit out in the sun and drink beer with friends, and neither understood the point of golf at all. And they shared a love for stupid humor movies, even though they couldn't agree on ranking them.

It was the most entertaining conversation Makenna had had in a very long time. Caden seemed genuinely interested in her answers. And he debated and argued every little point in a way that made her want to kiss him to shut him up. She liked the way she felt around this man, despite the fact she'd never laid eyes on him.

*C*aden couldn't remember the last time he'd had such an easy conversation or the last time he'd laughed or even smiled so much. It felt...good—which was remarkable. He tended to operate somewhere between "fine" and "pretty good" most days. And he'd long ago made peace with that. It was worlds better than the abyss in which he'd spent most of his teenage years.

"I gotta stand up and stretch," he said out of nowhere.

"Yeah, I know. This floor leaves a little to be desired."

"At least it's carpeted and not marble or tile. Your legs would be cold if it was." Caden reached his arms over his head and twisted his torso back and forth while he remembered the way her little gray suit skirt hugged her shapely bottom. His spine cracked when he turned to the left.

"Cold might feel good right now."

Makenna was right. It had gone from that over-air-conditioned feeling most office buildings had in the summer to comfortable to warm. It wasn't hot yet, but it was heading in that direction.

As Caden settled back on the floor and tried to find a position that didn't aggravate the tingles in his ass and hips, Makenna reopened the questions. "So, I work in this building, but what landed you in this fine elevator today?"

"Settling my father's estate. His law partner's office is on the seventh floor."

"Oh, I'm sor—"

"Don't be. My father was a very unhappy man for a very long time. And we didn't get along. He's gotta be in a better place now. Anyway, I just had to sign some paperwork."

He just barely heard Makenna's soft "Oh."

"So," he said, wanting to move away from yet another depressing topic, "first times—who, when, where, how good."

"What?" Makenna choked out an incredulous laugh. "Uh, I think not."

"Why not? We've talked about just about everything else. I'll even go first."

Makenna was quiet for a minute and then started moving around. She sounded closer than she'd been.

"What are you doing?"

"I'm not entertaining the idea of talking about this until I've at least broken bread with you. And I'm starving over here."

He'd been trying to ignore his stomach for the past...hell, he didn't even know how long. But her mention of food had him salivating.

Makenna was muttering, "Come on, come on, where is it. Not that bag." She nearly startled him with her triumphant "Ha! All right, Mr. Grayson, would you prefer a granola bar or a little bag of trail mix?"

He grinned, not expecting her to share with him, and he certainly had no intention of asking her to. "No, no. All yours."

"Come on, you have to eat something. I've got two, so there's one for each of us. Since this is my building, it's kind of like you're my guest. So you get to pick—granola bar or trail mix." Caden could hear her shaking the bags as she continued to say in a sing-song voice, "Granola bar or trail mix, granola bar or trail mix."

He smiled. "Okay, I'll take the trail mix."

"Done. Um, here?"

The package crinkled against the carpet as Makenna slid it in his direction. He reached his hand out in search of it. When they finally met somewhere in the darkened middle, Caden dragged his hand over hers. It was small and soft. He surprised himself by thinking he wanted to keep holding her hand more than he wanted the food. She didn't pull away. They both laughed nervously.

"We'll have to share the water, though. I only have one bottle."

"How much stuff do you have in there?"

"Hey, don't be knocking my bags. Without them, we wouldn't be sharing this gourmet meal right now."

"Agreed. Sorry," he said as he threw back the first handful of nuts and raisins.

They ate in silence and the salt from the trail mix made him thirsty. He felt awkward asking, but the idea of the water tortured him. "Can I have a drink now?"

"Of course. Let me make sure the cap's on tight so it doesn't spill." They executed the mid-elevator hand-off. Caden smiled as they once again paused with their fingers touching before pulling away.

He unscrewed the lid and tilted the bottle to his lips. "Oh, God. That's good."

"I know. I didn't realize how thirsty I was until I took a sip."

"Thanks for sharing your stuff with me."

"Of course. What was I going to do? Sit here and eat in front of you? Come on, you know me better than that. Then again, maybe not."

Caden thought he did know her...or at least he was starting to. Every story she'd shared with him revealed some part of her character —and everything he'd learned told of a person who was friendly and compassionate and giving. "No, you were right the first time," he finally said. "I do."

The trail mix was gone too soon, but at least it took the edge off. They passed the water back and forth until it was almost gone, then Caden insisted Makenna take the last drink.

They sat in the heat of the dark elevator for several minutes before Caden finally gazed in her direction and said, "Don't think your little ploy with the snacks distracted me from the current question on the table."

"Not at all. But you said you'd go first."

CHAPTER THREE

*M*akenna shifted onto her back and stared at the invisible ceiling. She had a big goofy grin on her face because Caden was about to tell her about his first time, while she had absolutely no intention of sharing hers.

"Okay. I'll start then. I am, after all, a man of my word. My first time was with Mandy Marsden—"

"Mandy?" Makenna wrinkled her nose and smirked.

"Hey, telling a story over here. Keep the editorial comments to a minimum."

"Oh, right, sorry. Please continue." Her smile grew wider.

"As I was saying…my first time was with Mandy Marsden, on her parents' living room couch while they were asleep upstairs. I was sixteen and had no idea what the hell I was doing. I remember it as being nice, but I imagine Mandy might have been…underwhelmed."

Makenna found the chuckle in his voice at the end there so endearing. She liked a guy who could laugh at himself. *He must be pretty confident in bed now to share a story like that*—the thought made her even hotter than she already was. "Sounds very romantic," she managed.

"Who knows from romance when you're sixteen?"

"Well, that's true, I suppose. Did you at least buy her dinner beforehand?"

"Does pizza count?"

She couldn't help but laugh. Caden was adorable. "For a sixteen-year-old, sure. I'll give you a pass."

"How big of you. Okay, then, your turn, Red."

She didn't answer.

"Red?"

"Next question."

She heard him roll over. His voice sounded closer. "No way. We had a deal."

"Could the court reporter please read back the transcript to ascertain Miss James never agreed to tell this story?"

He scoffed. "Okay, I realize we've been in here for a while, but please tell me you're not losing your mind already."

"Not at all, just getting the facts straight."

"Come on. What's the big deal?"

She was almost glad she couldn't see him—if his eyes were anywhere near as persuasive as his voice, she'd be a goner. "Just...no," she said through a laugh at his pleading.

"It couldn't be any worse than mine."

"Nope."

"Red."

"No."

"M.J."

"Hey, that's Makenna to you, mister. And the answer's still no." Even though her initials didn't bother her in the rest of her life, there was something about the way her name rolled off his tongue she really liked. She didn't want him to treat her just like everybody else did, just like one of the guys.

"This must be some story. You realize you're building expectations here."

She groaned. "No, no, no, no."

"Tell me and I'll take you out for pizza. You can even pick the toppings." They were just joking around, but Caden found himself hoping she'd agree to the pizza, even if it didn't get the story out of her. He wanted the hell out of this box, but he wasn't at all looking forward to walking away from Makenna. Or, more likely, her walking away from him.

Makenna didn't respond right away. Caden wished he could see the look on her face, the set of her eyes. "What color are your eyes?" he whispered, once again losing the filter between his brain and mouth.

"Blue," she whispered back. "And, yes."

"Yes, what?" Caden asked, distracted by the desire to reach out and touch her face. The whispering made their conversation feel intense, intimate. And all of a sudden his body roared to life. This time, though, his racing pulse and pounding heart were a result of arousal rather than panic.

"Yes, I'll have pizza with you. If you'll see a movie with me."

Caden imagined her words slipping over his body. He wished it was her small, soft hands instead. But he was happy she'd agreed to go out with him, and that she'd turned it into a full-on date. "Yeah. Pizza and a movie, then." He rubbed his hand over his hair as the dark concealed the smile reshaping his face.

"My first time was with Shane Cafferty," Makenna started, still whispering. "I was eighteen. It was two weeks after prom. We sorta dated all summer before we went off to different colleges. But, that night, we took a blanket out and laid it in front of the pitcher's mound on the high school baseball diamond. Oh, God, this is so embarrass-ing," she groaned.

"It is not, out with it." He was surprised she'd finally relented, but her opening up made him feel hopeful.

"He'd been on the high school baseball team. He was good—at baseball, I mean, God—anyway, taking a blanket out there at night was kind of our thing. The first time was sweet. Short"—she laughed —"but sweet. It got better, though."

"That's a good story. Much better than mine. Thanks for sharing. See, that wasn't hard."

She sighed. "No, I guess it wasn't." She paused for a few moments and then said, "You know, you have an unfair advantage over me. You saw me when I came into the elevator, but I was too distracted to see you."

"Yes." He smirked at her through the darkness. "I remember. But I didn't see your face either because your hair was in the way."

"What color are your hair and eyes?" She shifted while she spoke and her voice got a little closer.

Caden itched to reach a hand out and measure just how close she was. His senses told him she was within reach. The thought made his arm ache for the feel of her. "Both brown, although I don't have much hair to speak of."

"Wh…why?"

Laughter spilled out of him. It broke the quiet between them, but not the intensity. "I keep my head shaved."

"Why?"

"I like it that way." He wasn't ready to reveal all his oddities to her just yet, because he didn't want to scare her away. He was half contemplating taking out his facial piercings before she could see them, but decided, somehow, that felt dishonest.

"Like buzz-cut shaved or like baby's-bottom-soft bald?"

"Give me your hand," Caden offered. "You can feel for yourself."

Makenna gulped down her excitement at finally getting to do what she'd been dying to do most of the night. Her sight gone, she longed for another way to make a more tangible connection to Caden. And between the sex talk—G-rated though it might've been, and the plans for a date, and the whispering, and the feeling his body was close to hers, Makenna's body was starting to vibrate with a heady sense of anticipation that made her stomach flutter and her breath come a little faster.

Still lying flat on her back, Makenna gingerly reached out her hands. "Where are you?"

"Right here." Caden caught her right hand in his, and Makenna gasped at the contact. His hand engulfed hers as he pulled it up to his head.

Makenna's pulse raced as she smoothed her hand over Caden's head. His hair was shaved so close it felt soft and ticklish as she rubbed her fingers over it. Long after it was necessary, Makenna continued to stroke his hair. She didn't want to stop touching him. And when he scooted his body a little closer so she didn't have to extend her arm so far, she smiled, thinking he liked it, too.

"Tell me something else," Makenna said in a low voice, no longer whispering, but speaking soft enough she didn't chase away whatever magic was working between them.

"Like what?"

"Like...why a dragon?"

"Hmm." He leaned his head into her hand. She smiled. When he finally started speaking, his words came in an unbroken stream. "The dragon's my fear. I put it on my arm to remind myself I've tamed it. We, uh, we were driving home from a vacation at the beach. It was a little two-lane country road, and it was late at night because me and Sean had bugged our parents to let us have all day Sunday on the beach."

Makenna sucked in a breath at the gravity of what he was sharing with her. Her hand paused against his head as she wondered if she should say something, or if she should just let him talk. She was surprised to feel his big warm palm press her hand against his head, and took that as a sign he wanted her to keep rubbing him. So she did.

"My father was a stickler for going the speed limit. He never cared if twenty cars lined up behind him, blowing their horns and flashing their lights. You could pass on these back roads on the straightaways. People did it all the time. By the time we were about an hour away from the beach, it was all the way dark. I didn't see what happened at the time, but I found out later that a tractor trailer passed us, but moved back in his lane too soon. My father swerved to avoid getting hit."

Makenna's eyes welled with tears in anticipation of where the story was headed.

"The next thing I knew, the car was upside down. Wedged in a big irrigation ditch at the edge of a field. The passenger side took the worst damage when the car rolled, the side Sean and my mom were sitting on. I was the only one still conscious after the accident. But I couldn't move because a lot of our stuff from the back of the car—it was a station wagon, of all things—had tumbled forward into the back seat and buried me. My shoulder was dislocated, and I couldn't manage the leverage to dig myself out. I kept calling their names. But none of them would wake up. I passed in and out of consciousness a few times. Every time I woke up, it was dark and I was still trapped. We were there for about four hours before another passing tractor trailer finally spotted the car top-down in the ditch and called for help. By the time they got us out, Mom and Sean were gone."

"Oh, my God, Caden." Makenna willed him to feel the comfort and peace she so badly wanted him to have. From what he'd said earlier, she hadn't realized he'd lost his mother, too. She truly wished that wasn't something else they had in common. "I'm so sorry. No wonder..."

He gently grabbed her hand and slid it around to his cheek. Makenna whimpered when she felt him press his face into her palm. To her, his gesture seemed brave. She admired his ability to ask for what he needed. His cheekbone felt prominent under her fingers and a light stubble pricked against her palm. She rubbed her thumb gently back and forth.

"When I finally got over the worst of the claustrophobia, I got the dragon. I wanted to be strong for Sean. And I wanted him to know I wasn't going to live my life in fear, when he couldn't live his at all."

Makenna was swimming in emotion. The grief she felt for him was palpable; it ran down her temples into her hairline and constricted her throat. Her desire to protect him—to make sure nothing hurt him, scared him, took from him, ever again—came out of nowhere, but she felt the kind of kinship with Caden she'd always felt with her brothers. It didn't matter that she could still count the amount of time she'd known him in minutes.

And, God, she wanted him. She wanted to pull him down on top of her. She longed to feel his weight settle on her body, his lips on hers, his hands in her hair and gliding over her skin. It had been eleven months since she'd last been with someone, and never had she felt this kind of a connection. Makenna wanted her hands on him, too. Now that she was touching him, she worried she wouldn't be able to stop.

"Don't stop talking to me, Makenna. I need your words. Your voice."

"I don't know what to say is all. I want to take away your hurt."

His cheek lifted into a smile under her hand. "Thank you. But sometimes I think I need it. It reminds me I'm alive. And it makes the good times feel that much better. Like right now, being here, with you."

CHAPTER FOUR

*B*etween the lack of any visual reference, her soft hand stroking his hair over and over, and managing to share the story of his mother's and Sean's deaths without once coming close to panicking, Caden was almost dizzy with triumph. It was Makenna, it was all Makenna's doing. And he adored her for it. No one had ever gotten into the heart of him the way she had, and certainly never as fast.

Makenna's voice interrupted his thoughts. "You say the sweetest things, Caden Grayson. I swear."

Caden smiled against her hand, still holding his cheek, and finally chuckled.

"What's so funny?"

He shrugged, then remembered the body language would be lost on her. "Sweet isn't a word usually applied to me."

"Well, then, people don't know you."

He nodded. "Maybe so." Probably so. He'd be the first to admit he kept people away. He didn't like the feeling of burdening others with his baggage. Sometimes distance was easier than acting, or explaining.

"Definitely so," she replied.

Caden liked her argumentative nature. She was playful and feisty and had him talking and laughing more in the couple hours he'd known her than probably in the whole last month combined. With her, he'd never given distance a second thought.

Caden almost moaned when she slid her palm up his face and began stroking from his temple, back over his ear, and down to his neck. His mouth dropped open. His breathing picked up. He couldn't help but lean into her surprisingly sensual touch.

He closed his eyes for a moment and just gave in to the feeling of it. He could hear her breathing and didn't think he was imagining her breaths coming quicker, too. The possibility she might be longing for him the way he was longing for her all at once made him hard. He groaned low in his throat before he could stop himself.

"Makenna."

"Caden."

Was her voice filled with longing, or was that just wishful thinking? Surely he was projecting his desire onto her, right? He swallowed thickly and shifted his hips. His button fly was relaxed, but not enough to accommodate his hard-on without discomfort.

Then, her fingers exerted pressure against the back of his neck. But she continued on with the steady stroking, and he thought he must've imagined it. He just wasn't sure. He concentrated all his focus on the movement of her hand and...*I didn't imagine it that time, did I?* There it was again—her fingertips pulling him towards her.

Please let me not be imagining that.

He licked his lips and moved his head forward just an inch or two. God, he wanted to kiss her. His fingers itched to finally thread their way into all that red hair. His lips fell open in anticipation of claiming her mouth. He wanted to taste her. He wanted to feel her under him.

"Makenna," he rasped, a plea, a prayer.

"Yes, Caden, yes."

It was all the confirmation he needed.

He pushed himself across the carpet until his chest encountered her side. He slowly lowered his head so he didn't hurt her in his blind impatience. His mouth found a cheek first and he pressed his lips against the soft apple of it. She moaned and wrapped her arms around his broad shoulders. His right hand landed in a pile of silky curls, and the satisfaction he felt at finally touching her hair made him swallow hard.

"So soft," he murmured, meaning her hair and her skin and the mound of her breast pressing against his chest where he lay atop her.

Caden let out his own moan when her lips pressed against the skin in front of his ear. She exhaled roughly, and the rush of her breath over his skin brought goose bumps to his neck.

He trailed soft kisses across her cheek until he found her lips.

And then he couldn't go slow anymore.

And neither could she.

Caden groaned as his first kiss brought her full bottom lip into his mouth. Both hands found their way to her face, and he cupped his palms around her cheeks so he could guide their movement. Makenna's high-pitched moan accompanied her hands grasping at the back of his head and neck.

When her mouth fell open, Caden accepted the invitation like a starving man at a feast. He slipped his tongue into her sweet mouth and relished the tantalizing caresses their tongues traded. Makenna stroked his head and massaged his neck and gripped his shoulders. Caden pulled himself closer to her because, as much as it was, it just wasn't enough.

He needed to be closer. He needed more of her.

---

*M*akenna was floating in the pleasure Caden's touch brought. The darkness combined with the intensity of their connection made her feel like nothing else existed in the world. She'd never experienced this kind of passion before—at least, not from a kiss alone.

From the minute he murmured those sweet words about how good it felt to be with her, she knew she was going to have to kiss him. She needed to taste the mouth of the man who'd survived such tragedy, but managed to retain so much gentleness, so much sweetness. She thought they'd shared the most honest and enjoyable conversation of her life. She yearned for more, for a way to burn it into her memory for all time.

In her mind, Makenna was saying "Kiss me, kiss me, kiss me," but she wasn't as confident as Caden seemed to be about asking for what she needed. So she stroked his head and gently pulled at his neck. And the anticipation he might actually realize what she was suggesting had her shifting her thighs at the noticeable dampness on her panties. All of this, and she'd never seen him. At least, not with her eyes.

She gasped when the warm weight of his firm chest fell across her breast. His hand gripped long locks of her hair as his mouth pressed gently against her cheek. She couldn't hold back her moan at the goodness of finally feeling him like this. Needing more of him, she cradled his head, holding him to her, then slid her hands lower, reveling in the sculpted ridges of his broad shoulders and solid biceps.

Then his lips claimed hers. While Makenna loved the sweet butterfly kisses he'd traced over her cheekbone, her need to connect with him was too great to go slow. Her mouth fell open after their first kiss, and Caden didn't disappoint. He pulled more of his torso on top of hers and explored her wanton mouth with his tongue. Sometimes he thrust and sometimes she parried. Every movement caused her heart to slam against her rib cage and her body to tingle in anticipation.

When Caden pulled back and pressed smaller kisses on her lips, Makenna took the opportunity to pursue him this time. She grabbed the back of his head and lifted her own as she kissed his mouth and sucked on his bottom lip. She gasped when she felt something metal on the side of his mouth and was so turned on at the unexpectedness of it that she groaned and licked at it. His answering grunt reverberated into her lower stomach. His lips quirked into a quick smile as she lavished attention on what she finally realized was a piercing of some sort.

More of the puzzle that was Caden Grayson came together just then. Tattoo. Piercing. Buzz cut. He must look rough on the outside.

But he was a big, sweet, considerate, sometimes vulnerable softy on the inside. And she wanted to get to know both sides a lot better.

It was impossible to know how long they kissed in the darkness—time seemed to lose all meaning. But Makenna was breathless and needy and wet by the time he ran kisses and nips down her jaw line to her ear and, from there, down her neck. His short whiskers left a trail of fire against her skin as he moved. She curled her legs toward him, needing to feel more of him pressed against more of her. The groan he let loose when she hiked her knee across the back of his thigh made her whimper and rock her hips against him.

He pulled himself closer and slid his knee between her legs, keeping her from twisting her back the way she'd been. Not that she'd really noticed. Caden sucked the small diamond stud piercing her ear lobe into his mouth as his right hand ghosted over her body and settled on the hip wrapped around him.

"Oh God, Caden."

His cheek drew into a smirk where it pressed against her own, but she didn't mind him smirking when he licked and kissed and sucked at her neck the way he was doing. She tilted her head to the side to open to him, and ran her hands back up to offer encouraging caresses to his neck and head.

That was when she felt it. The fingers on her left hand clearly traced what could only be a scar on the side of his head. She hesitated for less than a second, but he apparently sensed it because he pulled back just a little.

"I'll tell you all about it," he whispered against her neck, "I promise."

She inhaled a breath to respond when the elevator jolted and light exploded in the small space.

Makenna yelped and clenched her eyes shut. Caden grunted and buried his face in the crook of her neck. After hours of staring into blackness, the light was painful, blinding.

Makenna was frustrated with the timing of the lights, relieved they were on, but fearful about what would happen to her and Caden now that they were.

And then the elevator shuddered. They plunged back into darkness.

They both groaned again and curled around one another as they tried to adjust to the strobing effect the lights left behind their eyelids. Makenna went from being blinded to seeing a swirling kaleidoscope of disorienting red and yellow spots.

"Shit," Caden rasped.

Makenna stopped worrying about her strained eyes and paid attention to him again, only to realize his body had gone rigid above her. *Oh no.* "Caden?"

His only answer was a strangled groan low in his throat and his left hand clutching a little tighter at her shoulder.

She understood what was wrong. She might've only known this man for a handful of hours. She might not ever have seen him. But she knew him. And she knew he needed her.

"Hey, hey," she cooed to him as she stroked his hair. "It's okay."

He didn't relax at all, but she sensed he was listening to her, or trying to.

"I'm here. And we're okay. We're gonna be okay. You're not alone." *This time*, Makenna added to herself. She was mentally cursing that teasingly temporary return of the electricity, because it'd offered the most glaring reminder of the whole night that Caden was trapped in a small, pitch-black metal box. She found herself furious on Caden's behalf. As she continued to stroke him and offer occasional murmured reassurances, mentally she cursed the inventor of the elevator, the electric company, her meter reader, and, while she was at it, threw in a few choice words for Thomas Edison, too, because, well, Caden wouldn't be trapped in a tiny electrical conveyance if good old Tom hadn't gone and found a way to apply electrical theory. She wasn't too happy with Ben Franklin and that damned kite, either.

Caden's shoulders finally unbunched. He shuddered and inhaled. Makenna let out a breath she didn't realize she'd been holding.

"I've got you, Good Sam," she said with a relieved smile.

He nodded infinitesimally, but they were so close that she felt it nonetheless.

"Come here," Makenna offered as she guided his head from where it'd been buried in her neck to her opposite shoulder so he could lie alongside her. She stretched to wrap her arms around him and was just barely able to clasp her fingers together as she held him.

---

*T*he shock of the flashing light set off a panic attack so unexpected, Caden had a hard time breathing. The only thing that kept him from losing his shit entirely was the calming scent of Makenna's hair and neck.

He didn't need to wonder why the light had set him off. All at once he was sucked fourteen years into the past, hanging upside down with his head wedged between the front center console and passenger seat, buried in a pile of baggage and vacation souvenirs. Something sharp stabbed into his side, making it difficult to take a deep breath without worsening the sting of it. His head rang and throbbed. Something wet ran down into his hair. And his right shoulder sat entirely too close to his jaw to be natural. For the longest time, the darkness and silence was eerily complete. But then the full horror of his situation would be fully illuminated by a flash of light from a passing car.

The first time it happened, Caden had been filled with relief and used much of what energy he still had screaming, "In here! We're in here!"

But no help came.

Not many headlights went by as the hour had become so late, but with each one Caden had his faith raised and dashed, his battered body further buffeted against the rocks of pleading hope and terrified disappointment.

As he passed in and out of consciousness, those rare moments were even harder to bear, because it became difficult for him to distinguish reality from nightmare. By the time a passing tractor trailer finally stopped to help several hours later, Caden was so sure he wouldn't survive the crash he didn't answer when the driver called out to ask if anyone could hear him.

"God, Caden, that's horrible."

He frowned and unthinkingly shifted his head to look up at Makenna's still-hidden face. "What?" he asked, his voice a dry scrape.

"I said that was a horrible thing for you to have gone through. I'm so sorry."

With a start, he understood he'd said out loud what he only thought he'd been remembering. And yet, here was Makenna, still holding him, soothing him, accepting him completely despite his infuriating childish fear.

For fuck's sake, he ought to be the one comforting her through this ordeal.

He leaned his head back into the crook of her neck and breathed deeply. Without having seen more of Makenna than her gorgeous red hair and her tight little backside, Caden was sure he'd be able to pick her out of a crowd by her luscious scent alone.

As he relaxed more fully, something she'd said came back to him. "Why did you call me 'Good Sam'?"

She squeezed her arms around him. He could hear the smile in her voice when she spoke. "Before I knew your name, I was thinking of you as my Good Samaritan. For holding the elevator door." She chuckled. "I really needed something nice to happen to me today, and you being patient enough to wait earned you the nickname."

Caden smiled. That he'd done something to make her day better unleashed a warm satisfaction through his body, easing the tight strain of his muscles. "Whatever you say, Red."

"You know, I'm close enough to smack you now."

He chuffed out a laugh, releasing more of his anxiety. "Go ahead, I might like it." Second by second, he was feeling more like himself again, relaxed enough that his body started responding to his memory of their phenomenal kissing. Not to mention the way she was wrapped around him. When Makenna coughed out a laugh, Caden smiled wider that she didn't come up with a witty retort. He liked that his comment flustered her.

Caden swallowed thickly and wished they had more water. He was too warm and covered in a sheen of panic-induced sweat, though neither discomfort gave him the first thought of pulling away from Makenna's equally overheated body.

One of Makenna's hands left his shoulder just as he heard the unmistakable noise of a yawn.

"Tiring of your stranded-elevator company already?" Caden asked, but also worried it could be true, particularly once she saw him.

"Never," she said through the tail end of the yawn. "Sorry. It'd been a long day hours before I had the pleasure of meeting you. And the heat is making me sleepy. And you're comfortable," she added in a small, tentative voice.

"So are you." He squeezed with the arm lying across her torso and tucked his fingers under her back to keep his hold firm. "Close your eyes, Red." Caden thought he could surely fall asleep in this woman's arms, but hated the idea of missing even one of what he was sure would be too few remaining captive minutes with her.

"I don't really want to," she protested in a whispered voice.

"Why not?"

She didn't answer right away, but finally said, "Because I'm... enjoying you."

Caden hid his smile in her neck and reached forward to press a rainfall of kisses on her soft skin. He traced his nose up the slender column of her throat to her ear. "Me, too," he breathed, enjoying her shiver. He pressed a kiss against the shell of her ear and added, "I'm sorry, for earlier."

One of her hands felt its way up to his face, where she tenderly cupped the hard angle of his jaw. "Please don't be. I'm just glad to be here for you."

He laid his head back on her shoulder. "But I want to be here for you."

"You are." He grumbled and she squeezed her arm around him. "Make you a deal: I'll help you through your claustrophobia, and you can help me with spiders."

"Spiders?" He chuckled.

"Those things have *way* too many legs to be acceptable. Don't even get me started on centipedes."

"Deal." He laughed, but inside he was beaming because her proposition only made sense if they were going to spend time together outside this damn elevator. And he really wanted that.

Hopeful, Caden pulled his hand out from under her back and stroked her long hair, threading his fingers through it from scalp to curled ends. When his fingers would linger over her scalp, she'd make a noise like a satisfied purring kitten, encouraging him to pet her over and over again.

Finally, her body relaxed under his. She fell asleep. And then it was his turn to feel satisfied—satisfied that this woman who hardly knew him and had never seen him felt safe enough in his arms to give herself over to the vulnerability of sleep. It was a trust he vowed never to break.

CHAPTER FIVE

*M*akenna awakened slowly and begrudgingly emerged from her dream. She'd been lying on a beach, the heat of the summer sun beating down on her, and her arms and legs had been entangled with her lover. She could almost feel his weight covering her.

And then she was awake enough to realize at least part of what she'd dreamed was real. The night came back to her in a rush. The elevator. Caden. The kisses. She smiled into the darkness.

She couldn't guess how long she'd been asleep, but it was long enough that her back protested the hardness of the floor.

"Hey." Caden's voice was gruff, thick with sleep.

"Hey. Sorry if I woke you."

"Nah. I've been in and out of sleep."

"Oh." Makenna covered a yawn.

"You snore," Caden said after a minute.

"I do not!" At least, she didn't think she did. It'd been a long time since she'd slept with someone else. She covered her eyes and groaned. When Caden chuckled, Makenna dropped her hand, turning her face in the direction of his.

"No, you don't. I just wanted to get a rise out of you."

"You suck," Makenna said through her own chuckle.

Caden shifted forward and pressed his lips against her throat. His kiss turned to suction as he drew her skin into his mouth. She gasped. After a few seconds he let go. "I *can* suck," he murmured as he kissed her again.

Oh my.

Her mind flirted with something witty, but all she could get out was a whimper as he pulled his lips away.

Caden shifted them, pulling Makenna onto her side facing him. She groaned, but not in pleasure. Her back screamed in protest.

"Are you okay?"

"Yeah, it's just…my back is kinda sore. Do you mind if we sit up?"

"Course not."

Makenna regretted losing the feeling of Caden's body, but sitting up relieved her back so much she moaned.

"Come here," Caden said, his voice now more distant from her.

"Where are you?"

"In the corner…you can lean against me."

Makenna smiled at his thoughtfulness—and his continued desire to touch her—and she crawled on her hands and knees toward where she thought he might be. Her fingers fell on a shoe, and she worked her way up his jeans-clad leg as she crawled between his bent knees.

Her hand touched his thigh, and he groaned. She bit her lip and smiled.

Carefully, she turned herself around and settled her body back against the hard plane of his warm chest. She hesitated for just a moment, then allowed her head to fall back onto his shoulder. He nuzzled against her hair. She could've sworn she heard him sniff, which reminded her of her earlier errant thought about running her nose up his throat. Pleased she could finally do what she'd wanted, she turned her face towards him and swam in the tantalizing scents of crisp, clean aftershave and man.

When he wrapped his arms around her waist, she sighed, then covered his arms with hers.

"Better?" he asked.

"Mmm, much. Thanks."

She felt him nod and smiled when he pressed a kiss onto her hair. Being with Caden this way—sitting so close, in his arms, him kissing her—it was totally crazy. She knew it was. So why did it feel so right?

Makenna was tired, but didn't think she could sleep. It was stifling in the elevator. She suspected the heat was as responsible for her exhaustion as the hour.

"Got any more questions?" she asked after a while, wanting to hear his voice again.

Caden chuckled and his chest rumbled against her back. "Hmm... where do you live?"

"You know the shopping center at Clarendon, where the Barnes and Noble and Crate and Barrel are?"

"Yeah."

"I live in the apartments above that.

"Those are pretty new, aren't they?"

"Yeah, I've been there about a year. It's great for people watching. I sit on my balcony a lot and watch the kids run around the playground and the people walk between the shops. How 'bout you, where do you live?"

"I got a townhouse in Fairlington. I work out of the firehouse there, so it's pretty convenient. Does your family live around here, too?"

"No. My dad, Patrick, and Ian still live outside of Philadelphia, where I grew up. And Collin's in graduate school in Boston." Makenna hesitated for a moment, then said, "My mom died when I was three. Breast cancer."

Caden hugged her tighter. "Shit, I'm sorry, Makenna. I went on and on—"

"Stop, really. I didn't want to say anything before when you told me about your mom, because...well, I mean, this sounds kinda bad to say. But I don't remember my mom. So, for most of growing up, she was more of an idea than someone I actually knew enough to miss. It doesn't compare to what you went through."

"It sure as hell does," Caden urged. "I don't care whether you're three or fourteen—a kid needs her mom. At the age you were, you probably needed yours more than I needed mine."

Makenna nuzzled back into Caden's chest, loving the protectiveness she heard in his voice. "I don't know. Maybe. But that's the thing. I don't know how he did it, but my dad was so great, he managed to fill his shoes and hers. Patrick is seven years older than me. He did a lot to help with me and Collin too. And my dad's sister moved to Philadelphia some time after my mom died. Aunt Maggie was always there when I had a problem I couldn't go to any of the guys with. So, while it's sad to think about not having had a mother, I had a good childhood. I was happy."

"Good," Caden whispered, "that's good."

---

*C*aden couldn't believe she'd lost her mother too. It explained a lot about her—she clearly understood loss, even if her experience was different than his. But he had no doubt hers had taught her the empathy and compassion she showed when he'd told his story. He thought maybe he finally understood what people meant when they talked about kindred spirits.

Makenna's back arched when she stretched and yawned, and Caden stifled a groan when her bottom pressed back into his groin. The friction was fantastic but too short. His imagination took off at a sprint. All he could think about was grinding himself into her tight ass and feeling the sensual curves of her hips in his hands as he held her to him.

He was surprised out of his fantasizing when she didn't lean against his chest again, but instead shifted around to face him. He could tell she was sitting on her legs because he felt her knees press against the inside of his thighs. The contact made his groin tighten. He clenched and released his fists, trying so damn badly to let her take the lead. He didn't want to push her past where she wanted to go. But her initiative was fucking sexy. When her hands landed on his chest, his cock twitched and fully hardened. He shifted his hips to make himself more comfortable. She leaned into him. He moaned his appreciation when her breasts fell against his chest as her lips found his chin.

"Hi," she whispered.

"Hi." He wrapped his arms around her body and hugged her to him.

Then her lips found his. Caden groaned as she focused first on the double piercing on the side of his bottom lip. He was relieved she seemed to like his spider bites, as they were called, though he suspected, for *this* woman, he'd rip them the fuck out if she didn't.

Her kiss was soft and slow, exploring, and he savored every pull of her lips, swipe of her tongue, and shifting press of her body. He ran his hands up and down her back enjoying the way the silk of her blouse skimmed against her body. When small moans and whimpers accompanied her kisses, Caden's erection twitched. He shifted his hips. He wanted more of her. He wanted to claim her, make her his.

But he also wanted to see her as he took her. He wanted to learn everything about her body. He wanted to watch her reactions as he used his mouth and hands to please her. And he definitely wanted her to have more than a quick fuck on a floor. She deserved better than that. Much better. And he thought maybe he wanted to give her everything.

Caden had to admit it. He was falling for Makenna. Before tonight, he would've put money against the idea of being able to fall for someone after only knowing them for one day. Good thing he'd never placed that bet.

Makenna's hands cupped his jaws. She leaned into him further, her breasts crushing against his chest. Caden threaded his left hand into the thickness of her hair and took control of the kiss, tilting her head back so he could get better access to her mouth. She tasted phenomenal and, combined with her sweat-heightened scent, was driving him crazy. He shifted his hips again, though she was frustratingly too far away to provide the friction he sought. She sucked hard on his tongue as she drew her head back. He growled and tugged a fistful of her hair. She gave in to his unspoken demand and tilted her head, then Caden laved his tongue against her throat, paying special attention to the spot just below her ear that made her squirm every time.

"I want to touch you, Makenna. Can I?"

She swallowed hard under his lips. "Yes."

"All you have to say is stop."

"Okay," she whispered as she cupped the back of his head with one of her small hands.

His left hand still tangled in her hair, Caden slid his right around her body and cupped the underside of her breast. He paused there, letting her get used to the sensation, giving her time to halt his movements if she wanted. He moaned his approval into the soft skin of her neck when she pressed herself into his touch.

He squeezed her gently and brushed his thumb back and forth. When he stroked her nipple, Makenna rose up onto her knees and reclaimed his mouth. He ravenously swallowed her appreciative moan and set about to elicit others by repeating the movement until she was whimpering.

The darkness intensified every sensation. The sounds of their pleasure were amplified. Textures sprang out against his fingertips. He was swimming in her scent. He couldn't wait to see her, but as he sat holding this sensual woman in his arms, he wasn't complaining he couldn't.

He slid his left hand out of her hair and raked it down her body to her other breast. She rested her forehead on his. He groaned at the feeling of her warm, firm breasts filling his hands as her hair cascaded around both of their faces.

In between panting breaths, she pressed kisses against his forehead as he fondled and stroked and teased her breasts.

She worked her lips and tongue down his temple and he braced himself for her reaction to what she'd find at the edge of his eyebrow. Finally, he felt her tongue, right there. She gasped. "Oh God, more?" she whispered.

Caden had no idea whether her reaction was positive or negative until he heard her moan as she lightly sucked the barbell piercing into her mouth.

He grunted his pleasure at her enthusiastic acceptance and thanked her by concentrating his fingers over her nipples. She cried out, her breath fanning into his ear. He couldn't help thrusting his hips again. He was hard and aching and didn't think he'd ever been as turned on before from kissing.

"Under," Makenna pleaded.

It took a moment for his brain to defog and realize what she was asking. *Hell, yes.*

Together they fumbled at the little pearl buttons on her blouse. Caden slid his fingers inside the satin of her bra cup and found warm erect feminine skin. The proof of her arousal felt incredible, but all his mind could think about was how good he knew she would taste.

---

*M*akenna thought she should be worried about how far this was going, and how much further it might go. But then Caden tugged at her hair or sucked on that sensitive spot under her ear or asked her permission to go just a step further, and she lost all capacity for restraint.

Time and again, Caden's mouth and fingers played her just the right way, as if they'd pleased her many times before. She already thought him an attentive lover, as he repeated every action that elicited a moan or a whimper or writhing from her.

She was hot and wet and needed his big hands on her body. She wouldn't let this go too far, but she had to have something, she had to have more. And she couldn't recall the last time she'd felt so sexy, so passionate. So alive.

The pads of his fingers were rough and felt phenomenal as they gently rubbed and tugged at her sensitive nipples. She could tell her bra was restraining his movements, so she freed her hands from wandering over his body and reached down to tug the satiny cups out of his way.

"You feel so good, Makenna," Caden murmured around their kisses.

She moaned as she felt him stroke his thumbs through the exaggerated cleavage created by the way her disheveled bra pushed her up and in. Needing to feel him too, Makenna's hands dropped to his stomach. She pulled at the softness of his cotton T-shirt until she could slip her hands underneath.

Caden groaned and squirmed when her fingers landed in the trail of small curls leading underneath his waistband. She played with them as she slowly walked her fingers upwards, then finally splayed her fingers out until her hands were flat on him. His stomach twitched and flinched under the teasing touches of her hands. Makenna rubbed her thighs together. She soon found his nipples and lightly scratched her short fingernails over them.

"Aw, hell, Red," he groaned.

"Like that?" She punctuated her question by fingering one of his nipples again while lightly tugging the other. When he grunted his answer, she smiled wickedly against his lips.

She was surprised and disappointed when his hands left her breasts. But then he slid them under her arms and lifted her up higher onto her knees.

"Oh, God, Caden," she cried out when he kissed a circle around her right breast, then rubbed his nose back and forth over her nipple. Her anticipation was nearly at its breaking point for the feel of his mouth there.

He didn't make her wait long. One of his arms embraced her, locking her to his mouth, while his other hand teased the unattended breast. He pulled her so tightly against him she finally had to free one of her hands from underneath his shirt to brace against the wall behind them.

His mouth on her was a riot of sensation. His tongue flicked her nipples. His teeth gently nipped. His lips sucked and tickled and taunted. His piercing bit thrillingly into her skin. Back and forth he went between her breasts until she thought she'd lose her ever-loving mind.

Makenna clenched her thighs together rhythmically, so far gone from his stimulation to her breasts she didn't care if he felt her shifting herself against him.

"Tastes so good, Makenna. Feels so good."

"God, you're killing me."

He plunged his tongue into her cleavage and slowly licked up her chest. It was erotic and thrilling and wanton. She groaned imagining him plunge that skillful tongue elsewhere.

His fingers returned to her nipples and pinched and twisted as he tilted his head back. Makenna braced her hands on his broad shoulders and looked down, sensing him all around her even though she couldn't see him. She lowered herself slowly until their mouths rediscovered one another in the darkness.

Caden pulled back a little and rubbed his rough cheek against hers. "I want to make you feel good."

"I feel so good with you."

"Mmm…can I make you feel even better?"

Makenna's head grew dizzy from the promise of what he was offering. She couldn't believe she was even considering it, but her body screamed at her for thinking she might turn him down. She nodded her face against his.

"Tell me, Red, you gotta say it out loud. I can't see your face or your eyes, and I don't want to make any mistakes here."

If she'd been just a little unsure a moment ago, she wasn't any longer. "Yes. Please…make me come."

"Oh, fuck, you can't say shit like that right now."

His words brought a smile to her face. She hoped she was affecting him as much as he was her. His words also made her feel bolder, so she teased him, just a little.

"I need to come, so bad. Please?" She bit her bottom lip at her brazenness.

Caden growled, "Mmm, yes." His hands flashed to her hips. He tried to pull her up onto his lap, but her skirt was too tight. Her thighs couldn't spread wide enough to straddle him. "Can I—"

He hadn't needed to ask. Makenna's hands were already at the sides of her thighs hitching her skirt up so she could put her legs over his. She was shaky with want and anticipation. He helped guide her.

They both moaned in needy satisfaction when the heated junction of her thighs settled over the bulge in his jeans.

Caden eased her into it. She adored him for it. He started back at her mouth again, exploring her with his tongue while his thumbs and forefingers teased her nipples. She couldn't resist licking and sucking at the metal on his lip, never imagining how incredibly sexy she'd find such piercings. And she especially loved how her attention to them made him grunt in satisfaction.

Now that Makenna had a source of friction, she had to use it. She ground herself against his considerable hardness and whimpered at how good he felt, there. His hands fell to her behind and rocked her against him even harder. With a firm grip on her ass, Caden helped her find a rhythm, encouraging her to use him for her pleasure.

Makenna moaned every time he pulled her against him, though that was nothing compared to what she felt when he finally lowered his left hand to the outside of her panties. His fingers there unhinged her. She cried out and swallowed hard and fought for a breath to ease the dizziness the pleasure caused.

He cupped her mound and grunted. "God, you're so wet."

"Your fault," she gasped.

His voice dripped with arrogance. "Happy to be blamed for this."

"Still smack you," she managed as his fingers began to move, to rub, over the soaked-through satin.

"Maybe later," he rasped. "God, you feel fantastic."

Moaning appreciatively, Makenna clutched herself to Caden's broad shoulders as he helped her thrust against him with one hand while he stroked her with the other.

"Oh, God." Everything—tension, butterflies, tingles, quivers—it all pooled in her lower abdomen.

"I wish I could see you come for me, Makenna."

"Oh!" was all she could manage to gasp out. He moved his fingers harder now, in a circle right over the nerves at the top of her sex. And it was just right. Exactly what she needed to get there.

"Yeah. It's okay, baby. Let go."

"Caden." She let out a high-pitched whimper as pressure built up under his tormenting hand. Her mouth dropped open. He sped up his movements just a little. Pressed just a bit harder.

Her orgasm was going to be tremendous. The whole middle of her body was already tense from the build up of tingling pressure that felt impossibly hard to contain. His fingers were so good. She concentrated hard on the way he was stroking her, on the connection between him and the center of her arousal, and gave herself over entirely to the pursuit of pleasure.

God, just a little more...almost...oh, God.

The elevator whirred and shook. The lights blinked back on.

CHAPTER SIX

*M*akenna groaned.

The light might as well have been a bucket of ice water—it was uncomfortable and dampened the fire that had raged in her body only seconds before.

She clenched her eyes shut against the unexpected brightness and buried her face in Caden's neck. The light seemed to affect him too. His now-still fingers remained wedged between their bodies, but his face was curled into her to block out the blinding onslaught of the lights.

Several moments passed. The lights remained on. Makenna guessed they were on to stay. Still tucked into Caden, she experimented with opening her eyes enough to get used to the brightness again. It was surprisingly hard. Her eyes protested, blinking and watering for what seemed like minutes.

Finally, she was able to open her eyes all the way. Her shoulders relaxed against Caden's broad chest. And then she realized.

Holy shit! I'm half naked. With a complete stranger. Who currently has his hand up my skirt!

A stranger I've never seen.

Who's never seen me!

What if he thinks I'm a troll? A plain *troll. Or homely—God, I've always hated that word. Homely. Homely. What kind of word is that to describe a person anyway? Oh God, I'm insane.*

The near miss of her orgasm didn't help either. Her body felt strung tight and like fluttery Jell-O all at the same time.

"I guess the power's back to stay this time," Caden said in her ear with a husky, strained voice.

"Um, yeah." Makenna rolled her eyes at her conversational brilliance, certain she was in the process of losing whatever mystique she'd had with the lights out.

Still resting her head on his shoulder, Makenna looked down between them and gaped. Caden's shirt was pushed up around his ribs and all down the left side of his toned stomach lay a swirling abstract tattoo that wrapped around to his back. It was stunning against his skin, which wasn't nearly as fair as her own. Before she really thought about it, her finger traced a curve of the black design. His stomach clenched, and he sucked in a breath at the touch. She smiled.

All at once, she *had* to see the rest of him.

Slowly, she lifted her head and sat back on his lap, keeping her eyes on his stomach all the while. She worried about what he might look like, then hated herself for even thinking about something so shallow. She finally resolved to set those worries aside. Makenna admired so much of what she knew of Caden already, there was no way she wouldn't perceive his internal beauty in his physical appearance, whatever it was.

She fought the instinctive desire to cover herself, to pull the two sides of the gaping silk closed, but she didn't want to hurt his feelings. She didn't want to close herself off to him after all they'd shared.

Her skin tingled all over, as if she could feel the path his eyes blazed as they moved across her body. Finally, she took a deep breath and trailed her eyes up from his stomach, over his tight-fitting, threadbare black T-shirt, across the hard angles of the strong jaw she'd nibbled, to his face.

She couldn't stop trembling, her body unexpectedly flooded with adrenaline as she drank Caden in through her final sense.

He was...*Oh, my God!*...so damn rugged and...masculine...and just...darkly beautiful.

The enticing angle of his jaw combined with full lips and high cheekbones and a strong brow framing intense brown eyes with impossibly long, full eyelashes. His shaved dark brown hair came to a widow's peak in the center of his forehead. Two small silver loops embraced the left side of his bottom lip. The piercing on his right eyebrow was black metal and shaped like a barbell.

He had a face that, with a certain set of his jaw and eyes, could easily appear harsh, intimidating. But she knew he was neither.

With a shaky breath and a hard swallow, Makenna got up the nerve to meet his eyes. He was watching her look him over, his eyes guarded. Not cold, but not warm either. Despite the intimate way they were still touching, Caden's shoulders bunched with tension, and the muscle in his jaw ticked. She got the distinct impression he was bracing himself for rejection.

She'd just been sitting there gawking without saying a word. Hating the idea he might interpret her silence the wrong way, she blurted out, "You're freaking gorgeous!" Her eyes bugged at her unfiltered honesty. She slapped a hand over her mouth and shook her head in embarrassment. She wished the lights would go off again as the blush roared over her skin.

He smiled. And it changed his whole face.

His eyes came to life, sparkling with amusement and happiness. Deep dimples creased his cheeks, bringing out a boyishness not otherwise apparent in his strong masculine features. He quirked an eyebrow at her as his smile shifted to a smirk so playful and sexy it curled her toes against the outside of his thighs.

She dropped her hands from covering her mouth and rested them against the firmness of his stomach. His playfulness brought out hers and, when she felt his hand twitch where it was wedged under her, she groaned and flew at him.

*C*aden's emotions were so all over the map he couldn't even catalog them. Panic had unleashed a torrent of adrenaline through his system when the lights flashed on. It was soon clear they were on to stay and, as the panic subsided—thanks once again to the calming balm of Makenna's soothing touch and grounding scent, frustration at the god-awful timing of the power's return made Caden grind his teeth as he attempted to acclimate his eyes to the brightness.

The position of his head in the soft curve of her neck allowed him to drink in Makenna's sexy nakedness. And she was...all peaches and cream skin and pert rosy nipples and feminine curves. A milky way of muted freckles ran across the top of her right breast and Caden swallowed against his desire to taste that decorated patch of skin with a long lave of his tongue. The creamy paleness of her thighs highlighted the tan on his dragoned arm where it was still wedged between them, his hand disappearing under the hem of her pulled-up skirt. Even from outside the silky fabric of her panties, Caden could feel the warm wetness of her arousal. His hand absolutely throbbed to resume its movements. He hoped like hell she'd give him the chance.

Caden was so lost in his pleasure at seeing her body he didn't at first realize she was pulling away until his headrest disappeared. He sucked in a breath and girded himself. His mind raced with worry over what she'd think of him. Makenna was a professional, educated, highly intelligent woman. Where she was well adjusted, he was anxious and withdrawn. She looked classy in her gray suit with its little white pinstripes, while he didn't even own a suit and rarely wore anything but jeans except when he worked. Her skin was pure and unblemished, while his was inked, pierced, scarred. Caden wore his past on his body; in fact, he'd used the pain of the tattoo and piercing guns to work through his survivor's guilt. He cringed and clenched his jaw as he wondered what her cop brother would think if they ever met.

Caden cut his eyes from her abdomen to her face as she sat back.

Unconsciously, he raised his knees to give her better support as she still straddled him. He watched her face and eyes carefully, looking for any clue, but he couldn't decipher her expression.

And Makenna...Makenna was so very pretty. The hair he already loved was a rich medium red that fell in a mass of loose curls over her shoulders. The way it was parted created a wavy cascade across her forehead and over the edge of her right eye. Her cheeks still bore a flush from their earlier activity, but her skin was otherwise pale and smooth like porcelain, which made her pouty pink lips stand out in contrast. He didn't think she had on any makeup, nor did she need it.

The longer she looked him over without saying anything, the more Caden tensed. His neck and shoulders stiffened as he forced his muscles to stay still under her intense gaze. He could imagine her mentally compiling all of his oddities: "Huge tribal tattoo covering half his abdomen, big dragon down the arm still trapped between my thighs, multiple facial piercings, big ugly scar on the side of his shaved head..." And that wasn't even all of it. *Great,* he could almost hear her thinking, *what the hell have I been kissing in here?*

He trapped the side of his tongue between his molars and bit down, using the pain to distract himself from his worries. If she didn't say something soon...

His jaw dropped open when her eyes finally settled on his. For being pale blue, they weren't the slightest bit cool, but instead exuded the same warmth he already associated with her personality. The weight of her gaze pinned him, as if time was halting and he was balancing precariously on the edge of a cliff, waiting to see whether he'd fall off or be caught by her acceptance.

When her words finally came, Caden couldn't interpret them at first, so different were they from the awkward polite rejection he was expecting.

Gorgeous. Freaking *gorgeous. Hardly. But, Christ, I'll fucking take it.*

Her embarrassment at her outburst released all Caden's tension. He smiled at her until she threw herself at him and literally kissed the silly grin right off his face.

He caught her in an embrace and wrapped his strong arms around her slender shoulders and held her against him. Their kisses went from urgent and needy to deep and languid. She pulled away to breathe, but he couldn't resist pressing his lips to hers for a few more chaste kisses.

She sat back from him and looked down. She fidgeted with her hands, which finally worked their way to the scalloped hem of her pink silk blouse and pulled the edges together across her chest.

Caden cocked his head to one side to figure out what her movements meant. He frowned when she crossed her arms as if to hug herself and worried at her bottom lip with her teeth. "Hey, Mak—"

Out of nowhere, the elevator began moving downward. Makenna gasped. A flashing light caught Caden's eye. The round L was blinking on the bank of call buttons. He figured the elevator was resetting itself by returning to the ground floor, which a more modern elevator would've done when the power first went out.

He squeezed Makenna's biceps. "I'm guessing we're gonna have some company when these doors open," he said, glancing down at her disheveled clothing.

"Oh, yeah, right," Makenna mumbled. She braced herself on his shoulders as she stood. He helped her up. Their movements together turned awkward and clumsy and...just felt all wrong. He frowned and rubbed his hand over his scar when she moved back to "her side" of the elevator and faced the far wall to put herself back together.

When the elevator came to a hard stop, Makenna glanced nervously at the doors as she smoothed over her hair with her hands, then leaned down to pick up her suit jacket.

Thump. Thump.

Makenna squeaked at the unexpected pounding, her hands flying to her chest. She stumbled a little where she'd been trying to step into one of her heels.

Suspecting, Caden started to say, "It's likely just—"

"Arlington County EMS," came a muffled voice. "Anybody in there?"

Caden answered with two pounds of his fist against the still-sealed crease between the doors. "There are two of us," he said as he leaned towards the door.

"Just stay calm, sir. We'll have you out of there in a minute."

"Roger that."

Caden looked to Makenna, worried about the noticeable silence that had come between them in the past minutes.

She stretched a hand forward hesitantly. "Um, sorry, you're…" She pointed at his feet.

Caden glanced down and saw he was standing on the strap of one of her bags. "Oh, shit, I'm sorry." He stepped back and leaned down to retrieve it for her at the same time she did.

They knocked heads. "Ow," they both groaned.

As they reeled back from each other, the doors inched apart. An audience of curious onlookers peered in as Makenna and Caden stood there holding their heads and looking awkward and relieved and embarrassed all at the same time.

---

*M*akenna felt like a complete idiot, not just for bumping into Caden, but also because the burning tightness behind her eyes told her tears were about to well up.

She thought she knew what his bright smile and sexy smirk and those yummy kisses had meant. But then he gave her those chaste little pecks that tasted like good-bye and didn't say anything. She'd told him he was gorgeous—*freaking gorgeous, thank you very much, and he was...is, so, yeah, there's that*—and he hadn't said…anything.

She just knew he'd be disappointed in her appearance. Caden was interesting and edgy and a little dark, and oozed a wounded sexiness that made you want to make his world all better. Makenna could only imagine how conservative, how boring, how *plain* she must look to him. For God's sake, she wasn't even wearing any makeup today. Well, she had been wearing lip gloss, but that had obviously come off a while ago…

She took a deep breath as she slipped her toe-pinching heels on. The doors finally eased open. The rush of cooler air felt fantastic against her overheated skin.

"M.J., are you okay?" Raymond asked, his kind, aging face full of concern.

She slung her bags over her shoulder as she mustered a smile for the building's evening lobby receptionist/guard. "Yep. Still in one piece, Raymond. Thank you."

"Well, that's good, good. Come on out of there already." He reached a wrinkled brown hand out as if she might need his assistance to walk.

Three firemen stood behind Raymond. Their laughter startled Makenna. She frowned at them, wondering what the hell they could possibly find funny about two people being trapped in an elevator for hours on end.

"Grayson!" One of them cackled behind his hand. "Don't worry, man, we're here to save you." The other firemen guffawed.

Makenna glanced over her shoulder in time to see the scowl on Caden's face.

"Laugh it up, Kowalski. You're a goddamned comedian." Caden clasped hands with the guy teasing him. They nudged shoulders in that guy-greeting kind of way.

Raymond led Makenna away from Caden and his fireman friends and chattered on and on about an electrical transformer failing and something about a secondary underground cable and…Makenna didn't really know what he was talking about because she was trying to listen to Caden's conversation.

One of the firemen broke away from giving Caden a hard time and walked over to her. "Are you all right, ma'am? Do you need anything?"

Makenna worked at a faint smile. "No, I'm fine. Just hot and tired. Thank you."

"Have you had anything to drink since you were in there?"

His question made Makenna's throat tighten. She *was* thirsty, now that he mentioned it. She nodded. "I had a bottle of water."

"Okay. That's good." He turned to Raymond. "All right, Mr. Jack-

son. We're all clear, then." The two men shook hands. "The fire
marshal will be by in the morning about these elevators."

"Yes, sir, I understand. I already let 'em know."

The fireman walked around Makenna and returned to the
animated conversation between his buddies and Caden.

"Raymond, will you watch my things? I need to use the restroom."

"Of course, M.J. You go right on ahead."

Makenna walked across the lobby, the click of her heels against the
marble floor sounded intrusively loud. A tingling sensation at the
back of her neck made her swear Caden was watching her, but there
was no way she was going to glance behind her to check.

She stepped into the bathroom, and the door closed slowly behind
her. The mirror drew her eyes immediately. She groaned at how tired
and rumpled she looked. Her hair curled in every direction, wrinkles
creased her skirt, and her collar lay askew from how she'd just thrown
on her jacket. She shook her head and veered into a stall, wondering if
Caden would still be out there when she was done or if he'd leave
with the firemen he clearly knew. She wasn't sure what she'd dread
more: him waiting for her and the awkwardness between them
remaining, or him being gone. Her stomach fluttered and clenched in
nervousness and hunger.

Makenna washed and dried her hands and then gathered up the
back of her hair in a handheld ponytail. Leaning forward over the
sink, she turned the cold water on and drank long relieving gulps
right from the faucet.

Her bathroom visit made her feel a little better. She took a deep
breath as she yanked the door open and walked back out into the
lobby.

His friends gone, Caden was leaning against the reception desk
talking to Raymond.

She blew out a deep breath. A wave of utter relief rushed through
her body. He hadn't left. He'd waited.

Then again, what else would a Good Samaritan do?

He smiled as she walked up to them, though this smile was nothing like the face-transforming one he'd given her after she'd blurted her opinion of him. This smile was tight and uncertain. She worried over what it meant.

Ugghhh, she groaned silently. *This is so ridiculous! How did we go from the best conversation of my life to...this?* Makenna decided her fears must be well founded—he must be worrying about how to let her down after...everything. Her deep sense of disappointment was probably out of proportion, but she couldn't help feeling it. She sagged under the weight of it.

Caden scrambled to collect her bags for her. She thanked him as she took them one at a time and hoisted them over her shoulder. They said subdued good nights to Raymond and soon found themselves standing out on a wide sidewalk in the little urban enclave of Rosslyn, just across the river from the heart of D.C. The night air was cool, refreshing. At the end of the block, a line of four Dominion Power trucks idled, their yellow lights circling and flashing.

"Um..." she began, as he said, "Well..."

They both chuckled.

Caden cleared his throat. "Where are you parked?"

"Oh, I take the metro. It's just two blocks that way." Makenna gestured behind her.

Caden frowned. "Is that such a good idea?"

"Oh, yeah. I'll be fine."

"No, really, Makenna. I don't like the idea of you walking to the metro and waiting in the station alone at this time of night."

Makenna shrugged, feeling warmed just a little by his concern.

"Let me take you home. My Jeep's just down the street here."

"Oh, well, I don't want to—"

He reached forward and grasped her hand. His touch provided almost as much relief as the water had earlier. "I'm not taking no for an answer. It's not safe for you to be walking around at this hour by yourself. Come on." He tugged at her gently, still allowing her to make up her mind.

"Oh...okay. Thanks, Caden. It's not too far."

"I know." He threaded his big fingers between her smaller ones. "Not that it would matter if it was."

She looked up at his profile and smiled. He was a lot taller than she was, and she liked tall men. He glanced down at her and squeezed her hand.

Caden led her around the corner of her building to a side street. He paused at a shiny black Jeep with no top and opened her door for her.

"Thanks." She reached inside and set her bags down on the floor of the passenger seat on top of a baseball glove. Her skirt made it a little difficult to get up and in. She blushed as she hiked it up a bit.

Caden shut her door and a moment later filled the driver's seat next to her. The Jeep rumbled to life. Makenna braced herself against the door as Caden pulled a U-turn out of the parking space. The breeze picked up tendrils of her hair and made them dance across her face. She quickly gathered the length of it in her hand to keep it from blowing too much.

"Sorry," Caden muttered as he turned onto the street fronting her building. "I go without the top whenever I can," he said in a low voice. "More open." He shrugged his shoulders.

As realization of what he was saying hit her, Makenna opened her mouth. But she couldn't find the words to tell him how brave she thought he was. So she just said, "It's okay. The air feels great."

Soon they were flying up Wilson Boulevard, the string of green lights and mostly empty streets making the trip quicker than usual. Sitting on his right side, Makenna had her first opportunity to really see the full extent of the long crescent-shaped scar that began over Caden's ear and jagged back to the edge of his hairline on his neck. In the flashing streetlights, she could tell the scar tissue didn't grow hair, making the curve of it stand out against the surrounding dark brown.

Caden must've sensed her gaze, because he glanced over at her and quirked a lopsided smile that made her stomach clench in want and disappointment that their evening was moments from ending.

A few quick turns later, the Jeep pulled into the circular drive of her condo complex. Makenna pointed out the entrance to the residences, and Caden eased into a space adjacent to the lobby door.

The usually calming sound of the central fountain bubbling was just discernible over the Jeep's idling. Makenna took a tired breath as the weight of the day pressed her back into the comfortable leather seat.

It was time to say good-bye.

CHAPTER SEVEN

*C*aden hadn't stopped cursing at himself since she'd disappeared into the bathroom. Somehow, he'd fucked things up with Makenna. Now she was acting distant and uncertain and even a little shy around him. And even though he hadn't known her very long, all of these seemed out of character for the Makenna he'd come to know and...really like. *His* Makenna was warm and open and confident. He had the distinct feeling he'd done something to clip her wings. And he was pissed as hell at himself, especially because he didn't know what to do to fix it.

And he was running out of time.

At least she'd agreed to let him drive her home. He spent the drive thinking about what to say to her and how to say it. Her stare didn't help his concentration. There was no avoiding the clear view she'd have of the ugliness of his scar. Plastic surgery when he was fifteen had smoothed out the worst of the tissue and mostly restored a natural hairline at the back of his neck, but it was still big and obvious and often made people first meeting him uncomfortable because it was hard to avoid looking at. It didn't help that the curved, thin line of ruined skin couldn't grow hair, which made it stand out even more.

He thought of the damn thing as his first tattoo—it certainly stood out as much as any of his colorful ink.

He let her have a good look, though. Because he didn't look normal and never would. And though she seemed to accept everything he'd revealed to her so far, he knew he could be a lot to take on board. He wanted her to be sure. So he only smiled over at her. He took out his tension on the gear shift gripped tightly in his right hand.

There was little he could do to drag out the trip to her condo. Even in mid-day traffic, it was no more than a fifteen-minute ride from Rosslyn to Clarendon. And, of course, when he wouldn't have minded some red lights, every one was green.

The Jeep idling at the curb, Caden shifted in his seat. "Makenna, I—"

"Caden—" she started at the same time.

They both smiled weakly. Caden swallowed a groan. Makenna's hair was windblown around her shoulders and her eyes looked tired, but she was so damn pretty. "You first," he said. *Chicken shit.*

"Thanks for keeping me such good company tonight." She gave him her first genuine smile.

Hope filled his chest. "It was my pleasure, Makenna."

She nodded and reached down to grasp the straps to her bags in one hand while her other went to the door handle. Caden's jaw clenched. "Okay, then, I guess...good night, then." She engaged the handle and pushed the door open.

His stomach rolled. She shifted herself and hopped down onto the sidewalk, then turned to drag her bags behind her. *What the fuck, Caden, stop her. Tell her.* "I'd like to—"

She shoved the door shut, drowning out his words, and leaned against the open window. He swore she looked sad but wasn't sure, just didn't know her facial expressions well enough to read them. Yet. *Please let there be a "yet."*

"It's okay. I understand."

Caden gaped, then pressed his lips into a tight line. *Understand? Understand what?*

She tapped her hand twice against the door interior. "Thanks for the ride. See ya."

"Uh, yeah." He ran his hand roughly over his scar as she turned, slung her bags over her shoulder, and walked across the wide sidewalk towards the brightly lit windowed lobby.

Uh, yeah? UH, YEAH?

When she was almost to the door, Caden threw the Jeep in first and pressed his foot on the accelerator. He pulled out into the drive. The growing distance from Makenna felt so damn wrong that Caden stopped in the middle of the street and looked back over his shoulder.

Makenna was standing in the lobby. Watching him.

He growled. *Fuck. This.*

Caden slammed the transmission into reverse. The tires screeched against the pavement as he jolted the vehicle back into the spot. He pulled forward just as gracelessly to straighten out. He wrenched the keys from the transmission and smacked the headlights off and heaved his body against the door, which he slammed shut.

Stalking around the back of the Jeep, he glared up at Makenna— glaring not so much at her as at his own idiocy for not making things right before the eleventh goddamned hour.

Her eyes widened. Her lips froze somewhere between a smile and an O. She pushed and held the door open for him.

And he hoped for all he was worth he was correctly reading the desire on her face.

He crowded right up into her space, pressed his body against hers —trapping her against the glass of the door behind her, plunged his hands into her hair until he was cupping the nape of her neck, and devoured her lips with his.

He groaned at the goodness of touching her again, like this. It was the first time anything had felt right since he'd held her on his lap in the elevator.

*A*nticipation stole Makenna's breath—and then Caden did with his forceful kiss. *Oh my God oh my God oh my God he came back! He came back!*

His demanding tongue tasted so damn good, and his piercing bit deliciously against her lip from the aggressive way he pursued her over and over. His hands tugged and massaged at her hair and neck. He just surrounded her. The difference in their height made Caden lean down over her. The way he forced her head back commanded her to open up to him. With the metal handle of the door pressing into her back, she felt completely enveloped in him, in his ardor, his scent. The world dropped away. There was just Caden.

Her hand fisted in his black shirt. He stepped closer. They panted. Their bodies heaved against one another. She moaned at the possessiveness of his grip. There was nothing shy or tentative or questioning about the way he was handling her. She felt claimed. She felt euphoric.

A tantalizing sound somewhere between a purr and a growl erupted from low in his throat. His hands continued to grip her, but he leaned his forehead against hers and pulled his lips away. "I'm sorry. I couldn't let you go."

"Don't be sorry for that," she rasped and swallowed. "Never be sorry for that."

"Makenna—"

"Caden, I—"

He clamped his lips over her mouth, their noses smashing. This time his sound was very clearly a growl. "Woman," he said against her lips, "would you let me talk already?"

The longing and frustration in his voice made her smile. She nodded. His lips quirked against hers, and he kissed her again, a series of quick pecks against her mouth.

By the time he finally started to talk, Makenna felt a little dizzy. His breath was sweet against her face. His stubble chafed at her cheek. He bored those deep brown eyes into her, pinning her against him in every possible way.

"I've never...you're just..." He heaved a sigh. "Aw, hell. I like you,

Red. I want to be with you. I want you to argue with me some more. I want to lie in your arms again. I want to touch you. I…I just…"

Hope and happiness filled and warmed her chest. He'd come back for her. He wanted her.

Smiling, Makenna reached a hand up behind her neck and grabbed one of his. He hesitated to release her, but finally let her pull his hand around to her mouth, where she pressed a big open-mouthed kiss onto the head of his dragon. She grinned up at him. "Come upstairs," she breathed. "I make a mean omelet. And I'm starving."

Her smile finally returned to brighten his face. He squeezed her hand and kissed her forehead. "Okay. I could definitely eat."

When Caden stepped away to allow her to turn back into the lobby, Makenna immediately missed the hard heat of his body all against hers. She squeaked when he grabbed at her bags, jerking her back a half step.

"Let me," he said as he pulled the straps away and slung them over his shoulder.

My Good Sam.

Out of habit, she stepped to the bank of elevators and pressed the button. This late at night, the door dinged and opened immediately. She turned to assess Caden's reaction before stepping in.

He rolled his eyes and motioned her forward, grumbling under his breath.

She was giddy things were turning out so differently than she'd feared just fifteen minutes before. Her joy bubbled over. She burst out laughing, then grasped his hand and pulled him into their second elevator of the night. "Come on. Lightning doesn't strike twice. Usually."

She hit the button for the fourth floor and stepped against him and nuzzled his chest. He stroked her hair and she melted.

The elevator reached her floor and opened up onto a rectangular space with halls running in opposite directions. She led Caden out and to the left, down to the fifth door on the right. "This is me."

She reached into her open purse still on his shoulder and found her key ring, then turned and opened the door. Smiling over her shoulder at him, she pushed into her apartment and flicked on the hall light, which illuminated her small tidy kitchen as well. She walked to the kitchen counter and dropped her keys, then turned and unburdened Caden of her bags, and plopped those onto the counter, too.

Sliding his hand around her neck, he kissed her again. Gently, adoringly. "Do you mind if I use your bathroom?"

"Of course not." She pointed behind him. "Just down that hall. I'm going to change out of my work clothes."

"Okay." He brushed her cheek with his big fingers. She leaned into the touch. Then he turned away.

Makenna floated across her small apartment to her bedroom. She stumbled into her walk-in closet, kicking off her heels as she went, and stripped off her rumpled and grimy clothes. She breathed a deep sigh of relief when she was finally naked. The idea of a cool shower took root in her mind and sounded so delicious she finally gave in. She piled her hair on top her head to keep it dry and just stood for a moment as the water streamed over her. Finally, she grabbed the bar of Ivory and ran it quickly over her skin. Minutes later, she was back in her closet and feeling a lot more like a human being.

She grabbed a pretty lavender lace bra and panty set, hoping against hope he'd actually see it, then slid into a pair of gray yoga pants and a soft lavender V-neck shirt. In her bathroom, she brushed her teeth and reworked her hair into a ponytail. She stretched her arms up over her head and luxuriated in feeling more comfortable than she'd been in hours.

When she strolled back out into the adjoining living room, she found Caden perusing her display of family photographs. She paused and leaned against the corner of the wall for a moment, just enjoying the look of him wandering around her apartment. He'd taken off his socks and shoes and now padded around barefoot, the frayed hem of his blue jeans just dragging on the floor. She was truly pleased he'd made himself at home in her space.

"Liking what you see?"

The blush roared up her cheeks. She chuckled and debated how to answer. It was late, she was tired, and she *was* interested. So she threw caution to the wind—he had come back for her, after all. "Yes, very much."

He looked over his shoulder and offered a lopsided grin that beckoned her to come stand next to him. She glanced up at the collection of photos he'd been admiring. "Those are my brothers." She pointed each of them out as she said their names. "That one's Patrick. Ian. And that's Collin. And me, of course."

"You're not the only Red in your family, I see."

Makenna laughed. "Uh, definitely not. Though, Patrick and Ian's hair looks more brownish than mine. Collin, though, had to deal with 'Carrot Top' comments all through school." She pointed to another frame. "The red was my mom's fault, as you can see." She watched Caden as he studied the picture of her mother holding Makenna on her lap just a few months before she'd died. It was her favorite because the family resemblance was so obvious. Her father told her all the time she looked just like her mother.

Lost in the image for a moment, she was surprised when Caden's hand tugged on her ponytail. She was even more surprised when her hair spilled down around her shoulders.

"Sorry," he murmured as he ran his fingers through her freed locks. "I spent all night imagining touching your hair."

Her blush returned, softer this time. His directness was one of her favorite things about him. She wasn't sure what to say in response, though, so she closed her eyes and just enjoyed the feeling of his strong fingers. After a few moments, she opened her eyes and found him staring intently at her. She smiled. "That feels nice. You're going to put me to sleep, though."

His smile made his eyes crinkle and shine. "That wouldn't be so bad, if you fell asleep with me again."

Makenna pressed her hands against her cheeks when she felt them heat again. Her pale skin tone showed everything. She grabbed his hand and pressed a kiss into his palm. "Come on, I promised to feed you."

*C*aden was ecstatic he'd read her right, that she'd wanted him to come back for her. He'd had to pull back from kissing her down in the lobby, because his imagination already had him buried inside of her against the windows. And he didn't want her to get it in her head he'd only come back for sex.

He wanted sex. That was true. The clingy form-fitting pants and the shirt that emphasized the firmness and roundness of her luscious breasts didn't help those desires. But he also wanted a chance.

Standing there in her apartment, feeling so welcomed and wanted, he was almost ready to believe she would give him one.

Still holding his hand, she walked them into the kitchen. "You can sit at the bar if you like. Want something to drink?"

"I'd love something to drink," he said, "but I don't need to sit. I can help." He watched Makenna move around her kitchen and admired the way her casual outfit highlighted her feminine curves.

She turned and smiled at his offer, then sat a cutting board and sharp knife in front of him. "You can help me chop, then. What do you like in your omelets?" She listed what she had. They settled on ham and cheese. The cold fizzy Coke she gave him relieved his parched throat.

Caden diced the ham while Makenna cracked the eggs into a glass bowl and beat them. He really liked working with her in the kitchen. It felt normal. And normal wasn't something he'd had a whole lot of in his life.

Makenna peeked over at him. They both smiled. He chopped. She stirred. Then he stole a glance at her. They both chuckled.

He was having fun with her, liked their flirting and the now-comfortable quiet between them. But it was hard not to touch her. His fingers itched to tuck her hair behind her ear. Her bottom looked so pat-able in her snug cotton pants. When she blushed, his lips yearned to taste the heat of it on her cheeks. Though, he knew if he touched her, he wouldn't be able to stop. So he busied his hands with his contribution to their meal.

Makenna wiped her hands on a towel and bent over. The sound of metal clanging made it clear she was looking for a pan. But all Caden could focus on was the way her backside pushed out toward him from how she'd bent at the waist. He took another long drink of Coke, but kept his eyes glued on her.

She grumbled and stood up, then placed her hands on her hips. "Oh, there it is," she said. She walked over to the sink and turned the water on. "Crap!" Something pinged against the floor.

Caden chuckled at the little show she didn't even realize she was putting on for him. His humor died in his throat, however, when she bent over again, retrieving the ring she'd apparently taken off and dropped.

He couldn't help it. All his focus on her rear had made him hard again. Their night together had turned out to be one long delicious tease, but now they were safe and cozy and alone in her apartment, so comfortably and intimately preparing a meal together. And he was going crazy wanting her.

Setting the little silver ring back on the counter, Makenna squirted some dish soap into the frying pan and quickly scrubbed it clean. Caden picked the towel up off the counter and walked up tight behind her. He wrapped his arms around her and plucked the pan out of her hands, then dried it quickly and set it aside on the counter. Makenna turned off the water.

Caden braced his hands against the edge of the sink on either side of her body and leaned the full press of him against her. Bending himself around her, he nipped and kissed her neck and jaw. She moaned and pushed her little body back against his.

He hadn't been so forward as to grind his erection into her, but she clearly felt it when she pressed herself back, because she gasped and clutched the edge of the sink in front of her.

Caden couldn't stop. The heat of her body against him, there, made it impossible for him to want anything other than all of her. He had to have her.

He had to have her, now.

CHAPTER EIGHT

The suddenly electric atmosphere in the kitchen rippled across Makenna's skin.

"Makenna," Caden whispered against her neck as he wrapped his arms around her.

She couldn't hold back the whimper that spilled from her open lips. His embrace felt so good, especially when he slid one arm up until it tucked under her breasts and the other down until his hand gripped one of her hips. She loved the way he used the leverage he gained from his firm hold to control the movement of their bodies.

The feel of him hard and needful behind her drove her insane with want. Her body readied itself immediately. She rubbed her thighs together as wetness settled against her panties.

With one hand, Caden cupped her jaw and drew her head to the right. Then he claimed her mouth, sucking on her lips and exploring her with his tongue. She let him lead, loving how commanding he was. He wasn't rough at all, but he took what he wanted. And she was willing to give him everything.

Makenna reached a hand back and grabbed his hip, her fingers extending further around to rest on the clenching muscle of his rear. Then, just to make sure her intentions were clear, she grasped his ass

and pulled him against her. She swallowed his groan as their kisses
grew more urgent, more desperate.

When he bent his knees and rolled his hips into her ass, she cried
out—a sound he elongated by kneading her breast and rubbing her
nipple over and over with the heel of his thumb.

Minutes passed as they writhed against each other within the firm
embrace of Caden's strong arms. His warm wet kisses were
languorous and dizzying. His quick breaths and throaty groans
sounded out a language her body understood, responded to, and
needed to hear again and again.

Her hands shook with the need to touch him. Finally, she reached
her free hand up and wrapped it around the back of his head so she
could stroke him encouragingly. He read her movements correctly.
His kisses came faster, harder.

When his lips moved to her jaw, then her ear, then her throat, her
chest heaved and her body ached with want. "Please," Makenna finally
begged.

She tried to turn in his arms but he gripped her tighter, for just a
moment. Then he relented, releasing his hold long enough for her to
move. She moaned in relief when she could wrap her arms fully
around his neck and hold him to her. He kept her trapped against the
counter, but she reveled in the tight press because it allowed her to
torment his obvious arousal with her thrusting hips and writhing
abdomen.

His hands blazed a teasing trail from her breasts to the sides of her
stomach to her hips, and back again. She squirmed under his touch
and needed more of it. Needed it on her skin.

She withdrew her arms and found the hem of her shirt. He pulled
his body off hers just enough to allow them to work together to
remove it. She dropped it to the floor, relieved to feel his big hands
exploring her skin with such enthusiasm.

Caden's eyes raked over what she'd revealed to him. Makenna
blushed at the intensity of his observation. "Aw, Red, you're so very
pretty."

Makenna's heart exploded at the affirmation his words provided.

Whatever insecurity about her ordinariness she might've still harbored in the back of her mind disappeared completely at his exclamation.

He dropped his head to her chest and licked and nibbled and kissed all along the lacy edge of her bra. As he flicked at her covered nipple with his rigid tongue, his arms reached around behind her. Her bra fell loose into their arms and soon it joined her shirt somewhere on the floor.

Makenna's moan was loud and needy when he cupped her breasts and alternated sucking on one nipple, then the other. Her hands flew to his head. She held him to her as she arched her back to offer him better access. His mouth was driving her insane. She'd never had someone lavish such attention to her breasts, and she'd certainly never felt so weak and wanton from it. She snaked one hand down his back and fisted his black shirt between his shoulder blades. "Off," she demanded as she tugged at it.

He reached back, his lips still greedily devouring a nipple, and wrenched his shirt off, only dropping his mouth from her when he absolutely had to.

"Oh, God," she murmured appreciatively as her eyes surveyed his broad chest.

There was so much more to him than she'd seen in the elevator. The large tribal tattoo that curled around the left side of his abdomen accompanied a beautiful open-faced yellow rose on his upper left pectoral muscle. The dragon roared up his right forearm, then the skin was unmarked until her eyes reached the very top of his bicep, where a red four-pronged badge sat with a tiny fire hydrant, hook, and ladder surrounding a gold number seven. His browned skin revealed the amount of time he must've spent without a shirt under the summer sun, and made the vibrant colors of his tattoos stand out even more.

Her original impression was so right—he was freaking gorgeous. She wanted to explore every inch of him, to trace every ridged muscle and every tattoo with her fingers and tongue.

Makenna's mouth went right to the rose. Her hands clutched the firm muscles of his sides. Caden threaded his fingers into her hair and held her to him. Her tongue ran around the edge of one of the lower yellow petals before trailing down and finding his nipple, which was right at the natural height of her mouth.

"So good," he rasped. He pressed a kiss onto her hair.

She flicked her thumb back and forth over the skin she'd made wet, so she could pay attention to his other nipple as well. He groaned at her teasing touch. She smiled at getting him back for how deliciously he'd tormented her earlier.

His skin felt so good under her fingers, and tasted better—just a little salty from how hot they'd been in the elevator. She imagined them in the shower together, using her own bare, soapy hands to wash the day off him. A smile formed where her lips were still pressed against his chest. *Another time*, she mused. *Please let there be another time.*

All this slow exploration made her ache. The cleft between her legs was wet and throbbing. Her body begged for the relief of his touch. And she hoped and prayed his body was making the very same pleas.

She sucked his right nipple into her mouth and flicked her tongue against it until he fisted his hand in her hair. She couldn't tell if he was holding her in place or trying to pull her away. Maybe both. But she could tell, either way, he liked it, because he grunted and rocked his hips into her.

Experimentally, she dropped her fingers from teasing his nipples and drew lazy circles over his abdomen, enjoying the way his muscles flinched and clenched under her light touch. His breaths quickened when her fingers swirled in the line of brown hair disappearing under his waistband. Without pausing, she continued down over the denim and cupped his considerable length in the palm of her hand.

"Christ," he groaned, then thrust against where she was rubbing him.

His fingers returned to her nipples. She whimpered and tilted her head back to look up at him. His eyes blazed. He leaned forward and pressed his lips against hers, then pushed his tongue into her mouth.

She went from rubbing him to squeezing him through his jeans.

"Makenna," he rasped, his voice soft and seductive, "I want you so much." He pulled back until they could see one another, then reached up and tucked her hair behind her ear. "What do you want?"

Reluctantly, she pulled her hand away from stroking him and brought both hands up to cup his face. "Everything. I want everything with you."

———

*B*lood pounded through Caden's body. His senses were on fire—her incredible scent, the sounds of her needy whimpers and moans, the satiny-soft feel of her skin under his fingers, the salty-sweet taste of her flesh. As he kissed and touched her, he watched her intently, eager to learn what she liked, finding pleasure in what gave her pleasure.

But when she started exploring him, he thought he'd lose his fucking mind. She'd tugged in silent demand for him to remove his shirt, which he'd done more than willingly, then she started devouring the skin of his chest after drinking him in through her eyes. Every movement of her mouth and hands was playful and sensual and set his body to throbbing, to begging for more.

And she'd given it to him. The press of her small, strong hand around his erection was irresistible. He hadn't held back from using the incredible friction he'd so badly needed and she'd so willingly provided.

And then she confirmed she wanted him too, just the way he wanted her. Her words resonated everywhere—a long-sought satisfaction calmed his mind and a comforting heat filled his chest. Those feelings were magnificent, life-giving—and more than he ever expected to experience.

In that moment, though, it was his cock that most reacted to her words, to the fulfillment they promised. And, as if her words weren't enough, she dropped her hands from lovingly holding his face and hooked the fingers of her right hand into his waistband, then turned and led them from the kitchen.

Caden smiled at her methods and followed her eagerly as she guided him past the small dining table, through the living room, and into her most private sanctuary. The room was square and dim, the distant kitchen light and the filtered light of the moon through the sheer curtains providing the only illumination.

She turned to face him, but didn't drop her fingers. Instead, she added her other hand and easily worked the line of buttons open. Looking him in the eye, she shoved at the heavy denim fabric where it hugged his hip and at the same time snaked her other hand inside his snug boxers until she gripped him skin-to-skin.

Caden's mouth fell open at the thrilling sensation of her soft fingers stroking his hard length. He held her gaze, pleaded with his eyes for her to continue on.

"Fuck. What are you doing to me?" She couldn't know it, but his question was about so much more than the wonderful movements of her little hand.

When she tugged at his jeans with her free hand, Caden quickly pushed them and his boxers down over his hips. He followed her gaze as she admired him. Her hand looked so good stroking him. He had to close his eyes against the erotic image so he could conjure up more control—he wanted this to go on for a long time. And she was already pushing him.

She let out a moan that dragged his eyes open again. He wasn't the only one squirming at the picture of her hand around his cock. Makenna's mouth hung open. A flush expanded out across her heaving bare chest. Every few seconds, her tongue darted out across her bottom lip.

Out of nowhere, she gripped his length more firmly and wrapped a hand around his waist, then walked them backward until her legs hit the bed. She sat down and pulled him another step closer until his groin was even with her face.

Caden gaped. Desire had never looked more beautiful than when she tilted her eyes up to him and sucked his head between her pink lips. He gasped as the wet heat wrapped around him.

"Christ, Makenna..."

He clenched and unclenched his hands and was surprised when one of her hands found one of his. She pulled his palm to her head. Drawing back from him for just a moment, she said, "Show me what you like."

Her offer astounded him and he grew in her mouth. Need led him to twist his fingers into her hair. But there wasn't anything she was doing he didn't love the hell out of. "Trust me, baby, you know what you're doing. I can't believe...your mouth is perfection."

She moaned around his length. He shivered at the sensation. The suction of her mouth and the teasing flicks of her tongue melted his insides. He gave into the urge and applied the lightest pressure against the back of her head with his fist. He resisted thrusting into her mouth though, not because his body wasn't screaming for him to do so, but because he wanted to let her lead this, and he didn't want to finish this way. And he was walking a very fine line.

Too fine, in fact.

If he didn't make her stop now, he wouldn't be able to resist the pleasure she was drawing out of him. He tugged at her hair, gently urging her to let go.

She released him and looked up with wet, shiny lips and a self-satisfied smile. He smirked, then leaned down and kissed her.

Still attacking her mouth, Caden dropped to his knees, and his hands fell to her thighs. After a moment, he walked his fingers up to her waistband.

"Lift," he ordered.

After he had peeled the last of her clothing from her, he sat back on his heels and drank in the beauty of her femininity. Very deliberately, he raked his gaze over her, over the plump rounded swells of her rising and falling breasts, over the soft curve of her porcelain stomach, down to the patch of damp red curls at the top of her sex.

*M*akenna's heart slammed against her breastbone. Each progression of their actions stretched her jangling nerves more taut and further readied her between her thighs. Once she'd had him in her room and in her hand, she knew she had to taste him.

She'd reveled in the warm heavy weight of him in her mouth, in the way his jaw dropped in pleasure, and in the deep groan that filled the room the first time she'd taken him all the way in to the back of her throat. The blaze in his eyes was so intense when she looked up at him it drove her harder. She wanted to bring him the pleasure he'd been bringing her all night. And, when she'd noticed a jagged four-inch scar just above his right hip, she redoubled her efforts, sucking him in deeper and running her tongue over him more vigorously.

This man had been through hell and back at a very young age. Yet, he'd survived without succumbing to the bitterness and resentment and despair that must've sometimes lured him. Instead, he was the kind of man who helped other people—for a living and as a matter of course. And he was relentlessly kind and quietly funny and more goddamned sexy than any man had a right to be.

So she'd wanted to do that for him. She'd wanted to concentrate all her efforts on bringing him pleasure. Again and again she'd hollowed out her cheeks and sucked hard as she brought her mouth up his entire length. Just as she reached his head, she'd abruptly stop sucking and plunge her mouth down around him again, taking him into the back of her throat. His ragged breathing and muttered curses were thrilling.

She almost whined when his gentle tugging pleaded with her to release him. But she was so eager to see where they'd go next she didn't think on it long.

Soon, she was watching Caden rake his eyes across her naked body. They were barely touching, but the moment felt so erotic. It was more than just sexual, though—Makenna was almost certain that within the mask of desire he wore was another emotion—adoration. And it made her feel so safe and secure to be with him this way.

God, he looked so freaking sexy kneeling between her legs. Caden Grayson was a big man, in every sense of the term. To see him before her like that...

And then he crawled closer. She had the distinct impression of a predator stalking his prey.

"Lie back," he encouraged as his hands walked up to her hips and his body settled between her thighs. She complied and reclined onto her elbows so she could watch him.

Then, with no pretense at all, his head dropped to the cleft of her legs. He laved a long hard stroke of his tongue through her wet folds, boring his eyes into hers all the while.

"Oh, Caden!" She felt his tongue all the way down to her curling toes.

"You taste as good as I knew you would," he murmured right against her. He lowered his face to her red curls and kissed her softly, then he further separated her thighs with his shoulders and licked her most sensitive skin over and over again.

Makenna's hands fisted against the soft green comforter under her. Weakened by the pleasure he so expertly provided, she dropped all her weight back against the bed and luxuriated in the play of his tongue against her. She uttered a near-constant string of encouragements and pleadings, but couldn't find it in herself to be the least bit self-conscious.

She'd had guys go down on her before, but no man had ever seemed as responsive to her body's cues as Caden. The way he paid attention to her soon had him treating her to an alternating rhythm of long hard strokes from her opening to her clit and intense bursts of flicks and sucks concentrated on the latter. Every once in a while the metal rings on his lip dragged across her labia. She found the unexpected sensation surprisingly decadent.

He was playing her body, commanding her pleasure, eliciting the same notes from her again and again. When he added his thumb to his efforts, stroking repeatedly over her clit while his tongue circled and dipped into her opening, every nerve ending concentrated itself at the center of her body.

"Caden, oh, my God. Oh, my God." Pure white-hot energy was flowing through her, rising in her, threatening to break her apart.

He responded to her words by rubbing her harder, faster, drinking from her more deeply.

"I'm...oh, I'm...."

She lost her words to a loud moan as a glorious explosion of sensation began under Caden's talented mouth and ricocheted through every cell in her body. Muscles flexed and contracted throughout her in a wave. She groaned as he refused to let up one bit, continuing to stimulate her over-sensitive skin in a way that extended her orgasm endlessly.

"Holy shit," she squeaked out between shuddering breaths.

When Caden pressed a line of kisses from her right thigh over her right hip, she felt the smile curling his lips. Then he playfully bit her hipbone. She screamed out a throaty laugh.

She liked someone who didn't have to be serious during sex, who could smile and laugh. It was just one more thing they had in common.

But she wasn't done with him yet.

Saving them the awkward conversation, Makenna flopped her right arm out on the bed and pointed to her night stand. "Drawer. Condom. On you. Now."

"Mmm. Yes, ma'am." He pushed himself into a standing position and kicked off his jeans which still hung around his knees.

Makenna licked her lips as he strode the three steps around her bed and reached into the drawer. His body was all taut lean muscle and moved with a quiet power. There wasn't enough light to make out the details of the designs, but she could see more ink decorated his shoulder blades.

Later, she planned to explore every inch of his amazing body. But just then, she needed him with her, in her. She needed a resolution to the hours of build-up between them.

Caden tossed the silver wrapper aside and unrolled the condom over his thick length. Makenna blushed though she couldn't look away—she'd always found that action particularly erotic. When he looked at her and smiled, she pushed herself back up to the pillows and held out a hand to him.

He crawled over top of her and lowered his weight onto her. She'd always loved that feeling, the weight of a man's body covering hers, and it never felt better than when Caden's tall muscular frame encompassed hers so fully, so lovingly.

Taking her head gently into his hands, he pressed closed-mouth kisses against her lips until she pushed her tongue out and encouraged his lips to part. She could taste herself on him, something else that had always driven her mad because it was like tasting the pleasure he'd given her all over again. When Caden groaned around her probing tongue, she kissed him more deeply and sucked hard on his tongue until he broke free of her and playfully bit at her jaw in punishment for her teasing.

He stroked his fingers over her hair, then rubbed her cheekbone with his knuckles. "Are you sure?"

She smiled and nodded. "I'm very sure. You?"

He chuckled. "Um..." He pursed his lips and looked up at the ceiling, putting on what she assumed was supposed to be a thinking face.

She reached her hand around him and not so lightly smacked his ass.

His eyes dropped back to her. His mouth fell open.

Makenna cocked an eyebrow. "I *told* you I would smack you."

The laugh he let loose sounded so purely happy she grinned even though she was trying to look put out.

"That you did. I like a woman who keeps her word." He kissed her again, softly this time. "Yes, I am very sure I want you, Makenna. Can I have you?" He gazed so intently in her eyes she almost thought he was asking for more than just permission to possess her body.

"Yes," she whispered, intending her answer as the reply to every way he might've meant his question.

*P*ushing himself up onto one elbow, Caden reached a hand down between them and stroked his fingers over Makenna's soft folds. He wanted to make sure she was ready. She was. Her responsiveness to him was thrilling. He centered his cock over her opening and met her eyes. And then he slowly pushed himself into her.

He groaned at the feeling of being inside of her, at the idea that maybe, just maybe, he'd found a place, a woman, he could belong to for all time.

The tight walls of her most private place gripped him fiercely, surrounding him in white-hot heat and velvet softness. He moaned low in his throat. "You feel so good."

When he filled her completely, he stilled and let them both savor the sensation.

She clutched at his shoulders. "So do you. God, I feel..."

He studied her face when she trailed off and watched a blush bloom on top of the flush their activities had already brought out in her skin. Now he was intrigued—he really wanted her to finish that sentence.

"What? What do you feel?" He strained to resist the instinct to move his hips.

She shook her head and flexed her hips, driving him deeper into her. It felt incredible, but he recognized the diversionary tactic for what it was.

He pulled his cock out until just the tip of his head was still inside her. Tremors shook his shoulders with the effort it took not to sink back into her. "Tell me."

She groaned. "Caden, I need you." He smiled at the pleading in her voice. She wrapped her legs around his hips and pressed her heels into his ass. But he was too strong for her to be able to force him to move. She pouted, but relented. "I *felt* so incredibly full."

His ego buoyed, he didn't hesitate to recreate the feeling for her, and plunged immediately back into her gripping heat. "Like that?"

"Yes, just like that," she moaned. "*God.*"

He remembered his earlier desire to see her when he took her and pushed himself up onto his arms. His hands settled on both sides of her ribs. He grunted appreciatively at the full view the position gave him.

He moved in her then, flexing his hips over and over, driving his rigid length into her slick tightness. Her muscles sucked at him as she shifted positions. He finally hooked his right arm under her left leg to force her more open underneath him. The change allowed him to plunge even deeper.

He shook his head at how good it all felt. "So tight. Christ, so wet."

She clamped her teeth down on her bottom lip and groaned as his repeated thrusts rocked into her. Her blue eyes were hooded with desire and flashed with a wondrous affection for him.

Caden returned her intense gaze. He caught her every movement, her every reaction to their joining. His mind began a catalog of information on Makenna he hoped he'd be fleshing out for a long time to come.

When she reached her wandering hands up to cup her own breasts and stroked her fingers over her nipples, he hummed in approval. "That's right. That looks so good."

He liked that she had the confidence to seek out pleasure during sex. She wasn't reserved. She didn't play games. Instead, she was real and completely guileless in the pursuit of their pleasure. Her honesty made her even sexier to him.

When Makenna's eyes dropped down to where they were joined, his eyes followed.

"Fuck," he murmured as he watched his wet cock slide in and out of her.

"We look...good...together," she panted softly.

"We look so fucking good together," he rasped. He gazed back up at her face. "You're so damned beautiful."

She smiled, beckoning Caden to kiss her. He released her leg and lowered himself back onto his elbows, then cupped his hands under her shoulders for leverage. He claimed her mouth until their need to breathe made it too hard to continue.

The room filled with the sounds of their lovemaking. The shifting of bodies moving together. Their panting breaths and impassioned moans. Every single sound reverberated directly to his cock and made him want her even more.

Enjoying the closeness of their bodies, Caden hunched himself possessively over her and slammed into her again and again. He rolled his pelvic bone into her clit with each thrust. The sound of her whimpering when he hit it spot on was the best reward.

"Sweet Caden," she whispered as she pressed a few open-mouthed kisses to his yellow rose. He lowered his head and reverently kissed her forehead.

When she wrapped her legs around him, the added depth tightened everything in his groin. "Fuck," he said through a dry swallow, "I want you...to come again. Can you do that for me?" he panted.

"Close," she rasped.

"Touch yourself. Come with me."

She groaned and reached down with her right hand. Her hand swiped down to the wetness he was bringing out of her. She separated her fingers into a V and slid them around him as he plunged in and out of her. "Aw, Christ." The added sensation shoved him closer to the edge. "*Red,*" he cautioned, his voice a raw scrape.

Her fingers moved, then circled over her clit. He lifted up just a little and glanced down. But he had to look away before the incredible sight of her touching herself did him in before she was ready.

"Just feel. Feel me filling you up. Feel your fingers stroking yourself."

A pleading whimper erupted from her throat. "Keep talking, Caden."

He moaned. The strain of holding back his orgasm flared. Then he blurted out the feeling most driving him crazy in that moment. "You're so tight, and it's so fucking good. Everything about you..."

He felt her tighten around his cock and he groaned. *Just a little more. Push her a little more.*

"Come," he growled through clenched teeth, "come on me."

The hand on his back clenched. Her short fingernails pinched as they sank into his skin.

"Mak—"

"Coming! Oh God!"

"Fuck, yes." Her orgasm roared through her. Her inner walls milked at him relentlessly. It was all he could take. "Oh, Christ." He thrust into her once, twice, a third time. His release erupted into her still-clenching depths. His muscles strained as the most intense orgasm of his life slammed through him. He stilled himself all the way in her and shuddered against her as his cock continued to twitch. "Makenna," he whispered as he panted into her soft wavy hair. He pressed kisses down onto the damp skin of her forehead, then allowed his head to fall into the crook of her neck when he gently pulled out of her.

Long, comfortable moments of blissful silence passed. Being with her had been incredible, but it was how at ease he felt with her that most had him hoping he could stay the night, and tomorrow, and the month…

Peace was not an emotion with which he was much familiar, but with Makenna, he had it. And he didn't know how he'd ever give it up.

CHAPTER NINE

*M*akenna was speechless. She'd guessed earlier in the evening Caden would prove an attentive lover, but she wasn't prepared for just how well he anticipated her needs, sometimes before she did herself, and how he made sure every one of them was fulfilled. It was a heady thing, being the center of someone else's efforts and attention. She felt giddy.

And he'd felt so good in her. He was the most well-endowed man she'd ever been with, and *Holy cow!* the pleasure she got from the sensation of fullness alone would've made the sex great. But the way he moved his body, the way he rolled his hips, the way his hands possessed her, the reflexive sweet kisses he dropped all over her—it all felt effortless, natural, with him, which was why she'd been able to orgasm again. She'd never before been able to come again so quickly after orgasming. But Caden had drawn it out of her with his body, his words, the deep need in his voice for her to join him when he fell.

Most of all, he'd made her feel desirable, beautiful, sexy. These feelings enabled her to be completely free with him.

She stroked light trailing fingertips over his back where he had collapsed on top of her. She wriggled a little and turned her head to kiss his stubbled cheek.

He lifted up from her neck and smiled at her, then pressed a series of soft, worshipful kisses against her lips. "You doing okay?"

She smiled. "I'm mighty fine."

His smile turned into a grin. "Yes, you are."

She gave him a quick peck. "You want something to drink?" she asked. "I have to get up to go to the bathroom anyway."

"Yeah, sounds good." He rolled off to her side and ran his fingertips from her neck down to her belly button. She squirmed, every part of her body now completely over sensitized from the immense pleasure he'd given her.

Makenna scooted off the bed and glanced back at him. He wasn't even trying to pretend he wasn't watching her nakedness stroll around the room. She smirked, knowing full well she'd be doing the same thing to him.

"You can use the bathroom in there if you want, I'll use the one out here."

He propped himself up on an elbow and gave her a very purposeful once-over. "Okay."

She shook her head and walked out of the room, chuckling.

After cleaning up in the hall bathroom, Makenna made her way back to the kitchen and smiled at the almost-dinner they'd made. She quickly returned all the ingredients back to the fridge, deciding she'd rethink whether everything ought to be thrown out when she had more brain power in the morning. Then she settled all the dirty dishes in the sink.

She scooped up the clothes they'd shed and piled them on the counter. Smiling, she pulled Caden's black shirt out and slipped it over her head. It was miles too big on her, but it felt great. She giggled like a school girl at the thought of his reaction.

She set a small tray on the counter and loaded it up with two bottles of water, some orange juice for her and a fresh can of Coke for him, and a big bunch of cold green grapes. She carried the lot of it into her room and found he'd switched on the lamp on her night-stand. He'd slipped his boxers and jeans back on and sat propped up against her headboard, his long legs stretched out in front of him.

"Nice shirt." He smirked at her, but his eyes smoldered.

"I thought so." She winked at him as she slid the tray between them and climbed up on the bed. "Help yourself."

Caden plucked a bottle of water off the tray and downed half of it in one greedy gulp. The sight of his Adam's apple bobbing in his throat made her squirm a little. She shook her head at herself as she grabbed her glass of juice and took a considerably smaller drink.

He recapped the bottle and sat forward, then broke off a stem of grapes. He threw two in his mouth and closed his eyes as he chewed.

Makenna reached down and plucked a handful off the stem. The sweet juiciness exploded in her mouth as she chewed. "Mmm. Good," she murmured.

He popped two more in his mouth and smiled. "Very."

A flash of red light behind Caden caught her eye. "Wow," she said. "It's 1:30. I had no idea." She gulped down the rest of her orange juice.

Caden glanced over his shoulder. "Um, yeah." He ate another grape and looked down at the two he was rolling around in his hand. His jaw ticked, that same way it had in the elevator when she'd first seen him.

Makenna frowned. "Hello?" He cut his eyes back up at her. "What just happened?"

His brow furrowed. "I...nothing. Really." He smiled, but it wasn't *her* smile.

Not again.

She cocked an eyebrow at him, trying to imagine what was wrong. "I call bullshit."

He chuckled and ran his hand over his scar, then sighed. "It's late."

She debated for only a second, then resolved the risk was more than worth it. Pushing the tray out of the way, she crawled over until she was kneeling in front of him. She cupped her right hand around his neck and her left hand around the back of his head, then gently tugged at him until the scarred side of his head faced her. Quite deliberately, she reached up and traced soft reverent kisses from his temple, along the scar over his ear, and all the way back to the very end of it at the hairline on his neck. She sat back on her heels and turned his face so she could see his now-flaming eyes.

Taking a deep breath, she asked, "Do you have somewhere to be?"

He shook his head.

"Because I'd like you to stay, if you want to. There wasn't any hidden meaning behind my pointing out the time. I was just surprised, just so you know."

He chuckled and nodded. "Okay. I'd like to stay."

She released a deep breath as relief and joy flooded her. "Good. And Caden?"

"Yeah?" He quirked a crooked smile.

"So there's no more weirdness or uncertainty...I like you." The warmth of a blush blossomed on her cheeks.

The smile she loved brightened his face and crinkled his eyes. "I like you, too."

Inside she was jumping up and down and screaming, "He likes me too, he likes me too!" Outside, she reached behind her and grabbed a few grapes. "Open," she said.

The dimples deepened on his face as his smile grew. He opened his mouth. She popped one grape in his mouth and two in her own, trying to suppress a smile while she chewed.

Then she thought for a moment. She wanted to know more about him—she wanted to know everything. So she sat back and looked at him, finally drawing her finger around the outline of his yellow rose tattoo.

"Tell me about this?"

---

*A*fter Makenna left to get them something to drink, Caden had cleaned up and gotten dressed, not sure what to expect, or whether to expect anything. He knew what he wanted. He wanted to stay the night. He wanted to fall asleep holding her. Not once in the last fourteen years had he felt as comfortable with another woman, as accepted. And they'd been so damned good together. All night long, everything had felt so natural with her. Now that he'd found that, found *her*, he wanted everything she'd give him.

And then she'd returned wearing his shirt. The black of it highlighted the contrasting pale porcelain of her legs and the fiery hue of her loose curls. Somehow, his body had found some last reserve of energy, because the sight of her in his clothes made his cock stir again. If he got the chance, he was going to give her his Station Seven baseball jersey with his name silk-screened on the back.

He'd been savoring the image of her wearing a shirt that would mark her as his when she'd pointed out the time. The air had left his lungs. *My time's finally up*, was all he could think. His gut clenched with unreasonable disappointment.

She'd noticed and called him on his shit—as she'd been doing all night. And he...loved her for it. *Yeah, I'm not even going to pretend it's something else.* Because, just then, as she kissed him—*kissed his scar*—and told him she liked him and pulled him back from the edge of a downward spiral, he thought he just might be in love with Makenna James.

Her finger tickled the outline of his rose. He told her its simple story. "My mom had a rose garden. Yellow was her favorite." He grabbed her hand and brought it to his lips.

Makenna pulled her hand free and pointed to the red cross on his upper bicep. "And this one?"

"It's the badge from my station."

She raked her fingernails over his left side. He flinched and swatted at her hand, making her laugh. "And this one?" she asked as she nudged him to sit forward so she could trace the big abstract tribal around to his back.

Something about her intense exploration of his ink felt incredibly intimate to him, but he just shrugged. "No story behind that one, really. I just liked it. And it took a long time to do."

She crawled in to kneel behind him. Her knees settled against the outside of his hips and her warmth radiated against his back.

He sucked in a breath and shivered when she pressed four kisses against the large Old English lettering on his right shoulder—the tattoo of Sean's name. It had been his very first tattoo—he'd lied about his age and used a fake ID to get it done on the day Sean would've turned fifteen. His chest felt full and tight at the same time, but above it all he admired and appreciated the way Makenna met his issues head on—kissing his scar, comforting him about the loss of his family, making him feel so accepted by wanting to understand why he'd marked himself again and again.

He anticipated her fingers before they fell on the lettering on his left shoulder. "What does this say?" She traced over the four traditional Chinese characters he'd had done on the fifth anniversary of the accident.

"It says 'never forget.' "

She kneaded his shoulder muscles, and he groaned and tilted his head forward. Her hands were surprisingly strong for being so small. After a while, her thumbs worked deep circles down either side of his spine until she reached the back of his jeans.

When she wrapped her arms around him and hugged, laying her cheek on his shoulder, he sank back into her embrace. It was an unusually peaceful moment for him. He felt so cared for. They sat that way for several long, comfortable minutes.

"Got any others?" she eventually asked.

He wrapped his arms over hers. "Another tribal on my calf. Wanna see?"

She nodded against his shoulder, then dropped her arms as he leaned forward and pulled up the leg to his jeans as far as he could. The black lines curved up and down the outside of his leg like feathers, or blades.

"Does it hurt?" she asked as she went back to massaging his back.

"It can. Some places more than others."

"Is that why you do it?"

He spun to the right and dropped his legs to the floor, his upper body twisting further around so he could search her face.

Despite being surprised at the abruptness of his movement, she leaned forward to kiss him. "Caden, I like your tattoos. I mean"—she paused and blushed beautifully—"I *really* like them. It's just…"

"Just what?"

"They hurt. And you said you got this one"—she stroked his left side—"because it took a long time to do. And the dragon was part of proving to yourself you'd beaten your fear."

He nodded, studying her face intently. She was choosing her words carefully. He could almost see her thoughts playing out on her face, a face he was learning to read better and better. A face he found so very lovely.

"I think—" She dropped her hands in her lap again and flashed her baby blues at him. "Well, it's like they're your armor."

Caden's jaw dropped. He didn't know what to say, because never, ever had he thought of all his ink that way. Instead, he'd thought of them as a way to remember, he'd thought of them as a form of penance, and he'd not minded, after a certain point, that they might keep people away. But he'd never specifically thought of them as offering him protection. But she was right. They allowed him to control the pain he felt—both physical and emotional—something that had been taken from him on that long-ago summer night.

Her observation was so in tune with who he was and what had happened to him he felt ready to turn over some of that control, to entrust *her* with some of it.

He lunged at her and tackled her against the headboard with the force of his kiss. He swallowed her surprised gasp as he pushed his tongue into her mouth, now tasting of the sweetness of grapes and oranges.

When he pulled back she was laughing and smiling. Her eyes scanned over his face. "These are sexy as hell, too," she said, fingering his lip and brow piercings.

He threw his head back and laughed. Her timing was perfect. She had a knack for injecting humor in serious conversations just when it was needed. Her giggle warmed him. He leaned forward again and kissed her, scraping his bottom lip over hers to make sure she felt his spider bites. She whimpered and he grinned. After a few moments he settled back against her chest again.

Minutes passed with Caden leaning sideways against Makenna's abdomen while she stroked his back and he played with the ends of her hair. "You have the prettiest hair I've ever seen, Red. And it smells fucking phenomenal."

"I knew it! I knew you sniffed my hair."

He tilted his head to look up at her, chuckling uncomfortably.

But the beaming smile on her face was all pleased. "Don't worry," she said when she saw his embarrassed expression. "I sniffed you, too. I love your aftershave."

He nodded and tucked his head back down against her. "Good to know," he said through a smile.

More comfortable minutes passed and she sighed. "I still owe you an omelet."

He chuckled. "Yeah, we kinda skipped that, didn't we?"

Her voice sounded like a smile. "Uh, yeah. I didn't mind, though." She kissed the top of his head.

"Me neither. And, anyway, I still owe you a pizza."

"Ooh, yeah." She wriggled underneath him like she was dancing. "And a movie, too."

"And a movie, too." Caden grinned where he leaned against her. She was making plans with him, plans for the future. He was fucking thrilled.

They lay together for a few more minutes, then Makenna yawned. "Let's get comfortable," she said.

Caden pushed off the bed and extended a hand to help Makenna. He picked up the tray. "I'll take this out to the kitchen."

"Thanks," she said as she pulled the covers down.

When he returned, she was lying under the comforter on the side where they'd been sitting. He came around the other side and shed his jeans before slipping under with her. "Oh, God." He chuckled. "That feels good."

She clicked off the lamp and then rolled over to him. He lifted his arm so she could fit into the nook along the side of his body. Despite the novelty of being with a woman like this, it all felt completely natural to Caden. And that made him cherish it all the more. Cherish *her* all the more.

I could get used to this, he thought as Makenna fit herself along his side and slid her knee onto his thigh. He was bone-achingly tired but happy beyond anything he'd ever imagined might be possible for him.

Just as his eyes drooped, she pressed a kiss against his collarbone and squeezed her arm across his chest. "I love...that elevator," she said.

With a sleepy smile and a full heart, he turned his head and kissed into her soft hair. "Aw, Red. I love that elevator, too."

Lovers at Dawn

CHAPTER ONE

*C*aden Grayson blinked awake and immediately knew three things.

He wasn't at home.

He wasn't alone.

And he'd just had the best night of sleep in longer than he could remember.

Maybe in fourteen years.

Peering down, he saw a tumble of red curls covering his chest and part of Makenna's face.

Damn. If that woman was a dream, he didn't want to wake up.

How the hell had he gone from getting trapped in a claustrophobic nightmare to having the best night of sex of his whole life? Shit like that just didn't happen to him. Never had. Oh, he was acquainted with luck all right. Just not the good kind.

But this whole situation was about a lot more than sex to Caden. He liked Makenna. He liked being challenged and accepted by her. He liked the way he felt when he was with her. Like right now, with her curled in against the side of his body. So damn soft and pretty against all his hard and ugly.

She stirred and murmured against him. Her breasts pressed into his side, and her thigh slid higher on his until her leg rested close to where he was getting hard. Her hand shifted across his chest far enough that she tucked her fingers underneath his back, embracing him fully.

It felt like a claiming, and fuck if it didn't make him want that. Something he'd never wanted before. Something he'd convinced himself he couldn't have and wasn't worthy of besides.

To be claimed.

To be wanted.

To be kept. Always.

After he'd lost his mom and brother, all he'd had left in the world was his father. But instead of bringing them closer, the tragedy of losing half their family had destroyed whatever father-son relationship they'd once had. His father did the bare minimum of what he had to do to get Caden to the age of eighteen. Then Caden had been unceremoniously pushed out the door. On his own and free as a fucking bird.

He'd never looked back.

Still, it didn't escape him that the flip side of the kind of freedom he'd found had been complete abandonment by his only living family.

Now, not even his father remained living anymore. So Caden was well and truly alone.

"Morning," came a raspy voice thick with sleep.

"Morning," he managed, his mind tangled in the downward spiral of his thoughts. "Sorry if I woke you."

"You didn't," she said, a smile plain in the tone of her voice. "Once my brain remembered that there was a gorgeous man in my bed, it woke me right up."

He grinned, appreciating again how quickly she could pull him out of his head. "*Freaking* gorgeous, if I remember right." She smacked his chest, and it made him laugh. "Just sayin.'"

Makenna lifted her head and looked at the clock on the side table. It read a few minutes after ten. "I can't believe I slept so late. Have you been bored to tears waiting for me to wake up?" She propped her head on his chest, and there was a shyness in her gaze he wanted to chase away.

"Not at all. I've only been awake for a few minutes. Anyway, I could never be bored with you half-dressed and laying on top of me."

She chuckled, and then there was only happiness in those baby blues. So maybe he wasn't the only one who needed the kind of reassurances she'd given him last night. "Is that so?"

"Trust me on that one, Red." He tucked a few strands of red curls back from her face. He wasn't sure what to say, what to expect. He only knew that he wanted more—more time with her, more of her sweet touches, more of how she made him feel. "What, uh, what did you have planned today?" Unlike his several-days-on, several-days-offer paramedic schedule, she worked a more traditional office job, so she probably counted on her Saturdays for downtime, friends, and errands.

She shook her head, making her curls dance across his skin and his blood heat. "Nothing really. The gym maybe? Oh, and there's a great little farmers' market I go to sometimes on Saturdays. I didn't have any plans. How about you? Do you work today?"

He traced his fingers over her shoulder and down her arm watching with fascination as goose bumps sprang up in the wake of his touch. "I'm off 'til tomorrow night and then I have a double. I often volunteer to do weekends so the guys with families can have them off, but my captain made me take the whole week off after my father..." He shrugged. "So, uh, no plans really."

"Hungry?" she asked.

"I could eat," he said.

"How about something more than trail mix and grapes?" She smirked.

He chuckled. "Yes, please."

She grinned. "There's a really good noodle place near here. Or we could do pizza like we talked about."

Now Caden was grinning. At the memory of their conversation, at the fact that she was doing just what they'd said, at the fact that it gave him hope. "Feed me pizza, Red."

Makenna pushed into a sitting position beside him and laughed. "Okay, Caden Grayson, then let's get dressed so I can put some slices in your pie hole."

He grabbed her around the middle and hauled her back down against him. Laughter spilled out of her, and he loved it. "My pie hole, huh?"

"Yeah," she said. "I grew up with three brothers, remember?"

"Oh, I remember, Makenna. I remember it all," he said, kissing the soft skin of her neck.

She sighed. "This isn't going to lead to pizza."

He laughed. "No, I guess not. Damn inconvenient stomach."

Makenna turned in his arms, her smile so bright and open. "I know, but we need fuel."

Oh, he liked the sound of that. "Damn straight we do." He gave her a slow, lingering kiss, making sure to rake his spider bites over her lip.

"I'm sorry, what were you saying?" she said, her voice all breathy and sexy.

"Pizza."

"Right, pizza it is," she said, sitting up again and scooting out of bed. Tussled hair fell over her shoulders. His T-shirt hung loosely on her body, her legs bare beneath. God, she was so pretty she struck him dumb. "Would you like to shower?"

Caden got out of her bed and stretched, getting hard again because of the way she was staring at him. Like she was *starving*. He stalked around the bed, laser focused on her.

"What?" she said, grinning and backing up.

In one smooth motion, he bent and lifted her into a fireman's carry.

She gasped and burst into laughter. "Why are you carrying me?"

He made for the bathroom. "I didn't want you to get away."

"I wasn't trying to get away!" She chuckled.

"One can never be too sure," he said, placing her gently on her feet back in the big walk-in shower. And even though he said it as a joke, it was the damn truth. "Yes to taking a shower." He stepped out of his boxers and chucked them outside of the stall, then stood and let her look her fill.

Makenna's gaze raked over him, and he felt it like a physical caress. "I think I'm overdressed," she offered, pulling his shirt over her head and dropping her panties until she was all beautiful naked curves before him. "Much better."

All he could do was nod.

She reached for the water knob. "How hot do you like it?" She slanted her gaze at him with a sexy little smile.

"However hot you like it, Red."

Water rained down on them, and steam slowly filled the space.

"I think..." She swallowed hard. "I think we might be a little delayed getting to the pizza."

It was all he needed to hear.

"Hell yes," he said, taking her in his arms. He pushed her against the wall as their lips met in a series of scorching open-mouthed kisses. Her arms went around his shoulders and her leg went around his hip. Caden's cock grazed her inner thigh, and he groaned at the too-brief contact. "What do you want, Makenna?" he asked around the edge of their kiss. She sucked on his tongue, drawing a grunt from deep inside him.

"You," she said.

"How?"

She took his cock in her hand and stroked his hard length before rubbing him against her. "Just like this."

Caden's hand dropped to that sweet spot between her thighs. "Are you ready for me?" he asked, his fingers rubbing circles around her clit before he dipped one inside her. She moaned at his touch and threw her head back at his invasion. Bringing her pleasure made him feel so fucking powerful that he wanted to do it again and again. "Oh, yeah, you're nice and ready," he said, his finger gliding in and out now.

"Caden," she rasped. His name on her lips in that desire-drenched way snapped the last tether of his restraint.

"Stay right here," he gritted out, hating to have to part from her for even one second, but needing to take care of her, too. She lowered her leg and nodded. Not giving a second thought to the fact that he was wet, he padded out to the beside table and grabbed another condom. He had it on by the time he stepped back into the shower.

And damn it all to hell the way she was looking at him and watching his hand move over his sheathed length nearly knocked him to his knees.

Caden positioned himself against her again, all skin on wet skin, and lifted her thigh over his hip. Not waiting another moment, he found her entrance and drove into her wet heat. "There it is." They both moaned. And as good as it was, Caden needed more. He needed to go deeper, get closer. Reaching down, he cradled under both of her thighs, lifting her against the wall right where he wanted her, right where he needed her until he was buried to the hilt. "Oh, fuck."

She held tight to his shoulders, her expression utterly wrecked. He met her hooded gaze, and those baby blues were filled with so much heat and need. Their gazes locked, their panting breaths on each other's lips, he fell into a rhythm that was two heartbeats away from frenzied.

"God, Makenna," he gritted out, feeling his control slipping so damn fast.

"Yeah, I'm right there with you," she breathed. "You're so good, Caden."

Even as his body drowned in all her sweetness, his brain latched onto what she'd said. Not *it's so good*, but *you're so good*. Maybe she didn't mean anything by it. Maybe it had just been a lust-drunk slip of the tongue. But his brain settled on hearing it as acceptance, not just praise, and it shoved him too damn close to this being over. He really wanted her to fall first, so he shortened his strokes until he was all but grinding against her.

"You're gonna make me come," she said, clutching tighter around his shoulders, her hips rocking within his grip.

"Good." He pressed wet, open-mouthed kisses on the corner of her mouth, her cheek, her jaw. "I want to feel you squeeze my cock," he said in a low voice against her ear.

The moan she unleashed was the sweetest victory, only bested by the way her orgasm stole her breath before it exploded back out of her again on a throaty shout. Her muscles worked him over until he couldn't hold back anymore, and then his hips were moving, flying, pulling all the way out before plunging deep again and again.

Sensation shot down his spine and nailed him in the back, driving him all the way inside her one last time before his orgasm had his cock pulsing and her name rasping from his lips. "Jesus," he finally managed.

Caden pulled back enough to search Makenna's expression. Her cheeks were pink. Her lips were swollen from their kisses. Her eyes were absolutely blown. She was fucking gorgeous. "You okay?"

"Mighty fine," she said, giving him a wink that made him laugh.

"We will always agree on that." He eased her feet to the floor and holding onto her to make sure she was steady. He kissed her then, soft and sweet. She molded herself to him, the hot water still raining down, the steam cocooning them from the rest of the world. He'd stay right here if he could.

"I'll be quick with my hair," she said, "and then you can have the hot water."

"No worries, Red."

"I don't want you to get cold," she said, working shampoo into her waves. The water almost made her hair appear brown.

He poured some shower gel into his palm. "Absolutely no fucking chance of that with you around."

She laughed and her cheeks went even pinker, which he found damn adorable given everything they'd just done. "I would've washed you," she said with a wink.

Next time, he thought. And he really hoped there'd be one.

When he'd woken up, he hadn't known what to expect. But the thing he most hoped for—a real chance—seemed more and more of a possibility the more time they spent and the more experiences they shared. But hope was such a dangerous fucking thing. He deflected all this overthinking with humor. "Wanting to get your hands on me again already?"

Her gaze raked over him, lingering on where his cock was stirring again. "Constantly."

He could work with that. He really freaking could.

***

*M*akenna felt like she must've stepped into somebody else's life twenty-four hours ago. Because she almost couldn't believe everything that was happening to her was real.

It wasn't just that she'd picked up a stranger and brought him back to her apartment for a night of incredible sex that was so unbelievable. That in and of itself was going to gobsmack her best friend, Jen, when Makenna told her. It was that she'd hooked up with him in the pitch-dark, and that the sex-fest had continued into her shower the next morning, and that it was Caden Freaking Grayson.

Makenna liked her predictable numbers and her books and her small group of friends. She was a strait-laced girl who wasn't known for doing crazy things or attracting the hottest guy's attention. And while she'd had one serious relationship, she wasn't the most experienced girl either.

And yet, here she stood in front of her mirror pulling her damp hair into a ponytail getting ready to spend the day with her...her what? Her one-night stand? The phrase sloshed around uncomfortably in her empty gut. That wasn't what they were. At least, it wasn't all that they were.

Or, hopefully, all that they were going to be.

They'd become lovers last night, but today, in the new light of dawn, maybe just maybe they were becoming something else.

She gave the reflection of her simple gray T-shirt and khaki shorts a final glance before heading out to the kitchen, where she found that Caden had washed the couple dirty dishes they'd made together. "Aw, you didn't have to do that."

He shrugged with one big shoulder, wiped his hands on a tea towel, and turned to her. "I don't mind." A small smile played around his mouth, and it softened the harsh angles of his face. "Where would you like to grab pizza? Have a favorite place?"

She grabbed her purse and keys. "I have two favorites. But the one with the easiest parking on a Saturday is probably Antonio's over on King Street. Ever go there?"

He grinned. "In the Bradlee Shopping Center? Hell, yeah. That place is *my* favorite, too. It's basically across the street from my house."

"It's fate," she said, laughing, even though, it was really freaking starting to feel like it *could* be fate. If she believed in that sort of thing. Which, until last night, she wouldn't have said she didn't.

At the end of her hall, she passed the elevator.

"Wait, Makenna..." Caden pointed, his brow furrowing.

"I'm not looking to meet anybody else in an elevator this weekend." She smirked, hoping that he wouldn't be offended that she'd planned to bypass the elevator in favor of the stairs. But on a Saturday, they were likely to stop at every floor and be squeezed in with the Emersons, their double-wide stroller for their three-month-old twins, and their two Frenchies, or with Mr. Henderson and his grocery cart, or with Mr. Jindal pulling his young grandsons in a wagon to go to the park. Or all three!

For a moment, she could see the indecision playing out on Caden's face before he gave her a pointed look. "That's right. Because that's *our* thing."

She smiled. "We have a thing?"

"Oh, Red, we definitely have a thing," he said, following her into the stairwell.

She laughed, absolutely tickled that they had a thing. You didn't have a thing with someone who was just a one-night stand, right? Their laughter and animated voices echoed their whole way down. When they got to the first floor, she didn't decide for him and instead asked, "I'm happy to drive us in my Prius or go in your Jeep." Even though she feared he'd find her Prius to feel tiny.

He opened the door to the lobby for her. "I'll drive. It's a nice day for the Jeep anyway."

As she climbed in, she couldn't help but wonder at everything that'd happened since she last got into his Jeep. Then, she hadn't been sure if he was even that into her. Now, he'd more than answered that question even though she still wasn't sure what they were. Or what he wanted them to be. But she resolved to stop worrying about how to describe what they were to each other and instead to just revel in it.

They crossed town talking about everything and nothing at all, the wind in her hair, and the sun on their faces. She studied Caden in profile, loving the angle of his jaw and the way his muscles moved under the dragon tattoo.

"What?" he asked, his hand rubbing over his scar.

"Just looking," she said with a grin.

"Is that good or bad?" he asked, his jaw ticking.

"Is it good or bad when you look at me?"

"I fucking like looking at you, Red."

"Same here. See? There you go."

He shook his head, but now he only appeared exasperated instead of self-conscious. Still, she imagined his scars must've attracted a lot of stares over the course of his life, so she people watched out the passenger window, so happy that she was nearly giddy.

Luckily, they'd already hashed out favorite pizza toppings the night before, so they made quick work of ordering and threw in an appetizer of mozzarella sticks so they'd have something to put in their stomachs until the pizza came.

"Hey, Caden, how the heck are you?" asked an older man who looked a lot like the cartoon character on the restaurant's logo. And there was a good reason for that.

"I'm doing all right, Antonio. How's business?" Caden asked, shaking the man's hand.

"Business is good, business is good. And who is your beautiful companion?" he asked, smiling down at her. He'd said hello to her before, as he did to just about every customer, but there was no reason he'd remember.

"This is my friend, Makenna," Caden said. She smiled and said hello. "Turns out Antonio's is her favorite pizza place, too, so I knew she was a keeper."

Antonio belly laughed. "I can't argue with that logic, my friend. Dessert's on me, so you two let me know."

Caden shook his head. "Aw, man, you don't have to do that."

The man's expression filled with affection. "You know I do. And it's my pleasure," he said, moving on to chat with some other customers.

"My station house isn't even a half mile from here so me and all the guys are always in and out of here," Caden offered.

Just then, their mozzarella sticks arrived and they both groaned. Makenna wasn't sure who dove in faster. "Why did he say he had to treat you to dessert," she asked around a bite.

"Oh, uh, they had a kitchen fire last spring and I worked on his son and nephew. He's been throwing me free stuff ever since even though I keep telling him not to."

How many people probably saw Caden as their hero? She couldn't imagine, but she bet there were a lot more Antonios out there. "I remember when that fire happened. You know, I've come to this shopping center more times than I could count. How often do you think we crossed paths?"

He sucked a bit of tomato sauce off his thumb and gave her an appraising stare. "No telling. But I can't imagine I wouldn't remember you."

She felt her cheeks go warm. "I doubt that, Caden Grayson. You're way more memorable than I am. And people everywhere know you. The firefighters last night. Antonio...."

"That's two times."

"Well, I've only been two places with you so far," she said, laughing. "So you're batting a thousand."

Their pizza arrived, interrupting their conversation. Not that either of them complained as they each pulled a slice onto their white paper plates.

"We are going to demolish this," Makenna said.

"I like a girl with goals," Caden said, smirking.

"That's not even a goal. That's a mission statement."

Now he was the one laughing, and then things got quiet while they both inhaled their slices. "You said two places *so far...*"

Butterflies whipped through Makenna's belly. "Did I?" she teased.

His gaze narrowed, and it was sexy when he was being all stern. "Didn't you?"

"I did," she said, smiling.

"So where else should we go?" he asked.

She didn't tease him again, not when it was clear they were both trying to feel this thing out. "I'm game for anything. Show me your place. Or drive me by your firehouse. Or we could go down to Old Town for ice cream."

"My place isn't much to see, really."

"Neither is mine," she said. She was proud of her place, but it was still just a little seven-hundred-square-foot apartment.

"Yours definitely is. It's warm and inviting and homey. Tons of pictures. Mine is basically bare walls."

"How long have you lived there?" she asked, diving into her second piece.

"Five years," he said. "My mom's father died and left me some money. We weren't very close, but I think that was more because of my dad not being very receptive to contact with my grandparents after the accident."

Sadness squeezed Makenna's gut. Caden had just lost so much, hadn't he? "It sounds like he wanted you to know that he thought of you."

"Yeah, I think that's right. He was a good man." He wiped his hands on a napkin.

Worried that she'd unexpectedly steered them into serious ground, she changed the subject. "So, what are your favorite desserts here? Because we are so getting dessert."

He chuckled. "The cannoli is fantastic, and the tiramisu is also very good."

"Oh, man, I love their cannoli," Makenna said, already making plans despite making serious headway on a third slice. It wasn't long before their pizza was gone and Antonio was bringing them each a cannoli. Makenna took a bite and moaned. "I'm so glad we got our own or else you might not have gotten much of this."

"I'd have sacrificed my half for you," he said, slanting her a glance.

"Because you're my Good Sam."

The corner of his mouth quirked up, and he looked at her for a long moment. "Yes, I am."

She wondered what the look had been about when she realized she'd called him *her* Good Sam. *Oh geez, Makenna.* The only thing that kept her from smacking herself in the forehead was that he'd agreed with her.

When the check arrived, he grabbed it before she could. "You treated me to dinner," he said, handing Antonio his card.

"It was trail mix!"

He laughed. "It was life-saving trail mix though."

"Well, thank you," she said. "This was amazing. The food and the company."

He winked. "Come on. I'll drive you over to my place." It was literally a two-minute drive. His neighborhood was a super cute community of all-brick townhouses situated around courtyards. He led them up to the door, unlocked it, then stepped back so she could go in first. "This is it," he said, closing the front door behind them.

The first floor was one big room for as far as she could see, with a couch, coffee table, and television stand with a big TV in the front half and a small table and chairs in the back. "The wood floors are gorgeous," she said.

"I got a buddy to help me refinish them when I first moved in," he said, leading her to the back where the dining area opened up to a small galley-style kitchen that looked more lived-in. Clean dishes on a drying rack. A stack of mail by the phone. Some apples in a bowl. "I got the place cheap because the prior owner had lived here for probably decades and it needed a lot of work and upgrades. Did as much as I could myself, sometimes with a lot of trial and error."

"That's pretty awesome, Caden. Your walls might be bare, but you can look around here and see everything you did to make this place comfortable and modern." She peered out his back door to where he had a plastic table and chairs set up on a little fenced-in patio. Turning back, she found him watching her. "What?"

"You always find the positive in everything," he said, his tone full of admiration.

Makenna shrugged. "I just call it how I see it."

"Is that so?" He pulled her into his arms.

"Yep." She smiled up at him. "I'm having fun with you."

"Me, too." He leaned down and kissed her. Once. Twice. "Have you ever been to Gravelly Point?"

"No. Where's that?"

"By the airport. Great sight-seeing and walking paths."

"That sounds fun," she said.

"Yeah? Okay, then. Lemme throw on some clean clothes and we'll go. You can come up if you want. The bathroom's upstairs if you need it."

"Lead the way."

At the top of the steps was a little landing with four doors, one of which led to his room and another to the bathroom, which she used while he changed. It was respectably clean, which she found remarkable since she'd grown up with three guys not that different in age from Caden and let's just say she'd always been very glad that she'd had a bathroom to herself.

She came out to find Caden wearing a white Station 7 T-shirt and unintentionally flashing his abs while he fastened the button on pair of gray cargo shorts. He totally caught her staring and gave her a wink as he went into the bathroom after her.

And the weird thing was…that none of it felt weird.

She was in a strange man's house for the first time ever, and she didn't necessarily feel at home, but she felt comfortable because she was with Caden. He just…didn't feel like a stranger. Not anymore.

Back in his Jeep, he slid on a pair of Aviator sunglasses. "Holy crap, I don't think I can handle you in Aviators," she said, letting the filter slip between her thoughts and her mouth again. But, come *on*. He was already ridiculously sexy and now…Aviators.

He peered over the top of the lenses at her. "That so?"

"Just drive already." She enjoyed the laugh she got out of him. She'd be happy to be silly if it made him laugh and smile like that. "Oh, and don't forget to show me the station," she said, tugging on his shirt sleeve.

"Yes, ma'am."

She laughed. "I am not old enough to be called ma'am."

"I'm just trying to obey over here."

"I like the sound of that." She waggled her eyebrows when he slanted her a glance.

"Do you now?"

"Mmhmm," she said, unable to restrain a grin. Him flirting while wearing Aviators? No. Just no.

Two blocks away, Caden slowed down and pointed out his fire-house. "We're not stopping or else the fire gods will see I'm here, rain down some sort of disaster, and yank me away from spending time with you."

"We definitely don't want that," she said.

"No we do not."

He told some stories about the guys he worked with on the ride over to the park he wanted to show her, and she enjoyed learning more about his life. It was clear that, even though he didn't have anything left of the family that he'd grown up with, that firehouse was his family now. And she was really glad for that. Her family played such a big part of her life that it made her sad to think of Caden without anyone in the world who cared for him or looked out for him. Her brother was a cop in Philly, so she knew a little bit about the kind of brotherhood that being a first responder created. Caden deserved that.

Gravelly Point was a park right on the Potomac River and across a small inlet from one of the runways at Washington's airport. "Wow, this is cool," Makenna said as they pulled into a parking place, a plane taking off right above them.

"I like to come out here sometimes," Caden said. "Got a blanket and some water in the back."

They met at the rear of his Jeep, where he had a lot more than that stowed. He also had a big first-aid kit, a change of clothes and shoes, flares, and some snacks. "Nice. You are prepared for anything."

He chuffed out a laugh and rubbed at the side of his head. "Yeah, I guess so."

It was the way he touched his scar that cued her in.

He seemed to do it when something made him uncomfortable or self-conscious. She looked at the stuff again. And realization punched her in the stomach so hard that it pricked the backs of her eyes with tears. Water, food, first-aid supplies, a blanket, flares...all stuff that you might need if you got stuck somewhere in your car.

Or trapped.

Like he'd once been.

Makenna went onto tiptoes to kiss his cheek. Because she had to do something. "Where do you like to sit, Good Sam?"

He grabbed the blanket and bottled water. "There's a clear view of the runway over here," he said.

It wasn't crowded, but there were plenty of people there enjoying the late September sun and the sparkling blue sky. They laid there for hours, just talking and touching and kissing. She loved the feeling of his big hand holding hers. The airplanes were loud once they were overhead, but it was fun watching them and the people-watching was good, too. She could see why Caden liked it there.

"I hate to say this, but I'm getting hungry again," she finally said.

He laid facing her, his head propped up on his hand. "Yeah?"

"Can I interest you in my favorite noodle place? We could get carry out and find a movie to watch. But, I mean, I know you might have stuff—"

"That sounds good," he said. "Really good. I'm all yours." Makenna really liked the sound of that. The sentiment made her belly go on a loop-the-loop.

An hour later, they were on her couch, eating Drunken Noodles and Pad Thai and watching *Field of Dreams*, which they both liked because they were baseball fans even though the end always made her cry. "It's a happy cry," she said when Caden brushed away her tears. "He sees his dad. Gets me every time. Stupid, I know."

Caden shook his head. "I've lost a parent, too, Red. It's not even a little bit stupid." The hug they gave each other felt like pure understanding, and it tugged at something inside her chest, something fundamental and surprising and scary.

Because how could she already have any kind of feelings for someone she'd just met?

They cleaned up, and even after twenty-four hours together, Makenna wasn't ready for him to go. "Stay with me?"

He pulled her into his arms. "I was hoping you'd say that." One day together turned into two, with him only departing when he had to go in for his shift on Sunday night. "I work a double."

"So you're off on Tuesday night?" she asked, leaning back against her kitchen counter, trying to seem totally casual and like she wasn't a little sad that the bubble of their weekend was over.

He braced his hands on both sides of her hips and met her eye to eye. "Mmhmm."

"Plans?"

He shook his head, his dark gaze intense and direct and full of desire…for her.

"Would you like some?" she asked, her stomach threatening to drop.

"With you? I'd fucking love plans, Makenna."

Elation shot through her. "Good. That's good. Well, maybe, grab some Antonio's and come after you get off?"

Amusement immediately played over his expression.

She frowned. "What?" Her wording finally hit her. "Oh, God, you know what I mean! Come *over* after you get off."

He guffawed so hard that his weight fell against her.

She smacked his shoulder. "You suck."

"You're the…you're the one who…" He couldn't get it out he was chuckling so hard. Good to know that her penchant for verbal nonsense didn't turn him off. And seeing him full-out cracking up was her new favorite thing. When he finally pulled himself together, he said, "I'll grab a pie and be over around 7:30."

"And cannoli?"

He nodded. "And cannoli."

"That sounds perfect."

He peered at the digital clock on the stove. "I don't wanna…"

"I know. You go. Have a good shift. And please be safe."

Nodding, he kissed her long and deep and so deliciously thoroughly that she almost couldn't breathe and the room spun around her. "Always," he said. And then he made for her door, stopping again before it closed. "Hey, Red?"

"Yeah?"

"New question. Best day ever. I'll start. The day I got trapped in that elevator with you."

She gasped, and he was gone. But that was okay, she'd be seeing him again soon and she'd tell him then—that hers was the very same answer.

CHAPTER ONE

*M*akenna James gasped awake, rushing up from sleep as if being tugged from deep under water. What had woken her—

Caden moaned next to her, thrashing against the pillow, a cold sweat on his forehead. Her heart already raced from being startled, but now it squeezed for a whole other reason.

She pulled herself closer and stroked her hand over the deep scar that jagged from his temple to the back of his head. A beam of early morning sunlight filtered through the window next to her bed, revealing his furrowed brow and clenched jaw. God, she hated the way his subconscious tormented him. "Caden? Hey, it's okay. Wake up."

Startled brown eyes flashed to her, not quite tracking for a long moment. "Red?" A scowl settled onto his gorgeous face when awareness returned to him. "Dammit. Sorry," he said, voice like gravel.

She smiled and shook her head, still stroking the close-shaved brown hair surrounding his scar the way he liked. "Nothing to be sorry for."

His arms came around her and he shifted her on top of his broad bare chest, her legs settling over his naked hips. "Damn nightmare." Caden blew out a breath. "I hate this. For you."

"I've got you." Makenna kissed him, reveling as she always did in the nip of his metal spider bite piercings against her lips. *And I love you.* Though she kept that thought to herself.

She'd realized weeks ago that she'd fallen for him, irrevocably and all the way, but she'd never given voice to the words. Something inside her warned against letting him know—yet—just how serious her feelings had become. Not because she believed Caden didn't care for her, too. A part of her worried that making a man so marked by loss confront how close they'd become might freak him out. Fourteen years had passed since he'd lost his mother and younger brother Sean in a car accident that had trapped and injured Caden and left him claustrophobic, scarred, and alone, and the memory of it still tortured him. As the nightmare proved. "Don't you worry about it."

"You're too damn good for me," Caden rasped, deepening the kiss, his big hands digging into her sleep-mussed red hair, his body coming alive beneath hers.

It wasn't the first time he'd said something along those lines, and the sentiment always made the center of her chest ache. How could he not see what she saw—a strong, amazing man who'd dedicated his life to helping others? "Never," she whispered around the edge of the kiss. "You're everything to me."

Her words unleashed a groan from deep in his throat. Caden lifted his head and pursued her lips, nipping and tugging and sucking until Makenna was hot and needy.

The nightmares didn't come every night. They mostly surfaced when Caden was stressed out over something. It didn't take much to guess what today's stressor might be—their trip to Philadelphia to see her father and brothers for Thanksgiving. The holiday was as close to sacred as things got in her family, her father insisting all four of his kids make their way home to give thanks for all they had in their lives, family most especially.

No way she could go without Caden, though. Not when his family was gone. And not when her heart demanded that Caden was family, too.

When she'd first brought up the trip, he'd actually thought she intended to go without him, and even said he'd just volunteer to work so the guys at the firehouse who had families could have off. Makenna made it clear that she wanted him to come with her, and she'd probably never seen him more resemble a deer in the headlights. Which she totally got it. Meeting someone's family for the first time was never easy. But once he'd seen how much spending the day together meant to her, he'd agreed like the sweet, sweet man he was. And so they were road-tripping it for a weekend of turkey, stuffing, and football with the testosterone-dominated James clan.

Caden's grip tightened in her hair as his hips surged beneath her. "I have to get in you. Do we have time? Please tell me there's time."

She smiled against his lips, the thick desire in his voice rushing heat through her veins. Grinding her core against his hard length, she said, "As long as we're quick." Though, truth be told, it wouldn't take much to convince her to linger in this man's arms. She was that far gone and he was that freaking hot.

A sound like a growl rumbled from Caden's throat. "Thanksgiving feasts are meant to be savored," he said, flipping them over and pinning her to the mattress. He helped her remove her panties and his Station 7 shirt with his last name 'GRAYSON' on the back. She'd long ago stolen it from him to sleep in—much to his satisfaction. And then he held himself above her and rocked his erection against the very place where she needed him most.

Makenna nodded. "I agree, but I'd rather not have to explain to my brothers why we were late." Which would be a total nightmare. They'd be like a pack of lions fighting over a meaty carcass, not giving up until they'd made her spill. Then, like the pains in the asses they could be, they'd spend the day making up all the juicy bits she wouldn't tell them to embarrass her—and Caden. No way was she letting that happen. Caden was nervous enough.

His expression darkened and his eyes shuttered, just a bit. Enough to reveal just how anxious he was about the trip.

"I want you, Caden," she said, hoping to pull him back from wherever he'd gone. She stroked her fingers down his strong back. "And I need you. However I can have you."

The shadows disappeared from his face and he finally nodded and quirked a half smile. "Hard and fast it is, then."

Yes, please!

He reached to the nightstand and pulled a condom from the drawer, then sat back to roll it on.

"Love it hard and fast," she whispered, watching him. Her gaze raked over the cut muscles of his chest and stomach and traced down from the yellow rose tattoo on his left pec to the large black tribal that wrapped around his side. Everything about him—his ink, his piercings, even his scars—was so damn sexy.

"Then hold on tight." The words had barely spilled from his lips before he was right there, probing her entrance, pushing into her, filling her with that delicious sensation of fullness that left her breathless, wanting, completed. He wrapped himself around her and leaned his cheek against hers. "So good, Makenna. Every time is so fucking good."

Buried deep inside her, he devoured her mouth in a molten-hot kiss, and then he pulled free but held his face just above hers. His hips rocked and thrust and ground, picking up speed and demanding that she take more of him, all of him. He stole her breath and her ability to think and her heart until there was nothing left of her that he didn't own.

Utterly and completely.

The depth of her emotions pricked at the backs of her eyes and made it so that all she could do was grasp his back and hold tight as his hips flew against hers. Because it was so much better than good.

How was it possible they'd only known each other for two months?

They'd met after spending a night trapped in a pitch-black elevator together, and their bond had been fast and deep—built on conversation that had revealed how much they had in common and a physical attraction that transcended appearances. If there'd ever been a silver lining around an otherwise bad situation, it had been having the freedom the darkness allowed to get to know him. And for him to get to know her. Since then, they'd been nearly inseparable.

Now, Makenna couldn't imagine her life without Caden Grayson. And she hoped she'd never have to.

---

*a*n hour later, Caden sat on the edge of the couch in Makenna's homey living room. His knee bounced. Tightness squeezed his chest. His teeth ached from how hard he was clenching his jaw.

What a fucking misfit.

Makenna was everything Caden was not—polished and out-going and able to put others at ease with her warm smile and her ready, open laughter. In the two months they'd been together, she'd totally embraced his friends and his interests and his world—inviting the guys at the firehouse over for dinner, cheering on his softball team, and even delivering a big tray of homemade brownies and chocolate chip cookies to the station. Hell, Makenna had all the guys there wrapped around her little finger at this point. And Caden was sure they looked at him and wondered how the hell he'd gotten so lucky.

Because he certainly wondered. Every damn day. And it made him sure it couldn't last. Or wouldn't. He couldn't be *that* lucky. At least, he'd never been before.

He shook his head and chuffed out a frustrated breath.

For the most part, he was a loner who was only comfortable around the guys he worked with and a small group of long-time friends. Over the last two months, Makenna had worked her way inside that small circle, after having broken down his walls and accepted all the bullshit she found behind them. He'd never been happier in his life. And he was having a damn hard time trusting it.

In his experience, happiness didn't last. Instead, it was ripped from you when you least expected, tearing you from the ones you loved and leaving you all alone. It was why he'd never before pursued a serious relationship with a woman. Until Makenna. Who was like a force of nature with her honesty and her positivity and her acceptance and her touch. He hadn't been able to resist the temptation of having something so good, something that might be able to shine some light on all his darkness.

"Okay, I'm ready," Makenna said, walking into the living room from the bedroom. She wore a beautiful smile and a lavender sweater over a pair of tight, sexy jeans tucked into knee-high brown leather boots. And, God, she was so damn pretty. Long, wavy red hair that he loved to play with swept across her face and settled around her shoulders. Her blue eyes were heaven in a stare, and saw right through all his masks. But instead of finding him unworthy—the way he felt—all that shined from those baby blues was affection and unconditional acceptance.

It slayed him. It really fucking did. Because she looked at him and never seemed to see all the defects he felt down deep.

"Great," Caden said, rising and swallowing the sour taste in the back of his throat. On the one hand, he wanted to meet her family. They were important to her, and so far in their relationship, he hadn't done nearly enough to meet her friends and get to know those she cared for the most. He owed this to her, and he wanted to be man enough—just once—to walk into a roomful of strangers and act like a normal freaking human being.

On the other hand, Caden was the furthest thing from normal. New people made him nervous as shit and he sucked at small talk. He never knew what to say, so he'd either clam up or end up with a foot in his mouth. Either way, he came off like an anti-social asshole. Much as he loved his ink and his facial piercings for a whole bunch of reasons, he couldn't say he was unhappy with the fact that his appearance scared some people off. Because being alone was miles better than being rejected, left, or abandoned.

Been there, done that, got the blood-stained T-shirt. Thank you very much.

Makenna came right up to him and wrapped her arms around his waist. "You look very handsome, Mr. Grayson." Her smile warmed his chest, and damn if her touch didn't make it easier to breathe. It had been like that from the start with Makenna—her presence easing his anxiety. He'd never had that with another person. He'd never even thought it was possible. "I hope you're not wearing long sleeves to cover your tattoos."

He was, though his dragon tattoo extended onto the back of his right hand, so there was only so much he could do about that. And they'd already had the conversation about his piercings—Makenna didn't want him to take them out for the visit, though he'd offered. "Just wanted to look nice."

Still holding one of his hands, she stepped back and gave him a long, slow once-over. Her gaze raked over his black dress pants and charcoal gray button-down shirt, a few of the nicer pieces he owned. A jeans-and-T-shirt kinda guy who worked in a uniform, Caden didn't have much use for dress clothes.

"So nice I'm tempted to take all this back off again." Her smile was pure temptation. "But seriously, I want you to be comfortable. Okay?"

Releasing a breath, he unbuttoned a sleeve and rolled it up. Repeated it on the other arm, revealing the whole dragon. Better already. On a roll, he undid another button at the collar. So much better. "There." He gave her a questioning smile.

"Perfection. And don't worry. They're going to love you. I promise."

He couldn't keep his eyebrow from arching. Highly fucking unlikely. "If you say so, Red." He tucked a silky wave behind her ear. Makenna's hair had been the very first thing he'd noticed about her.

Grinning, she nodded. "I do. Besides, with you being a paramedic and Patrick being a cop, I think you'll have lots in common to talk about. All of them love stupid humor movies, too. So it'll be just like us hanging out. Except with more penises." Pushing up on tiptoes, she pressed her body against him and hugged him tight.

Chuckling, Caden breathed her in, and her scent made his shoulders relax and his heart rate slow. *Get it together, Grayson. She needs this.* "Then let's do it," he said, forcing as much enthusiasm into his voice as he could.

"Yay," she said, with a radiant smile. "This is going to be great."

Nodding, Caden collected their bags and slung them over his shoulder as Makenna grabbed some things from the fridge. Maybe he could treat this weekend just like he did a run in the ambulance. When a call came in, Caden was able to focus on the crisis at hand in a way that blocked all the other shit out. In those moments, all that mattered was the person in need and what he could do to ease their pain and save their life. Just like someone had once done for him.

Surely he could focus, hold himself together, and do this for Makenna. "Of course it's gonna be great," he said, "because I'll be with you."

CHAPTER TWO

"So tell me about some of the weird calls you've responded to," Makenna said, smiling over at Caden. God, he was sexy sitting in the driver's seat of his black Jeep, big hands gripping the leather steering wheel. Though they were going home to visit her family, he was driving—he found her car, a little silver Prius, more confining than he could stand. They were halfway between her home in Arlington and her dad's place in Philadelphia and, as always, they never had trouble finding things to talk about. Heck, that was part of what drew her to Caden in the first place.

"There have been more than a few weird ones over the years," Caden said, quirking a small grin as he looked her way. "Let's see. There was the woman who got her hand stuck in the garbage disposal. Her sweater snagged on part of the internal mechanism. The sweater was cashmere and she was really pissed that we had to cut it."

Makenna grimaced. "Why'd she put her hand in the garbage disposal?"

"Dropped a ring down the drain," he said with a shrug of his broad shoulders. "We found it for her though." He pursed his lips and his eyes narrowed. "Oh. And once we got a call that a woman was hearing a man yell and scream through her apartment wall. We showed up with the police ten minutes later and he was fine. Turned out he'd been, uh, severely constipated and having a hard time...going."

Makenna burst out laughing. "That is gross. He must've been so embarrassed."

Caden chuckled. "I don't know. I think the woman who made the call was more embarrassed than he was. When we got there, she came out into the hallway with us because she was so worried about the guy."

"That's a big old case of TMI," Makenna said, enjoying the conversation. Being an EMT meant Caden confronted a lot of intense and often tragic situations, things about which he didn't always want to talk when he came home after a shift. So it was nice to learn more about this part of him.

Grinning so big it brought his dimples out to play, Caden nodded. Makenna loved how smiling made his face look so much younger and more relaxed. Between his head scar, the widow's peak of his shaved hair, and the piercings on his lip and eyebrow, his face could appear harsh, maybe even intimidating. Except when he smiled. "Then there was the guy who called because he thought his penis was going to explode. It turned out he'd borrowed Viagra without a prescription and taken three of them at once. Four days later, he still had an erection."

"Aw, God. What is wrong with people?" Makenna laughed and turned in her seat toward Caden.

"I don't know." Caden winked. "You'd be surprised how many strange calls we get. And dispatch gets the weirdest calls of all. People call to complain about fast food restaurants not getting their orders right, or to ask if the police could go to a movie theater and hold the show time up because they're caught in traffic, or to find out what the weather is. One old man called because he thought his house had suddenly started having a heartbeat. It turned out his new neighbors next door were in a band and he was hearing the drums. Oh, and then there was the old lady who called because her 72-year-old husband wanted to spice up their sex life by having a threesome. She wanted him arrested."

"Wow." Makenna shook her head. "I think I've called 9-1-1 exactly one time in my life, and it was when someone on the Metro thought they were having a heart attack. Even then I was nervous to dial the numbers."

"Well, that's how it should be," Caden said. "So many calls to 9-1-1 aren't emergencies at all."

Makenna reached over and laced her fingers with Caden's. Their clasped hands rested on his thigh, giving her a view of the dragon tattooed on the back of his right hand. "Okay, now tell me about some really great calls you went on."

"I've delivered three babies," he said, a small smile on his lips. "Those were my favorites. Such an amazing thing to be a part of, watching a life come into the world. You know? One of the couples named their son Grayson."

Her mouth dropped open. "Aw, Caden. That's so special. I can't imagine how scary it would be to know a baby was coming and not be able to get to the hospital." For a moment, Makenna's imagination ran away with the picture of this muscled, inked, pierced, scarred man holding a brand new baby in those big hands. What a sight that would be. She smiled.

"It was," he said with a nod. "I've also patched up a number of cats and dogs over the years, mostly pets that get trapped in house fires. Just to stabilize them until they get to a vet. But the people always appreciate it."

"Oh, be still my heart," Makenna said, squeezing his hand. "If I didn't already...like you, you would've totally won me over with your stories about babies and puppies." She looked out the windshield to the sunny blue sky beyond and hoped he didn't hear the way she'd tripped over her words. She'd nearly said she loved him. Because the feeling was always in the forefront of her mind these days.

He threw her a wicked grin. "How do you think Bear picks up so many different girls?" Isaac Barrett was a firefighter at Caden's station, and he was maybe the biggest player she'd ever met. But he was an also sweet and funny and loyal and would give a person the shirt off his back, and Makenna really liked him.

"Ah, so that explains it," she said.

"Pretty much." He lifted their joined hands to his mouth and pressed a kiss against her knuckles.

Heat lanced through Makenna's chest and her blood in equal measure.

Still holding hands, they settled into a comfortable silence. Makenna's gaze traced over what she could see of Caden's dragon tattoo, the one he'd gotten to remind himself not to let fear rule his life. She really admired the meaning behind many of his pieces, so much so that she'd been thinking of getting a tattoo herself. A lot. The idea whipped butterflies through her belly. She'd always been such a good-girl rule-follower that she'd never considered it seriously before meeting Caden. But, inspired by how he'd commemorated those he'd loved and lost on his skin, Makenna had been mulling over a few designs over the past couple of weeks.

I want to do this. The thought came firm and sure, and she felt the rightness of it down deep. "So, guess what I've been thinking about lately?"

"What's that?" he asked, his pierced eyebrow arching as he peered over at her.

It made her want to flick at his little black barbell piercing with her tongue. Her stomach flip-flopped as she gave voice to the idea. "Getting a tattoo."

Caden's gaze whipped toward her, his eyebrows cranked down over dark eyes. "For real?"

She grinned and bit her lip. "Yeah. I love yours and the more I think about it, the more I want to do it."

"What kind do you want?" he asked, his gaze dragging over her so hotly it almost felt like a physical caress.

"I've been thinking about a Celtic family tree. The one I like best is shaped like a circle and the tree and ground are made of Celtic knots. Some designs of it place initials below the ground or weave them into the branches, and that's really cool, too. Here," she said, dragging her finger against the screen of her smartphone. She opened an image she'd saved in her pictures and held it up so Caden could see. "This is one version of it."

His eyes flickered back and forth between her phone and the road ahead. "I like that," he said in a reserved tone. "A lot. How sure are you that you want to do this?"

"Pretty sure," she said. "I've been thinking about it a lot lately. It was just a matter of what to get. I wanted it to mean something, like yours do. So I thought about what means the most to me in the world, and it's family. Once I figured that out and found these designs, I was finally sure. But will you come with me if I get it done?"

He threw a blazing glance at her. "If you want to do this, I'd like to take you to my guy. He's the best there is. And of course I'll be there. In a heartbeat, Red."

She grinned and nodded. His presence would help steady her nerves. "Good," she said. "Maybe next week?"

"You just say the word," he said. "And I'll make it happen."

Makenna unbuckled her seat belt, stretched across the center console, and lingeringly kissed Caden's cheek, jaw, neck, letting her tongue sneak out to taste him while she was at it. He smelled good, like soap and mint and something spicy that was pure Caden.

He groaned and leaned into her touch. "Fuck, Makenna," he whispered. "I don't want you to stop but I really want you to put your seat belt back on."

She gave his ear lobe a final lick and settled back on her own side. "Sorry," she said as the buckle clicked. "I was just feeling really grateful."

He gave a little chuckle. "Well, I'll definitely take a raincheck on that. Besides, you can't put pictures in my head of you getting inked and then kiss on me like that while I'm driving."

"Why not?" she asked, biting on her lip to try to restrain the smile that threatened. And holy crap if the tone of his voice didn't make her wish he *wasn't* driving. Because she could think of some other very good uses for his hands....

The look he threw her—all blatant desire and frustration—shot heat over her skin. "Because it drives me crazy. And I can't do anything about it." He shifted his hips in the seat, drawing Makenna's gaze downward to the bulge forming in the front of his dress pants.

Slowly, she ran her hand down his chest and stomach to his lap.

"*Red,*" he rasped, his gaze drifting down to watch her hand rub and grip for just a moment. God, he was a delicious handful. Eyes back on the road, Caden shook his head and grabbed her hand, holding it in a ball against his chest. "I'm not chancing wrecking with you in the car." He threw her another one of those red-hot glances. "But you better believe we're revisiting this later."

*C*aden knew what Makenna was doing. For the past two and a half hours, she'd kept him talking non-stop. About his work. About tattoos. About Christmas. She'd teased him and made him laugh and generally kept his mind off of where they were going and what he was about to do—namely, meet her family. Which, of course, meant that she realized how anxious he was. And wasn't that a complete pisser.

Both because he didn't want her having to worry about such a thing and because she was right.

Following her directions, he veered off the highway into a suburb just south of Philadelphia.

"It's less than fifteen minutes from here," she said, excitement plain in her voice.

Caden nodded and tried like hell to ignore the tensing of his shoulders, the clenching of his gut, and the tightening of his chest. And man how he hated just how familiar these reactions were. Since the accident that had killed half of his family and left him alone with a bitter, angry, broken shell of a father at fourteen, Caden's body had always responded to stress this way. Working with a therapist years ago, he'd conquered the worst of his PTSD and anxiety and he had some techniques for battling the latter when it hit, but he couldn't stop it from happening or make it go away altogether.

Caden could never just be normal.

Something he could tolerate when it just impacted himself, but he hated it for Makenna's sake.

Holding the steering wheel in something close to a death grip, he silently counted backwards from ten, trying to remember his breathing techniques, trying to keep from freaking the fuck out before they even arrived. The last thing he wanted to do was embarrass Makenna in front of her family. Or embarrass himself.

It was vitally important that they like him—that they *accept* him—too.

Because Caden was falling for Makenna. Hard. Hell, he'd already loved her at least a little that first night they'd spent together. She'd kept him from having a full-on panic attack while trapped in that dark elevator, which had represented pretty much every one of his worst nightmares. And when she'd invited him in—to her home, to her bed, to her body for the first full night he'd ever spent in another person's arms, he'd probably already fallen most of the rest of the way.

Now, after two months of being with her, after two months of not being alone in every way a person could be alone—because of her, Caden felt like he stood on the edge of a tall cliff. One more step and he'd be free-falling head-first into a precipice from which he'd never return.

And it scared the ever-living fuck out of him.

Because he knew all too well how quickly and unexpectedly those he cared for the most could be torn from him. In the blink of a goddamned eye. And he'd have absolutely no say in it whatsoever. He wouldn't even see tragedy and heartbreak coming. Just like when he'd been fourteen.

Christ, Grayson. You're not helping things right now.

He heaved a deep breath and forced his fingers to loosen around the wheel. No, thinking about losing Makenna wasn't helping his state of mind at all.

"Hey," she said, squeezing his thigh. "Thank you for coming home with me."

The smile she gave him was so soft and pretty. It took the edge off of some of the anxiety building inside him. He could do this. He *would* do this. For her.

"You're welcome. I appreciate you inviting me." And he did. Despite all the churn in his head, it meant a lot that she'd wanted to be with him at Thanksgiving. It was nice not to be alone for once on a holiday. Hell, it was nice to be celebrating at all. His mom had always been the life of his family, and when she died, what was left of the Grayson family really died with her.

After she was gone, Caden's house never saw another Christmas tree, never baked another turkey, and never had another Easter basket waiting on the dining room table on Easter morning. Even after he and Sean had been way too old for baskets and Santa, she'd still marked presents "from Santa" and filled baskets that she insisted the Easter Bunny had delivered.

So being included in Makenna's family Thanksgiving celebration meant more than he could say.

Soon, Makenna was guiding them into a stately neighborhood full of big, older homes and manicured lawns and tall, mature trees. Most of the houses were made of gray limestone and sat back off the narrow streets, allowing room for wide covered porches and winter-bare gardens out front. Christmas wreaths and garlands of pine boughs and holly already adorned the doors and windows of some of the houses, making the neighborhood even more picturesque.

All of a sudden, curiosity replaced some of the anxiety flowing through Caden's body. Because all of this represented a part of Makenna he didn't know. He'd heard her talk about her father and brothers, of course, and he knew her mother died when Makenna was little, but hearing stories and actually *seeing* where she was from were two different things.

"My house is up here on the corner. Turn right, the driveway's on the side," Makenna said.

Caden rolled to a stop in front of the house and leaned to peer out Makenna's side window. Made of gray limestone, the place was beautiful. Three stories with a porch made for rocking chairs, windows flanked by black shutters, and soaring stone chimneys. An American flag fluttered in the cold breeze from its perch on one of the gray porch columns. "This is where you grew up?" he asked.

"Yep," she said, smiling at him.

He met her gaze, and loved the happiness he saw there. Well, he loved so much more than that, didn't he? Even if he hadn't looked at that reality too closely. "It's really nice."

She looked out her window. "It was a wonderful place to grow up. Just being here gives me the warm and fuzzies."

Be-beep.

Caden's gaze flew to the rear-view and found a car sitting behind him. "Oh, shit, sorry," he said, making the right turn.

Makenna chuckled. "Don't worry about it. Oh, just park on the street," she said when they saw that four cars already took up most of the driveway in front of the two-car garage.

Caden pulled the Jeep to the curb and killed the engine.

"Looks like my brothers are all here, but I don't know who the Beemer belongs to," she said, shrugging. When she turned toward him, she was wearing a smile so full of excitement and anticipation that he was surprised she was managing to sit still. "Ready to meet everyone?"

At that moment, he wanted nothing more than to make her happy, so he nodded. "Ready as I'll ever be."

Now he just hoped he didn't fuck everything up.

CHAPTER THREE

"I'm home!" Makenna called as she pushed through the back door into the rectangular mud room. A big bench seat with hooks took up one wall, and Makenna placed the jug of apple pie sangria and the tray of pumpkin roll on the bench as she hung her coat. Caden settled their bags on the floor and did the same. The house smelled like roasting turkey and savory stuffing and cinnamon, and it was so welcoming that her heart squeezed for the want of seeing her dad and brothers.

Her father rushed into the doorway that led to the kitchen. "There's my peanut."

Makenna laughed. "Dad," she said as they hugged. She didn't mind the ancient nickname. Not really. And, oh, it was good to see him. She stood back from the hug and took him in—his brown hair had a bit more gray in it since she'd last seen him over the summer, but otherwise he looked exactly the same. Bright blue eyes. Laugh lines from a lifetime of good humor. And wearing the old apron with a picture of a turkey breast and the words *I'm a breast man!* her brothers had thought was a hilarious gift at least ten years before. "I want you to meet Caden," she said, stepping aside to let the men shake.

"Caden Grayson, sir," he said as he shook her father's hand. She could hear the nerves in his voice, but she had absolutely no doubt about her father's ability to put Caden at ease. "Happy Thanksgiving."

"You, too. Call me Mike." Her dad clasped Caden's shoulder and guided him into the kitchen. "What can I get you to drink?" he asked, then rattled off a long list of choices.

"A Coke would be fine," Caden said, standing beside the big island in the center of the open, airy kitchen.

Makenna brought her contributions to dinner in and sat them on the counter. The rustic white cabinets, honey-colored granite counters, and warm wooden floors had always made this her favorite room in the house. But man, if she didn't like the room even better with Caden there. "I'll get it," Makenna said, grinning to herself as she leaned into the fridge. Everything was better with Caden.

Her dad engaged them in small talk about the traffic and the nice weather they were having and how much longer the turkey still had to cook, and Makenna could see the tension draining out of Caden's shoulder. She covered his hand with hers where it rested against the countertop.

Her dad took casual notice of the gesture but otherwise didn't react. Though she'd told her father all about Caden, she'd never brought a man home before, so it was new ground for both of them. "So, Caden, Makenna tells me you're a paramedic. What's that like?"

"It's..." Caden's brow furrowed for a long moment. "It's different every day depending on the calls we get. Sometimes it's long hours of hanging out at the station, but most days you can hardly catch your breath for running between calls. Depending on how critical the situation is, it can be hard and stressful, but mostly it's an amazing privilege to be there to help someone in a moment when they desperately need it."

Makenna's heart swelled at the passion in his voice. Despite all he'd been through—not just the accident and the loss of his mom and brother, but the life-long PTSD and having a father who hadn't been there for him, too—Caden was such a sweet, good man. Two months ago, he'd held the elevator door for her when nothing else in her day had gone right, and she'd called him her Good Samaritan. Then, she hadn't known the half of it.

Her father nodded as he pulled a big dish down from a cabinet, and Makenna could see that the thoughtfulness of Caden's response had impressed him. "I have a lot of respect for first responders. You're out there on the front lines."

"When you've had a stranger show up to help you during your darkest hour, the least you can do is be there for someone else during theirs," Caden said in a quiet voice. "I've always felt that I had to pay it forward."

Makenna slipped her arm around Caden's waist. Part of her couldn't believe he'd offered that up, because she knew he didn't like to talk about himself. And it made her so proud of him that it took everything she had not to pull his face down for a kiss. But maybe it was better not to freak her father out fifteen minutes after arriving.

"Makenna told me about the accident," her dad said, taking a drink from a bottle of beer. "I was sorry to hear it. That's a lot for a kid to go through. But I'd say you're doing your family proud."

Caden gave a tight nod and looked down, suddenly very interested in his can of Coke.

She squeezed him tighter, because her dad was right. But Makenna changed the topic because she knew the attention—and the compliment—probably made him uncomfortable. "Where are the guys?" she asked, moving to fill a glass with sangria. Full of apples, cinnamon, and spice, it was fall in a cup. Delicious.

"Downstairs in the rec room," her dad said, peering into the oven to check the turkey. "Watching football, I think."

After her mother had died of breast cancer when Makenna was three, her dad took over everything her mother used to do—including the cooking. And he was good at it, too. Not that she remembered much of her mother. Of any of them, Patrick had the most memories because he'd been ten when they lost her. But even his memories were mostly faint and indistinct. Which explained why she and her brothers worshipped her dad. He'd been everything to them.

"Oh, and you're not the only one who brought a date home." Dad grinned, loving knowing something she didn't.

"Who else brought someone?" she asked. Patrick was married to the police department, so she knew it wasn't him, and she hadn't heard about Ian or Collin dating anyone. What the heck?

"Wanna guess?" her father asked as he pulled two cookie sheets of appetizers out of the second oven. He settled them on the counter.

"No!" Makenna said. "Spill already."

Her dad smiled and scooped the southwest egg rolls, pigs in a blanket, and spinach-artichoke pockets onto a platter. "Collin."

Her little brother brought a date? Holy crap. "Someone from grad school?" Makenna asked.

Her dad nodded. "Shima. She's a real sweetheart. You should go make sure she's surviving your brothers and introduce Caden." He took a cautious bite of one of the egg rolls. "And take these down for me?" he asked, tapping the edge of the dish.

Makenna grabbed a stack of paper plates and napkins. "Did you know she was coming?"

"Nope. It was a surprise." Her dad shrugged. "The more the merrier at the holidays, though."

Nodding, Makenna reached for the appetizers.

"I got it," Caden said.

"Great to meet you, Caden," her dad said. "*Mi casa es su casa.* So while you're here, make yourself completely at home." Makenna gave her dad a grateful smile for welcoming Caden, not that she'd doubted he would.

"Appreciate that, Mike," Caden said, following Makenna across the room and into a hallway.

At the top of the basement steps, she turned to him, smiling. "Just remember, I am in no way responsible for the cretins you're about to meet."

"*D*uly noted," Caden said, giving her a wink. If they were anything like Mike, he might actually make it through this weekend. He followed her down the steps.

The basement family room was a big, comfortable space with overstuffed sofas and chairs grouped in front of a large flat-screen television. At the far end sat an old air hockey table. But he didn't have time to take much more in before five pair of eyes settled on them.

"Hey," Makenna said to a big round of greetings. Her brothers—clear from the various shades of red hair—all got up to give her a hug. Which left a fourth guy with blond hair and Ken-doll good looks who Caden didn't know. Makenna took the tray of appetizers from Caden's hands as she said, "Uh, guys, this is Caden Grayson." She introduced her brothers, but seemed suddenly nervous.

"I'm Patrick," the first brother said, holding out his hand. He was the oldest James brother—seven years older than Makenna if Caden remembered right. Tall with reddish-brown hair and a close-trimmed beard, he wore a friendly smile as they shook.

"Nice to meet you, Patrick. I've heard a lot about you," Caden said.

"I'm Ian," the next brother said, his expression not as friendly. He stepped back from their handshake fairly quickly and fell into conversation with the mystery blond man—who Makenna was staring at, a frown on her face.

The last brother had the brightest red hair, so red it was almost orange. "Caden, I'm Collin and this is my girlfriend Shima," he said with a friendly, open smile. Caden shook both of their hands.

Shima pushed her sleek black hair over her shoulder and smiled conspiratorially. "We can stick together today if the James clan decides to gang up on the newcomers."

Caden chuckled. "You've got a deal."

"Dad made some appetizers," Makenna said, holding it out to everyone before settling the tray on the coffee table. "So, Cameron, hey. Wow. How long has it been?"

The blond-haired man stepped up to her with a smile Caden didn't really like. An interested smile. Who was this guy and why did

Makenna seem unhappy to see him? "Too long, Makenna. You look great." He gave her a big, long hug. When the guy finally let her go, he tugged playfully—familiarly—at the end of a strand of her hair. "You haven't changed a bit."

With a chuckle, Makenna stepped back. "Oh, I don't know about that." She held her hand out to Caden. "Cam, this is Caden Grayson."

Cameron gave him a quick, assessing look that immediately set Caden's teeth on edge. They shook in a quick perfunctory greeting, and Caden couldn't help but wonder why it had just gotten so frosty.

Standing with Ian at his side, Cameron asked, "So what do you do, Caden?"

"I'm a paramedic," Caden said. "You?"

"I'm a cardiology fellow at Penn," he said.

"That's impressive," Caden said, taking a drink from his can of Coke. A doctor. And not just any doctor, but a specialist. Of course he was.

"Thanks. You have any interest in medical school?" Cameron asked.

"Nope," Caden said. "Emergency medical services is exactly where I always wanted to be." Which was the truth. When he was younger, he'd thought about pursuing a medical degree for about five seconds, but what he most wanted was to be there for people in crisis the way someone had once been there for him—out on the streets where things were messy and situations were still evolving and pre-hospital treatment was the difference between life and death. Plus, he hadn't wanted to spend all those years in school. He didn't have the patience for it.

"Huh," Cameron said with a shrug. "Well, good for you." His response plucked at Caden's last good nerve. Why did the guy make him feel like there was some competition he didn't know he was competing in?

Patrick joined their group. "You're in Arlington, is that right?"

Caden nodded, glad for the break from Cameron. "Yeah."

"Any chance you know Tony Anselmi? Arlington County police. I went to high school with him," Patrick said.

"Yeah," Caden said with a smile. "Our paths cross. I last saw him probably three weeks ago." As he and Patrick fell into a conversation about Tony and their respective jobs, Caden kept half his attention on the conversation between Makenna, Cameron, and Ian.

"You still crunching numbers?" Cameron asked her, his tone borderline condescending. Or maybe it only sounded patronizing because the guy rubbed Caden the wrong way. Caden frowned, knowing Makenna loved her job as a forensic accountant.

"Yup," Makenna said. "You still playing with people's hearts?"

Cameron burst out laughing.

"Geez, Makenna," Ian said.

"What? He's a cardiologist," she said.

"It's all good, it's all good," Cameron said. He tilted his beer bottle toward her as if in salute. "Touché."

Smiling, Makenna shook her head and sipped at her sangria.

Soon, they all settled onto the couches and chairs to watch football, which had never really been Caden's thing, though he didn't mind watching. Patrick sat in one of the big leather armchairs, and Ian, Collin, and Shima took one of the couches. That left him, Makenna, and Cameron for the other couch. She sat down first, which put him and Cameron on either side of her. Fantastic.

"So, how long have you two been dating?" Ian asked.

Makenna put her hand on Caden's thigh, and he appreciated the hell out of the claiming gesture. "A little over two months," she said, giving Caden a smile. Over her shoulder, he saw Cameron and Ian exchange a look. What the hell? Was he imagining this shit? Who was the guy, anyway?

"How about you two?" Makenna said, looking at Collin and Shima. "How long have you been dating?

The couple exchanged smiles, and then Collin said, "Since the end of the summer. We've known each other since we both started the Master's program, but got together at the welcome-back party in August."

"It's good when grad students date other grad students," Shima said. "Because then we don't bore other people silly with all our foreign policy shop talk."

Caden smiled. He liked Shima and was really glad she was there. "So, Ian, Makenna told me you're an engineer. What kinds of things do you work on?" he asked, hoping to get the middle James brother to warm up to him.

"I'm a civil engineer for the city of Philadelphia," he said. "I focus primarily on road, bridge, and tunnel projects."

"So it's all *your* fault," Patrick said with a grin.

Ian flipped him the finger as everyone laughed.

"Seriously," Patrick said, holding a hand out to Caden. "Have you driven around Philly much?" Caden shook his head. As a kid, his family used to roadtrip everywhere, but since the accident, Caden hadn't traveled much out of the DC area. "Well, trust me, driving in Philly sucks. I would know since I do it every day."

"Yeah, yeah, yeah," Ian said, glaring at his brother. "Same shit, different day."

"Cameron," Shima said, "what's your connection to the Jameses?" Caden wanted to high five her for asking.

"This knucklehead's my best friend," Cameron said, pointing at Ian. "Has been since grade school." Pause. "And Makenna and I dated for what?" He looked at her with a smile. "Three years?"

Dated? Three years? Caden looked at Cameron, who was wearing a satisfied expression that said he knew Caden hadn't known about their past. And he was right.

"Uh, yeah," Makenna said. "Three years."

Three years. Caden had never dated *anyone* for three years. Hell, Caden had rarely dated at all before Makenna. He took a long drink of his soda.

"We started dating my senior and her sophomore year of college," he said. Makenna just nodded. Caden ran the mental calculations. She would've been about nineteen when they started dating and twenty-two when they broke things off. Which pretty much meant there was no way in hell they hadn't slept together. *Whiiich* explained the way the guy had been looking and smiling at her, and how he'd hugged her longer than necessary. He was still into her.

"God, that seems like a million years ago," Makenna said with a smile. She took a long drink of her sangria.

"Nah," Cameron said with a wink. "Hey, do you remember that time when we—"

"Can I get some help setting the table?" came Mike's voice down the stairs.

"I'll help," Makenna called, grasping Caden's hand. "Wanna join me?"

"Yeah," he said. She could've asked him if he wanted to help her clean toilets with toothbrushes and he would've agreed. Anything to take a break from Cameron's smug face, and from the way the man's eyes followed Makenna's body as she rose from the couch.

CHAPTER FOUR

*U*pstairs, Makenna dragged Caden into the hall bathroom and shut the door. "I didn't know he was going to be here," she said. From the moment she'd looked up and seen Cameron Hollander standing there, she'd worried about Caden's reaction. Why hadn't Dad warned her? Although, she wasn't sure what she could've done even if she'd known.

"Okay," he said, and then he shrugged. His expression seemed unconcerned, but she knew he was capable of throwing down a shutter over his true feelings when he didn't want to confront them. Hell, separating himself from his emotions had been half of how he'd survived the aftermath of losing his family, so he was damn near an expert at it. "It's fine."

She dropped her forehead against his chest, wrapped her arms around his waist, and breathed him in. "It's awkward."

Caden chuckled as he stroked the back of her hair. "Only because he's still interested."

Groaning, Makenna shook her head, totally confused by Cam's presence and annoyed that it might make Caden uncomfortable. Finally, she lifted her gaze to meet Caden's. "Well I'm not interested in him, in case that needs to be said." It had been three years since they parted ways, and she'd been over Cam for a long time. He'd made his choice and she'd made her peace with it.

Caden's dark gaze studied her for a moment. He gave a small shake. "It doesn't, Makenna. Don't worry. Although if he stares at your ass or plays with your hair one more time, I won't be held accountable for my actions." The pierced eyebrow arched playfully.

She chuckled, but God, she really didn't want anything to mess up this visit or make Caden feel any more uncomfortable than she knew he already did. She was going to kill Ian, who knew that Makenna was bringing someone home. What the hell had he been thinking? "Would you like to know the story—"

The door handle jiggled.

"Someone's in here," she called.

"Okay," came Ian's voice.

"Let's go help with the table," Caden said. "We can talk later."

She nodded, and thrilled when he bent down and gave her a long, slow, wet kiss full of heat and passion and tongue. From the first time they'd kissed in the darkness of that elevator, his kissing skills had totally owned her. "I'm sorry, what were you saying?" she asked in a breathy voice when he pulled away.

The smile he gave her brought out his dimples. "I don't know, but you taste like apples and cinnamon."

"It's my sangria. You should try some."

"I think I will." His big hand slipped behind her neck as he kissed her again. A deep, exploring kiss. "Mmm, that's good," he rasped.

"God, I could kiss you like that all day," she whispered.

His grin was full of smug masculine satisfaction. "Could you now?" With a wink, he turned and opened the door.

Down the hall, they ran into Ian. "Were you seriously in the bathroom together?" he asked.

Makenna glared, not appreciating his standoffishness toward Caden downstairs. "Did you seriously bring my ex-boyfriend to Thanksgiving?"

"He's my best friend," Ian said, stepping past them. True, but it had been a lot of years since Cameron had celebrated a holiday with them.

When they were all younger, it hadn't been unusual for Cameron to be at their house for meals and sleepovers, including the holidays. But he hadn't last been there since before she and Cam broke up.

When her brother closed himself in the bathroom, she turned to Caden. "Sorry about him. Not sure what his problem is."

On one level, she wasn't surprised that Ian was the one to cause trouble where Caden was concerned. Because Patrick was so much older, she'd always idolized him and he'd always been an awesome big brother to her—they always got along great. And because Collin was younger and generally the easiest-going person you'd ever meet, she usually didn't end up having issues with him. But her and Ian—the two middle kids—butted heads over just about everything and anything, and always had.

"Loyalty, I'm guessing." He kissed the top of her head. "Stop worrying."

"Okay," she said. They went into the kitchen to find her father pulling the turkey out of the oven. "How can we help?"

"Collin and Shima started on the table. See if they want help and, if not, you can start plating everything. We'll be ready to eat in about twenty minutes. Just need to make some gravy."

"Okay," Makenna said, leading Caden into the dining room that hosted every meal whenever the whole family got together. Collin and Shima were setting out plates and silverware around the big formal table.

"Wait. You forgot Mom's runner," Makenna said.

"Oh, shit," Collin said. "Sorry."

"It's no problem," Makenna said, going to the glass-fronted hutch that sat on the far wall. She found the decorative cloth in the bottom cabinet. "When my mom died, my dad was really good about sharing all the traditions that had been important to her. My grandmother made this and gave it to Mom as a present, and Mom apparently used it every Thanksgiving." She unfolded the long rectangle with embroidered leaves and pumpkins and acorns. "We still like to use it."

Caden helped her spread it out down the length of the table between the place settings Collin had already set out.

"It's beautiful," Shima said. "It's really special that you still honor her this way."

"Yeah," Makenna said. "Collin and I were too young to really remember much of her, so it's nice to have things like this." She shrugged. "I've always felt like, if I can't have her, I have to hang on to whatever parts of her I can have. I don't know."

Caden's arm fell around her shoulders and he hugged her against him. "Shima's right. It's a special thing to do." The sweetness of his words unleashed warmth in her chest. God, she loved this man.

They made quick work of setting the rest of the table and then Makenna and Caden returned to the kitchen to help with the rest of the food. One by one, Makenna filled serving dishes and platters and Caden took them out to the table for her.

She and Caden had made a million meals together over the past few months, but there was something really special about the two of them working on a meal in the house where she grew up. It made Caden feel like part of the family, because to her he already was. Finally, the turkey was carved and the gravy was ready, and it was time to eat. Her father called everyone to the table.

Her father and Patrick sat at the ends, and Collin, Shima, and Ian sat on the far side. Cam went for the middle seat on the close side, which would put him between her and Caden. Not happening.

"Hey, Cam? Would you mind moving down one so Caden and I can sit together?" she asked, perturbed that he'd *made* her ask. She wasn't sure what he was up to with this visit, but she wasn't playing, whatever it was.

"Sure," he said, sliding over.

"Here you go," Caden said, pulling out the end chair for her so he'd end up between them.

She hid her grin as she sat next to her father and Caden took the middle seat. Score one for Caden.

Her father held out his hands, and they all followed suit. Out of nowhere, sitting at Thanksgiving dinner holding the hands of the two most important men in her life made her throat tight with gratitude and joy. Dad bowed his head. "Thank you, God, for fulfilling all our needs and blessing us with this food. Thank you for each person who shares this meal with us today. May our lives never be so rushed and busy that we don't remember to stop and be grateful, to see all the things we have in this life. Our family, our friends, our homes, our health, our jobs. And may those who are less fortunate get everything they need this Thanksgiving, and may we always do our part to make their lives better. Amen."

"Amen," they all echoed.

Makenna smiled at Caden and gave his hand an extra squeeze before she let it go. The incredible serendipity of getting stuck in that elevator with him was the thing she was most grateful for right now, because she couldn't imagine her life without him. His quiet generosity, his selflessness, his protectiveness, his sarcasm, the adoring way he looked at her, the way their bodies fit together—there were so many things to love about him.

Soon their plates were piled high and everyone was digging in. Makenna was well into her second cup of sangria and the warmth of it was spreading through her.

"Everything's great, Mike," Caden said. A chorus of agreements rose up all around the table.

"Shima," Makenna said. "Where are you from?"

"I grew up in New York," she said, "though my mother is from Japan. She met an American sailor and fell in love and here I am."

Makenna smiled. She really liked this woman and was super excited for Collin. "That's so romantic. There really is something about a man in a uniform."

"Why, thank you," Patrick said.

Rolling her eyes, Makenna laughed. "I didn't exactly have you in mind." She winked at Caden, who gave her a crooked grin. Even though his wasn't as fancy as some, he looked damn sexy in his uniform—especially knowing he'd be helping people and saving lives while wearing it.

Patrick pointed his fork at Caden. "They just relaxed the tattoo policy in our department last year," he said. "Used to be you couldn't have any showing. Now you can have one showing on each arm. They give you any problems with that?"

Caden shook his head. "Arlington doesn't have any policy regarding tattoos. But most of mine are covered anyway."

"Your dragon's beautiful," Shima said. "I've always wanted a tattoo."

Makenna's belly did a little flip, and then she decided to share the news, because she'd have to at some point anyway. "I'm going to get one."

Things suddenly got quiet at the table.

"Really? What are you going to get?" Shima asked, not yet cluing into the fact that all the James men were looking at Makenna like she had three heads—and looking at Caden like he'd introduced her to drinking the blood of bats. No one in her family had any tattoos.

Makenna glanced at her father, whose expression was largely neutral, though probably carefully so. "A Celtic family tree with all our initials. I wanted a design that meant something to me. And nothing is more important to me than the people at this table." Her father's gaze softened. Annnd she won him over.

"Just give it a lot of thought," her dad said. "But your idea sounds great."

"Thanks," she said.

"Why do you want a tattoo?" Ian asked, an edge to his tone that said he thought he knew.

"Because I like them."

"Since when?" he asked.

She nailed him with a stare and debated throwing her corn bread at him. Except that would be a terrible waste of corn bread. They might be twenty-seven and twenty-five respectively, but they still had the ability to bring out the twelve-year-old in each other. "Since a long time. I just wasn't sure what I would want before."

"A lot of guys on the force have them," Patrick said. She could've hugged him for the show of support. "They're pretty mainstream these days."

"My father has quite a few," Shima said. "A lot of military stuff, as you might imagine. Initials of friends who died. Some of them are very moving, to see what he found important enough to memorialize on his body."

Makenna nodded. Caden's tattoos were the same way. He had a yellow rose on his chest for his mother, Sean's name and Chinese characters that meant "never forget" on his shoulders, and the dragon on his hand and arm which was his reminder to fight his fear so he could live when Sean couldn't, among others. The accident had truly marked him inside and out.

"I need more sangria. Can I get anyone something while I'm up?" Makenna asked.

"I'd love to try some," Shima said. Collin and her dad asked for some, too.

"I'll help you," Dad said, getting up.

She grabbed her glass and rose, and she gave Caden's shoulder a small squeeze before she stepped away. What she really wanted to do was kiss him, but she didn't want to make him uncomfortable by doing it in front of everybody.

In the kitchen, her dad grasped her arm. "Are you doing okay with Cameron being here? I didn't know Ian invited him until they showed up," he said in almost a whisper.

"It's fine," she said. "Ancient history, anyway." And it really was. She hadn't thought about Cameron in ages.

"I'm sorry I didn't say anything before you went downstairs. I didn't want to make you uncomfortable in front of Caden." He shook his head.

Makenna pressed onto tiptoes to kiss her father on the cheek. "Don't worry about it, Dad. Really."

They poured everyone's drinks and carried the out to the table.

"Need anything?" she asked, leaning closer to Caden.

He shook his head. "I have everything I need." The look he gave her said his words weren't about the food.

Conversation flowed around the table. About her Aunt Maggie, who'd been a mother figure to Makenna when she was a kid—she wasn't there this year because she'd gone on a cruise with a group of girlfriends. About Dad's painting, something he'd been doing for as long as Makenna could remember. About Cam's fellowship and where he hoped to land when it was done next year. About Collin and Shima's masters theses. And so much more. The conversation was lively and easy, and Makenna appreciated how much Caden joined in with this big group of people he didn't know. She knew that wasn't easy for him.

"Okay, everybody," her dad said. "Go unbutton your pants and rest your stomachs for a bit and I'll get this cleaned up and pull our dessert." Everyone laughed.

"We'll help, Dad. You did all the cooking," Makenna said.

"I won't protest that," he said with a grin.

Everyone pitched in on clearing the table. Patrick and Dad focused on boxing up all the leftovers, and Collin and Shima reset the table for dessert. Ian took out the overflowing kitchen trash.

"I'll rinse, you load?" Caden asked, stepping up to the sink. Makenna nodded with a smile. This was their routine at home, and she kinda adored that he didn't give a second thought to doing it here. "What?" he asked as he handed off a dirty.

She just smiled. "Nothing at all, Good Sam."

He rolled his eyes, but the look on his face was all contentment. Not something she saw all that often, and she totally adored it. "Hey look." He nodded toward the window.

"Oh, it's snowing," Makenna said. Just enough had come down to dust the tree branches and grass. It wasn't sticking to the roads yet, but even if it did, they were staying until Saturday. Snow was especially nice when you didn't have to drive in it. "How much are we supposed to get, Dad?"

"Just a couple inches. Enough to make it pretty." He gave her a wink.

"This was the nicest Thanksgiving I've had in a long time," Caden said, drying his hands once they'd finished. "Thank you for letting me be a part of it."

The sentiment melted Makenna's heart. She wanted him to enjoy himself so much. He had holiday meals at the fire station or occasionally with friends, but it had been a lot of years since Caden had celebrated a holiday with family. And given how tight her own was, that broke her heart. Everyone needed somewhere to belong, and she really wanted to be that for him. And her family, too.

Her father gave Caden a big smile. "I'm glad to hear it, Caden. But it's not over yet."

"Everything's all set," Collin said. "Sugar comas to commence in three, two, one."

"That is if the tryptophan doesn't set in first," Cam said.

"Either way, we'll all be asleep in an hour," Patrick said, clapping their dad on the back. They settled back around the dining room table, treated this time to a smorgasbord that included Makenna's pumpkin roll, a pumpkin pie, an apple pie, and a carrot cake that Shima made.

"I'm seriously going to need some of each," Makenna said.

"Oh, good. I was hoping I wouldn't be the only one," Caden said, taking a piece of her pumpkin roll. He passed her the plate.

The food went around and the conversation resumed, and even Ian seemed done with making little digs at her and Caden. So Makenna finally allowed herself to relax about the visit. Caden was doing great, just like she knew he would, and her family had taken him into the fold. Just like she told him. There'd been absolutely nothing to worry about.

CHAPTER FIVE

*S*tanding in her childhood bedroom, Makenna shrugged into her favorite oversized sweatshirt, chilly after hours of watching movies with everyone in the basement. If Cameron hadn't been there, she would've just changed into pajamas given the late hour, but somehow it felt too familiar to do that given their history.

Why was he there? And what was he up to? All day, she'd felt him looking at her, watching her, trying to catch her eye. And all day, she'd pretty much ignored him and stuck by Caden's side, hoping to avoid giving Cam an in. Over the past few years, he'd texted or emailed her occasionally, and she heard stories about what he was up to from Ian when the family got together, but generally, they didn't have much contact anymore. Which was fine by her.

She tugged her boots off and ran a brush through her hair, then stepped out into the hall. When she rounded the bannister to go downstairs, her stomach dropped.

"Hey," Cam said, almost at the top of the steps.

"Hey," she said, waiting to go around him.

"Can we please talk for a minute?"

Alarm bells went off in her head. The final conversations they'd had several years ago hadn't been pleasant. Whatever this was, she wasn't looking forward to it. "I don't know."

"Come on, Makenna. Please?" He gave her *the look*, the one that once had melted her on sight.

She studied him for a moment—he had all-American good looks with blond hair, blue eyes, and a square jaw that was to die for, and wore a light gray V-neck cashmere sweater over a blue button down that made his eyes even brighter. Once, she'd thought there was no hotter man. And she'd been as attracted to his brain and his ambition as she was his looks. Not to mention his long association with her family, because she'd known Cam since her age ran in the single digits.

With a sigh, she nodded. "Okay. What do you want to talk about?"

He gestured toward her room. "Can we, maybe, talk somewhere more private?"

"I'd rather do it here," she said, crossing her arms. She was feeling a bit ambushed, which in turn made her irritated with both Cameron and Ian for setting it up. Because whatever it was he wanted to talk about was why he was here today. She knew that in her gut.

"Okay, then," Cameron said. "Well...the thing is..." He chuffed out a laugh. "I had this all planned, but now that you're standing in front of me, my tongue's all tied like I'm a teenager."

The self-deprecation was charming, as was the sheepish look on his face, but the sentiment set off more alarm bells.

He gave her a smile. "I miss you. That's the first thing I wanted to say. I miss you and I now know I made a huge mistake when I didn't take the fellowship in DC." Makenna's stomach flipped and the floor wobbled beneath her feet. "Actually, I knew it was a mistake almost immediately, but I was too immature and proud to admit it, and too scared to ask you to take me back."

No. Nonono. "Cam—"

"Please let me finish," he said with a tilt of his head. "I know I might not deserve it, but please?"

Heart racing fast, Makenna nodded. Even though she felt a little like she might throw up that second piece of apple pie she'd sneaked an hour ago. She didn't still have feelings for him, but that didn't make hearing this from someone she'd once loved any easier.

"I've done a lot of growing up and a lot of thinking about what I want in life. A prestigious match is still important to me, but not as important as having someone I care about to share my life with. I could've had that with you. I *should've* had that with you. And I still want it. With you," he said, his eyes blazing.

"Cameron, I'm with someone else now," she said, her insides all a-jumble at the surprise of this conversation. Never in a million years would she have expected this from him.

"I know," he said. "And I'm sorry for that. It's why I had to say something now, before you got serious with him. But you've only been dating for two months. We have a history that goes back twenty years. We were together for three of those. And we'd be married right now if I hadn't been a stubborn, selfish prick."

"I *am* serious with him," she said, the walls spinning around her. Once upon a time, she would've given everything to hear these words from him. But it was too late. She'd moved on. From Cameron and with someone else. With Caden. "We've been apart for three years, too. A lot has changed."

Cam stepped closer. "How I feel about you hasn't changed. Or maybe it has. It's gotten stronger. I have a good lead on a position in DC when my fellowship ends. I want to try for that position and move down there. I want to be with you. I want us to start over and build the life together we should've already had."

"You're not listening—"

"I am. I hear you. You think you're serious about this guy. But he's the blink of an eye compared to how long we've known each other. If you gave us a chance—"

Makenna stepped back, away from his intensity, away from his touch, away from these words that tormented her only because they no longer mattered. And once they would've meant the world. There was a sadness in that that hurt. A lot.

He moved with her, staying close. "Please, give us a chance. Give *me* a chance." He pulled something from his pocket. A ring box. "I still have it," he said, cracking the velvet top open to reveal a stunning emerald-cut diamond in a magnificent setting. She remembered how beautiful it looked on her hand. "I would give anything to be able to earn my way back into your heart, to have the chance to hear you say again that you would marry me."

Swallowing around the knot in her throat, Makenna closed the ring box in his hands. "Cameron, I appreciate what you're saying. I do. But I moved on. You made your choice and I made mine. And *three years* have passed. Caden and I haven't been together very long, but that bears no relationship to how much I care about him. I can't turn that off, and I don't want to," she said. She didn't want to hurt Cameron's feelings, in fact she hated that her words might hurt him, but he'd waited too long. Damnit, that wasn't her fault.

Cam clasped his hands around hers. "Don't say no. Please. Just think about what I'm saying. I'll wait. I'll wait as long as you need to figure things out." Desperation shaped his classical features into a tortured mask she'd never before seen him wear, and it made her realize how sincere he was being just then. Which meant he really had grown up a lot since they'd split.

Her heart ached for what they might've been. "I don't think I need to think about it, Cam."

"I'll wait, Makenna. Because I love you," he gave a helpless shrug. "I've loved you so much of my life."

She'd said those words to him once, but now when she thought of love it was Caden's face that came to mind. Caden's touch. Caden's eyes. "Where were you three years ago, or even two?"

He shook his head. "So lost. Clearly. Just think about it, okay?"

Her shoulders sagged. She didn't want to fight with him. She didn't want to hurt him. And she didn't want to ruin Thanksgiving. What was she supposed to say? "Okay," Makenna blurted, already mentally drafting the email where she told him they were through, for good.

She inhaled to say more when Cameron suddenly stepped fully into her space and pressed his lips to hers. Makenna was so stunned it took her a moment to realize what had happened.

She wrenched back and glared. "*Don't.* You know what? I don't need to think about this. I meant what I said. I'm with Caden right now. I have no intention of stopping being with him because we've had this talk."

He held up his hands. "I'm sorry. I'm really sorry. I understand. I just...I just miss you."

"I need to get back downstairs now," Makenna said, and without another word, she slipped around him and padded down the steps.

And then she locked herself inside the hall bathroom, pressed her back against the door, and slapped her hand over her mouth. What the hell just happened?

"Okay," Makenna had said. And with just that one word, Caden's whole world tilted on its axis and sent everything reeling.

He bolted from where he'd been standing near the bottom of the steps, having gone looking for Makenna to see if she wanted anything before he made himself a turkey sandwich. And he'd overheard her entire conversation with Cameron. The guy missed her, loved her, and wanted her back—well, that much had been clear most of the day, hadn't it?

Bee-lining through the house, he was glad everyone else was still downstairs. He made for the kitchen, then the back door, then his Jeep, just for space, just to escape, just to find some place where there might still be some oxygen left to breathe. Outside, he braced his hands on the hood of the Jeep, not caring about the snow or the way the cold wetness of it immediately made his fingers ache.

As if all that wasn't bad enough, to learn that Makenna had once agreed to marry that guy. That they would've *already* been married if Cameron hadn't made some mistake. Caden hadn't gotten all the details, but they didn't really matter. What mattered was that Makenna had loved Cameron enough to want to make a life with him. A life with a man who was Caden's opposite in just about every way— professional where Caden was blue collar, wealthy where Caden was just comfortable, all-American good looks where Caden appeared rough around the edges, confident and charming where Caden was awkward and clumsy.

Cameron was the kind of guy Makenna was attracted to when she met a man in the light of day. The darkness in that elevator had been Caden's saving grace, because it had allowed both of them to get to know one another without the preconceptions that appearances created—and he'd created some of his on purpose, hadn't he? Except once he'd gotten to know her within the freedom of that darkness, he hadn't wanted her to turn him away when she saw him. He hadn't wanted her to be put off by him.

And, miraculously, she hadn't been. He could still hear her calling him *freaking gorgeous* that night. And the memory of it still stole his breath and set his heart to racing. But if Cameron was the kind of man she'd once agreed to marry, then it proved that her attraction to Caden was a fluke. At the very least, not her norm. Didn't it? Did that matter?

Maybe it didn't. Or at least shouldn't.

But it made him doubt, for maybe the millionth time since they'd started seeing one another, whether he was good enough for her, whether he was right for her. He thought he'd put the worst of that behind him, because he knew it was his past and his anxiety and his fucked-up fears talking. He knew it was. But seeing an alternative future for Makenna held up in front of his face like this had reached inside his chest and his brain and his heart and stirred it all up again.

Stirred it up bad.

Jesus.

Breathe, Grayson. Just fucking breathe.

He braced wet hands on his knees, lowered his head, and counted backward from ten. *Ten.* Deep in, deep out. *Nine.* Deep in, deep out. *Eight.* If it hurt this bad to imagine Makenna with someone else, how much would it hurt to lose her? *Seven.* Deep, in, deep out. *Six.* I've lost everyone else, why would she be different? *Five.* Deep in, deep out. *Four.* You have her now, focus on that. *Three.* Okay, okay. *Two.* Deep in, deep out. *One.* Deep in, deep out.

Shit, his shoulders and chest were just as tight.

He did it again from ten, this time blocking out all the non-stop commentary racing through his head.

When he was done, he stood up and rolled his neck, his shoulders. She'd only agreed to think about what Cameron had said to her. She hadn't agreed to be with him and she'd made it clear that she was serious about Caden. *Focus on that.* Right. Okay.

Except hearing the echo of Cameron's declaration of love in his ear added another layer of stress to the whole situation. Because that dickhead had said it to Makenna again when Caden hadn't said it once yet.

In fact, the prospect of declaring how he felt scared the shit out of Caden. Because it felt like tempting the fates. *Hey, lightning, let me show you what I really care about so you know where to strike next!*

The past. Anxiety. Fucked-up fears. He knew it.

Didn't change that he felt that way though.

Which brought him back around to the gut check that maybe he wasn't good enough for her.

Because didn't Makenna deserve to hear those words? And if Caden couldn't give them to her ….

Then what?

Stop it. Get back in there and be with her. That's how you keep her.

He scrubbed his hand over the scar on his head. "Fuck," he bit out. And then he turned on his heel and got back in the house. He could pull himself together. *Nothing* had happened, nothing had changed. She'd show him.

"Hey, there you are," Makenna said, standing at the kitchen counter stirring a cup of hot tea. "I was looking for you."

"Just needed a little air," Caden said, joining her at the counter.

"Family proving a little too much?" she asked with a smile. She wrapped her arms around him. "Oh, you're so chilly. I better warm you up." Pressing herself tight against him, she held him closer and tucked her head in against his throat.

The embrace was fucking life.

He hugged her back. "Not too much," he said, clearing the roughness out of his voice. "I like your family. It's been a great day." And it was. He'd meant it when he told Mike he hadn't had a Thanksgiving this enjoyable in years.

"Would you like anything?" she asked.

His appetite for that turkey sandwich was long gone. "No," he said. "I'm good."

"Would you like to go be alone, just the two of us?"

He didn't even have to think. "That sounds like heaven," he said.

Makenna's smile was like the sun coming out from behind the clouds. *See how she's looking at you? Trust that look, Grayson. Nothing else matters.*

She grasped his hand. "Then come with me."

CHAPTER SIX

*W*hen they made it to her room, Makenna closed the door. "It's only a double bed, so I hope you're not too cramped tonight with me."

"We're sleeping together?" he asked, looking around her childhood room. Pieces of her youth remained tacked to the lavender walls and hung from her mirror. Ribbons, photographs, posters of bands. The room spoke of a person who grew up in the warm embrace of family, happiness, wholeness. "Your father doesn't mind?"

Chuckling, Makenna shook her head. "We practically live together, Caden, which he knows. I'm sure he's figured out that his twenty-five-year-old daughter has had sex before. Collin and Shima are sleeping together, too."

"Shima's pretty awesome," he said, wondering if Makenna would say anything to him about her conversation with Cameron.

"She really is," Makenna said with a smile. And then she unbuttoned her jeans, pushed them down, and took them off altogether, leaving her standing there in an oversized, faded red and blue Penn sweatshirt that was just long enough to cover her panties. "You should get undressed, too," she said, coming to him and starting on the buttons of his shirt.

Press and release, press and release. Until she was pulling his shirt from his dress pants and exposing his skin.

She gave a little moan and kissed the center of his chest. "Just like unwrapping a present." She trailed a line of kisses and licks from one nipple to the other.

"Fuck, Makenna," he whispered. "What are you doing?"

"Tasting you," she said.

The words were like a blowtorch to his blood. He was hard in an instant. "We can't," he said, though his hands went to the back of her head, encouraging her, guiding her as she continued to kiss and tease and drive him wild with her mouth.

"We can if we're quiet." Slowly, she dropped to her knees and bared him to mid-thigh. She took his cock in hand and gripped him firmly, tearing a soft grunt from his throat. "I've been wanting you all day," she whispered, her lips teasing his head with soft kisses. "Wanting to touch you and kiss you and hold you. I can't hold back anymore." She licked him from root to tip. Once, twice, three times. And then she sucked him into her mouth.

It felt so fucking good that Caden's hands flew to her hair, digging in, grabbing hold. She moaned at the contact and pushed herself deeper, burying his cock in the back of her throat. The intensity of it nearly took his knees out from underneath of him.

Makenna pulled off his length. "Lay down on the floor."

He was too far gone to debate the wisdom of having sex in her father's house. He needed this. He needed *her*. He needed the connection and the coming together of the act. Caden locked the door, took the rest of his clothes off, and spread himself out on the beige carpet.

She undressed, too, all that beautiful red hair spilling around the bare porcelain of her shoulders and making him think of peaches and cream. And, *fuck*, he was starving.

Caden grasped his cock. "Take me back in your mouth."

He didn't have to ask twice. Makenna settled herself between his legs and wrapped her lips around his cock. She sucked him deep and slow, than fast and shallow, her baby blues flashing up at him so fucking sexy. He needed to see her eyes, so he fisted her hair into a ponytail to keep it out of her face. He used his grip to urge her harder, faster, deeper. He needed it. *God*, he needed it. And she took it. She took everything he gave her and so much more.

"Fuck, Red, I'm gonna come if you don't stop," he whispered.

She pulled off him, her lips shiny and swollen. "I want you inside me first," she said, already crawling up his body.

Caden reached for his pants and fished a condom out of his wallet. Rolled it on with shaking, needy hands. Then he gripped her hip. "Take all of me, Red. Fucking take all of me." The words came from someplace inside him that was raw and wounded and so full of yearning.

"Yes," she whispered, sinking down, impaling herself on him inch by maddening inch. "Oh, God, it's so good."

"Jesus," he rasped. Every urge inside him had him wanting to flip her over, to pin her down, to drive himself into her until they were both screaming and coming and losing their minds. But there was no way that would be quiet. He had to let her lead this. His hips surged when she'd taken him all the way. "Ride me, Makenna. Use me."

She planted her hands on his chest and lifted herself up and down his length, her slickness coating him and creating the most delicious friction. Their breaths were the only sounds in the room, and the way she gasped and pressed her lips together and furrowed her forehead proved she was having to work to be quiet. "Shit, Caden," she breathed.

Their gazes collided, hot and needy. He gripped her hips and guided her into a new rhythm—forward and backward on his cock so that her clit ground against him. "Want you to come on me."

"Oh, yes," she gasped, her expression almost anguished in her desire. His gaze raked over her pretty face, her swaying breasts, the red hair between her thighs rubbing against his lower belly.

"Come here," he said, pulling her down to his chest. Caden banded an arm around her lower back and one around her neck, pinning her in place on top of him, and then he took over the grind, rubbing himself hard against her clit, his cock still deep inside. "Love being inside you," he whispered. "Love this closeness, with you."

"I'm gonna come. I'm gonna come," she cried.

Caden crashed his lips down on hers and filled her mouth with his tongue. Her whole body bowed on the orgasm, trying to break free from his arms. He held her tight and swallowed the moan that ripped up her throat as her pussy fisted him and fisted him and coated his cock and balls with her pleasure.

Her muscles went limp and she released a long breath. "Holy shit," she rasped. "Your turn. I want to feel you fall apart like that so bad. How do you want it?"

"Lay down on your stomach," he said, need and lust still stalking through his blood. "I'll be quiet, promise." They switched positions, and Caden spread himself out on top of Makenna. He took his cock in hand and entered her from behind. As he penetrated deep, he laid down on top of her, covering her from head to feet, all of him touching all of her.

"Oh, God, I love that," she whispered. "Love your weight on me. Love how filled up I feel."

Her words licked over his skin. "Gonna fuck you so deep, Red," he said against her ear, his hips surging and grinding into her ass. "So fucking deep." His arms wrapped around her head and shoulders for leverage, and his abs contracted on each thrust, hunching his body quietly around hers. Driving deep, deep, deeper. She arched her back and lifted her ass. "Oh, that's it," he said, balls deep inside her. "That's so fucking it."

"Caden," she breathed. "Jesus."

"Yeah, you're taking me, aren't you? My cock's so deep inside you." But as deep as it was, it wasn't deep enough. Never would be. Because he'd never be able to get enough of her. Not if he lived a hundred lifetimes.

That was how hard he'd fallen for her. The clarity of the thought was startling. For weeks he'd been hiding from the truth of it, not examining it too closely.

He drove the thought away. Not now. Not yet. Not with another man's words pinballing around his brain. He just couldn't... *Just feel. For once, just feel.*

Caden gripped her tighter, drove deeper, clenched his teeth against the grunts that wanted to tear up his throat. He gritted out whispered words into her ear, dirty little nothings that had her core growing tighter around him and his balls aching with the need to release.

"Faster," she whispered. "Faster and I'm gonna come again."

"Fuck, yeah." His hips snapped more quickly, the meeting of their skin making more noise now. But he couldn't hold back, couldn't resist giving her what she needed. And then she was coming once more, a moan spilling from her mouth. He covered her lips with his hand as her body clamped down on his cock. Then his own orgasm nailed him in the back and exploded him apart. He rode her slow and deep as wave after wave of sensation tore through him, not wanting it to end. Ever. "Jesus Christ," he rasped when their bodies finally stilled.

"So sexy to hear you come," she whispered.

"Shit, was I loud?" he asked, his head resting against hers, his heart still racing in his chest.

"No," she said, a smile plain in her voice. "Maybe we should sleep right here. That way if we get horny again, we can just pick up where we left off."

Caden chuckled. "You've got big plans for tonight, huh?"

She grinned over her shoulder. "Where you're concerned? Absolutely."

The words were just light-hearted joking, but he couldn't help but wonder if she meant them more broadly. If her conversation with Cameron was still pinging around inside his head, which it was, then surely it was doing the same to hers. Part of him thought he should tell her he'd overheard it, but part of him wanted her to choose to tell him it had happened. He eased off of her, removed the condom, and wrapped it in a tissue from a box on her nightstand. Then he gave her a hand off the floor and pulled her into his arms.

"Happy Thanksgiving, Caden. I'm so glad I got to spend the day with you. Of everything I have in my life, I hope you know that I'm most grateful for you this year."

He let the words settle like a balm into some of the raw places inside him, and they helped. But in his darkest places, he couldn't stop wondering if what her ex-fiancé had said to her could change that.

---

*C*aden felt better in the light of the morning. After the incredible lovemaking on Makenna's floor, they'd slept wrapped around one another all night, skin to skin, and both left him feeling claimed, owned, connected. She'd seduced *him* last night. She'd slept with *him* last night. She'd woke up in *his* arms this morning. That's what mattered. Not what Cameron wanted.

Why did the part of his brain that controlled Caden's fears and anxiety have to be so powerful?

No matter.

He could be stronger. For her.

Caden dried off from his shower and tugged on fresh clothes, glad to be back in jeans again. It made him feel more himself. He tugged the soft black Henley over his head, gave himself a onceover in the bathroom mirror, and opened the door to join Makenna downstairs.

Except the sound of his own name in a male's voice had him freezing in place and pushing the door most of the way closed again.

"She said she was serious about Caden, but that she'd think about it." Cameron. "I said my piece. There's nothing else I can do."

"Caden." Ian that time. He said the name with so much disdain that he might as well have said *Fucking Caden.* Their voices came from Ian's room right across the hall from the bathroom. Caden opened his door a little wider so he could hear them. Because if they were going to fucking talk about him, he was going to fucking listen. "If you want her, you need to fight for her. You think *he's* good enough for her? Because I don't. And I can't believe that my brothers do either. Tattoos and piercings all over his face? Did you see how the conversation flat-out halted when she said she was going to get a tattoo? That's all him. Great fucking influence. She deserves better."

Ian's hostility was a sucker punch to the gut, his words slicing deep at those darkest places. Caden's pulse pounded in his ears.

"I agree. It kills me to see her with him. For all those reasons and more. But I laid it all out for her. I didn't hold anything back. If I push her, she might shut me down all the way," Cameron said. "I gotta give her space on this. If it's gonna happen, it has to be her decision this time. She has to come to me."

"I hear you," Ian said, frustration plain in his voice. "You two were just so good together. I know things got messed up, but Makenna was so happy with you. I want that again for her. And for you. You're family. You've been family for twenty years. You deserve this and so does she. I'm glad you had the chance to talk to her, at least."

"Yeah," Cameron said. "Listen, I'm going to cut out before breakfast. I don't want things to be awkward with Makenna, and clearly Caden and I both being here is creating stress for her." There were some shuffling sounds, and then the door across the hallway clicked shut.

"You should be the one staying," Ian said.

Caden nearly held his breath. He pushed the door closed as much as he could without making it click and listened as footsteps and voices crossed to the stairs and disappeared altogether. When they were gone, he secured the door and fell back against it, his head aching, his chest hollow. He scrubbed his hand over the scar running in a crescent over his ear.

Hell if Ian's reaction wasn't exactly what Caden feared from her family. And was Ian right? Did Patrick and Collin feel the same way? Was Mike horrified at the guy his only daughter had brought home? Caden hadn't gotten anything but positive vibes from the other three James men, but maybe his radar was as fucked as his head.

Or maybe Ian was just an asshole. Caden got it, he did. Cameron was his life-long best friend and Ian wanted him to be happy. Fine. Whatever. That was one thing. But to dislike him because he thought Caden unworthy? That was another.

That was his true fear.

Jesus.

Just when he'd managed to get his head screwed on right about Makenna's conversation with Cameron.

Knock, knock.

Caden bowed off the door. "Yeah?" he said, pulling it open.

"Hey, there you are." Makenna's gaze scanned over his face, and her smile dropped into a frown. "Are you okay?"

"Uh, yeah. Yeah. Just finished getting ready." He flicked off the bathroom light.

"Dad's still making breakfast, so I thought maybe we could talk for a minute?" she said.

His gut clenched as dread snaked through him. "Sure. What's up?"

She took his hand, led him back to her room, and closed the door. Caden moved to the center of the room and crossed his arms, braced for the blow. "Are you sure you're okay?" she asked.

"What is it you want to talk about, Makenna?" The words came out more clipped than he'd intended, but he was hanging on by a thread right now. Very thin and fraying in the middle.

"Come sit," she said.

"That's okay." He forced a deep breath and stayed planted right where he was.

She frowned, her gaze studying his face like she was trying to solve a puzzle. "We fell asleep so fast last night that we never had a chance to finish the conversation from the bathroom." Makenna gave him a little smile, clearly trying to coax some reaction from him. "So." She sagged onto the edge of the bed. "The short story is that three years ago, Cameron and I were engaged for about five minutes. It ended when he gave me an ultimatum. I'd landed the job I wanted in DC and he had fellowship offers from hospitals here and in DC. It all could've worked."

Hearing her talk about the life she might've been leading right now —a life with another man—settled a weight onto Caden's shoulders. And the reason why was clear—he was *all in*. All in love with Makenna. Whether he wanted to admit it or not. Whether he wanted to face it or not. Whether he believed that meant certain doom for her or him or both of them, or not.

For fourteen years he'd been alone, purposely keeping others out, purposely living life as a loner, purposely avoiding relationships except with a select few friends. He'd hooked up with women over the years, but he'd purposely distanced himself from the ones who seemed to want more with him. Building a wall around himself had been a survival mechanism after his family had been destroyed, and then it had become a habit, one he'd never even tried to unlearn until Makenna.

"But Cam decided that the fellowship at Penn was more prestigious," she said, staring up at Caden. "And he said if I really loved him, I'd stay in Philly and find another job. Because he wouldn't do a long-distance relationship, so if I wouldn't stay in Philly, the whole relationship was off." She waved a hand. "We had a big fight. But it made me realize he wasn't the right man for me, because the right man would never ask me to give up my dream for his, especially when he had another great and still very prestigious option that would allow both of us to have what we wanted. So I took the job and moved to DC and we just sorta ended."

"Okay," Caden said.

"So that's the backstory." She heaved a deep breath.

He frowned. "The backstory to what?"

"To a conversation I had with Cameron last night that I want you to know about."

Caden swallowed. Hard. As much as he'd wanted her to tell him, now he was scared to hear what might come out of her mouth. "Which was?"

"Cameron asked for a second chance," she said, her fingers fidgeting with the hem of her sweater. "And said he wants to try again and that he still loves me. I wanted you to—"

"Do you still love him?" he forced himself to ask.

She flew off the bed and came right up to him, one of her hands settling on his crossed arms, one cupping his face. "No. Not for a long time. I told him that I'm with you, that I'm serious about you, that it's too late and too much time has passed." Makenna shook her head, her eyes pleading. "You're the only one I...that I have feelings for. I care about you so much, Caden. Please tell me that you know that."

"Are you...are you sure that you don't want to consider what he's offering?" Voicing the question made Caden nauseous, but if he didn't ask her, he'd just wonder about it. Better to get it all out in the open. His anxiety needed to hear her say the words. "He's a high-powered specialist. He'll be able to give you a good life. And he's known your family forever."

Makenna blanched and her whole face frowned. "Oh, my God. I don't want to consider his offer. I don't want him. I want you. I have a great life with you right now. Caden." She forced his arms to part and pressed herself against him, both of her hands cupping his face. "You're the only man I want. You."

For a moment he didn't say anything because he couldn't. Relief made his throat go tight and his chest ache with pressure.

"Do you remember the night we met, before we went to bed? I mentioned how late it had gotten and you thought that was me trying to tell you to go?" Caden nodded. That night had been so amazing with her that he hadn't been able to avoid wondering when the other shoe would drop. He'd thought it had been that moment. "Do you remember what I said?"

"You called bullshit on me," he said, the memory pulling a little of the heaviness off his shoulders.

Makenna smiled. "I totally did. And I said, just so there's no more weirdness or uncertainty, I like you." He nodded, the memory tugging at the corner of his lips. "Well, I'm saying it again right now. Just so there's no more weirdness or uncertainty, I like you. A lot." She nailed him with a stare, her blue eyes blazing.

"Shit. I get caught in my head sometimes, Makenna," he said, throwing out a lifeline.

She caught it. "Oh, Caden, I know you do, but it's okay. I hated to even dump all this on you, but I also didn't want to keep it from you. That didn't feel right."

Knock, knock.

"Yeah?" she called, not letting him break the embrace.

Patrick popped his head in the door. "Dad said breakfast is ready."

"Be right there," Makenna said. Her brother ducked back out. "Are we okay?" she asked.

Caden blew out a breath, some of the tension bleeding out of his body with it. It was just, on top of Ian's comments, he'd been so ready for more bad news. Instead, she'd given him her honesty and understanding, and it made him love her even more. No sense in denying that's what it was anymore.

"Yeah. I'm sorry," he said, feeling a little drained. Life was a lot fucking easier without all these emotions coming at him all the time. Makenna had opened him up, and sometimes it made him feel like an exposed nerve that was too sensitive, too vulnerable, too unprotected.

He was always going to be a lot to take on board, wasn't he?

"You don't have anything to be sorry for," she said. "I'm sorry you even have to deal with any of this."

"No, I'm glad you told me," he said. And he was.

Sometimes his brain got stuck on a loop of negativity, spiraling him down and down and down, and having her words saying the things she'd said was the best cure for when that happened. He needed her words, just like he'd needed them that night they'd been trapped in the elevator. Then they'd kept him from succumbing to his claustrophobia. Now they kept him from handing a microphone to his darkest fears so they could convince him those fears were real. Both times, she'd pulled him back from the brink.

"And for the record, I like you, too. A lot." His feelings ran deeper than that, obviously, but he was too bare, too raw, to contemplate confronting his fears by saying anything more just then.

Her smile was radiant. "Best thing I've heard all day." She rested her hands on his chest. "Look, if you want to go back to Virginia, we could leave today. I know Cameron being here made this trip more stressful than it should've been."

Caden immediately shook his head. "No. No way. I'm enjoying your family." Well, most of them. "And I know you love being here. I don't want to go home early." No way would he do that to her. He knew how important her family was to her.

"I would go, for you." Earnest blue eyes stared up at him.

He knew she would, and it was part of why he loved her. He shook his head. "And I'm staying for you."

CHAPTER SEVEN

*D*espite the rocky start to the morning, Makenna had a great day with Caden and her family. Breakfast, a late lunch full of yummy leftovers, and an afternoon of board games that had everyone laughing and teasing. With Cameron gone, the whole atmosphere changed from tense to easy, at least that was the way it felt to her. She was itching to confront Ian about inviting him, but she didn't want to create new tension. It could wait until after the holiday.

It was late as their group walked out of the movie theater after seeing the last showing of a new action flick, their bellies full of Chinese food and popcorn—everyone had been ready for a change of menu after several meals in a row of turkey and stuffing. The sidewalks were crunchy with rock salt and patches of ice that hadn't been shoveled away.

Four inches of snow had fallen yesterday, which wasn't bad for Pennsylvania. But then freezing rain had fallen over night after the streets had been plowed, so driving had been more hazardous today then it'd been yesterday, but luckily her dad and Caden hadn't minded bringing them out to the movies.

"Be safe heading home, kids," her dad called as he, Ian, Collin, and Shima passed Caden's Jeep and headed over to Dad's Ford Explorer.

"Will do," Caden said, unlocking the doors. Makenna hopped in the back seat so Patrick could have the front.

Yawning, Makenna secured her seatbelt and sagged back against the seat as Caden pulled out of the lot. He followed her dad's car through the commercial area around the mall to where the surroundings became suburban and then almost rural-looking on the way to their house.

As the lights receded, Makenna's eyelids grew heavy. And against the backdrop of Caden and Patrick talking, she finally stopped fighting it and let herself drift off.

A sudden jerk startled Makenna awake. Screeching tires. The Jeep fishtailed hard in one direction and then the other.

"Fuck," Patrick bit out.

The Jeep came to a hard stop, jolting Makenna against her seatbelt and knocking the breath out of her.

Both men seat turned to her. "Are you okay?" they asked.

"Yeah. What happened?" Her eyes focused on the scene out the front window. Two cars sat just off the road at an intersection. One was an Explorer. "Oh, my God. Dad." She ripped at the seat belt buckle.

"Makenna, call 9-1-1. Patrick and I will check it out," Caden said. He flew out of the driver's seat, ran to the trunk and grabbed something, and then ran toward the accident. Patrick was already opening her father's car door.

She pressed the phone to her ear as she jumped out of the Jeep. Caden had managed to stop in plenty of time, his Jeep just off the road. He'd placed an orange cone at the back corner of his vehicle.

"Nine-one-one, what is your emergency?" the dispatcher answered.

"I'm calling to report an accident," Makenna said, jogging toward the scene, heart racing. She recounted what'd happened and let the dispatcher know that an off-duty police officer and paramedic were on scene.

"Can you put me on with either of them when they've assessed for injuries?" the dispatcher asked.

"Yes. Let me get them," Makenna said. She didn't know how either Patrick or Caden did this kind of thing every day, because just the act of calling 911 had adrenaline flowing through her system until she was shivering. It was more than just the cold, she knew that much for sure. Dread flowing through her, she approached the driver's side of her father's truck and could see that the front end was crumpled.

Patrick leaned into her father's door while Caden stood in the rear driver's side doorway, a big medic kit opened next to him. She peered in to see Collin, bleeding from the forehead and grimacing. Oh God.

"The dispatcher would like to talk to one of you," she said.

Patrick held out his hand, and she passed him the phone. He rose and stepped away from the vehicle.

Makenna leaned in and gently touched her father's arm. The air bags had deployed inside the car. "Daddy, are you okay?"

"Yeah, yeah, peanut. The seatbelt just took the wind out of me. I'll be fine," he said, his voice like gravel.

"Hang tight, Collin. I don't want you to move until we can get your neck immobilized, okay?" Caden asked, snapping off one pair of gloves and putting on another. "Let me check your dad. I'll be right back."

Makenna stepped away to let Caden pass and Ian came around from the passenger side. "Are you okay?" she asked him.

"Yeah. Shima and I are fine. Collin didn't have his seat belt on, though," Ian said, the words not critical, just worried.

As she watched, Caden listened to her father's heartbeat and took his pulse, and then he unbuttoned her father's shirt and examined his chest in the dim overhead light.

"How are they?" Patrick asked Caden, phone still pressed to his ear.

"Collin has a mild head injury, a scalp lac, and a probable rib fracture," Caden said in a calm, confident voice. Makenna's chest squeezed with worry as Patrick relayed the information to the dispatcher. Caden continued, "Mike has an elevated heart rate and chest pain reproducible on palpitation and movement, which means a possible sternum fracture. At least, that's what I can tell without more diagnostics."

God, both of them needed to go to the hospital. Makenna couldn't believe this was happening. Her brother repeated Caden's diagnosis.

"EMS is within range," Patrick said. "I hear the sirens."

Makenna had just cued in to them, too.

"All right, Mike. Cavalry's almost here. They'll get some pain meds in you and you'll be good as new. Just try to sit still," Caden said.

"Thanks, son. I'm okay," her dad said, the strain in his voice belying the words.

Caden snapped off his gloves and moved to the back seat again. As worried as she was about her father and brother, she was also fascinated to see Caden in action—confident, totally in control, rushing in to help without having to be asked. Exactly what he was trained to do.

A few minutes later, two police cars, two ambulances, and a firetruck rumbled into the scene, their red and blue lights circling over everything. As the crews got out of their vehicles, Patrick met up with the police and Caden joined the paramedics as they unloaded stretchers and backboards from the rear of their rig. He was deep in conversation with them, clearly recounting what he'd learned about the men's conditions.

Makenna leaned into the driver's seat. "The ambulance is here. Just hang on," she said.

Her father gave her a tight smile. "Don't you worry."

When the paramedics approached the car, Shima cleared out of the back seat, and one of the paramedics went around and took her place, the other leaning in through Collin's doorway like Caden had done.

Makenna and Ian stepped back too, making space for the crews to do their job. Caden fell in beside her, his gaze running over her face. "Are you sure you're okay?" he asked, taking her cheek in his hand. "I know you were asleep when it happened. I tried to stop as gently as I could."

"I'm fine. Really. What happened?"

Caden frowned. "The damn ice. The second driver tried to pull out of the cross street without sufficient lead time and his back tires caught ice, which stalled him half-way out. So your dad had to swerve to avoid him, but he hit a patch of ice, too, and caught the vehicle's back quarter panel before going off the road."

"It was lucky Dad responded so quickly," Ian said. "I thought for sure we were going to broad-side him."

Nodding, Caden said, "It could've been a lot worse, that's for sure."

"It's bad enough," Makenna said, her throat going tight.

"Come here," Caden said, pulling her into his chest. "They're going to be all right. You'll see."

"Thanks to you," she said, peering up at him. "This would've been so much scarier if you weren't here."

He shook off the compliment and rubbed her back.

Soon, the two paramedic crews had Dad and Collin loaded onto stretchers. They told Caden where they were going and said the family would have to follow by separate vehicle. As the crews loaded the stretchers into their rigs, Patrick waved Ian and Shima over to the police, who seemed to be asking them questions.

Patrick joined her and Caden. "You four go ahead to the hospital. I'll finish up here and one of these guys will give me a lift home to get my car when we're done."

"Okay," Caden said. The two men shook.

"Thanks for everything, Caden. It means a lot," Patrick said. "Keep me posted."

"We will. Wish I could've done more," he said.

When Ian, Shima, and Caden had given statements, they loaded up into Caden's Jeep and made the quiet drive to the hospital. Shima sat next to Makenna, concern radiating off of her, and it touched her to know how deeply concerned Shima was for her brother. She really cared.

But getting to the hospital didn't give them any answers, because while Dad and Collin were being evaluated, all the rest of them could do was wait. Within an hour, Patrick had come, but they still hadn't heard from anyone in the emergency department beyond filling out some forms on both the James men's behalves.

Caden was a godsend through it all. Grabbing coffee for all of them. Staying close to Makenna's side. Holding her hand. Explaining to everyone what was likely happening to Dad and Collin respectively so they'd all understand why it was taking so long—the scans they both required were probably part of the hold-up.

This would've been so much harder if Caden hadn't been there. More than that, it felt like he *belonged* there. As part of the James clan. At her side.

"Mike and Collin James family," called a woman's voice.

They all stood at once, her and Patrick going fastest to join the woman near the doors to the ER.

"I can only allow one person back for each patient," she said.

Makenna turned to Ian. "Do you mind if I go with Patrick?"

"No," Ian said. "Just text me when you know more."

Giving Caden a quick hug and a kiss, Makenna agreed. She gave Shima a nod, too. "Will let you all know as soon as we can." And then she was rushing to her father and youngest brother's sides, heart in her throat to know that they were going to be okay. She couldn't lose any of these men that she loved. Not her father, not her brothers, and not Caden.

Because the pain of it would absolutely shatter her.

CHAPTER EIGHT

*I*t was morning before they got home. Turned out Makenna's dad didn't have a sternum fracture; he was just badly bruised—which was good news. Collin did have a broken rib, but his head scans had been clear and the scalp lac didn't include any injury to the bone beneath. When they got back to the James house, everyone helped get Mike and Collin settled before falling into bed.

"You were my hero last night, you know that?" Makenna said, half asleep next to Caden in her small bed. Even exhausted she was so damn beautiful, with the morning light bringing out all the shades of red in her hair.

Caden shook his head. He'd never be comfortable with that word. Hero. Because he was always questioning if he'd done enough, been good enough. Heroes were brave and fearless, neither of which described his anxiety-ridden ass. He knew himself well enough to know that was true. "I was…just doing my job. It's what I do."

"That doesn't make it any less heroic," she said, rolling closer so that her chin rested on his bare chest. Makenna traced her finger over his rose tattoo. "People live because you get up and go to work, Caden. That's…that's amazing."

There was truth in what she said, but it still made him uncomfortable to think about it that way. He always thought of it more as a debt owed, as paying back the universe for what someone had done for him. And not just anyone, but David Talbot. That was the name of the paramedic who had first arrived on the scene of his family's accident fourteen years before. That was the name of the man who'd saved Caden's life and pulled him back from the brink of madness.

Their car had flipped into an irrigation ditch that ran along the side of a country road, making it so that passing cars couldn't see it in the darkness. For hours, Caden had been pinned upside down in the back seat, his head wedged between the front center console and passenger seat, his shoulder dislocated, something stabbing him in the side.

He'd called out his family's names for a long time, but no one ever answered. He'd screamed for help every time the lights of a passing car flickered through the gloom, but no one ever came. Caden had passed in and out of consciousness for hours until he could no longer distinguish reality from nightmare. By the time a long-haul trucker finally stopped in the early light of morning, Caden hadn't responded to the man's calls to see if everyone was all right because he hadn't believed the voice was real.

His mind hadn't stopped playing tricks on him ever since.

"I'm just glad I could help," he finally said, leaning up to kiss Makenna on the forehead. He ran his fingers through her soft hair. He never had tired of playing with it, and didn't think he ever would. "Let's get some sleep."

Makenna kissed his chest and pressed herself tight along the side of his body, her head on his shoulder. They fell asleep quickly, but the combination of the accident and the anxiety caused by the overheard conversations had twisted his subconscious into knots that played out in some of the worst nightmares he'd had in years.

They all started out the same—with his father losing control of the car and it flipping in a series of crushing, body-bruising jolts until it finally landed upside down, the impact throwing Caden's body so hard that he became pinned in place, unable to move.

It was the endings that were different.

In one, no one ever came to rescue Caden from the accident, and he was still there now—a living hell he could never escape, blood still dripping down over his face from the wound on his head.

In another, his brother Sean's eyelids flipped open in his lifeless face, his eyes sightless in death but so accusing as they stared at Caden. Sean moaned, "It shoulda been me. I shoulda been the one to live," before disappearing into thin air.

In the one that just had him gasping awake, it was Ian who first showed up on the scene, and when he looked in and saw Caden hanging there, he just said, "She deserves better than you," and walked away as Caden screamed and screamed.

Jesus.

Caden looked to his side to find that Makenna had turned over at some point. She must've been exhausted for his bullshit not to have disturbed her, because he knew his nightmares often woke her up. Just another thing he hated about himself, for her sake.

He blew out a long breath. Caden was so fucking exhausted. And it was an exhaustion that had absolutely nothing to do with last night's lack of sleep. It was an exhaustion he carried in his very soul, one that weighed down his spirit with grief and survivor's guilt and self-doubt, and he didn't know how he'd ever fix that. Or what it should mean if he couldn't.

Finally, Makenna stirred beside him. "Hey," she said, giving him a sleepy smile.

God, she was so very pretty. It struck him dumb every time. "Hey."

"Did you sleep?" she asked.

"Yeah," he said. Some, anyway. If she hadn't heard his nightmares, he didn't need to burden her with them.

"I must not have slept enough," she said, making a face. "I'm kinda nauseous."

"It's three o'clock in the afternoon," Caden said. "We've missed two meals. Maybe food will help."

They threw on clothes and found Mike, Patrick, and Ian congregated around the island in the kitchen.

"Daddy," Makenna said, rushing up to him. "How are you feeling?"

He huffed out a little laugh. "A little beat-up, but I'll be okay, peanut."

"I wish I could stay longer," she said, leaning her head against her father. With a grimace, Mike put his arm around her and softly hugged her in. The gesture was so casual in its intimacy and tenderness that it stole Caden's breath. Not because there was anything particularly unique about a father hugging his child, but because after the accident, Caden's father never once hugged him again.

The accident had left his old man with his own demons, leaving no room for the father-son relationship they'd once had. And it had made a much younger version of himself believe that his own father wished Caden hadn't survived either. He'd felt like such a burden to the man, for years. It was part of why he'd started donning the armor of his ink.

"Don't you worry about it," Mike said. "Collin and I are going to be fine."

"Do you want to stay and take the train home when you're ready?" Caden asked. He felt bad that his having to work tomorrow cut the weekend short, but the price of getting the holiday off was a series of back-to-back twenty-four/seven shifts for the next few days.

Makenna blew out a breath and braced her hand on the counter. "I don't know. I have to work on Monday anyway."

"Are you okay?" Patrick asked. "You're kinda green."

"No sleep and no food," she said.

"What do you want?" Caden asked. "I'll make you something."

"We were just talking about food, too," Mike said. "We still have plenty of leftovers."

"Why don't you two go sit down?" Caden said to Mike and Makenna. "We can take charge of dinner." He looked at Patrick.

"Absolutely," Patrick said.

Makenna pressed up onto tiptoes to give Caden a quick kiss as she passed him. "Thank you." It was the first time they'd done something more than hold hands or sit close together in front of everyone, and Caden braced for a reaction. But there was none. Not even from Ian, who'd been very quiet around him since the accident.

The three of them heated up the food and set it out on the table.

And even though Ian's derisive words were still pinging around the back of Caden's brain, he liked this family. Despite Ian's snubs. Mike was loving and friendly and generous. Patrick was a good guy and a straight shooter, and they worked together as well in the kitchen as they had on the scene the night before. Collin was talkative and funny, easy going and accepting. And Makenna...Makenna was everything good and light and loving.

Soon they were all gathered around to eat, including Collin and Shima, who came down when the smells of turkey and stuffing started wafting through the house. Collin was moving a little stiffly and looking a little bleary-eyed but otherwise he'd be fine. And Caden was glad. He'd hate to see anything happen to the family Makenna loved so much. Because she deserved everything.

The meal was subdued compared to the conversation of the day before, but it was real. Real life. And for the first time, Caden actually let himself imagine being a part of it.

The past couple of days had kicked Makenna's butt. First, the unexpected conversation with Cameron. Then, the accident. Then, the stomach virus she'd picked up that had left her queasy and exhausted. And finally, she'd barely seen Caden in the four days since they'd gotten home because he'd had back-to-back shifts that had allowed him to get the holiday off in the first place.

All of which made her very glad that they'd have tonight together. He'd made the arrangements for her to get her first tattoo, and Makenna was thrilled. And a little nervous. Okay, a lot nervous. But Caden would be right there with her.

The work day finally over, Makenna took the elevator to the first floor—her favorite elevator, the one that made her smile every time she took it because she'd met Caden in it—and made her way to the Metro. Outside, it was already dark, and the cold air bit at her skin. But she was all pure frenetic energy looking forward to tonight.

Back at her apartment, she was thrilled to find Caden home.

Wearing jeans and an ACFD T-shirt, he was in the kitchen unpacking containers from plastic bags. "Hey," she said. "What smells so good?"

"Hey, Red," he said in a quiet voice. He turned toward her. For a split second, something in his gaze looked wrong, almost disheartened, but then he gave a little smile and his whole face changed. "I stopped at the noodle place."

"You okay?" she asked, wrapping her arms around his neck.

"Yeah," he said, hugging her back. "Last night's shift was non-stop and I couldn't seem to stay asleep today."

"Ugh, I'm sorry," she said. "Well, thank you for getting food. I love the noodle place." *And I love you.*

She thought it so often these days that the words lived on the tip of her tongue. After the conversation about Cameron, Makenna had been so tempted to just tell Caden how she felt, but there'd been moments over the weekend where he'd seemed stressed, and she could tell he was at his limit. They'd get there. She knew they would. The way he looked at her, the way he took care of her, the way he made love to her—it all said he felt the same way she did, even if he hadn't given her the words.

"I know," he said with a wink. "That's why I stopped there." His lips found hers, warm and exploring. She reveled in the little bites of his piercings against her skin as he kissed her again and again.

"Mmm, good appetizer," she said around the edge of the kiss.

He grinned. "Food then tattoo. Then we can come back to appetizers after."

"Fine," she said, feigning being put out. "I guess I can live with that plan."

"You excited?" he asked, returning to the counter.

Makenna couldn't hold back her smile. "Really excited. Heath sent me the final version of the design today," she said. "Wanna see it?"

"Of course," he said, grabbing silverware from a drawer. Heath was the tattoo artist who'd done most of Caden's work over the years. "He's great, isn't he?"

She dropped her bags on the edge of the counter and fished out the sketch. She found the sheet and made sure it was the right one before she handed it to Caden—because she had two versions of it in her bag. One for Caden to see, and one that Heath was actually going to use to make the stencil. She'd cooked up a little surprise that he couldn't know about until the ink was done, and she was nearly bursting at the seams.

Caden studied the design for a long moment. "This is fantastic, Makenna. How big are you thinking?"

"That's the size," she said, imagining what it was going to look like in the center of her upper back. The circle surrounding the Celtic knot tree was about five inches round. At first, she'd thought she wanted it to be smaller, but Heath had talked her into a somewhat bigger piece so that the holes in the center of all the knot work would remain distinct as the tattoo aged.

"It's gonna be fucking beautiful. But then, it'll be on you, so of course it will." He leaned down and gave her a nuzzling kiss on the cheek. "Do you want to get changed and I'll set everything out?"

"Yeah," she said. "Sounds great." The kitchen, dining area, and living room were one big room, with her bedroom door toward the far end. She paused there and looked back. Caden moved around her little kitchen, comfortably and familiarly, and he just looked so freaking good there. In her space. Well, *their* space now.

He still had his townhouse in Fairlington, but he rarely slept there anymore. And it was so bare bones in furnishings that he preferred they not sleep there because he feared she'd be uncomfortable. A part of her wasn't sure why he even kept it at this point.

"What?" he asked, giving her a skeptical look.

She grinned and leaned against the door jamb. "I rode our elevator today."

He shook his head. "Anything interesting happen?"

"Oh, I got trapped with a smoking hot stranger and made out with him in the dark. The usual," she said.

He smirked. "That never happens."

Makenna threw her head back and laughed. Still smiling, she changed into jeans and a pink camisole with a low back, and then she threw a warm, chunky caramel-colored cardigan over that.

She found Caden sitting at the set table, containers of food over-flowing with several types of noodles. It smelled amazing—savory and spicy and like she could eat everything she saw.

For a moment, the look on his face made her think he was upset about something, but then he saw her and his expression transformed into a sexy smirk. "Smoking hot, huh?"

Laughing, she took the seat next to him. "You fishing for compli-ments, Grayson? I already said you were freaking gorgeous."

"Yeah, but that's not the same as smoking hot." He arched a brow, and damn if his playfully smug, expectant expression wasn't hot as hell with his brow piercing and the widow's peak of his dark hair.

She picked up her fork. "Okay, then how about this? You are so freaking gorgeous and so smoking hot that you make my heart race and my mouth water and my panties melt. Every time I see you. How's that for a compliment?"

Caden's smile was slow coming but so damn sexy. "I like tattoo night."

She laughed and shook her head. "So do I."

CHAPTER NINE

$\mathcal{H}$eroic Ink was located on the edge of Old Town Alexandria, the oldest part of the town that had started as a port back in colonial times. Located on a quaint street full of boutiques and restaurants, the tattoo studio had a well-known reputation for its expertise in military tattoos of all kinds, which explained all the military memorabilia and photographs of service men and woman tacked in a giant collage to the front of the registration desk.

When they walked in the front door, the blue-haired woman at the desk recognized Caden right away. "Well, hey you," she said. "It's been way too long."

"I know, I know," Caden said, his hand at the small of Makenna's back. "Rachel, this is Makenna James. She's here for Heath."

"Hi Makenna," Rachel said, holding out a heavily tattooed hand. "So nice to meet you."

Makenna smiled and shook Rachel's hand. The woman was stunning and so cool. With short two-toned blue hair, a nose piercing, and ink everywhere, you could look at her for an hour and not take everything in. And she had such an inviting smile. "Hi Rachel. I'm excited to be here."

"This is your first one?" she asked, placing a form on a clipboard in front of her.

"Yes." She grinned at Caden, who was totally watching her as she took everything in.

"Well, let's get this party started," Rachel said.

Before long, Makenna was seated backward on a chair, her hair twisted up in a knot on the top of her head, and Heath was applying the stencil to the center of her upper back, just below her neck.

Heath was kind of the quiet type, which probably explained why he and Caden got along. But he could also be funny and wickedly sarcastic, and he was cute besides. He had short brown hair and a full beard and moustache, and lots of ink peaked out beneath his band T-shirt and holey jeans.

Heath handed her a mirror. "Want to check out the placement?"

Makenna walked to the full-length mirror near her chair and looked over her shoulder. Butterflies raced through her belly. The design was beautiful and she loved it, but a part of her couldn't believe she was having this done. She never would've been brave enough to do this without Caden.

She didn't mind when he walked up to look, because Heath was leaving her little surprise off until he was almost ready to do it.

"What do you think?" she asked Caden as she studied the design in the mirror. Beneath the tree, the roots were made up of the initials M, E, P, I, M, C—for the six members of the James family, including her mother, Erin. "I think it looks perfect."

"So do I," he said, his gaze fixed on her skin. "You ready?"

"So ready," she said.

The kiss he gave her was deep and wet. He whispered in her ear, "I'm already getting turned on thinking about you getting inked."

Well now *she* was turned on. "Appetizers after, remember?"

He nodded, his crooked smile bringing one of his dimples out to play.

Heath gave her a few instructions and then his tattoo machine came to life on a low buzz. "Let me know if you need a break. This one's going to take a little while, so it's completely fine." From the corner of her eye, she caught him dipping the tip into a little cup of black ink, and then leaned in, his gloved hand falling on her back.

Makenna bit her lip at the first contact of the needles. It kinda hurt, like something almost sharp scratching you, but it was tolerable. "Not too bad," she said to Caden, who was sitting in a chair right in front of her.

"There will be more sensitive places, but nothing you can't handle," he said, his dark eyes full of a sexy look that was part pride, part satisfaction, and part lust. Appetizers were going to be *good*.

"How you doing, Makenna?" Heath asked.

"Good," she said, staring at Caden. "No problem."

"So Caden said you two met in an elevator," Heath said, amusement plain in his voice.

"We really did. We were trapped in it for over four hours," Makenna said, smiling. It was a little weird to talk to someone she couldn't look at, but she couldn't move while he was working. "In my office building. I rode it just today."

"That's quite a way to meet someone," Heath said with a chuckle. "How come nothing like that ever happens to me?"

"Maybe you don't ride enough elevators," Makenna said.

The tattoo machine pulled away from her skin. Heath laughed. "I guess I don't," he finally said, leaning back in.

The needles hit a sensitive spot along her spine that had Makenna grimacing. Originally, she'd been thinking of putting the piece on her shoulder, but when she'd decided on the bigger size, she thought it would look better in the center. Heath had warned her that the central placement meant inking over bone, which could hurt more, and it sure did.

Caden braced his elbows on his knees so he could lean closer. "Want to play twenty questions?" he asked.

She smiled, knowing he was trying to distract her and appreciating the heck out of the gesture. "Are there still questions left we haven't asked each other?"

"Probably," he said. "For example, I don't think I've ever asked you your favorite sex position."

"No laughing," Heath said, as Makenna tried to hold back her humor. Heat filled her cheeks. "Also, TMI. However, I like TMI, so feel free to answer, Makenna."

Since the needle was away from her skin, she did laugh that time. "Okay, so maybe there are questions we haven't asked." She winked at Caden as Heath got back to work. "And, to answer the question, the second part of the night on my floor."

Caden's gaze went molten. He flicked at the spider bite piercings with his tongue. And that had parts of *her* going molten, because she knew how freaking talented that tongue was.

"Yours?" she asked, arching an eyebrow.

"The same night, but the first position," he said, flicking at his piercing again. So, his favorite was her on top of him. That had been hot too. The position gave her a fantastic view of so much of his ink and all of his piercings, not to mention his darkly handsome face as she took him into her body again and again. She could still hear his voice saying, *Ride me, Makenna. Use me.* And just the memory made her need to squirm in her seat.

"What's your favorite holiday and why?" she asked.

"Thanksgiving," he said immediately. "Because this Thanksgiving was the best of any holiday I've had in years. Almost the best I can remember."

Aw. That answer hit her right in the chest and made those words want to jump off her tongue again. "Mine has always been Thanksgiving, too. Although Christmas is a close second. Those are the holidays that always bring family together again."

Caden nodded. "What is one thing you'd change about your life if you could?"

She studied him for a moment, wondering if this was just a playful question in the game or if he was still wondering about her feelings for Cameron. But the answer was an easy one. "I wouldn't change anything about my life."

Eyebrow arched, he gave her a skeptical look. "There has to be something."

Makenna thought about it for a long moment, then took a few

seconds to breathe through another sensitive patch of skin. "Um, then, I would've wanted my mother to have lived longer so I could've known her. But then, honestly, if she had lived I wonder if my relationship with my father would've been as close. I would hate to lose that. Do I get to ask that one back?" She didn't want to put him on the spot in front of Heath, but he'd asked the question and had to know she'd want to ask it of him, too. That was how they'd played this game in the elevator that night, the game that had helped bring them so close together.

He gave a tight nod and waved a hand at himself. "I'd get rid of the anxiety and the claustrophobia and all that bullshit."

"I get that," she said, hating that he wanted to change anything about himself when she loved him *so much* just as he was. She didn't want perfect, she just wanted him. In all his gorgeous, funny, considerate, and sometimes angsty glory. "But you do realize, if you hadn't been claustrophobic the day we met, you might not have asked me to talk to you in that elevator. You might not have needed my help, and then we might not have gotten to know each other."

He tilted his head, his eyes narrowing in a way that brought out the harshness in that utterly masculine face. Finally, he gave her another nod. "Fair enough. Your turn."

Wanting to lighten the mood, she thought of something funny to ask. "What's your favorite line from *The Princess Bride*?" She was already smiling as some of her favorites came to mind. Funny movies of all kinds were their thing.

Caden grinned. "When Vizzini says, 'Inconceivable!' And Montoya says, 'You keep saying that word. I do not think it means what you think it means.' Oh, or maybe when Vizzini says, 'Stop rhyming and I mean it,' and Fezzik replies—"

"Anybody want a peanut?" all three of them said in unison. The needle pulled away from her skin and they all laughed.

"There are too many good ones in that movie," Heath said.

"It's true," Makenna said, her cheeks hurting from smiling. "I like the priest who pronounces 'marriage' as 'mawage,' and of course the classic, 'My name is Inigo Montoya. You killed my father—"

"Prepare to die," they all said again to more laughter.

The questions went on for a long while. They talked about silly stuff like favorite ice cream flavor, what they'd eat for their last meal, and what other countries they'd want to visit, since neither of them had ever been outside the States. They asked about more serious stuff like what job they'd want if they couldn't do their current one and what the top items on their bucket lists were. As always, the conversation was fun and engaging, animated and moving. They'd always given great talk.

"I'm about two-thirds done," Heath said. "Let's take a little break."

"Okay," Makenna said, standing up to stretch. She was tempted to look in the mirror, but she really wanted to wait to see the finished tattoo.

Caden stepped to her side as if to look.

She whirled away. "You get to see when I get to see—when it's done," she said, not knowing if Heath had added the part Caden didn't know about.

"So it's like that, is it?" he asked with a smirk.

"It's exactly like that." She gave him some smirk right back.

"You're doing great, you know," he said. "It's a big tattoo for your first time."

She checked to make sure Heath wasn't right behind her, and then said. "I like it big. You should know this."

The smile he gave her said he wanted to devour her. "Is it time for appetizers yet?"

"Ready to wrap this up?" Heath said, sitting down on his rolling stool again.

"Definitely," Makenna said, taking her seat. "And for the record, Caden, it's almost time."

———

*C*aden had really enjoyed sharing this experience with Makenna, and he was still kinda blown away by the fact that she wanted to do it in the first place. He knew that she really liked his tattoos, but she'd told him that she'd always been afraid they would hurt. And here she'd barely reacted the whole time.

He wasn't surprised, though. Makenna was soft and sweet, but she could also be tough when she needed to be—like when she was calling him on his bullshit, or like how she was so well adjusted about the death of her mother.

"There," Heath said after a while. "All done."

The smile Makenna wore absolutely owned Caden. It really did.

"Can I see it now?" she asked. Heath handed her the mirror, and she walked kinda backward toward the full-length. "I get to see it first," she said, grinning at him and sticking out her tongue. For a long moment, she studied herself, moving the hand-held mirror this way and that, and then her eyes went glassy. "I really love it," she said. "Heath, you are so talented. It's amazing." Her joy was palpable, and it lit Caden up inside.

"Caden, I like this woman a lot. You're welcome to bring her around absolutely any time," he said with a wink.

Makenna laughed. "I mean it, it's great. So much better than I even imagined."

"Well, you're welcome," Heath said.

"Do I get to see it now?" Caden asked, curiosity getting the best of him.

"You do," she said, her expression suddenly shy. She turned around, and Caden came closer.

The black ink was stunning against her fair skin. And she was right, Heath's work was meticulous as always, crisp and clean and executed perfectly. The Celtic knots were beautiful, and the way the tree blended with them was interesting and unique. Across the bottom, six initials in an old-looking font formed a curve among the tree's roots—M, E, P, I, M, C. Caden looked closer. The second M had a smaller letter hanging off of it on a little flourish. C.

"Say something," she said.

He met her gaze in the mirror. "It's incredible," he said. "And it looks fantastic on you, just like I knew it would. What's the little letter C?" That hadn't been on the design she'd shown him earlier.

Meeting his gaze in the mirror, her expression went so, so soft, and she gave a shy little shrug. "The C...is for you."

The words hung there for a moment, and it was like the room sucked in on him. "For me?" he heard himself say as if from a distance. Blood rushed through his ears.

She nodded.

"But...but this...this is your family tree," he said, the room going a little Tilt-a-Whirl around him.

In an instant, she was right in front of him, hands on his chest and bright blue eyes staring up at him. "To me, it feels like you *are* part of my family, Caden. And I wanted you there."

"I...I...don't know...." He shook his head, entirely overwhelmed and overcome. "I mean, that's amazing of you to do. I just can't believe you did it," he said, not exactly sure what he was saying.

And then something else occurred to him. She'd put his initial on her body. It wasn't exactly the same as his name, but close enough. And he'd always heard that tattooing a lover's name jinxed the relationship. It was bad luck. And for him, was there any other kind?

It was a stupid superstition, of course. But it was like him resisting telling her "I love you" because he didn't want to tempt the fates, or the gods of mayhem, or whoever was responsible for bad things happening to good people. His brain was already imagining the ways that little curve of a C could be easily changed into something else—a heart, a clover, another knot.

And Jesus, here he was thinking about not wanting to tell her that he loved her when she'd permanently claimed him on her very skin.

"No one's ever done something like that for me, Makenna," he finally managed, his brain still only vaguely connected to his mouth. "It's...it's amazing."

Her smile was pure joy. "I hope you don't mind. Once I thought of it, it just felt so right. So I went with it. You'll always be a part of me."

"Let's get you bandaged up," Heath said, waving her over to the chair again.

Caden watched him work on Makenna and listened to him give her aftercare instructions, but he did it all as if he was watching it from across the room, from somewhere outside his body. His heart raced and his chest went tight.

Clearly, the tattoo of his initial plucked at his anxiety, but what he said was true—no one had ever done something this special for him. Ever. It was just that, *offuckingcourse*, that made him scared.

Terrified, actually.

After everything he'd lost, how could he have something so, so good for keeps?

CHAPTER TEN

*C*aden was ravenous for Makenna the minute they walked through her apartment door. He was on her in an instant. Pressing her back against the kitchen counter. Dropping her purse to the floor. Tugging off her coat.

He was using her. He knew he was. Using her to help shut down all the bullshit in his head. Because when he was with her, when he was *in* her, it all went away. It always fucking went away.

But she seemed to be right there with him. Shoving off his jacket, burrowing her hands under his shirt, jerking it up. They worked it off together.

Their kisses were urgent, deep, rough. He devoured her—her skin, her tongue, her moans. He couldn't get enough of her.

"Still…too…many…clothes," Makenna rasped around the edge of a kiss, her hands pulling at the button to his jeans.

"God, I need you," he said, his mind an overwhelming blur, his chest still too tight from before.

"I'm right here," she whispered. "Right here."

But for how long?

The thought came out of nowhere and struck him stupid. He

froze, then blinked. As if someone had just unexpectedly punched him in the face.

"Caden?" Breathing heavily, lips swollen, Makenna peered up at him in the dim glow thrown off by a light mounted on the bottom of one of the cabinets.

He hoped the dimness hid the parts of him he didn't want her to see. Like the darkness had in the elevator.

"Need you," he said again, diving back into the kiss. He pulled her with him as he walked them haltingly toward her bedroom. They were a tangle of hands and kisses and shedding clothes. By the time they'd reached the bed, Caden was hard and aching and desperate to bury himself inside her.

"Condom. Hurry," she said.

He couldn't have agreed more. He had it on in a flash and then he turned her to face the bed. "Kneel," he rasped.

Makenna crawled onto the bed, her back arching so fucking beautifully, her ass right there and waiting. Her tattoo flashing at him from under the protective plastic wrap in the ambient light coming in through the window.

He couldn't wait.

He couldn't.

Taking his cock in hand, he found her opening and pushed home.

She took all of him. Just like she always did.

Buried deep, her body accepting every bit of him, her moans proclaiming her pleasure, all the noise between his ears ceased. Just fucking went quiet.

And it was such a relief that all he could do was give in to the goddamned incredible perfection of it.

His hips started moving, slower at first, but quickly faster, chasing, needing. He grabbed hold of her hip with one hand and her shoulder with the other, his focus centered on her tattoo—on his C. On the way she'd claimed him when he couldn't even—

No.

He slammed his eyes shut and focused on the slick friction of her body accepting his, on the softness of her skin against his. The sounds of harsh breathing and colliding bodies and the stream of moans spilling from her lips filled the room, and he focused on those, too.

It did the job. Too well. Because out of nowhere his orgasm was an unstoppable force. "Fuck, I'm coming," he gritted out. His cock jerked with each spasm, his hips moving in punctuated thrusts as it played out. He was almost numb from the intensity of it. "Shit, I'm sorry," he said, easing out of her. It was the first time in all the times they'd been together that he hadn't taken care of Makenna first.

Because you weren't really with *her just then, were you?*

She turned onto her side, her smile apparent in the dimness. "Why would you apologize? That was freaking hot."

He disposed of the condom, then returned to her on the bed. "Let me make it up to you, Red," he said, slipping in behind her, his hand sliding over her hip.

"Caden, maybe you can't see the blissed-out expression on my face in the darkness, but trust me, I'm not complaining right now." Humor was plain in her voice, which meant she hadn't clued in to how out of it he was.

"I want you to come," he whispered in her ear, making sure he didn't press against her tattoo. It would be tender for a few days. He pulled her thigh over his, opening her core to his touch. "I always want you to come." She was wet and hot, and her hips pressed into his fingers as they swirled in a firm circle over her clit.

On a long, low moan, she pressed her face back against his, enough that he could make out her expression. Eyes closed, she did look blissful, happy, trusting. And instead of that making him feel better, it suddenly made him feel like a fraud. Because he couldn't give her all of him, could he? He wouldn't reveal all of himself to her, would he? He shouldn't burden her with all the doubts and fears and uncertainties that had been building up inside him lately, should he?

Eyes tightly shut, he leaned his forehead against hers and concentrated on stroking her just like she liked it. He needed to give her this. At least this. If not everything she deserved.

She deserves better than you.

"Oh, God, I'm coming," she said, her hips surging. "Oh, God." Her body shuddered through the climax, and then she sighed on a long breath. "Wow. Appetizers rock."

Caden had to clear his throat to get his voice to sound half normal. "Yeah they do."

She chuckled and turned over, burying her face against his chest. They lay there for a long moment until she finally yawned. "I'm so tired."

"Me, too," Caden said, though probably not for the same reasons.

"Can we just fall asleep like this?" she mumbled.

"Anything you want," he said, wishing it was true. Because he wasn't dumb. A woman who wanted you to meet her family and who tattooed your initial onto her body wanted more. Maybe wanted everything. And he felt so amazingly privileged that Makenna James maybe wanted all that with him. But he also felt undeserving.

Always.

"I guess I gotta take care of the tattoo first," she said, pushing herself up. She stroked her fingers along the tribal tattoo on his calf. "Will you help me?"

"Of course," Caden said, scrubbing at the scar on the side of his head. "Be right there."

"Okay." She threw him a small smile over her shoulder before she got up. The light came on in the bathroom, sending a stream of brightness into the bedroom.

Which meant it was time to shake the fuck out of it. Because just like in that elevator, the darkness was only going to hide him for so long.

---

*N*ausea had Makenna tearing out of bed and dashing across the room. She threw up everything she'd had for dinner the previous night and possibly some stuff she'd eaten two weeks ago given how many times she wretched.

Damn. When she'd felt better yesterday, she'd assumed she was over the stomach virus. Maybe she ought to go to the doctor. Shuddering, she flushed the toilet, then pulled herself up to the sink to rinse out her mouth.

Which was when it occurred to her.

She was late.

No, she couldn't be—

There'd been that one time a condom broke as Caden pulled out, but Makenna had had a period since then. True, it had been light. But her periods had always been like that—light one month, heavier the next; coming twenty-eight days later one month, then thirty-one the next. Which was why she hadn't given the lateness much thought.

Except this nausea had her thinking.

No.

No.

Shit.

Thoughts reeling, she shuffled back into the bedroom, completely unsure what she was going to say, to find the bed empty. "Caden? Hey? Where'd you go?" She found the other rooms dark and empty. What the heck?

Flicking on the kitchen light, she found a note on the counter.

Red—

I didn't want to wake you. Realized I needed something from the house before my shift so I left early. Talk to you later. –C

Makenna frowned. In all the time that they'd been together, he'd never left before morning. On a sigh, she combed her fingers through her hair. Not that it meant anything. Oh, screw it, she was just out of sorts from her maybe-but-probably-not-bathroom-revelation. Back in the bedroom, she disconnected her phone from its charger and shot off a text.

Missed waking up to your freaking gorgeous face. Have a good day! xo

She didn't get a message right back, but he never texted while driving, and he was probably on his way to the station given the time. She sagged down onto the edge of the bed.

Could she really be pregnant? Her stomach did a flip flop that made her wrap her arms around herself. Crap. There was no way she could make it through the entire work day without finding out.

Forcing herself up, she threw on some leggings, a sweatshirt, and a pair of gray knit boots, and ran a brush through her hair. She bundled into her coat and grabbed her purse, and then she was a woman on a mission. This was one of the things she loved about where she lived— the little urban enclave of Clarendon had everything you could need, most of it within easy walking distance. Including the Walgreens, just two blocks away.

Soon she was standing in front of a shelf full of pregnancy tests. And, good God, why were there so many? Pluses, minuses, one line, two lines, words, symbols.

This is ridiculous. Right? I don't need these.

Except. Maybe I do?

Pull down your big girl panties and pee on a stick and you'll know for sure.

Right.

On a sigh, Makenna grabbed one test that claimed to be able to provide the earliest results. And then she picked another that not only gave the words "pregnant" or "not pregnant" but also estimated how many weeks had lapsed since her last ovulation. Awesome.

She made it back to her apartment in no time flat, and for the first time since she'd met Caden, she was glad he wasn't there. Only because she didn't want to burden him with a possible baby scare without knowing there was definitely something to worry about in the first place. If she thought he wasn't ready to hear *I love you*, she could only imagine that his unreadiness to hear *I'm pregnant* would probably have to be multiplied by a factor of, like, a gajillion.

Dumping the bag out into the bathroom sink, Makenna had the oddest thought—she didn't know what she wanted the results to say. Which made no sense given that she was twenty-five and they'd been together less than three months, but the thought was there all the same.

With her heart in her throat, she opened the boxes and laid the plastic sticks out in a row—two of each kind. She used them all, just to be quadruple sure. And then she waited. And her pulse raced. And her belly flipped.

And then the results came in.

Plus. Plus. Pregnant 3+. Pregnant 3+.

Makenna stared at the little windows like she was trying to decipher Sanskrit.

Plus. Plus. Pregnant 3+. Pregnant 3+.

She was pregnant. And it had been more than three weeks since she'd ovulated? How far along was she? She sank down onto the closed toilet lid and dropped her head into her hands.

Oh God. Ohgodohgodohgod.

Okay. Don't freak out.

Right. I'll do that right after I freaking freak out!

"Stop. Think this through," she said out loud. An idea came to mind and she went in search of her cell phone. She called her doctor's office and found out how to get a blood test—might as well start with confirming this.

She quickly showered and dressed for work so she could stop on the way to get the blood test and have a chance of getting the results back before the weekend. Because even though she knew—home pregnancy tests were way too accurate to get four false positives—she still wanted the official result. And she suspected Caden would, too.

Staring into the bathroom mirror, her gaze dropped to her stomach.

"I'm pregnant," she whispered to herself, as if she was revealing a secret. And she guessed she was. Because no way was she telling Caden until she knew everything there was to know.

CHAPTER ELEVEN

*T*he nightmares were getting worse. They'd tormented him during the little bit of sleep he'd gotten the night before, so he'd gotten up and paced the living room, ultimately leaving rather than face Makenna's knowing eyes in the morning. And during the long period of no calls they'd had during today's shift, he'd drifted off, only for the nightmares to come at him again.

They all started the same.

It was the endings that were different.

In one, it was him and Makenna in the backseat when the car flipped, and it was Makenna who didn't survive while he did. He called her name over and over, but she never answered.

In another, Sean morphed into Makenna from an earlier version of the dream. It was her eyes that accused him. Her voice that said, "It shoulda been me. I shoulda been the one to live."

In a completely new spin of his subconscious, Caden became his father and Makenna, his mother. When the car flipped, Makenna suffered his mother's fate, her head battered against the side window, her neck breaking, her death instant. And not only was Caden trapped hanging upside down knowing that everything he'd ever loved was gone, but knowing, too, that it was his own fault.

He'd lost control. And she'd paid the price.

So by the time a call came in to the station, Caden's head was a fucking wreck. Which probably explained why he had his very first on-the-job panic attack while responding to the scene of an accident. It was the hair that did it. The female driver's long red hair.

His mind had done its usual thing, and for several long moments, he'd been absolutely sure his worst fears had come true. Makenna was dead in that car. His chest went tight, his breathing shallowed out, and he froze.

It didn't matter that Makenna rarely drove her car. Nor that the car in the accident hadn't been the same as Makenna's little Prius. Or that there was absolutely no reason why Makenna would be on Duke Street near Landmark Mall at four o'clock in the afternoon when she worked miles away in Roslyn.

His brain didn't trade in logic in moments like those.

Embarrassment aside, it was even worse that he could've jeopardized a patient's life. In the end, the woman's injuries weren't that serious. But that wasn't the point. He was fucking out of control, and he didn't know what the hell to do about it. He hadn't been this bad in years.

Then again, he hadn't had anything to lose in years, either.

Now he did. And *he* was losing it.

When they returned to the station house, his captain called him into his office.

Exhausted and strung out, Caden dropped into the chair in front of his captain's desk. In his forties and prematurely gray, Joe Flaherty had been Caden's supervisor all nine years he'd worked in this house, and he was aware of Caden's background. A few of the guys were, too.

As a rule, Caden didn't flake out—he showed up early, he left late, he picked up extra shifts, he covered for the guys with families, he left his rig clean and well stocked, and he did the job to the best of his ability. They all knew he was solid. Well, until today.

"What happened out there, Grayson?" Joe asked, his voice concerned, but not unkind.

Caden scrubbed at his face. "I've been having trouble sleeping,"

Caden said. "Nightmares about the accident have been coming back lately for some reason." He shook his head, wanting to be honest, but not wanting to say more than he had to. He met Joe's gaze head on. "When I first saw the woman, I thought it was Makenna."

A thoughtful expression on his face, Joe nodded. "We all see someone we love in the face of a patient at some point, so don't beat yourself up about that," he said. "You talking to someone about the nightmares?"

He shook his head again. Caden hadn't sought any kind of therapy in years. He'd worked things out. Gotten himself under control. Learned ways to handle his shit.

Only, clearly, that wasn't all true anymore, was it?

"Maybe you need to consider it. Given your history, I always expected you to have issues responding to MVAs. The real miracle given the life-threatening nature of your accident and your PTSD is that you didn't. And I watched you."

Caden knew that was true. And he'd understood why. On some level, he'd actually appreciated it. Before his first times out there, he hadn't known how he might respond either. But he'd been so driven to repay the debt, to help how Talbot had helped him, that he'd never had an issue. Accident scenes had never been a trigger for him the way they could be for other crash survivors.

The accident had scarred him physically, but the emotional trauma stemmed from its consequences. From losing his family. From surviving what they hadn't. From being alone with their corpses—because he hadn't known until later that his father had actually lived. From being left alone, in the car and all the years after, when his father checked out on him. From the fact that it took so long for someone to come help him that he hadn't known they were real.

Caden nodded. "I hadn't realized things were getting to me as bad as they apparently are. I'll handle it."

Joe's eyes narrowed. "Don't try to go it on your own. If your PTSD is flaring up enough to cause nightmares and give you a panic attack, something is stressing you out. Go talk to someone. That's an order. Don't make me pull you off shifts."

A rock parked in his gut, Caden rubbed a hand over his scar. "Yeah. Okay."

"Now go home," Joe said. "Get some sleep. And ask Makenna when she's gonna bring around more of those chocolate-iced brownies."

"I'm still on," Caden said.

"And I'm telling you to cut out. C-Shift will be on soon, so we're covered. That wasn't a suggestion." Joe arched an eyebrow.

Well, fuck. Caden hadn't been sent home once in nine years. And even though nothing in Joe's tone or expression made him think there was anything punitive or even irritated about the command, Caden still felt he was letting down his captain, his station, his family—the only one he had.

This was the one place where he'd always had things together.

Standing took way more effort than he wanted to admit. He came to attention, spine straight, head up.

"Dismissed," Joe said.

Caden made quick work of going home—to his townhouse in Fairlington that was just three blocks away. Makenna wouldn't be at the apartment yet, and he was way too raw to be around her just then anyway.

Which was why he texted her a lie.

Came home sick. Flu or something. Gonna sleep it off here for a few days so I don't get you sick. Talk to you later.

He stared at the words for a moment, then he hit *Send*. Maybe it wasn't that much of a lie after all. Something *was* wrong with him. And he didn't want to burden her with it. At least not until he figured out what had happened, what it meant, and what he needed to do about it.

---

*M*akenna was going a little crazy. Sitting in a ball on her couch, she'd been flipping cable channels for fifteen minutes without seeing a single thing worth watching. How was that even possible? But that wasn't what was really driving her crazy.

No, she was going crazy because she hadn't seen Caden in three days. They'd been texting all weekend, but he was still sick and not wanting to make her sick. It was killing her not to go help him, but he kept insisting she not come.

On top of that, she was going crazy because she'd gotten the official results from her doctor, and they'd confirmed what she already knew. She was pregnant.

But they'd also told her something she hadn't known—based on her bloodwork, she could be as far along as eight weeks. Which meant it really had happened when that condom broke back in October. *Knowing* she was pregnant was the only thing keeping her from helping Caden whether he wanted her to or not. She probably shouldn't chance getting sick.

Given how far along she was, the doctor's office managed to fit her in for an ultrasound appointment for Tuesday. And part of what was making her crazy was not knowing whether she should tell Caden before Tuesday so he could go with her, or get the ultrasound by herself and make sure the baby was healthy before raising it with him. She knew she was probably overthinking the whole thing and not giving him enough credit, but all this alone time had hit at the worst possible moment and had her conjuring up every bad outcome possible.

And all the craziness was compounded by the fact that she didn't feel like she should tell anyone else *before* Caden. She'd resisted calling her best friend, Jen, who was out of town on a Christmas shopping trip with her mom anyway. Besides Jen, her other closest friends had been college roommates, none of whom lived in the D.C. area. At any rate, she wasn't so close with them anymore that she would've felt comfortable calling and dropping the *Hey, I'm pregnant and scared my boyfriend is going to freak out* conversation on them. In this moment, part of her wished she had more girlfriends, but she'd always had an easier time making guy friends. She'd always blamed that on growing up surrounded by men.

Which had her wondering what she was going to tell her family— and when. Patrick had always been a great sounding board for her.

Because he was so much older than her, Ian, and Collin, he'd helped his dad out a lot when they were all young. Later, he became almost a mentor to Makenna as she made decisions about college and careers. And her dad had never been anything but incredibly supportive, even when she was the first in the family to move out of the Philadelphia area. But telling one James man could be akin to telling them all, and that definitely wasn't something she was ready to do yet.

Which was why at four o'clock on Sunday afternoon she was still in her pajamas and an entire pound bag of peanut M&Ms lay demolished on the end table next to her.

At least peanut M&Ms had protein.

Sorry lil' nut. I'll do better.

Makenna sighed.

And then she decided she'd had enough.

A woman on a mission, she turned off the TV and marched directly to the shower. Once clean, she awkwardly worked to apply Aquaphor to her tattoo, which had moved from being sore to being itchy. She threw on some comfortable clothes, stuffed her feet into boots, and grabbed her purse and coat. And then she headed to the store.

She had a care package to put together.

At the very least, she needed to *see* Caden, even if she didn't stay.

Thinking of what she liked to have when she didn't feel good, she roamed around the supermarket picking up chicken noodle soup and crackers, popsicles and ginger ale, tea bags for hot tea and bread for toast, among other things. As little as Caden had stayed there over the past two months, he couldn't possibly have much food in the house, which made her feel bad for not doing this sooner. She threw in pain medicine and throat lozenges and Pepto Bismol.

And then she passed the aisle full of holiday items. Gift wrap, decoration, candy, and toys made it look like the North Pole had exploded in the middle of the Giant. Makenna grabbed Caden a bag of peanut M&Ms, because he liked them, too. A shelf of stuffed animals caught her eye, and even though it was a little corny, she was drawn closer.

What said *Feel better!* more than a cuddly stuffed animal? The fact that she was considering giving it to a big, tattooed, pierced, and scarred guy made it kinda funny, too—and anything that might make him smile seemed like a good idea to her. Besides, Caden might look a little rough around the edges, but he was a big teddy bear inside. And she'd always loved that dichotomy about him.

And then she saw the perfect little guy.

He was a brown bear with black stitching here and there like he'd been hand-sewn or put back together. He had a sweet face and an even sweeter red patchwork heart on his chest. And something about all that stitchwork and the heart reminded her of Caden. Without letting herself overthink it, Makenna grabbed him and threw him in the cart.

It was a short trip from the store to Caden's townhouse. She'd always loved where he lived in Fairlington. Built in the 1940s to house workers for the then-new Pentagon office building, the neighborhood was all red-brick collections of townhouses grouped around small cul-de-sacs. They were charming and close to everything and some of the units were surprisingly spacious, including Caden's, which had two bedrooms and a finished basement.

As she parked her Prius in one of the visitors' spots, that got her to thinking.

Here she'd been wondering why he didn't get rid of *his* place. Given the baby, it would make much more sense for them to get rid of hers. Caden's house had easily twice the square footage of her apartment, and he didn't even use the room next to his bedroom, which would make a perfect nursery.

As she stared at the front of his house, her belly did a little flip. Obviously, she was getting ahead of herself. But thoughts of where the baby would live represented just one in about a million things she now had to consider. Well, they. *They* now had to consider. She had to stop thinking about this like she was on her own.

She had Caden.

And right now, he needed her.

Makenna collected all the bags from the car and hefted them up to his front porch. She had to sit some down to knock on the door.

It opened in less than a minute.

"Makenna? What are you doing here?" Caden asked, clearly surprised to see her. Wearing a pair of old sweatpants and a thread-bare T-shirt, he was a sight for sore eyes, making her want to throw her arms around him and burrow into his chest. But he also had dark and almost sunken circles under his eyes like he hadn't slept in days, and something about his color wasn't quite right. He really did look unwell.

"I missed you too much to stay away anymore, so I brought you a care package. Well, it kinda grew into a care grocery order, but same difference." She smiled, though inside she was bursting to tell him their news. "I won't stay if you're not up to it, but at least let me put this away for you and maybe make you a bowl of soup or something." Was she imagining it, or did his face look thinner, too? God, she really should've come sooner.

He frowned but nodded, then reached down and grabbed the bags she'd rested on the porch. "You didn't have to do all this," he said, leading her inside. "But thank you."

"Of course, I did," she said as they walked through the open living and dining room to the small kitchen at the back of the house. "I've been dying to come take care of you, but I didn't want to wake you up if you were sleeping or something. But then I started worrying that you were over here needing help or food or medicine and would be too stubborn to ask for what you needed." She gave him a knowing smile.

He chuffed out a little laugh as they settled everything onto the counters. "Yeah. Well. You know me."

"So what's been going on? Is it a stomach virus? The flu?" she asked as she started unpacking the bags.

Brow furrowed, Caden crossed his arms and leaned against the counter. "Yeah. Uh, my stomach. But, it's starting to feel better." Looking down at the floor, he gave a little shrug.

And there was something so...almost...defeated in the gesture and his posture that Makenna immediately stopped what she was doing and went to him. "I don't care if you're sick. I'm hugging you." She gently wrapped her arms around his waist and held him. And damn if he didn't *feel* a little leaner, too. "Have you been getting sick a lot?"

Caden's arms came around her on a long sigh. Like he'd been needing her. "Nothing I can't handle," he said in a low voice.

Which probably meant he'd been puking his brains out. Poor guy. "You don't have to handle this on your own, you know. I would've come sooner. I would've slept over here to take care of you."

"Didn't want to be a burden." He nuzzled his face against her hair.

Heart clenching, she pulled back to look him in the eye. "Caden, you could *never* be a burden to me. No matter what you needed, I would be there for you. Every time. You can always count on that. Do you hear me?" How did he not know this by now? The question had her wanting to lay *all* her feelings on the line. If he knew she loved him, he'd know all of this was true. But she definitely wasn't doing that when he wasn't feeling good.

He stared at her a long moment, almost like he was weighing her words. Finally, he simply said, "Yeah." He kissed her forehead. "Thank you."

"Don't thank me. This is me officially taking care of you. Do you think you could eat something?"

"Probably," he said.

Makenna kissed his cheek, and his stubble tickled her lips. "This is kinda cute," she said, stroking her finger along the couple of days' worth of growth.

"Oh yeah?" He lips almost quirked into a smile. "Good to know."

"Yep," she said, returning to the groceries. She had everything unpacked within a few minutes. "What would you like?"

His gaze roamed over the choices. "Soup and crackers would be great." He stepped closer. "I can't believe you brought all this. Ooh, M&Ms." He picked up the bag.

Makenna laughed. "You might want to wait on those until you're not getting sick anymore. It would be a shame to ruin M&Ms by knowing what they look like when you vomit them."

"Nice," he said with a smirk.

"Just saying. Okay, you go sit, and I'll get everything ready," she said, shooing him from the kitchen. "Oh, wait. One other thing." She handed him the bag with the bear in it.

"What's this?" he asked.

"A feel-better present," she said, unable to hold back her grin. He was going to think this was so silly. And it was. In a good way.

Caden stuck his hand in and pulled out the stuffed animal. "You got me a teddy bear," he said, his face *finally* breaking into a little smile. He rubbed his hand over the scar on the side of his head, something she'd seen him do so many times.

"Everybody needs a teddy when they're sick," she said. "That's, like, totally common knowledge. He can keep you company when I'm not here." Which wouldn't be often, but still.

Nodding, Caden gave her the softest look. "Thanks, Red. I...I don't know what I'd do without you."

She smiled, so glad she'd come to see him. He needed this. They both did. "Well, don't worry about that. Because you won't ever have to find out."

CHAPTER TWELVE

*M*akenna walked alone into her doctor's office on Tuesday morning. After going back and forth, she'd decided the best approach was to gather all the information she could before telling Caden she was pregnant. Most importantly, she wanted to know that the baby was healthy. Assuming that was the case, she planned to tell him tonight after work. Tell him everything.

It was time. And she was bursting at the seams.

She checked in at the desk and took a seat. A number of other people were waiting, and two of the women were obviously pregnant. Excitement shivered through Makenna's chest. That was going to be her in not too many months. At the side of one of the women, a man sat whispering into her ear, making her laugh. He rested his hand on her belly as they spoke.

And that...that would be Caden. Who hadn't had a family in so very long. God, she hoped he was excited about having one now. Even if he was scared—hell, she was too—she hoped his excitement would outweigh it. Because at the end of all this, they were going to have a tiny product that was a part of them both. And that was amazing to Makenna.

The waiting room door opened. "Makenna James?" called a nurse wearing a set of pink scrubs.

She followed the woman to an exam room, her heart racing a little faster with each passing moment. Because she was about to see her child for the very first time.

Before too long, she was wearing a paper gown and her long-time gynecologist entered the room with a nurse. "Makenna, nice to see you again," Dr. Lyons said.

"Nice to see you, too," she said, smiling at the woman's always upbeat personality.

"Are you here alone today?" the doctor asked as she scrubbed her hands.

Makenna nodded. "I wanted to make sure the pregnancy was okay before telling my boyfriend."

"Okay," Dr. Lyons said, "well, let's get started then." The doctor explained how the internal ultrasound worked and then Makenna laid back with her feet in the stirrups—which always felt incredibly awkward no matter how many times she'd had to do it in her life.

But all of that fell away as an image appeared on the screen and a fast beat rung out in the room.

"Hello, little one," the doctor said, taking some measurements on the monitor.

Tha-thump tha-thump tha-thump tha-thump tha-thump.

"Is that the heart beat?" Makenna asked, the sound planting itself inside her chest and squeezing.

Dr. Lyons smiled as she made some adjustments with the ultrasound wand. "It sure is. Sounds perfectly normal, too."

"It's supposed to be that fast?" Makenna's gaze locked on the screen where the doctor had zooned in on a grainy, peanut-shaped object with tiny nubs protruding from the sides.

In her mind, she heard her father calling her *peanut*, and now she knew why.

That was her baby and he was totally a little peanut. Well, he or she.

"Based on the measurements here you're nine weeks and three

days along, and your estimated due date is July seventh. Everything looks to be progressing normally." Dr. Lyons smiled. "So I think you're safe to share your news."

Makenna couldn't pull her gaze away from the screen. Suddenly, the whole situation crashed down on her and she caught her breath as tears pricked her eyes. "This is so incredible. I wish I'd brought him now."

"There will be plenty more to share with him, including more scans," the doctor said as she removed the wand. The image stayed on the screen. "And I'll send you away with parting gifts." The imagining machine made a *whirring* sound and spit out a strip of paper. Dr. Lyons handed it to her.

Pictures of their peanut. Makenna pressed them to her heart, any uncertainty she might've felt about having a baby disappearing. "I can't wait to show him. So everything's okay?"

"Yep. I want to put you on pre-natal vitamins and we'll get you set up with your pre-natal appointments. We'll see you back in four weeks." The doctor discussed some pregnancy dos and don'ts and gave her some information sheets to take home. God, there was a lot to learn about all this, wasn't there?

When they were done, the doctor walked to the door, then turned back with a smile. "Have fun telling your boyfriend tonight. I hope it goes great."

"Thanks," Makenna said. Dr. Lyons left, and Makenna slid off the table. Looking down at the pictures, she just felt so amazed and overwhelmed and excited. "I hope it goes great, too."

---

*A*s Caden climbed the five flights of steps up to Makenna's apartment, he felt like years had passed since he'd last been there. He certainly felt like he'd *aged* years since he'd last been there.

What a wasted wreck he'd been the past few days. His PTSD hadn't flared like this for years. For most of the weekend, he hadn't slept, and when he had, the nightmares had been torturous. His mind was like a maze full of dark corners and dead-ends and looming shadows. He'd had no appetite, and the two times he'd tried to eat, he'd thrown it back up again. Luckily, Makenna had left on Sunday evening before he'd lost the soup and crackers she'd brought him. Aches racked his body like he really had been sick, and he'd had a non-stop headache since Friday night that made it hard to think.

All of which was why he was hoofing it up the steps. In the lobby, he'd stood in front of the open elevator door for a long moment before his central nervous system had threatened a full-on lock-down, and he'd known he just couldn't get in that little box. No matter how short a ride it would be. *That's* how out of control his bullshit was right now.

The last twenty-four hours had been his first shift back to work, and getting out of bed to get his ass down to the station had taken Herculean effort. Not to mention making it through the shift itself. It felt like he was walking through molasses-filled air that made his limbs heavy and his muscles tired.

He'd finally given in and made an appointment with his doctor.

As he stepped out into the fifth-floor hallway, Caden recalled feeling this bad once before.

When he'd been eighteen. During the weeks leading up to high school graduation, when he hadn't yet known exactly what he was going to do with his life but had at least known he couldn't keep living with his bitter shell of a father. The uncertainty of the situation and his father's near-total abdication of parental responsibility for or interest in Caden had been bad enough. But it was also what would've been Sean's sixteenth birthday, and the combination sent Caden into a downward spiral that had ultimately resulted in a diagnosis of depression.

And *fuck* if Caden wasn't feeling the similarities with that time more than he wanted to admit.

It felt like such a colossal defeat after having held himself together for so long. And now *everything* seemed to be coming apart at the seams.

It was all almost more than he could bear. And didn't that make him feel weak and worthless. He was better than this. He *should* be better than this. Sonofabitch.

He slid his key into the lock on the apartment door, eager to see Makenna. It had helped seeing her Sunday night, when she'd been so sweet as to bring him that care package. She was the light to Caden's darkness and had been since they'd been trapped in that elevator. If anyone could take some of the weight off his shoulders, if anyone could make it easier for him to breathe, it would be her.

Stepping into the apartment, he was instantly surrounded by the rich, spicy smell of tomato sauce, and for the first time in days, he actually felt hungry. "Red? I'm home," he called.

Makenna rushed out of her bedroom, wearing a pair of jeans and a blue sweater and the most beautiful smile. "There you are," she said, rushing right up to him. She flung her arms around his neck. "God, I've missed you."

"I missed you, too," he said, reveling in the press of her soft heat against all his cold hardness.

Loosening her hold, she pushed onto tiptoes and kissed him in a soft meeting of lips that quickly deepened to more. "Really missed you," she whispered.

Caden managed a little chuckle as he slid his hand into all that gorgeous red hair. "I can tell."

Makenna pulled back and gave him a smile. "Are you feeling better?"

He nodded, because what else was he going to do? And being with her did make him feel better, so it wasn't really a lie. "What smells so good?"

"I made spaghetti sauce and meatballs. All I have to do is cook the noodles and dinner will be ready. You hungry?"

"I could eat," he said. He'd kept down the small cup of corn chowder he'd eaten for lunch at the firehouse, so he was hopeful that his body would let him have this.

"Good," she said, slipping away to the stove. She turned on the burner under a big pot. "Make yourself comfortable. Everything will be ready in less than fifteen."

"Okay," he said, heading for the bedroom. He changed out of his uniform into a pair of jeans and a T-shirt, and then he sagged down to sit on the edge of the bed. Exhaustion settled over him like a lead blanket. God, what was wrong with him?

You know what's wrong, Grayson.

Yeah, he probably did. Goddamnit.

But for the next few hours, he was going to let all that go and just be with Makenna. If that was possible. He hauled himself off the bed and returned to the kitchen to help get dinner ready. Soon, they were seated at the table with mounding servings of spaghetti, sauce, and meatballs. Crusty, warm garlic bread filled a little basket, and Caden took a big piece for himself.

"This looks fantastic," he said.

"Good. Eat up. There's tons left," she said.

They dug in and ate in silence for a while—which was really unusual for Makenna. She'd always been the one initiating conversation or keeping it going. The talkative yin to his quiet yang.

Looking at her, he asked, "How was your day?"

"Oh." She looked up. Gave a little shrug and a nervous laugh. "The usual," she said, waving her fork.

Since he was the king of nervous awkwardness, he recognized it when he saw it. "Is everything okay?"

She scoffed. "Yeah. Of course." Her smile was just a watt too forced.

He arched an eyebrow and nailed her with a stare.

"Okay, fine," she said, setting her fork down. "I have some things I'd like to talk about, but I was trying to wait until we were done eating."

Caden didn't love the sound of that. He set his fork down, too. "What do you want to talk about?"

She heaved a deep breath, like she was bolstering herself for what she had to say. A boulder parked itself in his gut. "So, I have an idea. We've pretty much been living together for the last two-plus months, right?" He nodded, wariness clawing over his skin. "And I've been wondering why you're keeping your place because you're always here

—which I love, but it's a waste of money, really. But when I was at your house the other night, it occurred to me that if we were going to think about fully moving in together, it would make more sense to move into your house since it's bigger. And then I'd get rid of this place." The words spilled out of her in a rush.

He stared at her for a long moment, his brain struggling to catch up, to process. "You want to move into the townhouse with me?"

"Well." Makenna gave a shy little shrug, one that revealed just how much she wanted it. "I've just been thinking about it."

Caden swallowed around a constriction in his throat. She wanted to move in together. Permanently. For a moment, it felt like maybe there wasn't enough air, but he forced a couple of deep breaths. The idea wasn't *that* big of a deal since they'd pretty much been living together. Right? Though, it took things to a whole other level. And it also took away his ability to retreat into his own space if he fell apart like he had this weekend. That realization sunk tension deep into his shoulders.

"Makes sense, I guess," he managed. "Let's think about it and decide what's best."

She twisted her lips. "Okay," she said. "It just doesn't seem to make as much sense to keep a smaller place when you have such a nice house right by where you work."

He braced his elbows on the table and clasped his hands together. And tried to ignore the pool of anxiety threatening to bubble up inside him. "Although it's further away from yours."

"True, but I don't mind," she said, her hands fidgeting on the table top.

"Well, like I said, let's think about it. Your place is a lot homier than mine."

Makenna smiled and waved a hand. "That's just because you haven't decorated much. But once we moved some of my furniture in and maybe did some painting and hung some pictures, your place would be homey, too. Your townhouse is great, Caden."

Tightness parked itself in the center of his chest. Why was she pushing on this right now? And why did it make him feel like the walls were closing in on him? "Okay," he said, picking up his plate and getting up from the table. "Dinner was great, by the way. Thank you." He walked into the kitchen, needing space so he didn't flip out when his stress really had nothing to do with her or her idea. He was just in a bad fucking place to be thinking about permanence, which made him feel like an asshole.

She followed him. "Gah, I'm going about this all wrong."

"Going about what?" he said, that rock getting a little bigger in his gut.

Makenna closed the distance between them, her hands falling on his chest, her baby blues looking up at him with so much affection. For a moment, she appeared to struggle for words, and then she said, "God, I'm being a tongue-tied idiot right now."

"Whatever you have to say, just say it," he said, dread prickling like ice all down his spine. Her unusual nervousness spiked the anxiety inside him and tightened the knot in his chest, making his breathing shallow out.

"Okay. Here goes. Caden, I…I love you. I love you so much that I can barely remember my life before you. I love you so much that I can't imagine my life without you. I've been dying to tell you, but I know we haven't been together that long. Though, to me, the number of weeks that I've known you feels completely meaningless to how attached my heart has become," she said, her voice urgent and so damn earnest. "I love you. And I'm *in* love with you. That's what I really wanted to say."

He heard the words as if through a long tunnel. They came to him slow and detached, as if his brain had to translate them from some other language to one he could understand, to one he could trust.

Makenna loved him.

Makenna had said the words. Words her actions had been communicating for weeks. Hell, maybe more.

The gates that held back the darkness in his psyche had been badly battered the past few days, and hearing her declaration destroyed what was left of them. All his fears, all his doubts, all his insecurities came rushing forth until he was drowning, suffocating, going under fast.

On the face of it, his reaction made no sense because she'd given him what he wanted—her love, her commitment. But it was getting what he wanted that made him so afraid.

Because deep inside, he was the fourteen-year-old boy who believed he should've died so his twelve-year-old brother—the best friend he'd ever had—could live. He was the kid sick with survivors' guilt who desperately wanted his father to acknowledge him instead of *choosing* to abandon him. He was a man who'd been taught that life didn't give you what you wanted, or if it did, it took it away again.

The past. Anxiety. Fucked-up fears. Caden knew it, but he couldn't fight it. His heart wasn't whole. His feet weren't steady. His brain wasn't right.

He wasn't right. And in that state, he didn't trust himself with loving her.

He grasped her hands and pulled them away from his chest. "Makenna, I—" But no further words came out, because it was like his brain had frozen. He knew what he felt, but he didn't know what to say. How to put it into words, or whether he even should. He was fucking paralyzed.

"You don't have to say it back," she said, something sad and maybe even a little disappointed flashing through her eyes. "I didn't say it with an expectation that you would say it back."

So she'd expected him to fail her. And that's what he was doing. Like he needed more proof that she deserved better.

He gasped a breath, all the stress of the past week crashing down on him like a ton of bricks. Or maybe it was more like a house of cards, because in this moment Caden felt like a fucking fool to have ever believed that he was capable of being one of two when his half of that equation was so damn damaged.

"Makenna, it's just, this is all..." Shaking his head, he stepped back, out of her grasp. His skin was suddenly too sensitive to allow her touch. Hell, the clothes on his back felt too rough, too heavy, too confining. "It's just a lot. It's just fast," he said, not even sure of the words coming out of his mouth.

A look of hurt flashed across her pretty face, and even though she tried to hide it, tried to recover, he knew what he'd seen. "It doesn't have to mean anything—"

"Yes, it does," he bit out, hating that his emotional bullshit was making her discount her feelings. To try to make him feel better. "It means fucking everything." He grasped at his chest, the lack of oxygen setting off a burn right in the center. His head throbbed out a punishing downbeat.

"Caden—"

"I'm sorry," he said, wincing as he tried to suck in a deep breath. "I can't...I gotta...go. I just need some space. Okay? Some time?" His fight or flight instinct was kicking him in the ass. Hard. "I...just need some space. I'm sorry."

Then he was out the door, his whole world imploding around him. Because he'd probably just destroyed the best thing he'd ever had. But maybe that was as it should be, since he clearly couldn't handle it anyway.

And Makenna deserved someone who could.

CHAPTER THIRTEEN

*M*akenna stared at her apartment door, the sound of it closing still echoing loudly all around her. What the hell just happened?

She clutched her stomach, just that moment realizing she'd never even gotten to the point of telling Caden about the baby. And, Christ, how was she supposed to do that now? When hearing that she loved him sent him into a full-out panic attack. Never in all the time she'd known him had she ever seen his face go so pale and distant and just...blank out like that. Like she was looking at a shell of the man she knew.

Given how marked by abandonment he was, she'd always worried that hearing her say she loved him might trigger his anxiety. But she never thought it would be this bad.

On instinct, she dashed for the door and wrenched it open, but the hall was empty. She sagged against the door jamb and stared at the emptiness.

Every urge within her told her to run after him. But he'd asked for time and space. Would going after him make things worse? Would it push him away? Was it worth the risk?

The thing was, Makenna understood a lot about how Caden

reacted to things. And, after doing some reading on the subject, she understood a lot about how his anxiety and PTSD worked—that didn't mean she always knew how to handle it, and she certainly had no imaginings that she could fix it, but she understood that he faced these struggles. Hell, his need for a distraction from his claustro-phobia and anxiety was what had led them to get to know each other in the first place.

And she didn't love him *despite* of all of his issues, she loved him *because* of them. Or, rather, because they were part of who he was. And she loved who he was. With everything she had.

Which meant she should probably give him the space he needed. Even if it left her heart an aching, bruised mess.

She walked back into her kitchen and let the door fall closed behind her.

Dropping her head into her hands, Makenna fought back tears. She'd gone about that conversation all wrong. At the table, she'd gotten nervous about the big things she had to tell him so she'd blun-dered into the conversation about moving in together. Which no doubt must've seemed to Caden like it came from out of left field. And then she'd piled on her feelings.

"Okay, don't panic," she said to herself. Her words sounding loud in the quiet space. "He'll be fine. We'll be fine." She just had to keep telling herself that for however long he needed.

Desperate to keep busy, she mechanically worked through putting the sauce and meatballs into bowls for lunch and to freeze, and then she dove into doing the dishes.

When she was done, she gave in to the yearning inside her and sent Caden just one text:

Take as much time and space as you need. I'll be here no matter how long that is. xo

She hit *Send* and then went to bed, hoping against hope that he'd feel better in the morning.

But the morning didn't bring any word from Caden. Nor did the afternoon, or the next night. Or any day that week. By Friday night, Makenna was a wreck of worry and heartache. She couldn't bring herself to go home and face her empty apartment. She was worried for him that he was in such a bad place, and she was worried for herself that it might be so bad he'd never make his way back to her.

And she didn't know what to do.

So she went back to her apartment building to get her car. She wasn't sure where she was going or what she was even thinking. Or maybe that was just kidding herself. Because within twenty-five minutes, she was driving down Caden's street, and then past his small cul-de-sac. She slowed down enough to see that his place was dark and his Jeep wasn't parked in its usual spot. So next she made her way to the Station 7 Firehouse just a few blocks away.

His Jeep wasn't there either.

Her car idling along the curb on the far side of the street, Makenna stared at the building, a golden glow spilling out into the street from some of the windows.

Part of her was sorely tempted to go in and see if any of the guys knew where she might find him. Or at least knew how he was. Had he even been going to work? But another part of her worried that going to his job to ask after him was crossing a line. Certainly a line that violated his request for space, and possibly one that could impact his livelihood.

She couldn't bring herself to do it...but maybe she could call one of the guys she'd gotten to know a little better. Isaac Barrett! He'd come to her house one night for dinner with Caden and a few of the other guys, he'd often made a point of talking to her when she'd come out to the station's softball games earlier in the fall, and he'd given her a big hug when she'd dropped cookies and brownies off at the firehouse. She wouldn't call them close, but maybe close enough to ask a couple hopefully casual-sounding questions.

Luckily, she had his cell phone number from when he'd RSVP'd for that dinner. She found it in her contacts and pressed *Send*.

Two rings, then, "Hello? Bear here."

"Bear, it's Makenna James, Caden's—" She momentarily got tripped up on what to call herself given what was going on between them. "—uh, girlfriend."

"Makenna of the wonderful brownies," he said. "To what do I owe this pleasure?"

"Hey, I'm sorry to bother you but I was wondering if you might know where Caden is." There. That sounded casual. Right?

"Gimme a second," he said. Muffled words she couldn't make out sounded in the background, and then a door closed. "I'm back. So, Caden took a leave of absence. Didn't you know?"

A leave of absence? Makenna's belly slowly sank as a feeling of dread spread through her. Caden was so dedicated to his job, so much so that it seemed more like a calling to him. She couldn't imagine him walking away from it. Unless he absolutely had to. "Unfortunately, no."

"Is he okay, Makenna?" Bear asked. "His last coupla shifts, he was running way ragged."

"He'd been sick," she said. "But, I don't know, maybe there's something else."

"Yeah," Bear said in a knowing voice. "I hope everything's okay."

"So do I," she said, her throat suddenly thick with tears. "If you hear from him, is there any chance you'd let me know? I'm...well, I'm worried."

"Count on it," Bear said. They hung up.

Sitting in her car in the darkness, Makenna finally gave into the tears she'd been holding back all week.

---

*H*is Jeep parked in a spot behind Makenna's building, Caden didn't know what he was doing there. His head and his heart were still a fucked-up wreck, and he had no idea what he'd even say if he saw her. He had no more clarity, no more certainty, no more faith in himself than when he'd left there Tuesday night. And the last thing he wanted to do was hurt her more than he'd undoubtedly already done.

All he knew was that he'd been drifting through life for days— more ghost than human—until he'd finally gravitated there.

Like she was the sun to his dark planet.

Not at all sure he was doing the right thing—for her—he hauled his ass out of the Jeep and made his way to her place. By the stairs again, *offuckingcourse*.

His head had gotten so bad that he'd not only admitted just how bad to his captain, but he'd taken a leave of absence. For the first time in nine years of doing this job, he didn't feel that he was fully competent, and the last thing he wanted was to make a mistake that would cost someone everything. He wouldn't be able to live with that.

And he was holding on by a very thin string.

He'd also given in and gone to the doctor for meds, and even went back to see his old therapist. Dr. Ward was in his late forties now, and his hair was a little grayer and his waistline a little wider, but otherwise, he looked pretty much like Caden remembered.

So far, Caden had only had one session with the guy, and it had worsened his nightmares. Talking had always been like that for him—stirring shit up so that it got worse before it got better. But he had to try something. Because feeling like this wasn't tenable.

When Caden got to the apartment door, he knocked. Waited. Knocked again. He had a key, of course, but given how he'd left things on Tuesday night, he thought he owed her the respect of knocking. When she still didn't answer after knocking a third time, he let himself in.

Everything was quiet and dark—only the under-counter lamp in the kitchen threw off any light.

Caden heaved a deep breath. An ache ballooned inside his chest. An ache for Makenna. He missed her something fierce. It felt like a part of himself had been ripped away, the edges still jagged and raw. But that's what he was—all jagged, raw, festering wounds from one loss after another.

And it didn't seem like a single one of them had healed.

He wandered through the darkness and into her bedroom. He sat down on the bed. Makenna's scent was stronger here. Her vanilla skin lotion. Her strawberry shampoo. The coconut hand cream she rubbed on before bed each night. He breathed those hints of her in, needing to carry some small part of her with him.

Knock, knock, knock.

Frowning, Caden forced himself up and to the front door. A quick peak through the spyhole revealed a delivery man of some sort. Caden opened the door.

"Makenna James?" the delivery man said. At his feet sat a huge vase of red roses.

"She's not home," Caden said, staring at the flowers.

"Would you please sign for me then, sir?" He thrust a clipboard at Caden, who scrawled an unintelligible line at the X. The guy retreated down the hall.

Caden bent down and grasped the crystal vase. Carried it to the kitchen counter, the door slamming closed behind him. Placed it down. And stared some more—at the little envelope sitting among the fat, red blooms.

With a sinking feeling in his gut, he pulled the envelope free and opened it. The card read:

Take as much time as you need. I'll be here. And I love you. ~CH

CH. Cameron Hollander. Sonofafuckingbitch.

Without returning the card to the envelope, Caden slipped both back into the plastic holder, his gaze glued to the other man's words.

Caden hadn't been able to deal with Makenna saying she loved him and hadn't been able to give her the words back, yet here was Cameron giving them to her again and again. Which was exactly what Makenna deserved.

Jesus Christ. Hands braced against the counter, Caden found himself having to breathe through a sudden clenching tightness in his chest.

Makenna deserved...someone like Cameron. Someone whole, someone unbroken, someone with his shit together. Caden was not that man. Hell, right now, Caden wasn't even the man Makenna had met in that damn elevator. At best, he was a ghost of his former self, and that guy hadn't even been fully squared away.

Maybe Makenna didn't want Cameron like she once did, but she deserved someone who could do what Cameron could—and what Caden couldn't.

And that was all Caden needed to know.

Disappointment and frustration and sadness and anger whirled inside him. He forced himself away from those fucking flowers before he hurled them across the room just for the satisfaction of seeing them shattered and broken—a mirror of how he felt inside.

Not quite sure what he was doing, he stalked back to the bedroom. Flicked on the light. Stood there. On the nightstand next to his side of the bed lay a military thriller he'd been reading a few pages at a time before going to sleep.

He grabbed it.

Suddenly, he was grabbing everything of his that was there. Uniforms. Clothes. Shoes. Toiletries. He didn't deserve to be in Makenna's life, not when he couldn't give her what she needed, what she wanted, and what she deserved. He had to do the right thing. For her.

His chest in a vise, he stuffed all of his belongings into a black trash bag.

Standing in the middle of the kitchen, he stared at the fucking flowers one last time. And then he left a note—and his apartment key —on the counter beside them.

CHAPTER FOURTEEN

a little after ten o'clock, Makenna finally made her way home. After leaving the firehouse, she'd driven to her favorite Mexican restaurant and had dinner sitting at the bar—a table for one just feeling more depressing than she could stand. Next, she'd gone to the bookstore for a while, but finally left when she realized she was browsing the bargain books for thrillers Caden might like.

Opening the apartment door, the first thing she noticed was that the overhead kitchen light was on. As was her bedroom light. "Caden?" Her heart swelled inside her chest as an ocean of sheer relief rushed through her. "Caden?" she called again as she hurried back to the bedroom.

But the place was empty.

She returned to the kitchen. Because the second thing she'd noticed was a huge vase of roses sitting on the counter. Among the blooms, she could just make out the words, *I love you. ~C*

"Oh, God," she said, her throat going tight. Caden had been there. He'd come to tell her he loved her. And all the while she'd been avoiding coming home.

Makenna pulled the card from the plastic holder. And her stomach dropped to the floor.

Take as much time as you need. I'll be here. And I love you. ~CH

CH. Freaking Cameron. Crap.

Makenna's shoulders sagged. Not Caden. Not Caden, after all.

And then she noticed something else.

A note next to the vase. Dread skittered over her skin as she lifted and read it.

You may not want him, but you deserve more than me.

It wasn't signed, but she didn't need it to be. Makenna recognized Caden's handwriting. And beneath the note lay his apartment key.

Caden *had* been there.

She frowned, her thoughts racing. *You deserve more than me?* What did that even mean? And why did he relate it to Cameron, whose card he'd obviously opened and read? And why had he left his key?

Dread wrapped around her now like a second skin. Caden's note and key clutched tightly in her hand, she walked back to the bedroom. Slowly, tentatively, like something might jump out at her. She wasn't sure what she was looking for as she stepped into the room. Everything looked the same as when she'd left this morning.

Then Makenna walked into the bathroom. It only took a split second for her to notice what was different. Her toiletries were the only ones on the counter. His toothbrush, toothpaste, and razor were gone. She opened the medicine cabinet. His floss, mouthwash, and shaving cream were gone. Pulling back the shower curtain revealed that his body wash was no longer there.

A raw ache settled into her chest. "No," she said, rushing into the bedroom again. "No, no, no." She flung open the walk-in closet door. Caden was a pretty basic guy when it came to clothes. A few pair of jeans, a few shirts, his uniforms. So he'd never taken up much space in her closet. But what space his things had taken was now vacated. His clothes and shoes were gone.

"No, Caden, no," she said, tears straining her voice. *Don't give up. Don't give up on us.* "Damnit."

Makenna raced back to the kitchen and fished her cell from her purse. She called Caden. Again and again it went to voicemail until she finally gave in and left a message. "Caden, please talk to me.

What's going on? I don't understand. I'm here for you. Please just let me in. Whatever it is, we can fix it." She debated for a long moment, and then she added, "I love you."

She pressed *End* and hugged the phone to her chest.

Numbness settled over her. Numbness and denial.

Without getting changed, she laid down on her bed, phone in hand. *Call me. Call me. Call me.*

The next time she opened her eyes, the first gray light of day spilled through her windows. She woke up her phone to see she hadn't missed any calls or texts.

He'd packed up and walked out of her life, and he wasn't returning her messages.

As Makenna lay there in the darkness, she couldn't help but face the truth of what was happening. What *had* happened. Caden had left her because he thought she deserved something more than him. Caden had left her because he didn't think he was enough for her. How many times had he said something along those lines? And he was still saying it, despite the fact that she'd told him she loved him, that she was *in love* with him, and that she couldn't imagine her life without him.

If those sentiments weren't enough to make him believe that she wanted him—wanted *them*—she didn't know what else she could possibly say or do to convince him.

Makenna's numbness wore off in a cold rush.

Pain lanced through her blood until she was consumed by it. Her heart. Her head. Her soul. Curling into a ball, she sobbed into her pillow. She cried for herself. She cried for Caden. She cried for what they'd been—and everything they could've been still.

And then she thought of the baby—and of the fact that Caden didn't even know it existed—and she cried for the little life they'd made, too.

What was she going to do?

What were *they* going to do? Her and the baby.

She didn't know. Not yet. But she was going to have to figure it out. She was going to have to be strong for her son or daughter. And for herself.

And she would. But today she was going to let herself grieve. Because it wasn't every day that she lost the love of her life.

CHAPTER FIFTEEN

*A*ll weekend, every time Caden woke up, he played Makenna's voicemail.

Caden, please talk to me. What's going on? I don't understand. I'm here for you. Please just let me in. Whatever it is, we can fix it. Pause. *I love you.*

He dragged the little arrow backward with his thumb. *I love you.*

And again. *I love you.*

And again. *I love you.*

CHAPTER SIXTEEN

*C*aden couldn't do anything but sleep. Even though nightmares tormented him. Even though his muscles ached from lack of use. Even though life passed him by.

Although that hardly seemed to matter. Ghosts weren't alive anyway.

Every so often, he got up long enough to take a piss, choke down his meds, and stare aimlessly into his refrigerator. Sometimes he ate. Sometimes he watched television.

But then his thoughts and his fears and his failures became too painful to endure.

So he went back to bed.

CHAPTER SEVENTEEN

*T*he banging wouldn't fucking stop.

At first Caden thought it was his head, which would've been par for the goddamned course, but then he heard someone shouting his name. Over and over and fucking over.

Dragging himself from bed was an effort he barely had the energy to make. He shuffled out of his room and down the steps, his legs feeling weak, his muscles aching from disuse.

He looked through the spyhole. "Fuck," he bit out.

"I'm not leaving until you open this door," his captain yelled. "I'll break it down if I have to."

Pound, pound, pound.

Caden knew Joe Flaherty enough to know he was good to his word. And that he'd broken down more than one door in his career as a firefighter.

Kicking aside the big pile of mail that had collected on the floor under the mail slot, Caden unlocked and opened the door, just a little. "Captain. What can I do for you?"

"Let me the hell in," Joe said, pushing the door open further and stepping in to Caden's living room. "Jesus fucking Christ, Grayson." The older man stared at him, his expression shocked.

Caden looked down at himself, at his bare chest and stomach and the dark gray sweatpants hanging loosely on his hips. "What?"

Joe's eyes widened. "What? *What?* Are you telling me you don't know you're a goddamned skeleton?" He raked his hand through his graying hair. "I called. Over and over. But I knew I should've come sooner."

Confused, Caden shook his head. "I don't...I'm sorry...what—"

"Do you have any idea what day it is?" Joe asked, hands planted on his hips.

Caden thought about it. And thought some more. He tried to remember the last time he knew what day it was. He'd left Makenna's on a Friday. And then slept for days. He'd tried to get up for an appointment with his therapist, but hadn't been up to it. That had been on a...Thursday? And he'd been up some other times for a bite to eat or to stare mindlessly at the television. But...uh, no. He had no idea. Rubbing his hand over his scar, he shrugged.

Joe turned on the lamp beside the couch and sat heavily. "Sit down, Caden."

Frowning, Caden shuffled to the couch. Sat. Braced his elbows on his knees. God, his head was heavy.

"What's going on?" Joe asked, his face a mask of concern.

Caden shook his head. "Nothing."

The other man's expression slid into a scowl. "Do I need to take you to the emergency room? Because I will haul your ass out of here in a heartbeat—"

"What? No." Caden scrubbed his hands over his face. "I know I'm off right now, but I'm...I'll..." He shrugged again, not knowing what to say. He'd walked out on Makenna mid-spiral and hadn't been able to do anything but hold on until he hit bottom. Was he there yet? Hell if he knew. Although he could hardly imagine feeling much worse than he did just then. Physically, emotionally, mentally.

Everything fucking *hurt*, like he was agony personified.

"You're off? You're not off, Caden. You're clinically depressed, if I had to guess. And looking at you, I really don't need to do that. What have you lost? Twenty pounds? Thirty? Jesus. When was the last time you ate?"

"I...I don't...I can't keep anything down." Caden dropped his gaze to the floor. "But I'm not hungry anyway."

"Of course you're not. That's the depression. Fuck, I'm sorry I didn't come sooner. I should've known..." Joe heaved a breath. "How bad is it?"

Caden kept his eyes down. Really bad. Way worse than it'd been when he was eighteen. Or maybe he was misremembering just how empty and painful and isolating and pointless and worthless depression had previously made him feel. "Bad," he said, his voice little more than a whisper.

"Thoughts of hurting yourself bad?" Joe asked.

Humiliation roiling through his gut, Caden couldn't look Joe in the eye. Yeah, he had those thoughts. The ones that sometimes taunted him with the promise of freedom from all this fucking misery. He hadn't considered them seriously, but he couldn't deny having them.

"Shit. Okay. What are we going to do about this?"

"We?" Caden's gaze cut to his captain.

"Yeah, *we*. You think I'm leaving you alone like this? You're coming to my house today, and tomorrow you're either going to your doctor or to the hospital. And I'm taking your ass. And I'll keep taking you until you get this under control. In fact, I'll help you pack a bag. You're staying with me until we turn this thing around." Joe arched a brow and nailed him with a stare.

"Cap—"

"None of that's up for discussion, Grayson. In case that isn't clear." Joe glared at him, but it was a glare Caden had seen many times before, when something hadn't gone quite right on a call—one born of concern, and maybe even a little fear.

"Okay," Caden said, too tired to fight the man. "I got meds, but I've missed some."

"Did you take one today?" Joe asked. Caden shook his head. "Then do it. How long have you been on them?"

He'd gone back to his therapist the day before he'd walked out of Makenna's life. "The tenth, I think it was."

Joe nodded. "Good. That's good. Even if you've missed some, that's two weeks' worth of medicine. Fucking shame antidepressants take so long to build up in your system. But at least you have a jump on it."

"Wait," Caden said, frowning. "Two weeks?" His eyes went wide. "Shit. What day is it?" His leave of absence ended on the twenty-third so he could take shifts to let the guys with families have the Christmas holidays off.

His captain clasped him on the back of the neck and gave him a look filled with so much compassion that Caden actually got a little choked up. "It's Christmas, Caden."

Christmas? *Christmas?*

"Fuck," he said, shoving into a standing position. Adrenaline punched through his system, leaving him wired and wobbly. "I...I'm sorry...*fuck*...I can't believe...I missed...everything."

"Don't give it a second thought. That's how I knew something was wrong," Joe said, standing up beside him. "You've never missed a day of work in almost ten years until all this happened. And then Bear told me that Makenna had called a few weeks ago because she didn't know where you were. Knowing you'd checked out on work *and* her, I knew something was wrong."

Makenna.

Hearing her name out loud was like a punch to the gut. Caden pressed his fist against the jagged throb in his chest.

Makenna.

The sob came out of nowhere.

Caden slapped his hand over his mouth, horrified to fall apart in front of Joe, to show him just how weak he really was.

But it was like her name unlocked something inside him, and it felt like whatever it was had been the very last thing holding him together. "Fuck," Caden choked out, falling heavily to the couch. He dropped his face into his hands, a vain effort to hide the unhideable. His tears. His sobs. His grief.

His failure.

Joe was right there with him. Hand on his shoulder, the man sat beside him. "It'll get better. Just hang on. We'll get you through this."

When Caden could manage to talk again, he shook his head. "She's gone," he rasped, sliding his wet hands to cradle his throbbing forehead. "I...I fucked everything up."

"Don't worry about that. Worry about you. Fix you. Then you can work on whatever else you want. But it starts with you." Joe squeezed his shoulder. "And I'll be here to help."

Caden tilted his head to the side just enough to see Joe's face. "Why?"

His captain nailed him with a stare. "You really gotta ask?"

"Yeah," he rasped.

"Because you're a great part of my team, Caden. Excellent at what you do. More than that, after all these years, I consider you a friend. And if all that wasn't enough, you're a good fucking human being, and I'm not losing you to whatever bullshit lies your head is telling you. I know you don't have any family, so I'm officially stepping in and stepping up. I will fight for you until you can fight for yourself. You hear me?"

The words reached inside Caden's chest...and eased him. Not a lot. Not permanently. But enough to take a deep breath. Enough to let his shoulders loosen. Enough to begin to think beyond the next five minutes.

Caden respected the hell out of Joe Flaherty. Had for his entire adult life. And if Joe believed all that about Caden, maybe there was truth in what he said. And if Joe was willing to fight for Caden, maybe Caden could figure out how to fight for himself, too.

It starts with you.

That idea connected to something deep inside Caden. He didn't know what it was. He didn't know what it meant. But he grasped onto it, and he grasped onto Joe's support. Because he had to grasp on to something.

Before he lost himself forever.

CHAPTER EIGHTEEN

*M*akenna pulled her car into her father's driveway, her stomach a nervous, nauseous wreck. For once, that wasn't her morning sickness talking. It was the looming conversation she needed to have with her dad and brothers. The one that informed them she was pregnant and nearly twelve weeks along. And that the father was out of the picture.

Two weeks had passed since Caden had left his key. Two weeks since she'd left that voicemail. Two weeks of silence, although she had sent him a Christmas card. One last attempt to reach out.

No. Don't think about Caden.

Heaving a deep breath, she nodded to herself. She couldn't think of him without getting upset. And angry. And confused. And worried. None of which made her love him any less, though, which just made her so, so sad.

Enough. It's Christmas.

Right. It would've been their first.

The thought made her eyes sting.

She forced her gaze to the ceiling of her car, pinching off the threatening tears.

When she'd reined herself in, she retrieved the shopping bags of gifts from her back seat and made her way inside.

"There's my peanut," Dad said when she walked into the kitchen, the nickname making her throat tight. The smell of pancakes and bacon surrounded her—Dad had made the same thing for Christmas breakfast every year since forever.

"Hi," she managed. "Merry Christmas."

Patrick sat at the breakfast bar, the newspaper spread out in front of him and a coffee mug in his hand. "Merry Christmas," he said, an affectionate smile on his face. "Wondering when you were gonna get here."

"I know," she said, guilt eating at her. She'd never missed a Christmas Eve at home before, but the holiday had really hit her hard the day before and she'd just needed the time to herself. So she'd called and blamed her inability to make the trip on a bad headache. "I'm sorry I didn't make it yesterday."

"Feeling better?" her dad asked. She nodded. He wiped his hands on a tea towel and took her bags. "Let me help with these," he said, carrying them into the living room for her. She followed him in and was just about to comment on how pretty the Christmas tree looked when he turned with his arms wide open.

Swallowing the words, Makenna fell into his embrace, needing it like she hadn't needed a hug from her father in years. Needing the support and the protection and the unconditional love she'd always found in this man, who'd managed to give her and her brothers everything they needed in a family, even though they'd all lost their mother.

"Merry Christmas, Daddy," she said.

"It is now that all my kids are home." He put his arm around her shoulders and led her into the kitchen. "Hungry?'

"Famished, actually," and she was. Being here was good. Being here helped. It beat back the loneliness she'd been battling. It proved she wasn't alone, no matter what. It distracted her from her troubles. And it reminded her that, as much as she'd lost, she had so very much to be grateful for, too.

"Where are Collin and Ian?" she asked, bumping her shoulder against Patrick's. He pulled her into a one-armed hug.

"They were getting cleaned up. Should be down any minute," her dad said as he poured a few circles of batter onto the griddle.

"How's Caden? What's he doing today?" Patrick asked.

Makenna was prepared for this one. "Since he had Thanksgiving off, he had to work Christmas." At least that's what he'd said back at Thanksgiving. She wasn't sure if he was back to work or not. She hadn't let herself call Bear again, and he hadn't called her.

Patrick nodded. "I hear that. I'm on tonight, but at least I have the day."

Footsteps on the stairs sounded out, and then Collin and Ian joined them in the kitchen. Another round of hugs and greetings and Christmas wishes ensued.

"How are you feeling?" Makenna asked Collin. His hair had grown in enough to begin to cover the scar on the side of his forehead.

"Doing okay. Still having some headaches, but it's better than it was," he said. "I wish Caden had come. I would've liked to thank him for everything he did while I was actually with it."

Makenna hugged herself and forced a smile. "You did thank him. Anyway, he'd tell you he was just doing his job."

"Still," her father said, pointing with his spatula, "he made a bad night better. Him and Patrick both. I'll never forget that."

A knot of emotion lodged in Makenna's throat. "Can I have blueberries in my pancakes, Dad?"

"Heck, yeah. Blueberries, chocolate chips, M&Ms, whatever you kids want," her dad said with a laugh.

That set off a flurry of conversation about the pancakes that thankfully got them off of talking about Caden. Makenna ducked her head into the fridge as she looked for the blueberries and the strawberries Collin wanted.

Christmas breakfast was its usual fun and rowdy affair. They talked, joked, laughed. Her dad told stories from when they were kids, including a few about their mom. That was part of their tradition.

Their mother might not be with them anymore, but she was still a part of them. Her dad made sure of it.

And that was the moment it really hit Makenna that her baby was going to grow up without a parent just like she had.

She made a quick excuse and slipped away from the table, hoping her exit hadn't appeared as hurried as it felt. She made a beeline for the hall bathroom and locked herself inside. And damn if her first thought wasn't about the time she'd locked her and Caden inside the very same room so she could talk to him about Cameron.

She sagged back against the door, silent tears rolling down her face. She fought against them, knowing if she let the flood gates open she might not be able to close them again. Her quiet sniffles and shuddered breaths filled the room.

Maybe the baby wouldn't grow up without one of his parents. Maybe once she told Caden about the baby, he'd at least want to be involved in the kid's life.

Because she absolutely had to tell Caden. She knew that. And she planned to do it. The question was when. She hadn't told him yet because she'd been hoping he'd realize he made a mistake and come back to her—and if he did, she wanted it to be for *them*. Makenna and Caden. *Not* because she was pregnant with his baby.

So, at some point, she was going to have to talk to him again. To see him. At the very least, she wanted to give Caden the opportunity to see the baby during her next ultrasound. He deserved that. He deserved to be involved, to know his child.

That appointment wasn't for another six weeks, but Makenna was already excited because it was the one where she could learn the baby's sex. She'd already decided that she wanted to know. For some reason, when she thought about the baby, she always thought of him as a boy. Maternal instinct or pure randomness? She'd find out soon.

Pull it together, Makenna.

Right.

She cleaned up her face and took a deep breath, then walked out the door.

And nearly walked into Patrick, standing in the hallway. Arms crossed. Clearly waiting. "Wanna tell me what's wrong?" he asked.

Leave it to Patrick to realize something was wrong. "Nothing," she said, giving him a smile.

He arched an eyebrow, his frown deepening.

Makenna sighed. "Later."

"Promise?" he asked. She nodded, and he pulled her into his arms. "Whatever it is, I'm here for you."

A quick nod against his chest, and then she pulled away. "Come on. It's time for presents."

*L*ater came faster than Makenna hoped. Certainly faster than she was prepared for. Though, honestly, there was really no way to prepare for what she had to tell her family.

They'd exchanged presents. Watched *A Christmas Story*—because it really wasn't Christmas without Ralphie wanting a BB gun and shooting his eye out. Helped their dad make their traditional beef tenderloin dinner. And now that they'd eaten and dinner was all cleaned up, Patrick kept giving her that eyebrow.

If she didn't say something, he would.

"Can we all sit in the living room for a minute? I need to tell you guys something," Makenna finally said, her belly flipping.

"Is everything okay?" her dad asked, coming around the kitchen island to her.

"Yeah, but, can we just go sit down?" she asked.

The guys all gave her strange looks, but everyone followed her in and took seats around the room, Dad and Patrick on either side of her on the couch. The Christmas tree stood in front of the big window and threw off a multi-colored glow from the hundreds of lights strung through its branches. She'd missed decorating it yesterday, the day the James family had decorated its tree for as long as she could remember.

"What is it, Makenna?" her dad asked.

Makenna's heart thundered against her breastbone and a tingly nervousness fluttered through her. "So, I have some news."

Beside her, Patrick heaved a deep breath.

She met his gaze, and then her dad's, and then Collin's and Ian's. "I'm pregnant." Makenna nearly held her breath waiting for their reaction.

For a moment, no one said a thing, and then her father moved closer. "Um." A series of emotions flickered over his face. "A baby is, uh, pretty amazing news, Makenna. But why do I feel like there's more?"

She hugged herself and nodded. "Because—"

"What does Caden have to say about this?" Patrick asked, his expression as serious as a heart attack. His narrowed eyes had her feeling like he'd already pieced this story together. It was the damn police officer in him.

"He doesn't know," she said, giving him a look that pleaded for his support.

"*What?*" Ian said.

"Why not?" Collin asked.

Everyone started talking at once, and her father hushed them all. "Tell us what's going on," he said, taking her hand.

"Um." She swallowed around the lump in her throat and fought back the emotion threatening to overwhelm her. "So, we broke up a few weeks ago. I'm not really sure what happened, to be honest. Caden had been really sick and stayed at his house. And then when I saw him after he was better, he just seemed off. He said we were moving too fast for him, and that was it. I'd just found out that I was pregnant and in the midst of everything, I didn't have a chance to tell him. And then I didn't want to tell him if that was the thing that would make him come back."

His expression full of concern, her father nodded. "How far along are you?"

"Almost twelve weeks," she said. "I'm seeing a doctor and everything looks good."

"Are you going to tell him?" Collin asked. All three of her brothers wore the same look on their faces—part concerned, part angry, but trying to rein the latter in.

"Yeah," she said. "I'm going to invite him to my next ultrasound, which isn't for over a month."

"So, you're keeping it?" Ian asked. Only the gentleness of his tone kept her from flipping out on him.

"Of course, I'm keeping it. This is my baby, too." The one bright spot of certainty in all of this was knowing without question or reservation that she *wanted* this baby. No matter what, he'd been conceived in love. And she already loved him. And if this was the only part of Caden she got to have, she was holding on tight with both hands. "So, that's...that's my news," she managed.

"Aw, you're going to be an amazing mother," her dad said, wrapping his arm around her shoulders. "And we'll be here for you every step of the way."

The unconditional support beckoned the tears she'd been holding back. Finally sharing this news with her family took such a weight off her shoulders. "Thanks," she whispered.

"And I'm sorry about Caden," her dad said as he pressed a kiss to her forehead. "I know this isn't easy."

She gave a quick nod, sniffling. "I'm sorry, too."

"Do you want me to talk to him?" Patrick asked, sitting forward next to her.

"About?" she asked, studying her brother's face.

He braced his elbows on his knees. "Just feels like something doesn't add up, Makenna. The guy I met on Thanksgiving was *way* into you. Then two weeks later, he's just up and done?" Patrick shook his head. "Something doesn't add up. And I'd kind of like to know what it is since Caden's presumably going to be in your life whether you're together or not."

Makenna was torn, especially since his instincts were on the money. There was more to it. And it had to do with Caden's history. In saying she deserved more than him, he'd all but laid that out. But his pain felt too private to share with them, even if it would help explain hers. "Let me think about it," she said, scrubbing at her cheeks. "But I appreciate it."

"Okay," Patrick said, clearly unhappy not to get the go-ahead. "Just say the word."

"Dad's right," Ian said. "You're gonna be great, Makenna."

"Yeah," Collin said. "And we're gonna be the most awesome uncles ever."

That set off a round of jokes and plans for the baby that had Makenna crying again, this time with happy tears. "Thank you," she said, her cheeks hurting from smiling. "Thank you for being here for me."

"That's what family's for," her dad said. "No matter what."

"No matter what," Patrick said, nodding.

"Absolutely," Ian said.

"No matter what, Sis," Collin said. "Except for changing poopy diapers. That's all Patrick."

Of course, her brothers couldn't pass up a good opportunity to make jokes about poop, which had them all laughing again. The tension bled out of Makenna's shoulders as she shook her head at them and laughed along. She was going to be okay, because she had these four amazing men standing at her side.

But who did Caden have?

CHAPTER NINETEEN

The new year hadn't made Caden a new man, but at least he was eating more and showering regularly and basically fucking functioning. Thanks to Joe. And twice-a-week sessions the past three weeks with Dr. Ward. And the wonders of modern pharmaceuticals.

Most of the time, it felt like he was making a slow climb up a steep mountain carrying a big-ass rock on his back, but at least he was climbing. That was a victory in and of itself. And he was working on giving himself some credit. Baby steps, man, that's what he was all about these days.

Sitting on the bed in Joe's guest room, Caden dragged the cardboard box full of unopened mail in front of him. Joe had brought it over from Caden's house after his shift the evening before. Now that Caden was rocking out all this basic functioning, it was time for him to try to take care of a few other key parts of his life. Like paying his mortgage. And keeping the damn electricity current so his place would have heat. Last thing he needed was to come home from this little sojourn at Chez Flaherty to find his pipes burst and his basement flooded.

He sorted through the box. Bill, bill, bill. Junk, junk, junk. Magazine, magazine. An invitation to the wedding of one of the guys at the station. More bills, some of them stamped *Second Notice*. Tons of fucking junk. A Christmas card.

He did a double take at the return address.

A Christmas card from Makenna.

He stared at it for a long moment. He'd walked out on her...and she'd sent him a Christmas card?

His gut clenched. He flipped the envelope over. Stared at the sealed flap. And finally ripped through it.

The card actually made him smile—and he couldn't remember when he'd last done that. It had a picture of a miserable blond-haired boy wearing a pink bunny costume and read, *He looks like a deranged Easter bunny!*

From *The Christmas Story* movie. A freaking classic.

Leave it to Makenna.

As fast as he'd managed that smile, it slid back off his face. They could've watched that together, sharing stupid humor movies like they always had. More than that, they could've celebrated Christmas together. Their first. If Caden hadn't fallen the fuck apart.

How much more of his present and his future was he going to let his past destroy?

Fuck.

He heaved a deep breath. *Eyes on the prize, Grayson.* Getting better. Getting whole. Rebuilding his life. And making right all the things he'd done wrong.

Hesitating just one more moment, he opened the card. There was no printed text on the inside, just Makenna's looping handwriting.

Dear Caden,

I just wanted you to know that I'm thinking of you. And if you need me, I'm here for you. I can't say I understand what happened between us, only that I'm willing to listen. I don't deserve more than you, because there is nothing more than you for me.

I still love...that elevator.

Merry Christmas,

Makenna

Caden read it over and over until he had the words memorized. He could still hear her voice saying *I love that elevator* that very first night they'd met. After hours of being trapped in the elevator and the most incredible sex of his life, she'd invited him to stay the night with her. When they'd settled into each other's arms, she'd blurted out, *I love...* And then she'd covered herself by adding *that elevator.* Caden had thought it was cute. It had given him hope that maybe she was feeling him with the same crazy intensity that he'd been feeling her. And in the days and weeks that followed, that had seemed to be true.

Until, somewhere along the way, he'd stopped trusting himself, the situation, his happiness, and maybe even her. He knocked his numb-ass skull back against the headboard. In that moment, he wouldn't have been surprised if a cartoon lightbulb suddenly appeared over his head. He'd stopped trusting her...not to abandon him. And so he'd done the leaving.

He'd made his own worst fears come true.

Brilliant fucking job.

Blowing out a long breath, he rubbed his fingers over what she'd written. *There is nothing more than you for me.* Could she really believe that? And could he get himself to a place where he did, too?

He picked up the envelope and found the postmark—she'd sent the card on December twentieth. Almost four weeks ago. He knew it was expecting too much to hope she might wait for him, to wait for him to be better. Not just for her, but for both of them. Especially when she had no way of knowing that he was trying to find his way back to himself, so he might earn a chance to come back to her.

He looked at what she'd written again. Once, twice, he swallowed around a lump that had lodged in his throat, and then he whispered, "Aw, Red. I still love that elevator, too."

*T*he next week, Caden moved home and started back to work. He'd been off for almost six weeks and he was starting to go stir crazy sitting around Joe's house. It was time to get a life. His.

Truth be told, he was fucking nervous about walking back into the firehouse again. No doubt the rumors were flying about what had happened to him, especially given how bad a shape he'd been in those last few days on the job. And if the guys didn't have an idea of what might've been going on with him before, they'd probably get the gist just by looking at him—while he'd gained twelve pounds back so far, he was still down twenty from where he'd been at the beginning of December.

A shadow of his former self, maybe, but no longer a ghost.

Never again.

But his nerves would have to fucking suck it. Because he needed the work—not just for the money, but because he *needed* to help people. Right now, he was all about playing to his strengths, and doing his job had always been one. That much he could definitely give himself credit for.

He shouldn't have been worried.

To a man, they were nothing but happy to have him back. Even better, the day was a marathon of calls, one after the other, but it was smooth sailing all the way. Clocking out at the end of the shift made him feel ten feet tall. It had been just the confidence booster he needed.

And it gave him a little hope, too.

If he could get back on his feet at work, maybe, just maybe, that meant he could make things right in other parts of his life as well. Above all else, he wanted to make things right with Makenna.

Thinking of her made him ache, but less and less with unworthiness, guilt, and fear. No, this ache stemmed from the hollowness caused by their long separation, by her absence from his life. He missed her so bad that his chest often throbbed with it, like he'd left a part of himself in her hands. And he unquestionably had.

He just needed a little more time. A little more time to get himself right. A little more time to make peace with the past. A little more time to become the man that Makenna deserved and Caden wanted to be.

He just needed a little more time.

———

A few nights later, Caden was sitting at his kitchen table writing out bills and suddenly found himself staring at the dragon tattoo on the back of his right hand and arm.

He saw it every day, of course. But for some reason, he hadn't actually *seen it* in a very long time. He hadn't remembered why it was there.

The tattoo had been a declaration and a promise. A declaration to himself that he'd conquered his fears, and a promise to his brother, Sean, that Caden would be strong, that Caden wouldn't live his life in fear when Sean couldn't live his at all.

"I forgot to be the dragon, Sean. But I won't forget again," he said out loud.

Which gave him an idea.

He placed a call, got lucky making an appointment, and booked it out of the house. Caden made it to Heroic Ink within twenty minutes.

"Glad you called, man," Heath said, extending his hand. "Been slow as fucking molasses in here all day."

Caden returned the handshake. "This is win-win then because I really wanted to get in tonight."

"Well, come on back and let's rock and roll," Heath said. "Flying solo?"

"Yeah," Caden said, the reference to Makenna not making him sad and regretful—for once, but making him even more confident in what he was about to do. Because clearly, he was in need of a new reminder, a new declaration, a new promise. And ink had always been part of his process for coping and healing.

"So tell me what you're thinking," Heath said, gesturing to the chair at his station.

"It's text. I want it on my left forearm, big as you can make it." As he sat, he handed Heath a sheet of paper he'd written on in the Jeep.

Heath nodded. "Want any embellishments? Flowers? Ribbon? Flourishes. Have any thoughts on font?"

"I'm open. You know what looks good, and I always like what you come up with. Just so the words are bold and the most prominent thing about the piece, I'll be happy," Caden said.

"Gimme ten to pull something together," Heath said, opening up his laptop. It didn't even take ten minutes. "What about something like this?"

Caden's gaze ran over the design on the screen. It was different from anything he'd imagined, so naturally it was perfect. "Do it. Just like that."

The first dig of the needles into his skin was like a balm to his soul. He'd *always* loved the feeling of getting a tattoo. He *liked* the pain because it reminded him he was alive. Enduring it always made him feel stronger. And each new piece always left him feeling like he'd donned a new plate in the suit of armor he'd spent a lifetime creating.

This one was no different.

What Heath had designed was intricate, and good-looking lettering took time, so Caden was there a long while. But he was totally fucking content. For once. Even though tattoos on the forearm hurt like a mofo.

About two and a half hours later, Heath said, "All done."

Caden hadn't been watching because he wanted to wait for the full effect when the tat was done. Now, he looked.

Solid black cursive words sat at an angle on his forearm in groups of twos, reading from his wrist to his inner elbow:

One Life / One Chance / No Regrets

Open-faced red roses flanked the top and bottom of the words and wrapped around his arm, while red and black flourishes curved out from some of the letters and around the flowers. The center of the bottom rose morphed into a clock with Roman numerals to remind him that time was always ticking—and wasting, if you didn't play things right. The way Heath had combined the elements looked phenomenal.

Caden might've survived that accident fourteen years before, but he'd never really understood why. He'd never really felt he had anything specific to live *for*. Meeting Makenna had changed all that, even if Caden had been too mired in the past to see it at the time. But now that he was working so hard to get himself healthy again, he saw it with a clarity that was startling.

Caden wanted a chance for a life with Makenna. And though he knew there was a chance she wouldn't take him back after what he'd done, he at least had to try.

"Fantastic work as always, Heath. Thank you," Caden said.

"Anytime. I hope it gives you what you need," Heath said, leaning in to bandage the piece.

"Me too," Caden said. "Me too." And though so much remained uncertain, Caden couldn't help but marvel at how far he'd come these past six weeks. Because, sitting there in that chair with his arm on fire, Caden's soul felt lighter than it had in longer than he could remember because he'd renewed his commitment to Sean.

And, more importantly, to himself.

CHAPTER TWENTY

*L*ying in bed on his day off, something Caden's therapist had
said at his last session pinged around in his brain: *Find ways to
close the door on the past.*

Caden had been thinking about it for days, wanting to find a way
to do just that so he could start looking forward instead of always
looking back. It was the last thing he needed to figure out before he'd
feel ready to go after what he wanted.

Makenna James.

His gaze drifted to the stuffed bear on his nightstand, the one she'd
given him to make him feel better. All these weeks, he'd kept it close—
well, he hadn't slept with the damn thing because he was a twenty-
eight-year-old man, after all—but he liked having something she'd
touched close by.

And Makenna was what Caden most wanted. If she'd have him.
And who the hell knew. Given the way he'd bailed on her—abandoned
her, really, he might as well call a spade a fucking spade—he wouldn't
blame her for slamming the door in his face.

Dr. Ward's advice had stemmed from discussing Caden's realization that he'd let the past control him so much that he'd made his own
worst fears come true. The question was, what the hell did it mean to

close the door on the past? How was Caden supposed to do that? All the people involved in the accident that he'd let define his life were gone. And he'd never been one who'd found any answers or solace in talking to gravestones.

The only thing that left was the scene of the accident itself.

Caden had never once gone back. Had never even thought about it. Truth be told, it scared him more than a little.

Which was probably why he should do it.

He gave it one last thought, and then he hauled his ass out of bed, showered, and got dressed. In his spare bedroom, he rooted through boxes of his father's things looking for the file from the insurance investigation into the accident. His father had died last August, and Caden hadn't kept many of the man's belongings—only the paperwork related to settling the estate, family photo albums that Caden hadn't even known his old man still had, and a few things from around the house that Caden had always associated with his mother. What he'd wanted of Sean's belongings Caden had claimed years before.

Caden was on his fifth box when he found what he was looking for. He pulled the thick folder from a stack and flipped it open. His gaze skimmed over things Caden didn't really want to re-read in detail—the specifics of his mother's and brother's injuries, first and foremost—until he found the location information for the accident that had occurred along Route 50 in Wicomico County, Maryland.

Bingo. Time for his biggest—and hopefully last—journey into the past.

The ninety-minute ride to the general area flew by, probably because Caden wasn't looking forward to confronting what he had to confront, but it took longer to find the actual stretch of highway where his family had crashed.

The investigation file listed a mile marker, which was the first piece of information he had to narrow his search, and there were also pictures of the accident itself. He'd seen them—and the whole file— before. When he was sixteen, he'd found the file and read it cover to cover, needing every gory detail like a junkie needed a fix. Caden had thought knowing would help, but it had just provided fodder for his subconscious to twist into nightmares and guilt and fear.

So he didn't spend a lot of time looking at the photographs now—except to take note of the fact that the ditch and field where the car had landed were immediately after a long line of trees, which was part of what had kept anyone that night from seeing the over-turned car for so many hours.

First, Caden saw the mile marker, and then he found the tree line. He pulled the Jeep onto the side of the road. Sitting in the driver's seat, Caden surveyed the scene, but beyond his knowledge of the photographs, not a thing there looked familiar. And why would it? The accident had occurred late at night and, by the time daylight broke, Caden had been out of his mind.

Taking a deep breath, Caden got out of the Jeep and walked around to the grass. The irrigation ditch was still there, creating a deep slope downward just a few feet off the edge of the road. He climbed into it. Stood there. Crouched down and placed his hand against the frozen earth where two people he'd loved had died.

Not a day goes by that I don't think of you, Mom and Sean. I'm sorry I lost you. I love you. And I'm trying so damn hard to make you proud.

Closing his eyes, he let his head hang on his shoulders.

A tractor trailer roared past, and the sound of it was familiar enough to send cold chills down Caden's back. But Caden wasn't trapped in that car. He *wasn't*. Not anymore.

He rose to his feet and looked around for one last minute. There weren't any ghosts there. There weren't any answers there. The past wasn't there.

The realization brought both relief and frustration. Relief that he'd come to this place and found it to be...just a place. Just an ordinary roadside sitting under the winter gray sky. Frustration because going there hadn't brought him any closer to figuring out how to close the door on the past.

What else could give him any sense of closure?

Back in the Jeep, he flipped through the investigation file. A name caught his attention. David Talbot. The paramedic who'd been the first person Caden was aware of on the scene of the accident. What Caden most remembered about the man was the kindness of his voice, the reassurances he kept offering, the way he explained everything that was happening even though Caden hadn't really been capable of following it. The man's words had helped ground Caden after a long night of not knowing what was real, and Caden had always been convinced that David Talbot was the only thing that had kept him from going insane. And staying there.

Holy shit, why hadn't Caden thought of Talbot before? Would the guy even be around? Maybe it was a long shot after fourteen years, but Caden's gut said there was something to this idea. It certainly couldn't hurt.

A quick search on his smart phone revealed that Talbot's firehouse in Pittsville was only a few minutes away. Caden made his way there not knowing what to expect, or whether he should expect anything at all.

The Pittsville Volunteer Fire Department was a two-building complex with the main firehouse having five bay doors, all of which stood open. Yellow and white fire and E.M.S. apparatus occupied each bay, and a line of pick-up trucks filled the lot off to one side. Caden pulled his Jeep in line with the trucks and hopped out.

His pulse kicked up a notch as he approached the firehouse, and his chest filled with an odd pressure borne of anticipation. He stepped into the bay housing a heavy rescue truck and headed in the direction of voices, but something caught his eye. A big number 7 on the side of the truck.

Prickles ran over Caden's scalp. Pittsville's fire department was Station 7? The same number as the station he worked in. The same station number he had tattooed on his biceps. What were the fucking chances?

"Can I help you?" came a voice from further inside.

Caden turned to see an older man with a beard and moustache standing by the end of the truck. "Yeah, sorry. My name is Caden Grayson. I'm E.M.S. over in Arlington County, Virginia," he said, extending a hand to the other man.

"Well, how 'bout that. Welcome. I'm Bob Wilson," the man said as they shook. "What brings you over our way?" he asked with a smile. One of the things Caden loved about working in fire and E.M.S.—the community you could find with others in the same line of work.

"Something personal, actually. An accident that happened fourteen years ago." Anticipation made Caden's gut feel like he was riding a roller coaster about to crest the highest hill. "Any chance a paramedic named David Talbot is still around?"

"Dave? Hell, yeah. We tried getting rid of the guy but he just sticks to us like fleas on a dog." Bob smiled and winked.

"Shit, really?" Caden said, disbelief at this...*good luck* washing over him. "I knew it might be a long-shot."

"Nope. We're all pretty much long-timers here," Bob said, gesturing for Caden to follow. "Come on back. He's here. We had a call earlier, so you got lucky. Otherwise you woulda had to track him down at home."

As they made their way deeper into the big building, nervousness suddenly flooded through Caden's veins. The last time he and David Talbot had seen each other, Caden had been a wreck in every sense of the word. If anyone in Caden's life had seen him at his lowest, at his worst, at his most vulnerable, it was Talbot. Caden was so unprepared for the possibility of ever meeting this man—this man who represented such a positive force in Caden's life—that he wasn't sure what he was going to say.

Bob led them into the firehouse's dining room where eight men were sitting around the table talking and laughing, empty plates sitting in front of them. "Everyone," Bob said, "this is Caden Grayson. He's E.M.S. over in Arlington County, Virginia." A round of greetings rose up, and Caden gave a wave. "He came to see you, Dave."

Caden's gaze did a fast scan around the table, but he couldn't immediately identify Talbot. And then the man at the far end of the table turned to look at him, and Caden was suddenly sucked fourteen years into the past. When a man with a friendly face and a calming voice had put a traumatized fourteen-year-old kid at ease and saved his life.

"Me, huh?" Talbot said, rising and coming over to Caden. He extended a hand. "Dave Talbot. What can I do for you?"

Caden returned the shake, the oddest sense of déjà vu washing over him. "Well, Mr. Talbot, it's about what you've already done for me. Fourteen years ago, you were the first on the scene of a single-vehicle accident. And you saved my life."

What Caden needed to say was profoundly obvious, and he didn't even feel awkward about saying it in front of the other men who were all blatantly curious about what was going on.

"I know a long time has passed, but I need to say thank you. And I need to tell you that what you did for me that day made me want to help people, too. It's why I went E.M.S. I know we don't always get to know what happens to someone after we transport them to the hospital, so we don't get to know the impact we might've had. I wanted you to know that yours was huge. And I appreciate the hell out of it every day." Bone-deep satisfaction spread through Caden at getting to pay respect to this man after all this time.

You could've heard a pin drop in that room.

Dave was visibly moved by Caden's words. The older man studied Caden's face then looked at the scar that jagged along the side of his head. "Well, I'll be damned," Dave said, his voice strained. "Overturned station wagon?" he said, almost as if thinking out loud.

"Yeah," Caden said, a lump lodging in his throat.

"I remember you," Dave said, clasping Caden's arm. "It's a real pleasure to see you, son." He shook his head and cleared his throat, emotion plain on his face. "This is a helluva thing right now. Damn."

"I remember that call," another of the men said, coming around the table to join them. "Some of them stick with you, especially when there are kids involved, and that was one for me." The man extended a hand. "Frank Roberts. I was real sorry for what you went through."

"Frank," Caden said, returning the shake. "Thank you. That means a lot."

"I was on that one, too, said a white-haired man sitting at the table. Damn impressed that you're in this line of work after that accident. A lot of people wouldn't be able to do that. Wallace Hart, by the way," he said, giving a little wave.

Caden nodded, just about as gobsmacked as he could be that these men were not only still here but actually remembered him, too. Remembered what had happened. His father had never been willing to discuss the accident. Hell, his father had barely talked to Caden beyond that which was strictly required for basic life logistics, so to find people after all this time who'd been there, who knew what'd happened, who'd known Caden then. Dave was right. That *was* a helluva thing.

"You have time to sit?" Dave asked. "I could grab you a cup of coffee. And we have pie."

A little overcome by their reaction to him, Caden nodded. "Does anyone say no to pie?"

"Not if they're in their right fucking mind," Frank said to a round of laughter.

Some of the men cleared out, leaving Caden, Dave, Frank, and Wallace at the table. The other three men all had a good twenty or more years on Caden, which maybe explained why they talked to and looked at him in almost a fatherly way. They asked about the aftermath of the accident, about what he'd done after school, about his training and station, and about his personal life—whether he had a family of his own.

"Not yet," Caden said, finishing the last bite of his apple pie. "Truth be told, I had someone, but I messed it up. I've struggled with PTSD and anxiety ever since the accident, and I let it get the best of me. I've been working on how to make it right. How to make *myself* right. I guess that's what led me here." It felt right to be honest with them. And, frankly, he was in the middle of a more meaningful conversation about his life than any he'd ever had with his own old man.

Sitting next to him, Dave nailed Caden with a stare. "Let me tell you something, Caden." He paused for a long moment. "We talked about you around here. Those of us on that call, we were all affected by what we encountered out there that morning, and we talked about it more than once. I'll tell you straight, every single one of us was surprised as hell that you survived that accident. Your father, too, though the rear section of the car was in the worst shape. I can still picture how flattened it was. Like it had gone through a compactor." The other men nodded. "Whatever difficulties you've faced, I imagine you came by them honestly after that. But you need to know that you surviving, that was a miracle to my mind."

"Yeah," Frank said. "You were damn lucky." Wallace nodded.

Lucky.

For so long, Caden hadn't believed such a thing existed, not for him. And here these men all agreed that's what he'd been. Had he been looking at it wrong all these years?

Emotion clogged Caden's throat and momentarily stole his ability to speak. He nodded. "I appreciate that because...because sometimes I've had to ask myself why I survived when my mother and brother didn't." He shook his head.

"It's the wrong question," Dave said. "A better one is, what happened *because* you survived? And I'll tell you. Because you survived, you went on to become a paramedic. And what you did today for me, by coming in here and telling me what my help meant to you? There are people out there who feel the same way about you. You may never meet them—hell, you probably won't, that's the nature of the thing—but they're out there for you just like you were for me. And I want to thank you for that, for what you said. Because this job makes you confront a lot of hard things and it takes you away from your family at all hours and it puts you in harm's way, so it's good to know that what I do—what we all do," he said, gesturing at all of them seated there, "matters."

"Amen to that," Wallace said, raising his coffee cup and taking a swig.

As Dave's words sank in, Caden felt a little like he'd walked cartoon-like into a pole he hadn't seen coming. The idea that Caden might matter to someone as much as Dave did to Caden, the idea that what Caden did for his patients might impact them the same way Dave's care had impacted Caden all those years ago...it was fucking *revelatory.*

His scalp prickled and his heart raced. All these years that Caden had wasted feeling worthless and guilty, wondering what the point of his surviving had been, he'd always thought of his work as paying a debt he owed. And there was truth in that. But there was truth in what Dave said, too.

What Caden did mattered to a lot of people.

Which meant that *he* mattered, whether he felt it or not.

Damn. *Damn.*

That idea parked itself on Caden's chest like a thirty-ton ladder truck. That shit wasn't going *anywhere.*

It was like sunlight breaking through heavy black clouds, the golden rays streaming in and touching everything in their paths. Illuminating things that had been dark for so long. Shedding light on things long forgotten. It was a lightness of being that Caden couldn't ever remember feeling before. Soul-healing relief rushed in behind the light, along with the unimaginable—forgiveness.

And not just for himself.

Had Caden's father ever had anyone to talk to about the accident? Because if Caden felt guilt just for surviving, what must his father have felt for being the one behind the wheel?

The question was another eye-opener, one that had his heart letting go of some of the anger Caden had carried for over half of his life. And more of that light streamed in.

Before long, he was exchanging contact information with Dave and the others and saying his good-byes. And Caden felt like he'd finally figured out Dr. Ward's advice. Because an hour with the men who'd saved his life had done more to give him closure on the accident than anything else in the past fourteen years.

"Hey, Caden," Dave called as Caden was heading out of the bay.

Caden turned. "Yeah?"

Dave gave him a serious look. "If I've learned anything, it's that little matters more than family and love. Do whatever you have to do to win back that girl."

"I'm going to do everything I can," Caden said.

And after today, he finally felt like he might be ready.

CHAPTER TWENTY-ONE

*M*akenna left her four-month check-up and knew the time had come—she had to tell Caden about the baby. The ultrasound appointment was in two weeks, and there was no reason to keep putting the conversation off, except that she was nervous as hell about doing it.

Driving through the early evening darkness, Makenna made her way to Caden's house. This conversation couldn't happen by phone or text or email. She had to do it face to face—not just because it was the right way to go about it, but because she needed to see Caden. To see how he was. To see how he reacted to the news. She just needed to see *him*.

Because Caden Grayson was an ache inside her that wouldn't go away.

She pulled into his cul-de-sac to find his house dark and his parking place empty. Echoing the trip she'd made over a month ago, she drove to the little firehouse on the other side of Fairlington—but this time she found his Jeep.

He'd gone back to work.

Makenna's chest swelled with emotion. If he'd gone back, that must mean he was okay, and that made her happy. But the fact that he'd gone back to work—but not come back to her—really must mean that whatever sliver of hope she'd been holding out for them was completely pointless.

If he was going to come back, he'd have done it.

At least, now she knew.

Anyway, that's not what telling him about the baby was about. More than that, she didn't want Caden back if the baby was the only reason he wanted to be in her life. So. Fine.

As she parked her car along the curb, the clock on the dash said that it was nearly 5:30. His shift probably ended at seven tonight or seven tomorrow morning, depending on the schedule—the firehouse had an overlapping shift system to ensure they were always staffed and could give the guys adequate days off after working twenty-four hours at a time. Which meant she could either go in there and talk to him. Or she could wait.

After waiting two months, she would've thought the idea of a few more hours would've been nothing. But knowing Caden was just across the street in that building—so close—after all this time apart nearly had Makenna crawling out of her skin.

She'd given him time and space. Just like he'd asked. Now she was done with that. This baby was coming whether either of them was ready or not.

Without letting herself overthink it any further, Makenna shut off the car and got out. Flurries whirled around her, and she ducked her head against the freezing wind and zipped her thick coat up to her neck.

On a nice day, the guys often had the doors to the bays open, their trucks on display. But those doors were closed up tight against this weather, so Makenna headed to the office door on the side. Belly going for a loop-the-loop, she let herself into the reception area, setting off a buzzer. No one stood behind the counter.

After a few seconds, a young guy she didn't know came in from the back. "Can I help you?"

"Hi," she said. "Is Caden Grayson here?"

"Grayson? Yeah." He gave her an appraising look that rushed heat into her cheeks. "I'll get him."

The guy disappeared into the hallway beyond. "Grayson!" he yelled, making Makenna's cheeks burn a little hotter. "Visitor."

Makenna stuffed her hands in her pockets and blew out a shaky breath.

An exchange of words down the hall caught her ear—because she heard Caden's voice. Hearing it was a relief and a heartache. She braced in anticipation of seeing him walk through the door.

And then he did.

Be strong, Makenna.

"Hi," she said, drinking him in with her eyes. He looked…so fucking good. Gorgeous, as always, with that strong jaw and that masculine face and those broad shoulders. He was a little thinner, but the dark circles were nearly gone from beneath his eyes and everything about him seemed…lighter somehow. Like he stood taller, moved easier.

"Makenna, what are you doing here? Are you okay?" he asked, coming around the counter to her. He stopped an arm's length away.

"I'm sorry to bother you at work, but I—"

"No, I'm sorry." He rubbed his hand over the scar on his head. "I didn't mean it that way. Just surprised, is all."

"I know. I was hoping we could talk for a minute. It shouldn't take long," she said. Well, actually, it was going to take the next eighteen years, at least. But what needed to happen just then shouldn't take long.

"Uh, yeah. Yeah, of course," he said. "Come inside with me?"

Her heart squeezed as a little voice inside her said, *I'd follow you anywhere, Caden. Don't you know that?* But all she said was, "Sure."

She followed him around the counter, a ridiculous little thrill fluttering through her when their arms brushed as they walked down the white cinder-block hall.

For some reason, that sensation made her think of the first time she ever touched him. That night they were trapped in the elevator. After maybe two hours, they'd both gotten hungry and shared two snacks and a bottle of water that Makenna had in her bag. Because they couldn't see one another to hand off the water, they'd slid it back and forth across the floor until they encountered the other person's hand. By then, she'd already learned just how much they had in common and become intrigued by Caden, and those little touches from a man she'd talked to but never seen had been thrilling.

Walking beside Caden after so long apart, that night seemed like it'd happened a million years before.

Laughter and trash talk spilled out of a room off to the left. Having been to the station before, Makenna knew it was the kitchen and dining room. A quick peek in as they passed it revealed that the table was full, and all the guys had plates of food in front of them. She caught Bear's eye as she and Caden walked by.

"I'm sorry I interrupted your dinner," she said, peering up at Caden.

"Don't be," he said in a quiet voice.

At the end of the hall, they turned to the right. "Let's, uh, let's go in here," he said, pushing a door open for her. He flicked on the light, revealing two rows of bunk beds along the walls, all neatly made.

The door shut, closing them in together.

Makenna's heart tripped into a sprint.

Caden's gaze raked over her and finally settled on her face, his eyes filled with an intensity she didn't understand. "You look really great, Makenna."

"Uh, thanks," she said, the compliment catching her off guard. "You look good, too. Better." Better than before, she thought, but she didn't want to get caught up in talking about the past when what she needed to discuss with him was the future. "So—"

"Did you have a good Christmas?" he asked, stepping a little closer.

She tilted her head, trying to read him. "Um. Sure. I went home to Philly. It was…it was nice."

On top of the awkwardness, an odd tension filled the space between them, like they were magnets that didn't know whether they were supposed to attract or repel.

Because the attraction was definitely there—at least for her. Her body was hyperaware of his. How much taller than her he was. How close he stood. How broad his chest was. How his hands fisted and his jaw ticked.

He reached out and fingered the end of her hair, then seemed to think better of it and pulled his hand away. "Your hair's gotten longer."

The fleeting touch had Makenna's heart pounding in her chest. Desire and yearning roared through her, and she didn't know whether to be annoyed at herself for responding that way or climb him. Or both.

"Yeah," she managed. "I just haven't gotten around to it." She shrugged, because why they were talking about her hair, she wasn't sure. "Look, Caden," she said, wanting to take control of things. "I need to—"

Dooodo, dooodo, dooodo

The tones of the station alerting system sounded loudly in the small space and blue and red lights on the ceiling started flashing—the color combination communicated that they had a fire and medical call. Caden had taught her that the first time she'd visited there. The dispatcher's voice spilled from a speaker in the ceiling with the details of the call.

"Shit," Caden said, his face going serious but his eyes filled with something that looked a lot like disappointment. "I'm really sorry, but I gotta go."

Makenna's stomach fell. "I know," she said. "Duty calls."

"I'd rather stay and talk to you," he said, stepping closer, so close that she could've leaned forward and his chest would've easily cushioned her weight. "I don't know how long I'll be. This day has been a bear, and the freezing rain we're supposed to get tonight probably means more of the same," he rushed out.

She caught the scent of his clean, crisp aftershave. "Will you promise to call me? When you have time to talk. As soon as you can?" Makenna nailed him with a stare.

Heated brown eyes blazed down at her—or maybe that was her

projecting what she felt and what she wished. "I'm on tomorrow, too, but I can promise that."

"I mean it, Caden," she said.

And then he stole her breath. He cupped the back of her head in his hand and pressed a kiss to her forehead, then one to her cheek. He nuzzled the side of her face. "I promise," he said.

Oh God. His heat, his touch, this confusing moment of bliss. It ended in an instant.

"I'm sorry. You know your way out, yeah?" he said, already opening the door.

Stunned, all Makenna could do was nod. "Be careful," she called.

But he was already gone.

And Makenna had no idea how to interpret what'd just happened.

---

*F*uck. *Fuckfuckfuck.*

That was the general tenor of Caden's thoughts as he and his partner pulled out of the bay in response to the call. He couldn't believe...so much. That Makenna had come to see him. That he'd had her right there in front of him. And that they'd been interrupted before he could say even one of the things that needed to be said.

And before she could tell him why she'd come. Curiosity curled through his gut. Why *had* she come to see him? After all this time? He was dying to know, but wasn't sure what the next thirty-six hours of his double shift might entail for him given the shit show bad weather usually created. And he didn't want to leave anything up to chance. Glad he wasn't driving for this one, he pulled out his phone and shot off a text.

It was damn good to see you, Red. Do you maybe want to get together Friday night to talk? I'm serious about keeping my promise.

Not just the one he'd made to call her, but the one he'd made to himself to live with no regrets.

He hit *Send* and nearly held his breath.

Makenna responded in less than a minute. *I have an on-site meeting in Loudoun County on Friday and won't get home until late. Saturday morning? It was good to see you, too.*

That last line made him smile, even though having to wait an extra night was going to kill him. The only reason he hadn't driven right from the Pittsville FD to Makenna's apartment the day before was because he'd wanted to touch base with his therapist first. Just to make sure he'd thought all this through the right way. Because when Caden went to Makenna, he wanted it to be for keeps. If by some miracle she was willing to give him a second chance, he didn't want to do anything to fuck it up. Ever again.

He texted back. *Saturday morning works. Your place, or?*

My place. Be careful, Makenna replied.

You, too, Red. Caden's fingers itched to type more. But he'd wait. Because now he knew exactly when he'd have his shot to get the life he most wanted.

And this time, nothing was going to stand in his way.

CHAPTER TWENTY-TWO

*T*he traffic on 66 was heavy but moving as Makenna made her way home on Friday night from the off-site meeting she'd had out west of D.C., which was surprising given the snow and freezing rain they'd had on and off all day. Being from Pennsylvania, Makenna wasn't uncomfortable driving in the snow, whereas people in D.C. tended to either crawl along or drive like maniacs who didn't think frozen surfaces and black ice could possibly affect them. But so far, so good.

Makenna's stomach did a little flip. Only one more sleep until she'd see Caden tomorrow and finally get to tell him her news. *Their* news.

As if she wasn't nervous enough, seeing him on Wednesday night had confused the hell out of her. His compliments, his touches, his *kisses*. The text he'd sent saying how good it was to see her. What did all of that mean?

And was she being a complete and hopeless idiot for wanting it to mean that he still had feelings for her? Because she would've given almost anything for that to be true. Even after everything.

It didn't seem to matter what she told her heart, because it wouldn't stop wanting the sweet, sexy, damaged man she'd met in the darkness.

A song came on and she hummed along until she couldn't hold back from singing the catchy tune on the chorus. Paying close attention to the road, her gaze shifted from the cars in front of her to her rear view mirror as she sang.

A tingling sensation in her belly. Again.

Makenna didn't think anything about it.

Until it happened again. Harder. Like... *Oh, my God!* Like something moved inside her.

Could that have been the baby? She was suddenly sure it was.

"Was that you peanut?" she asked out loud, a smile breaking out on her face like she hadn't felt in weeks. She nearly held her breath for the sensation to happen again, because the first fluttery feeling of her baby moving inside of her was one of the most amazing things she'd ever felt. "Do that again, you little bugger."

The rest of the song played out, and the baby didn't move again, but that didn't keep Makenna from grinning until her cheeks hurt.

Slam!

Something hit the rear quarter-panel of her car on the driver's side, and Makenna barely had time to make out the shape of a dark SUV spinning out of control before she was struggling to control her own car. The impact of the other vehicle sent her Prius into a slow sliding circle. She turned her steering wheel in the other direction, trying as hard as she could to keep from losing control.

"No, no, no, no, no."

Her efforts were keeping the car from spinning out, but the hit had pushed her onto the snow-covered side of the road untreated by the plows and salt trucks. Her tires lost traction, and the car wouldn't respond to her handling or to the brakes she reluctantly engaged as other cars' brakes lights came on ahead of her.

"Oh God, oh God, oh God," she said out loud, because she wasn't going to be able to stop. And flashing headlights behind her revealed she wasn't the only one out of control.

Airbags exploded in front of her with a cracking *pop*, and then her car became a pinball.

She hit a car ahead of her and slammed into the airbag. There was no time to think or feel or react. *Pop.* The side airbags deployed, and she was hit again. Again. Again. The car jolted this way and that. Screeching tires and blaring horns and other crashes sounded out all around her until Makenna couldn't tell from which direction they came. Another hit, the hardest yet. Suddenly the car was on its side and rolling.

And all Makenna could do was scream.

---

*C*aden's cell phone rang a little after seven, and he picked it up to see the firehouse's number on his screen. "Grayson here."

"Caden, it's Joe. I know you just pulled a double but there's a multi-vehicle MVA on 66 I expect us to get called in for any minute now. I sent Olson home an hour ago with the flu so we're short and I know you're close," his captain said.

Caden was already shoving on his boots. "I'll be there in five."

By the time Caden was parking his Jeep, the doors on the fire-house bays were rolling up. Both emergency vehicles had their lights flashing as men suited up and climbed in. Caden hightailed it through the falling snow to the rig and grabbed his gear. "Let's rock and roll," he said as he jumped into the passenger seat of the paramedic unit.

From the engine truck, Joe gave him a salute.

"Catch me up," Caden said to Brian Larksen, driving the rig beside him. They'd run many an incident together over the years.

"Multiple vehicles. Possibly as many as ten. Two overturned. One, Two, and Three are on the scene or en route," Larksen said, referring to the county's other fire stations. "Four and Ten were called out with us."

"Christ, what a mess." Caden said. "Well, one patient at a time."

"Just like we do," Larksen said, hauling ass onto Interstate 395 behind the engine truck.

Even with Friday night traffic and the snow, they made it to the scene in just under fifteen minutes. Not bad for being outside their usual area of operation.

And, Jesus, the scene was a fucking disaster.

Even from a distance, Caden could see the responders struggling to access vehicles smashed one against the next. A delivery truck was on its side half in the grass, where the road sloped down toward the exit ramp for Westmoreland Street.

They caught up with their guys at the engine, awaiting orders from the chief running the incident. Orders came quickly, and Caden and Larksen were tasked with attending the driver of the delivery truck. They got their gear and booked it to the truck. The crash had blown out the windshield, making access to the passenger cab easier than it otherwise would've been.

"Sir, my name's Caden Grayson. I'm with Arlington E.M.S. and I'm going to help you," Caden said, leaning in through the jagged edges of the busted window. The male driver was laying against the passenger door, which was road-side down, likely revealing he hadn't been wearing his seat belt. The man looked up, and the side of his face was like hamburger. "Just lay real still for me. We're gonna get you out of there. What's your name?"

"Jared," the man rasped.

"Getting him out of there is going to be a bear," Larksen said quietly, handing Caden a flashlight. Caden nodded, his brain already working through the logistics on this one. They might need an assist. Caden knocked out the rest of the glass along one edge so he could lean over without cutting himself.

"Jared," Caden said, leaning in further. "I'm going to take your vitals. Can you tell me what hurts?"

"My face and my arm," the man said. "I got dragged against the road here."

"Do you think anything's broken?" Caden asked, getting the man's pulse and heart rate, and checking the dilation of his eyes.

"No. I don't think so," Jared said.

"Okay, buddy, just hang in there. I'll be right back," Caden said, unfolding himself from around the window. He was updating Larksen and gathering supplies when Jared's voice sounded from behind him.

The man was trying to climb out.

"Whoa, whoa," Caden said, turning to support the man's shoulders as he leaned out the window, blood streaming down his face and onto Caden's jacket.

Larksen was right there, and together they lifted him out and laid him down on the road.

"Grayson!" a voice called.

Caden looked around until he saw Bear jogging toward him, but he ignored the other man because they had to get these wounds treated, particularly the one on Jared's face. White bone glinted through the gore, and now Jared was struggling to maintain consciousness.

"Grayson," Bear said, running up beside him.

"What?" Caden said, laser-focused on his patient.

"I need you to come with me," Bear said.

He held out his bloody gloves. "Little busy here."

"Shit, Caden. I need you to come with me *now*." Something about Bear's tone slid ice into Caden's veins.

"I got this," Larksen said. "Deal with whatever it is and come back."

Caden rose, rolling off his gloves and dropping them to the ground. "What's the problem?"

Bear took him by the arm and led him away from the truck and further onto the grass that divided the highway from the exit ramp that curved off down a little hill. "She's conscious, but she's trapped, and she's—"

"What the hell are you talking about, Bear?" Caden asked, agitated at having been pulled away.

"Makenna," Bear said, pointing down the slope, where a little car sat upside down and propped at an angle against the hillside.

The world sucked in on Caden until he couldn't see anything else. He took off like a shot, sprinting his way down the slippery embankment, his heart in his throat, his gut a sick knot, his brain paralyzed with fear.

No, no, no, not Makenna!

Firefighters were working on opening the badly mangled driver's door so they could extricate, so Caden slid around to the passenger side where a team of paramedics was working.

"Makenna!" he called. "Makenna?"

"Caden?" she cried, her voice warped and wobbly.

A gray-haired EMT from Station Four named Max Bryson peered awkwardly out of the door. "Caden, she's been asking for you." Caden swallowed hard as the man climbed out of the crumpled, upside-down front passenger seat. "She's stable for now. I can't tell about the baby though, I'm sorry. They'll have her out in just a few. Car's stable if you want to get in with her."

"Baby?" he asked, his brain scrambling to catch up with the man's words.

"Shit, you didn't know?" Bryson asked.

Makenna's pregnant? Caden's head was spinning.

But he wasn't what mattered.

Caden crouched down to the narrow opening of the crushed passenger seat immediately. "Makenna?" Jesus, it was tight. And that was as much thought as he gave that before crawling in beside her because fuck his claustrophobia. Nothing was keeping him away from her.

He couldn't quite get his whole body into the space, but he was close enough to see that she was hanging upside down by her seat belt, her body curled by the way the loss of roof height forced her to bend.

Christ, she was bleeding and cut up and shaking. White powder from the airbag deployments dusted her hair, face, and clothing.

Every one of her injuries lashed at his soul. "Makenna, talk to me."

"Oh, God, it r-really is y-you. Caden, I'm-I'm s-scared," she said, looking up at him, her face wet with tears and blood from a wound that had been bandaged on the side of her forehead.

He reached for her hand, but found it wrapped in gauze and splints. "It's me. I'm here."

"The baby," she whispered, her tears coming harder. "I don't w-want to lose your baby."

The words reached into his chest and squeezed so hard he could barely breathe. He had so many questions, but now wasn't the time. "Everything's gonna be okay," he said, willing it with everything inside him. Life owed him this, goddammit. This one thing. Her and his child coming out of this okay. The fucking bullshit in his head had robbed him of so much already. Not this. Not this, too. He crawled closer so that he could rub her hair. "You're pregnant, Red?" The wonder of those words raced through him.

"I'm s-sorry," she cried. "I should've t-told you sooner, but I...I..." Her face crumpled.

"No, no," he said, stroking her hair. "Don't worry. I won't let anything happen to you or the baby, okay? I promise." Jesus, she was pregnant. *Pregnant.* With his baby. He'd be fucking ecstatic about that if he knew they were both okay.

With a loud crunch, the driver's side door abruptly wrenched open. Makenna flinched on a moan.

"Hey, Red, look at me. They're going to get you out of here. Just hold on for another minute," Caden said, looking into her beautiful eyes. It killed him to see so much pain and fear there. "Take a nice deep breath for me." She did. "Another," Caden said, breathing with her, calming her down.

"Okay, Makenna," Bryson said, leaning in the doorway. "We're gonna cut your seatbelt free and ease you out of there. Caden? You think you can support her legs from in there so I can get her out by the head and shoulders?"

"Yes," Caden said without hesitation. Although it was going to force him to squeeze all of himself into the tight space so he'd have leverage to hold her. They didn't want her to fall to the roof of the car when they cut her free. He got into position, his shoulder bracing her thighs. His head was crammed against the jagged roof.

Which was the first moment it occurred to him that he and Makenna were stuck together in a crashed upside-down car. *Déjà fucking vu.*

The moment Bryson cut the belt, Caden was all that was holding her. Makenna gasped as her weight shifted. "I've got you, Red. I've got you."

Judging by the way her legs turned, Bryson was slowly moving her upper body toward the opening. She groaned and her hands flew to her belly. "Please, please, please, please," she whispered over and over again.

And Caden was right there with her. *Please let them both be okay.*

As Bryson started to move her out of the car, Caden slowly lowered her legs into his arms, and then another guy outside grasped her legs until she was free.

Getting himself back out of the car took longer than he had patience for, but he essentially had to soldier crawl under what was left of the caved-in passenger door opening. And then he scrambled around to the far side and went to his knees by Makenna's head.

As he leaned over her, words spilled out of his mouth in a desperate rush. He couldn't let another second pass without her knowing. "I love you, Makenna. I've loved you from the very beginning, since you laughed in that elevator and eased my fears, since you shared your first-time story with me and made me laugh, since you accepted me even when I couldn't accept myself. I'm so fucking sorry," he said.

"Caden?" she said, her voice slurring. Her eyelids fluttered and sagged.

"Yeah, Red, it's me," he said.

Her head lolled to the side.

"Loss of consciousness," one of the medics said. "Let's get her moving."

Caden rose as the men lifted the stretcher. "I'm going with you," he said to Bryson, daring the man with his gaze to challenge him. He didn't. Jogging along with the stretcher, they made for Station Four's paramedic unit. Caden glanced around for his team, and saw Bear in the distance. The guy looked his way and gave him a wave and a nod. It was all the okay he needed, and if there was hell to pay for leaving, Caden was more than willing to pay it.

Because everything he loved lay broken and bleeding at his side. Here he'd thought he had time...time to get himself right so he could be the man Makenna deserved. Now, all he could do was hope he wasn't too late.

CHAPTER TWENTY-THREE

*C*aden was climbing the walls. Once they'd reached the emergency department, the staff had made him wait while Makenna was triaged and treated. But there was one thing he could do to fill the crawling time. Her family needed to know what'd happened.

At Thanksgiving, Caden and Patrick had exchanged information. He found her brother's number and waited as it rang.

"Patrick James here," he answered.

"Patrick, it's Caden Grayson, Makenna's—"

"I know who you are, Caden." The ice in the other man's tone made it crystal clear that Patrick knew what'd gone down between him and Makenna. "To what do I owe the call?"

"Makenna was in an accident. She's stable but in the hospital. Came in by ambulance fifteen minutes ago," Caden said, hating to be the bearer of this news when he knew how close Patrick and Makenna were.

"Fuck," Patrick said. "What happened? Is she injured? How's the baby?"

Patrick knowing about the baby made Caden feel grateful that Makenna hadn't been dealing with that all on her own. Caden should've been there, but at least she'd had her family. "She was semi-conscious and banged up when she came in but her injuries weren't serious, although they haven't determined the baby's condition yet. Ten-car pile-up on Interstate 66. Makenna's Prius got flipped over a guard rail and overturned." Caden scrubbed his hand over his scar as he paced in the busy waiting room.

"I'm going to get the family together and we'll get down there as fast as we can. Where are you?" Patrick asked. Caden gave him the hospital information, and then Patrick said, "Thanks for calling me, Caden. I appreciate it. But I need you to be prepared to answer some questions for me when we get Makenna squared away. You hearing me?"

"A hundred percent. I'll be happy to tell you anything you want to know," Caden said. "I love her, Patrick. I fucked up, but I love her."

A long pause, and then, "We'll see you soon." Patrick hung up.

Caden couldn't spare any worry for the James men's reactions to him, not when every cell in his body agonized over what was going on with Makenna. Besides, any anger they bore toward him he'd earned with his mistakes. So he understood that he'd have to work to earn back their trust. He'd be fucking happy to grovel to anyone who wanted that from him if it would make Makenna and their baby okay.

Their baby. Every time he thought about Makenna's pregnancy, the wonder of it smacked him upside the head anew. Sheer awe lit up his chest. There was fear inside him, too, he wasn't going to deny that. Fear for this little, vulnerable life, maybe struggling to survive. Fear that he would be responsible for protecting and guiding that life. Fear of the million unknowns that could rain down on you at absolutely any moment.

As tonight proved.

But the wonder, the awe, the light—the love—all of it was so much bigger than the fear. So much more powerful. It was the fiery bright-ness of the sun against the cool glow of the moon.

No matter what happened, Caden had a family. Right this very minute. For the first time in over fourteen years.

And he wanted that family more than he'd ever wanted anything in his life.

"Makenna James family?" a blond-haired woman wearing scrubs called from the doors to the emergency department.

Caden rushed over. "I'm her boyfriend," he said. The word was so fucking inadequate compared to what she was to him—his everything.

The doctor guided him inside past patients waiting in cubicles, on gurneys, and in chairs. "I'm Dr. Ellison. Makenna's awake and stable. She's cramping a little and the baby's heartrate is elevated, but otherwise the baby seems to be fine. The next twelve to twenty-four hours will give us more information." They turned a corner into a hallway with curtained rooms. "She needs an X-ray on her hand and a CT scan for the head injury. We've got those orders in, but radiology's backed up so we're in a holding pattern. Hopefully it won't be too long." The doctor stopped at the edge of a curtain. "Any questions?"

Only about a million, but none that he needed the doctor to answer. "No, thanks."

With a nod, Dr. Ellison drew back the striped curtain and stepped into the small room. And there was his Makenna, bandaged and bruised with IVs protruding from her hand, but alive and awake. And without question the most beautiful thing Caden Grayson had ever seen in his life.

---

*M*akenna felt like she was moving slower than everything around her, or maybe that was just the pain meds they'd given her. Sounds came as if from a distance. The walls seemed a little wavy. Her limbs were like lead.

The curtain to her room suddenly opened and the doctor walked in…*with Caden!*

"Makenna," Dr. Ellison said, "I have Caden here for you. I've updated him on your condition. We're just waiting on radiology, okay?" The woman patted Makenna's arm.

"Okay," Makenna said in a weak voice, her gaze glued to Caden. He wore his uniform, his coat dirty with mud and blood here and there. "Thank you."

"Press the call button if either of you need anything," Dr. Ellison said, and then she was gone.

Caden shrugged out of his coat and dropped it on a chair, and then it was like he was stuck there at the edge of the room. She ached for him to come to her, but all she could manage was his name before she started crying. "Caden..."

He was to her in an instant, his body folding over her, his forehead settling against hers. "I'm sorry, Makenna. I'm so fucking sorry," he said.

Makenna shook her head as her mind struggled to process his words. "It wasn't your fault," she said. "I was just glad you were there. I was praying for it, actually, so hard. When you showed up, I wasn't sure whether to believe you were real."

Caden reached behind him and dragged a chair as close to her bedside as he could. He sat heavily and cradled her hand against his big chest. "I'm not talking about the accident," he said, dark eyes blazing. "I'm talking about how I left you, how I shut you out, how I lost myself and didn't know how to own up to it with you." He swallowed thickly, his Adams apple bobbing in his throat. "I'm talking about making you go through finding out you were pregnant all by yourself, making you worry for even a second that you would have to raise a child by yourself." He shook his head, and she'd never seen his expression more earnest.

Relief flooded through her that he'd accepted the idea of the baby so readily, and that he seemed to want to be involved. Which meant that her little one wouldn't have to grow up with only one parent as Makenna had, after all.

"Do you remember what I said after they pulled you from the car?" he asked, his eyes on fire with an intensity that reached inside her chest and just...owned her.

But Makenna couldn't remember anything after the scare of her car door screeching open. They'd cut her loose from the seat belt, and then... It was all a blur. "No," she whispered. "What did you say?" Her heart tripped into a sprint because the moment felt weighted with a significance she didn't understand and didn't want to read too much into. She wouldn't be able to withstand the disappointment and heartache. Not after the scares this night had entailed.

"I said...I said that I love you, Makenna. I said—"

"Because of the baby," she threw out, fear getting the best of her. But she had to know.

"Yes, because of the baby—"

"Caden—"

"Makenna, I've been in love with you since the night we met. I'm as sure of that as I am that I let my family's accident dictate my life in ways I wasn't even aware of—until I totally crashed and burned. I love you so much if feels like a part of me is gone when we're not together. I love you because you're beautiful and kind and smart and funny. Because you accepted me when I didn't even accept myself. Because your heart is more filled with empathy and understanding than anyone I've ever met. I don't make any sense without you. Not anymore. Because you're in me, and I want you there. I want you there forever. You *and* the baby. Our baby."

"You...you love me?" she asked, trying the words out as emotion ballooned inside her chest. "Then why...*why?*" Awkwardly, she tried to scrub away the tears from her face, but the bandages on one hand and the IV in the back of the other made it nearly impossible.

Caden grasped a tissue from the box on the rolling tray, and then he leaned in and dried her tears for her. It was such a ridiculously tender gesture that Makenna sucked in a breath.

"Why did you walk away?" she asked again.

With a heavy sigh, Caden sat back down and took her hand again. He pressed a lingering kiss to her knuckles, the little caring gestures lending credence to his words. "The short answer is that I lost myself, I let myself spiral until I couldn't control it, and then I became clinically depressed."

"Oh, Caden," she said, the knowledge that he'd been hurting so badly cutting right through her.

He shook his head. "I'm better now, so don't worry. I've been working on getting myself back on track for months. And I *am* better, Red, I need you to know that. Better than I've ever been since the accident." Another kiss to her knuckles. "I let a lot of things chip away at my confidence until I'd convinced myself I didn't deserve you—"

"I don't love Cameron, Caden. I don't want him. And I want you to know I've asked him never to contact me again," she rushed out.

"I know you don't love him. I know you were honest and sincere in everything you said to me. Problem was, I couldn't hear what you were saying, or I couldn't let myself believe it. I don't know. And that's another thing I should apologize for," he said, lips pressing into a hard line. "That I let my lack of faith in myself affect the faith I had in you. And I fucking hate that I did that. Because you did nothing to warrant it. It was all my own bullshit. But that realization was why I was waiting to come back to you, to come back and ask for a second chance. I wanted to come back to you whole. I wanted to be healthy. I wanted to be confident I wouldn't make the same mistakes all over again. I couldn't do that to you."

"And are you all those things now?" she asked, hope and pride rising up inside her. Because there was something in the light in his eyes and the strength of his words that had already answered the question.

"Yes," he said, nodding, his gaze burning into hers. "For the first time, yes. I had been planning to see you this weekend, even before you stopped by the station Wednesday night." He gave a little shrug. "You showing up felt like a sign. That it was time. And that I was ready."

Makenna closed her eyes and inhaled a deep breath, all the stressful uncertainty she'd been carrying sloughing right off her shoulders. It was the most beautiful relief, even as exhaustion from the night stole over her body. Looking at him again, she gave a small smile. "I'm so proud of you, Caden."

"So," he said in a low voice. "Do you think...could you give me a second chance to be in your life? To love you? You and the baby?"

"Oh, Caden, I've just been waiting for you to say the words," she said, her throat going tight. "I want you in my life more than anything, and not a second has passed since we've been apart that I haven't loved you with everything that I am." She rubbed her knuckles along the prominent ridge of his cheekbone and wished her body was in a condition that would let her do what she really wanted —to climb into his lap, wrap herself around him, and never let go. "I'm going to love you forever. I'm not going anywhere, no matter what."

"Jesus, Makenna, I was so damn scared you'd be done with me for good," he said, stretching over her to give her a hug.

"You never have to worry about that, Caden. But you have to promise me you'll never shut me out like that again. You have to let me be there for you the same way you were here for me tonight, when things are at their very worst and everything seems to be falling apart. I want to be there for you. I *need* to be there for you. And you have to promise to let me. Because I can't lose you like that again. I won't."

Caden pressed their clasped hands to his heart. "I promise," he said, a fierceness in his gaze. "I want and need that too, and I promise. I'm so sorry."

The smile she gave him was all joy and love. "Then it's you and me, 'til the end. In the darkness and in the light."

The words healed places inside him he didn't ever think would get better. "You and me, 'til the end," he repeated. And then he sat back enough to gently lay his head on her stomach. "You and me and this little guy." He pressed a kiss against her belly.

Seeing him nuzzle her stomach, with the little baby bump just starting to show, was something she'd feared she'd never get to experience. And it was so sweet it stole her breath. She gently stroked his close-shaved hair. "I'm so relieved that you're happy about the baby."

"I'm fucking ecstatic, Makenna. You two are the luckiest, best thing to ever happen to me." He eased off of her and grasped her hand again. "How far along are you?"

"Seventeen weeks on Sunday," she said, a little thrill going through her at getting to share this with him after all.

"Wow," he said, a smile dawning on his face. It brought out his dimples. "Do you know if it's a boy or a girl yet? How have you been feeling?"

"I don't know the sex yet, but my ultrasound appointment is next week. That's why I came to see you at the station. I wanted you to know about the baby so you could be involved, and I wanted to invite you to that appointment because I thought you deserved to meet your child. Aside from tonight, I've been feeling good for the past month or so. Earlier my morning sickness was terrible, but it passed." And now, talking about how she was feeling, Makenna realized that the cramps she'd had earlier had gone away. Hope flooded through her. They were going to make it out of this night after all—together and stronger for it.

"I'm sorry I wasn't there to help, Makenna, but all that changes right now," he said.

"Makenna James?" a man said as he came through the curtain. "Time for your scans."

"Oh, that didn't take too long after all," she said, ready to know just how bad her hand was and whether the bump on the head she'd gotten that'd required three stitches was anything more serious.

"Can I come?" Caden asked, standing.

"Unfortunately not, but you can wait here. She won't be gone long," the orderly said.

"Okay," Caden said, his brow furrowed. "Just give me a minute." And then he folded down the rail on her bed, leaned over her, and pulled her gently into his arms. For a long moment, he just held her. Held her so damn close. The embrace was love and life and belonging, and it eased so much of the hurt she'd been carrying around inside her. "Love you so much," he whispered. Finally, he let her go. "Sorry, I couldn't resist."

"Never be sorry for that," Makenna said with a smile as the orderly unlocked the brakes on the bed and wheeled her out of the room.

The orderly was right—the hand X-ray and head CT didn't take long. Even better, several hours later she received the news that her head scans were clean and only the first two fingers on her right hand were broken—the doctors had feared breaks throughout her hand, but it appeared to be mostly sprained. Those airbags had clearly done their job, because everyone who knew what'd happened to her repeated how lucky she was.

And every time she looked at Caden, Makenna agreed.

She drifted in and out of sleep, each time finding Caden right by her side, sometimes awake, other times asleep, his head against her hip, his hand curled around hers. Makenna didn't think she was imagining the new peacefulness he wore on his gorgeous face. Sleep had never been peaceful for him, and seeing him rest so quietly was further proof of everything he'd said.

The next time she woke up, she found her father sitting in a chair at her other side.

"Daddy," she whispered.

"Oh, Makenna. I've been trying so hard to let you sleep." He came to her side. "But I've been dying to see your eyes so I could know you were really okay," he said, so much emotion on his face. God, it was good to see him.

"I am. Or at least I will be," she said, filling him in on what the doctors had told her.

Her father blew out a deep breath and pressed a kiss to her cheek. "I hate to see you hurting."

"Don't worry," she said, his concern lodging a lump in her throat.

"Ha," he said with a wink. "Tell me how that works out for you when this little one comes."

Makenna smiled. "I suppose that's fair."

Her father's gaze dropped to where Caden slept. "So, things are..."

"Things are good, Dad. Really good. We have a lot more to talk about, but I understand what was going on and I know that we love each other. And that's all I need to know for right now. The rest we'll work out together," she said, needing her father's support.

Dad brushed a strand of hair back off her face. "Sometimes, you remind me so much of your mother. She'd be so proud of the woman you've become," he said, making her eyes well up. "You're all big heart and kind soul. And don't ever change."

"Aw, Dad," she said, her eyes leaking again.

Just then, Caden pushed into a sitting position. "Sorry I fell—" he said. His eyes went wide, and he was on his feet in an instant. "Mike. Uh, Mr. James."

"Mike is fine, son," Dad said, nailing him with a stare. "You here for my baby girl now?"

Caden nodded. Part of Makenna felt bad for him, but a bigger part of her was proud of how confident he was standing before her father. "Yes, sir. A hundred percent. When Makenna's better, I'd like to tell you what happened if you're open to it. I know how important you are to her and, well…" He nodded. "I'd just like to try to make things right."

Her father walked around the bottom of the hospital bed and came to stand in front of a much taller Caden. "It looks like you already have, but of course I'll hear what you have to say. We all will. Because you're part of the family now." Her father held out a hand, and when Caden took it, Makenna couldn't stop smiling. "Congratulations on the little one."

"Thank you, Mike. That means a lot," Caden said. Was Makenna imagining it, or were Caden's cheeks turning pink, just a little? How freaking cute was that?

"Listen, Patrick's probably climbing the walls," Dad said. "Let me head out so he can come back. They'll only allow two at a time."

"I can go so you can stay and visit," Caden said, gesturing to the door.

Her father shook his head. "Your place is right here." He clapped Caden on the back then looked at Makenna. "Get some sleep. I'll see you in a while."

"Thanks, Dad," she said.

When he left, Caden leaned against the rail of her bed and bent down to kiss her forehead. "Your father's a helluva guy."

She grinned. "Yes, he is. And so are you." Makenna only hoped that things went as well with her oldest brother.

The thought seemed to beckon him, because the next instant, Patrick walked into the room and came right up to her on the opposite side of the bed from Caden. "Makenna, Jesus. You scared the hell out of all of us." He kissed her on the forehead. "You okay?"

"Yes, I'm going to be fine. Thank you so much for coming down," she said.

"I wouldn't be anywhere else. None of us would. You know that," he said, still not acknowledging Caden. Makenna's shoulders sagged, but they had to work this out between them.

An awkward silence stretched out and Makenna was debating how to make all this right when a fluttery tingle flitted through her belly. And again.

"Oh! It's happening again," she said, grabbing Caden's hand. She flattened it against her belly. "I don't know if you'll be able to feel it but this is the second time I've felt the baby move."

Caden's face was a mask of joyful anticipation as he leaned over her. He shook his head, his smile bringing out his dimples.

"Damn," she said. "I guess we're gonna have to get used to the kid not doing things when we want him to, huh?"

Chuckling, Caden nodded. "Sounds about right."

"So, you're in this, then?" Patrick said, finally looking at Caden. "You know what, let's take this into the hall so we don't disturb Makenna."

Caden straightened and met Patrick's intense gaze eye to eye, then nodded.

"Guys, it's okay," Makenna said, worry slinking through her.

"Don't worry," Caden said, kissing her on the forehead. "We'll be right back." They disappeared into the hallway, but they didn't go so far that she couldn't hear a lot of the conversation.

"I'm *all* in," Caden said. "I know I made mistakes, but I've worked to fix them, and I won't make them again."

A long pause, and Makenna could imagine the hard-ass expression on Patrick's face. *Cop face*, she always called it. "She deserves everything, Caden." Makenna's heart melted at her brother's protectiveness.

"I couldn't agree more. And I'm going to make sure she has it. That they both do," Caden said. Just a few short hours ago, she'd worried she'd never hear Caden say something like that ever again. Now here he was, making amends with her family and holding his own. More proof of how far he'd come.

Another long pause, and she couldn't hear what they were saying.

"Yeah, well, if I do, I'll kick my own ass." Caden's voice, followed by laughter.

"You got a fucking deal," Patrick said.

A moment later, they returned to her room. "Everything okay?" she asked.

Caden and Patrick exchanged a look and a nod, and then Caden gave her a smile. "I'm here with you, Red. Everything's finally perfect."

CHAPTER TWENTY-FOUR

"This is my favorite Valentine's Day ever," Makenna said, sitting in the rocking chair as Caden drove in the last screw on the baby's crib. What could be more romantic than the father of her child whole-heartedly throwing himself into decorating the baby's nursery? They'd been working on it for hours, both of them perfectly content to just be at home together on this day that was all about cele-brating love.

They'd gone with a red, yellow, and light blue color scheme and a fireman and Dalmatian dog theme. Makenna's guess had been right—they were having a boy. Caden had teared up upon seeing the ultra-sound and learning the news—it was one of the sweetest things Makenna had ever seen.

Caden's smile brought out his dimples. "Oh, yeah? Me too."

She popped a piece of chocolate from a big box he'd given her into her mouth, and looked around at what used to be Caden's spare bedroom. She'd moved into his house the week after she'd been released from the hospital. Caden had insisted, and Makenna had fallen in love with him even more for how much he'd been doting on her.

"There," he said. "All done." He rose and slid the crib into place against the wall, then settled the mattress inside.

"It's coming together so nicely," she said, looking up at the mobile with its hanging fireman's helmet, Dalmatian, fire hydrant, and fire truck. "Such a cute room."

"I have an idea." Caden disappeared for a moment and returned with the stuffed bear she'd gotten him all those months ago. "I think this guy should go in here. The baby's very first bear. A gift from his mom and his dad."

"Have I told you lately how sweet you are?" she asked as he placed it in the crib.

He gave her a sheepish smile and knelt in between Makenna's thighs. "Our son deserves everything." He pressed a kiss to her belly—she wasn't very big yet, but there was no mistaking that she was pregnant. "And so do you."

She rubbed her hand over her short hair. "We all do," she said. "And we have it."

Leaning closer, Caden cupped her cheek and kissed her, a slow press of lips and a soft slide of tongues. "You taste fucking delicious," he said.

"I do?" she whispered, her arms wrapping around his neck.

He nodded and deepened the kiss. Then he tracked kisses from her cheek to her jaw to her ear.

"Watching you being all handy and domestic is really hot," she said, smiling.

He chuffed out a laugh against her neck. "Like that, do you?"

"A lot." She nodded.

"Any time you want me to hammer, drill, or screw, you just let me know," he said.

Makenna laughed. "I want those all the time, Caden. Don't you know?"

A mischievous grin on his face, he rose and pulled her up with him. Kissing her again, he walked them out of the nursery and into their bedroom. Boxes of her stuff lined one wall—slowly, but surely, they were getting her settled in. "Tell me what you want." His dark eyes blazed at her.

"You," she said, pulling her shirt over her head. "Just you."

He kissed her shoulder, the swell of her breast, her nipple through her bra. "You have me," he said. "You always have." He unclasped her bra and flicked his tongue over one nipple than the other.

Before long, they were both naked and Caden was pressing her back onto the bed. He dropped to his knees and pushed her thighs apart. The look on his face was pure masculine hunger as he leaned in. He kissed her thighs, her hip bone, the skin just above her pubic hair, driving her crazy and making her need him even more. And then he pressed a firm kiss against her clit, and Makenna couldn't help but thrust her hips.

"You want me to put my mouth on you here?" he asked, his breath ghosting over her most sensitive skin.

"God, yes," she said, looking down her body at him. He was so fucking sexy, his big shoulders filling up the space between her thighs, that harsh face peering at her with such intensity.

"Say it," he said. "Tell me what you want."

"I want you to make me come with your mouth," she rasped.

"Fuck, yes," he said, and then he was on her. Licking, sucking, relentless, driving her out of her mind. He penetrated her with one thick finger, then with another, his fingers moving inside her as he sucked hard on her clit and flicked it with his tongue. His lip piercing pressed against her flesh, a feeling that always drove her wild.

Makenna cried out and grasped his head, holding him to her, pressing him down. "God, I'm going to come already."

He growled his approval and sucked her harder, faster.

She held her breath as her orgasm washed over her in wave after wave. "Holy shit," she rasped.

"Again," he said, a mischievous glint in his eye, his pierced eyebrow arched. He angled his fingers inside her and hit a place that sent her flying.

"Jesus," she rasped. "That's so freaking good."

As he worked his fingers deep inside, he flicked his tongue over her clit hard and fast. He reached his other hand up her body and grasped her breast, his fingers stroking and squeezing her sensitive nipple. Makenna's body wound back up fast, arousal and lust and love lancing through her for this man. This gorgeous, sweet, damaged man. Her Caden.

"So good, so good, so good," she said, her hips moving, her heart racing.

"Come on my tongue, Makenna," Caden gritted out. "I want it."

The need and arousal in his tone shoved her closer to the edge. And then he angled his fingers to stroke that spot inside her again and again.

She came on a scream, her body shaking and the room spinning. Turned out that pregnant sex had some fun benefits—she found it easier to have multiple orgasms and they were so much more intense. Makenna reached her hands out to Caden.

He crawled up over her and pushed her up against the pillows until he could settle between her parted legs. "Love you so fucking much," he said, taking himself in hand. He leaned down and kissed her, an urgent kiss filled with heat and love and need, and then his cock was right there and sliding deep.

"Love you, too," Makenna moaned, arching beneath him. Hearing him say that would never get old. Finding him in that elevator had been such a gift.

Arms braced on either side of her shoulders, Caden's hips moved in a slow, grinding rhythm. His gaze dropped down to where he disappeared inside her. "Looks so fucking hot," he rasped. "Feels so good inside you."

She ran her hands down his strong sides to his ass, his muscles clenching beneath her grip. "Harder," she whispered, needing more of him, needing all of him.

"Don't wanna hurt you," he said.

"You won't," she said. "Need you so much."

"Jesus," he said, coming down all the way on top of her. His hands slid beneath her ass, tilting her hips, and then his hips were flying—hard, fast, delicious. Every impact ground against her clit until Makenna was panting and digging her fingers into his shoulders. "You own me, Red. Do you know that?" he whispered against her ear. "There isn't a part of me that isn't yours completely."

The words squeezed her heart and made her soul fly. "I feel the same way, Caden. You're everything to me."

"Fuck," he growled, his hips moving faster. "It's too good."

She wrapped her legs around his hips and dug her heels into his ass. "Come in me. I want to feel it."

He circled his hips, the new sensation suddenly pushing her closer to orgasm. "Oh, God."

"Yeah?"

"Don't stop," she whispered. "Don't stop."

"You gonna come for me again?" he asked, kissing her ear.

All she could do was moan as sensation twisted faster and faster low in her belly.

"Aw, so fucking tight," he rasped.

And then she was crying out and coming, her body gripping his.

"Yes, Makenna, yes. I'm coming. Coming so fucking hard," he said, his voice low and gritty. His cock pulsed inside her as his hips slowed and jerked.

When their bodies calmed, he eased from inside her and rolled them over until she was laying half on top of him, his arm around her shoulder and holding her close.

"I never thought I would have all this, Makenna," he said, kissing her forehead. "It's more than I ever hoped for." He tilted her chin up so he could look her in the eyes, eyes that were lighter and more unburdened than she'd ever seen them. Since they'd moved in together, he'd told her everything he'd done to get himself healthier while they'd been apart. And she was so proud of him, proud that he'd had the courage to look all that darkness in the face and still manage to find the light. *"You're* more than I ever hoped for."

She stroked her hand over his scar, her chest so full of love for this man she wasn't sure how she contained it inside her. "I'm going to spend the rest of my life making you happy."

He pressed her hand to his mouth and kissed her palm. "You know what, Red? You already do."

CHAPTER TWENTY-FIVE

5 *Months Later*

"Oh, Makenna, he's healthy and beautiful and just perfect," Dr. Lyons said as their son made his entrance into the world. The baby cried, and the sound crawled right into Caden's heart and made it fuller than it'd ever been in his whole life. How had he gotten so lucky?

"Good job, Makenna," Caden said, pressing a kiss to her damp cheek. "You did it. I'm so proud of you."

"He's here," Makenna said, clutching Caden's hand. "He's really here."

The doctor laid the baby on Makenna's belly and clipped off the umbilical cord while a nurse dried him off and put a striped cap on his little head. And, God, he was so little. Little and beautiful and amazing.

"Would you like to do the honors?" the doctor asked Caden, holding the scissors out to him.

"Yeah?" Caden asked, smiling. Makenna grinned and nodded, and

Caden cut the cord, bringing his son fully into the world.

Finished rubbing him down, the nurse covered the baby with a blanket and lifted him higher so Makenna could hold him in her arms. Seeing Makenna hold their son for the first time was something he would never forget. He shook his head as he looked at the two of them, just so filled with awe. This...this was his family. Leaning over, he stroked her hair. "He's beautiful."

"He really is," she said, her voice shaky. "Hi, Sean, it's so nice to finally meet you."

Caden gently cupped his hand around Sean's little head. Sean David James Grayson. It was a big name for such a little guy, but they'd both fallen in love with it as a way to recognize the important people in their lives—his brother, the paramedic who'd saved Caden, and Makenna's family. Wherever they were, Caden hoped his mom and brother would be proud.

The nurse gave the three of them wrist bands and took the baby's footprint and weighed him, and then asked, "Would you like to try to feed him, Makenna?"

"Yes," she said, her face lighting up. It took a couple of tries, but Sean caught on pretty fast. And the wonder on Makenna's face was so fucking sweet that it made Caden's chest ache.

Caden held the boy's tiny hand, the little fingers curling around one of Caden's. And it gave him the best idea. Because today he was making this family official. He had the ring and the approval of her father and brothers—even Ian, who finally seemed to have warmed up to the idea of Makenna being with Caden—and now was the perfect time.

After a while, the baby pulled away and fussed, and Makenna nuzzled him, cooing and talking until the boy calmed down. For long moments, she and his son just stared at one another as she spoke quietly to him. Watching them, Caden had never felt happier or more grateful in his whole life.

"Your turn to hold him," she said, smiling up at him.

Caden's heart tripped into a sprint. Sean's little body barely filled the crook of Caden's arm. He was so little, so vulnerable, so beautiful, with a head of silky brown hair peeking out from beneath the cap and blue eyes that Caden hoped stayed that color. Part him and part her.

When the baby started to cry, Caden shook him gently in his arms and walked in a slow circle by the bed. "You and me are going to be good friends, little man. I'm going to teach you everything. I love you," he said, "you and your mom both."

The baby's little arm escaped from the blanket, and when Caden had his back to Makenna, he slipped the ring from his pocket and put it in the baby's palm. Sean's fingers closed tightly around it. "You can do the honors for me," he whispered, then he turned to Makenna, nervousness suddenly racing through him. "He's perfect, Makenna," Caden said, laying the baby on her chest again. "And I think he has a gift for you."

She gave Caden a questioning smile and grasped Sean's hand. The diamond glinted and Makenna gasped as she slipped it from his little grasp. "Oh, Caden."

Heart in his throat, he went to one knee beside her hospital bed and took her left hand in his. "Makenna James, you are everything I want and need in this world. I love you with all my heart, and I promise to devote myself to loving you and taking care of you and building a wonderful life for you and Sean. For the three of us together, as a family. You are the best thing that ever happened to me, and I would be the happiest man in the world if you would agree to be my wife. Makenna, will you marry me?"

"Yes," she said. "Oh, Caden, Yes."

Caden took the ring and slid it on her finger. Finding where he belonged in this world—and that it was with her—was a gift bigger and more meaningful than he'd ever imagined possible. He rose and kissed her, softly, sweetly, with so much love.

"I'm the luckiest man who ever lived. Thanks to you." He kissed Makenna again, then kissed Sean's head. "And you, too."

Makenna smiled even as her baby blues filled with happy tears. "I love you, Caden. So much."

Caden smiled back, his heart so damn full. "Aw, Red. I love you, too. Forever."

CHAPTER ONE

*O*ne year ago this week, Caden Grayson had gotten trapped in a pitch-black elevator. And between the darkness and the tightness and the way it triggered memories of the most terrifying moments of his life, it had been his worst nightmare come true.

And his utter salvation.

Because he hadn't been alone in that elevator.

No. Not by a long shot. Makenna James had been trapped in there with him. And it seemed impossible to him that she'd been a stranger in that moment, because now she was the person who knew him best in the world. Maybe even better than he knew himself.

Certainly, she'd changed everything about his life and what he thought it would be. Which was why he found himself staring at his own reflection with a bit of wonder. Because he was wearing a classic black-and-white tuxedo, and today was his wedding day.

Stepping out of the bedroom he shared with Makenna, he almost walked into Makenna's brothers. Wearing tuxedos of their own, Patrick, Ian, and Collin James all looked at him at once, eagerness on their faces.

"Can we get him yet?" Patrick asked, glancing at the closed door on one side of the hallway.

Grinning, Caden checked the time on his cell phone. "Yeah. I guess it's about that time."

The three James men immediately made for the door. Quietly, they all walked into the fireman-themed room with its red, yellow, and light blue color scheme. Caden and Makenna's son's room. Caden's *son*. Sometimes, the goodness of that stole Caden's breath. He had a son.

Peering into the crib, Caden felt like he shared the awe he felt with Makenna's brothers. Because they were all looking at Sean Grayson like he was the most amazing thing they'd ever seen. Three-month-old Sean lay on his back, his pudgy little limbs totally at ease, his face slack in sleep. A shock of dark brown hair stuck up in every direction from his little head. Caden didn't have a lot of experience with loving families, but all the James men—including Makenna's father—doted on the boy to no end. Jokingly fought with each other to get to do it, actually. Caden wouldn't have had it any other way. He wanted Sean to have everything that Caden had been denied for so long. And much, much more.

Caden reached in a hand to rub Sean's chest and belly. The baby's eyes flew open and he immediately stretched in a motion that was half excitement, half startle. But then Sean realized he had an audience, and the little guy graced them with one of the smiles he was giving more and more often and cooed and waved his arms. To a round of laughter and smiles, Caden picked the little man up, kissed his soft head, and marveled for maybe the millionth time at the little life he held in his hands. The life he'd made with Makenna.

It didn't take long for the four of them to change Sean's diaper, feed him a bottle Makenna had left for them, and get the baby changed so that he was wearing a long-sleeved onesie that made him appear to be wearing a tiny tux of his own.

"We clean up good," Caden said to Sean, lifting him into his arms. "We are going to knock your mom's socks off." In truth, it was the other way around—Caden's chest was tight with the anticipation of seeing Makenna walking up the aisle. To him.

As Ian and Collin left the room, Patrick put a hand on Caden's arm. The two men had gotten close since Makenna's car accident seven months before had scared the hell out of them all. "You're really good with him, Caden. And you're really great for both of them. Just want you to know that. I hope you do."

The words of acceptance and approval hit Caden right in the chest. He wasn't used to receiving them, and maybe never would be. But he appreciated the hell out of them. He extended a hand to his soon-to-be brother-in-law. "Thanks, man. That means a lot."

Downstairs, they found Makenna's father, Mike James, and Caden's captain at the firehouse, Joe Flaherty, shooting the shit.

Both men rose as they entered the living room, Mike coming right over to take his grandson. "Let me see this little guy. Did you have a good nap?" he asked Sean.

"He did. The kid sleeps like a champ," Caden said.

"That's because he's such a good boy," Mike cooed against Sean's cheek. "And because he knows he has a great mom and dad who will always look out for him."

Caden clapped Mike on the back, the words making it too hard to respond. How the hell had he gotten so lucky as to find Makenna *and* her family? Because family was something he'd thought he might never have again. And despite the rocky times that Caden and Makenna had weathered, her family had embraced him with both arms and the big heart that every member of the James clan seemed to have—even Ian, who hadn't been as accepting at first.

A big smile on his face, Joe turned to Caden and held out his hand. "I don't think I've ever seen you in a tux before."

"I know," Caden said, laughing. "I barely recognize myself."

Joe clasped Caden's hand tight. "Well, I recognize you. You're exactly the man I've always known you to be, Caden. And I'm damn proud of you."

Shaking his head, Caden worked to clear his throat. Because he knew Joe was talking about more than the clothes. He was talking about the major depression that his captain had helped him get through last winter, the one that had brought him right to the brink of losing everything. Which was why Joe was the clear choice to be his best man. "Shit," Caden whispered. "I have you to thank for that."

"You can always count on me to have your back," Joe said, giving him a pointed look. Caden nodded and scrubbed a hand over the scar on the side of his head.

"Goes for me, too," Patrick said, joining them.

"For all of us," Mike added. Meeting each of the men's gazes, Caden nodded again, the room feeling a little bit like it was closing in on him. Not out of anxiety, exactly, but because he was still new at dealing with so much raw emotion—and having it be the good kind. Overwhelming, but good. "Now," Mike said. "We better go. My baby girl's waiting for you."

"Right," Caden said with a laugh. "And that waiting ends today."

---

*S*tanding in the small room that led out to the hotel courtyard, Makenna James was a flurry of nerves. Because she'd spent her first night apart from her son. Because she was dying to be back in Caden's arms. Because she was getting married today. Well, in just a few minutes, now.

"You look so beautiful, Makenna. Your mother would be so proud of what a wonderful woman you've grown up to be," Aunt Maggie said. Dressed in a teal blue dress that matched her eyes and with red hair nearly the color of Makenna's, Maggie was the obvious choice to be her maid of honor. After her mom died when Makenna was three, Maggie had stepped in to help her dad with the four James kids, becoming the only mother-figure Makenna really remembered.

"Thank you, Aunt Maggie. That means a lot. Part of me wishes she could be here, but part of me thinks I have so much good in my life that I shouldn't wish for even one thing more." Makenna smoothed her hands over the full skirt of her wedding gown. Sleeveless with a sweetheart bodice and silver jewels forming a sash around the waist, the dress made her feel like a princess.

"You deserve it all," Shima said, smiling, a bouquet of yellow roses in her hands. Yellow roses, just a small way to remember Caden's own mother who he'd lost in an accident so many years before. Shima was Collin's girlfriend, and with all the trips her brothers had made to visit the baby over the summer, Makenna and Shima had gotten close. Almost like sisters. And Makenna hoped they might be just that one day.

Makenna squeezed Shima's hand. "You're the best. The next one of these we attend could be yours, you know." She laughed as Shima blushed.

"We'll see about that," Shima said, ducking her head so that her sleek black hair fell around her face.

Outside, the music changed, the wedding march marking Makenna's cue. "Oh. It's time."

"Yes, it is," Maggie said. "And you have a beautiful family waiting on you to start its forever."

"I do," Makenna whispered, the wonder of it all nearly stealing her breath.

The wedding planner opened a set of French glass doors that opened out onto the hotel's outdoor, brick-lined courtyard, a little secluded garden in the middle of Old Town Alexandria. Shima stepped out and marched down the aisle, and then Maggie.

And then it was Makenna's turn.

The moment she passed through the doors, her gaze latched onto Caden's handsome form waiting for her in front of an arch woven with ribbon and roses. His expression went from serious to open wonder to outright happiness, his smile bringing out his dimples and making him appear young and so carefree. It made her heart feel too big for her chest. He'd always done that to her, hadn't he?

And, damn, could her man wear a tux. Between his broad shoulders and his trim waist, the fine black suit fit him like a glove and made her giddy with excitement. This man was going to be her husband. This man was going to be her *forever*.

The next thing Makenna knew, she was standing at the top of the aisle, her eyes still locked on Caden's even as her father gave his blessing to the couple and kissed her on the cheek. Joe Flaherty and

Makenna's brothers stood up for Caden. One of Makenna's greatest joys was how Caden had been embraced by so many people since they'd met. He deserved that, and so much more.

Makenna's gaze searched out Sean and found him in Patrick's arms. Wearing a onesie that made him appear to be decked out in a little tux of his own, Sean sucked on one of his fists. She nearly laughed at how cute the baby looked as she took Caden's hand and stepped up onto the brick dais in front of him. Her son was going to be every bit as handsome as his father, but with her blue eyes.

"You look so pretty, Makenna. I think you stole my heart right out of my chest," Caden whispered, his dark eyes blazing at her.

"And you looking just as freaking gorgeous as ever," she whispered back.

The officiant's words were lovely, but all Makenna wanted was to exchange vows with Caden and proclaim publicly that they belonged to one another forever. And then they were doing it. Trading rings and making promises that would last a lifetime. Makenna thought she just might make it through the ceremony without crying until Caden's voice cracked on the words, "In good times and in bad." And then her damn eyes wouldn't stop leaking even as she couldn't stop smiling. Because sometimes life was so good you could barely take it all in.

"May I present Mr. and Mrs. Caden Grayson," the minister said to the applause of the small gathering. "You may now kiss the bride."

Caden's tongue flicked at the small spider-bite piercings on the side of his bottom lip. "I've been waiting for this part."

"Have you, now?" Makenna said just before Caden's lips came down on hers, soft but claiming, tender but full of banked heat, way too short but promising more. Promising everything.

They pulled back from the kiss wearing huge smiles. Makenna grasped Caden's lapel and pulled him down so she could whisper in his ear, "You're mine forever now."

"That's the best thing I've heard in my entire life, Makenna," Caden said, his lips against her cheek.

As they stepped off the dais, Sean's fusses turned into a cry.

"Give him to me," Caden said to Patrick. "He can walk with us."

When Sean settled in against Caden's chest, Makenna couldn't restrain herself. She leaned in and hugged her men, the three of them forming a little circle of love and family and forever.

Together, they walked down the aisle. Everyone rose to their feet, clapping and cheering for them. Her family. Most of the guys from Caden's firehouse. David Talbot and the other men who'd saved Caden's life fifteen years ago and who he'd found again last winter when he was fighting to find himself. People from Makenna's accounting office and a few girls with whom she'd gone to college. It wasn't a large gathering, but it was everyone and everything they needed.

The reception passed in a happy blur of toasts and dances and pictures and moments that quickly passed into memories. Shima caught Makenna's bouquet. And Patrick caught the garter Caden had slipped off her thigh. Makenna was absolutely tickled at both. When someone requested Aerosmith's *Love in an Elevator*, the party really got underway. And they danced until Makenna's feet hurt and Caden had shed his suit coat and rolled up his sleeves, baring the tattoos she loved, and Sean fell asleep in Grandpa's arms despite the noise.

"You ready to get out of here yet?" Caden asked, hugging her from behind.

Makenna turned in his arms and found his dark eyes absolutely on fire. Her heart tripped into a sprint. "More than ready."

Of course, it took a while for them to say their good-byes and make their way out of the room, and it wasn't easy leaving Sean for a second night in a row. But Makenna knew he was in good hands.

And for this night, she was all Caden's. Body, mind, and soul. Because after all he'd lost, he deserved nothing less.

---

*C*aden's heart was hammering in his chest as he led Makenna into the elevator. The honeymoon suite was on the tenth floor of the hotel, but he had a stop to make along the way.

"Do you think everyone had a good time?" Makenna asked, her face bright and alive and so very pretty. The doors slid shut.

"Yeah," Caden said. "I think they did. And so did I."

Makenna smiled. "Me, too."

Floor two. Floor three.

Caden reached out and pressed the *Stop* button. The elevator lurched to a halt somewhere between the third and fourth floor. Right where they'd met a year before. An alarm bell rang, then cut off.

"Oh. What are you..." Makenna glanced from the panel of buttons to Caden and back again. "Why did you do that?"

"Because," he said, taking her hands. He'd cleared this with the hotel manager, but he didn't have long. "I need to say something to you. Something more than our vows. And I wanted to do it here."

"Are you okay, Caden?" she asked, a flash of worry in her baby blues.

Caden backed Makenna against the wall, boxing her in and nailing her with a stare. "God, Makenna. I am so much more than okay. Even though this isn't the elevator we got trapped in, I thought an elevator was the best place to make some additional promises to you."

Her expression went soft and so full of emotion. For him. "What?"

He stroked a red curl back off her face. "I promise that I'll always believe in your ability to help me when I'm trapped—in an elevator or my own mind."

"Oh, Caden," she said, her head tilting as she looked up at him. "I will."

He nodded. "And I promise to keep myself healthy so that you won't need to help me that way."

"I believe in you. I know you will," she said, her words a strained whisper.

"And I promise to be your soft place to land when life gets hard or you lose something important to you. Because you've done that for me so many times already."

A quick nod, and then her hands landed on his chest. "God, I love you."

"I love you, too. And that's why I wanted you to know. I want to make an amazing life for you and Sean, for all of us. I'm not scared anymore. And that's why I wanted to trap us in here long enough to let you know." Caden gave a little smile as a tear broke free from the corner of one of Makenna's eyes. He caught it with his thumb.

"You're the best thing that ever happened to me, Caden."

"Hey, that's my line," he said.

Makenna chuckled. "You're not the only one who found everything they ever wanted."

Grasping her face, Caden leaned down and claimed Makenna's sweet mouth in a kiss. Her arms rounded his neck, pulling him in harder, closer. It was a kiss full of promise and commitment and tenderness, but when Makenna moaned, heat ripped through Caden's blood.

"Need you so much," he said.

Makenna's hands stroked the back of his head as she nodded. "Can't wait to feel my husband moving inside me."

"Christ, Red." Caden stabbed at the *Start* button as desire lanced through him. The elevator moved again, but their kisses didn't wait. What started sweetly was now full of scorching, demanding need. When the doors eased open, they spilled into the small lobby outside of their suite, their bodies never coming apart. When Makenna's dress made it difficult to walk her backward toward the door, Caden swept her up into his arms.

She threw her head back and laughed. "Are you carrying me across the threshold?"

"Absofuckinglutely," he said with a wink. And then he was pushing open the door and carrying her into the beautiful room. Though it couldn't hold a candle to his wife. His *wife*.

It was the first time his brain had truly absorbed the gravity of that word. And it made his need for her surge until he was restraining himself from flipping up all those gorgeous white skirts. But, no. She deserved more than that. She deserved to be laid out and savored. Tonight and always.

But that didn't mean he could slow down. "Turn around," he said, turning her so he faced her back. She scooped her hair out of the way and he worked at the row of tiny buttons, kissing the peaches-and-cream skin he revealed as he opened them one by one. When he was finished, he helped her step out of the dress and laid it reverently over the chaise lounge in the corner. When he turned around again, he stopped short to find her wearing a strapless white satin bra and a tiny pair of panties with intricate light blue embroidery and piping. "God, you're stunning."

Makenna reached behind her back and unhooked her bra, then let it tumble down her arms. "And you are the sexiest man I've ever seen," she said as she came to him. As she worked his shirt off, excitement flooded into Caden's gut. Because he had another surprise for her. He knew the minute she saw it. "Caden, is this...you got a new tattoo." Her eyes flashed to his.

Caden smiled even as his cock ached for her tight heat. "For you. Another promise."

Across his heart, just beneath the yellow rose he'd gotten for his mom years before, he'd had this inked into his skin in all black:

IX.XXII.MMXII

'TIL DEATH

Makenna kissed the still-tender skin. "And not a moment sooner."

Caden's heart swelled in his chest. "Love you so fucking much, Red."

She grasped his hand and led him to the bed. And then he was laying Makenna out, baring her skin, baring his own, until all that separated them were their heartbeats.

His hard cock dragging against her soft legs, Caden kissed his way down Makenna's body. He licked at her nipples. Placed playful little bites that made her squirm all down her ribs. And finally nuzzled his face against the triangle of red hair at the top of her thighs. He couldn't help but remember that first night she'd invited him in—to her home and her body. And wonder at just how far they'd come.

But now wasn't the time for memories.

Opening Makenna to him, Caden settled his shoulders between

her spread thighs, needing to give her pleasure. Wanting to give her everything. He kissed up the inside of both thighs until Makenna's hand fell on his head.

"Please," she rasped.

He couldn't stand for her to beg for what he was only too happy to give. He placed firm, flat licks of his tongue from her opening to her clit. And then again. And again.

Her other hand fell on his head, desperation clear in her clutching touch.

He sucked her clit into her mouth and flicked at it with his tongue. Furiously. Insistently. One hand reached to play with her nipples while the other pressed her belly down, forcing her hips to tilt upward to his demanding mouth.

Her hips rocked as her hands held him tighter, and then she was screaming his name and coming and writhing beneath him. And it was fucking glorious.

"That was too fast, Red. I think you can do that again," he said, peering up her body.

"My heart might stop," she said, her face breaking into a grin.

He shook his head. "Nah. And even if it does, I might know a paramedic who could start it right back up." He winked at her.

Makenna laughed. "I want you in me."

He kissed her clit. "Then come again and you can have me."

"Fuck, Caden," she said, her head falling back to the bed and her body arching.

He flipped them so that she straddled his face. "Use me. Ride my mouth until you come."

Grasping his head with one hand and bracing herself against the bed with the other, Makenna rocked her hips so that her clit ground against his tongue and lips. He grasped her ass and helped her move, pressing her down, letting her know he could take her weight. A moan wrenched out of her that had blood pounding through his cock, especially when she ground down harder and held her breath.

He growled against her soft flesh and banded his arms around her hips so that she was trapped in place. And then he sucked her clit so frantically that the orgasm stole her breath and made her collapse on top of him.

Licking his lips, Caden turned her boneless body over so that she lay under him on her back. "That sounded good."

"Fucking delicious," she said, her eyes soft with satisfaction.

"Yes, you were." He grinned and kissed her, lingering over her lips until he was nearly dizzy with desire. Taking his cock in hand, Caden stroked at his erection, his head and his fist bumping against Makenna's core. "Don't let me hurt you." When their schedules and energy and Sean's sleeping allowed, they'd loved one another many times since their son's birth, but Caden hadn't been inside Makenna since then. They'd wanted to save their bodies coming fully together again for their first time as husband and wife.

"You won't. I'm so ready for you. Make love to me, Caden," Makenna said.

In answer, he pushed inside her, inch by scalding hot inch. And it was like coming home. "Fuck, that's good. Always so damn good."

Makenna moaned and wrapped her legs around his back, holding him tightly, forcing him into a slow, deep grind that had both of them panting until the only sounds in the room were their fevered exhales and the soft shift of skin against skin.

Caden curled his arms under Makenna's shoulders and hunched himself around her, wanting deeper, *needing* deeper. "Fuck, I never want this to end."

"Don't stop. God, don't stop," Makenna rasped, arousal straining her voice. "Gonna make me come again."

His hips ground down on her harder, faster, and he pressed his lips to her ears, knowing she loved his words. "Do it. Come on me. Show me what I do to you, Red. Fucking come on me."

A high-pitched whine ripped from Makenna's throat and her body went taut.

"Christ, that's it. Squeezing my cock so tight," he said through a groan. And then Makenna's body was fisting him over and over until Caden was nearly blind from the goodness of it.

"Want you...to come in me," Makenna said, her voice breathy, her legs falling wide around him. "Want to feel my husband pour himself into me."

Her words kicked him in the spine and had him driving into her, his skin slapping against hers, his arousal as tight as a corkscrew. "You're mine, always," he gritted out.

"And you're mine," she replied.

The sentiment blew Caden apart into a million pieces and reassembled him as a new man. A man who would never have to walk alone again. The orgasm went on and on until Caden got light-headed and his body shuddered. And then he settled his weight atop Makenna and embraced her in a whole-body hug. "Never gonna let you go."

"Good," she said, stroking his back. "Wouldn't let you if you tried."

"I still love that elevator, Makenna," he said, pressing a kiss to the racing pulse in her neck.

She laughed. "I still love that elevator, too."

They lay there like that until they eventually fell asleep. And then they found one another again and again and again. All night long.

And though their story started as two separate hearts in the darkness, their forever would be fully in the light. Well, Caden wasn't so different of a man that he didn't know the darkness would sometimes return. No one was intended to die with their hearts still intact. But whatever came at them, they'd get through it together.

He pressed a light kiss to Makenna's forehead, not wanting to wake her. "You and me, 'til the end. In the darkness and in the light."

Her eyes opened and her whole face immediately filled with a smile. "Did you say something?"

Caden grinned and shook his head. "Just that I love you."

he End

ABOUT THE AUTHOR

Laura Kaye is the New York Times and USA Today bestselling author of over forty books in contemporary and erotic romance and romantic suspense. Laura grew up amidst family lore involving angels, ghosts, and evil-eye curses, cementing her life-long fascination with storytelling and the supernatural. Laura lives in Maryland with her husband and two daughters, and appreciates her view of the Chesapeake Bay every day.

Visit Laura Kaye & Become a VIP Reader at
http://www.LauraKayeAuthor.com/

facebook.com/Laurakayewrites
twitter.com/laurakayeauthor
instagram.com/laurakayeauthor

MORE CONTEMPORARY ROMANCE BY
LAURA KAYE

Hard Ink Series
HARD AS IT GETS
HARD AS YOU CAN
HARD TO HOLD ON TO
HARD TO COME BY
HARD TO BE GOOD
HARD TO LET GO
HARD AS STEEL
HARD EVER AFTER
HARD TO SERVE

Warrior Fight Club Series
FIGHTING FOR EVERYTHING
FIGHTING FOR WHAT'S HIS
WORTH FIGHTING FOR
FIGHTING THE FIRE

Blasphemy Series
HARD TO SERVE
BOUND TO SUBMIT

MASTERING HER SENSES
EYES ON YOU
THEIRS TO TAKE
ON HIS KNEES
SWITCHING FOR HER – COMING IN 2022

Raven Riders
HARD AS STEEL
RIDE HARD
RIDE ROUGH
RIDE WILD
RIDE DIRTY
RIDE DEEP - COMING IN 2022

Hearts in Darkness Duet
HEARTS IN DARKNESS
LOVE IN THE LIGHT
HEARTS IN DARKNESS COLLECTION

Stand Alone Titles
DARE TO RESIST
JUST GOTTA SAY

Made in United States
North Haven, CT
26 July 2022

21825854R00183